TAILS UP!

BY
Ray R. Kepley
With
Illustrations By Duane Blehm

Dedication

TO

my wife and daughter

AND

to all red-blooded characters who may
be interested in what the Buffalo and
Indian days were like.

Library of Congress
Catalog Card Number
80-81060

ISBN 0-9604248-0-6

ELLIOTT PRINTERS
GARDEN CITY, KANSAS

ii

CONTENTS

PART I

West From Civilization

Illustrations

CONTENTS

PART II

At The Sod Ranche

Illustrations

CONTENTS

PART III

The Arickaree Campaign

Illustrations

Preface

TAILS UP!
"Just a Few Words to Begin With"

When a Buffalo scents trouble his tail instinctively goes up. By 1868 it is a fair statement to say his Tail was Up, the great herds of wild buffalo were approaching the "beginning" of the end. In the next ten years they were almost exterminated from the face of the earth as civilization advanced across their grazing lands, the Great Plains. As the buffalo went, so went the Plains Indian; by reason and by instinct he foresaw the end of his old way of life and his domination of the buffalo grazing grounds. He went on the offensive—his Tail was Up. While the White Settler, the cause of it all, cautiously but determinedly moved into the Wide Open Spaces with a quiet excitement at what he found and a future he envisioned. As the oppressor he soon became the oppressed—and with him too it was Tails High.

This is a historical story, it attempts to follow in an orderly fashion the recorded and accepted history of the Kansas and Colorado Plains in the year of 1868. To many people of today, the happenings of that distant time are cloudy and uncertain. This story seeks to clear up some of those uncertainties. Unlike many "Westerns" no fantasies or impossible situations have been knowingly written into it. To the best of my knowledge and research, the hard facts of History, Geography and Human Behavior have no conflict with the story's credibility.

There is at least one area I feel I should ask the reader to bear with me. In writing the dialogue in a way to bring a true flavor of the times and characters I have deliberately used the rough language of the hard every day world which includes profanity and vulgarity. This, I know, will be distasteful to some. It can be said, "this is the age of enlightenment." If you are not aware such words exist and have been in common use for ages, then it is time you learned. But under no circumstances do I wish this to be considered a "dirty book". Accordingly to you gentle people I offer my apology and give the following explanation. I am

vi

attempting to tell a factual tale of a time and place where Sunday School verses and endearing words were seldom heard but where the rough and ready swearing of the bullwhackers, Muleskinners and their like was as common as the rising of the sun. To replace their epithets with mousier words with little or no feeling is like substituting a beep for the crack of a rifleshot.

In this story as already noted, emphasis is on history and geography. An extra effort has been made to see that it is correct in those respects, the historical events and details of the land surface which can be checked by records, maps and data of all sorts have been carefully scrutinized. The vast collections of the Kansas Historical Association have been the main source of reference. Although many other references have been used too, the tale could never have been told with any degree of truth without the Kansas Collections.

Those of us who were here in the early years of this century are privileged to have had a little "peek" at what the old times may have been like. The little "peek" I had, always aroused a great interest, hence this story. To those of you who have not been so privileged, I hope you find it factual, enlightening and interesting. To you older readers who had a bigger "peek", I humbly dedicate this work and herewith throw myself on your tender mercies.

Well, with these few words to begin with, here finally is the story. It is the tale of a young man who felt the "Daniel Boone" urge to come west in the spring of 1868, and as it is told by him. In a manner of speaking he soon had his tail high.

TAILS UP!
PART I
West From Civilization

CHAPTER I

How It All Started

This year of 1924, having turned my 82nd year, I have decided to write the story of my early day experiences on the Plains. As the years have passed I realize the full story of the Sixties and the Seventies has never been told. A few old timers like myself are the last remaining links of a long gone era, and each of us left, has an obligation, I feel to add his bit of history so this generation and generations to come may know of life in this great country of ours in those early days.

I was born and raised in Davidson (part of old Rowan) County in North Carolina, son of a country doctor and farmer, the third of five boys and one girl. Our parents worked hard that we might be educated above the ordinary level of that day, it having been my privlege to spend two terms in Medical School. But I shall always think that was a mistake as I was never cut out to be a man of medicine. However, shortly after the beginning of the War between the States I was admitted as an orderly in the hospital where my father was a doctor, there eventually I served as surgical assistant until the untimely death of my father in "64". By then heartsick and completely fed up with my part in the War, I managed to pull wires and get myself transferred as a private to the Infantry. There I served under General

Lee and was with his straggling army until nearly the end of the fighting but must admit that I had little real battle experience, being relegated most of the time to the supply and transportation end of the army. In the spring of "65" my outfit was captured by Sheridan at Five Forks. I remember the doughty Union General lined us all up and gave us a nice speech in which he praised us as the best fighting force he had encountered and stated further if his own men had shown as much ability and fortitude the war would be over. Then the General promised substantial inducements to any man who would forsake the Confederacy and join his forces. Hopeless and ragged, but loyal and proud, only a few turncoats from our side stepped across the line. The General thanked us anyway for our attention and sent us away to spend the rest of the War in a Federal Prison Camp.

After the War the next few years were full of work and readjustment, things went well with our family, considering the hard times but gradually I developed a feeling of restlessness. My war service had intensified a craving for more exciting life, especially after reading Harpers Weekly and other publications describing the wonders of the West. That was the beginning; the bug had hit me hard, and it wasn't long before I commenced putting away every cent I could for the trip west.

In March, 1868, the time came. I kissed my mother and sister goodby and with a lump in my throat, shook hands with my four brothers, picked up my belongings and started on my long journey. The trip by rail and steamboat was in itself an adventure for a young fellow unused to travel in that swift and modern fashion. Still, I must admit I was smitten at times with a feeling of homesickness and sometimes apprehension as to what might be my fate in this far away land, a feeling I never completely overcame until I had spent years in the wide and lonely west.

Kansas City, at the junction of the Missouri and Kaw Rivers, was my destination. On the way up the River I met a pleasant old gentleman from that city who gave me a glowing report on his community. Though certainly a friendly courteous man he may have been inclined to some salesmanship on that subject, Kansas City, so he told me was the New York of the West, Leavenworth and other River towns were merely whistling stops for

2

Missouri river steamboats and even St. Louie would be outstripped by K. C. as soon as the Union Pacific, now being built across the Plains was completed. He told me he owned a controlling interest in the "overland freighting" firm of Tyler & Randall, which was now preparing to haul supplies over the Santa Fe Trail to points in Colorado. He suggested I try there for a job.

Kansas City in those days though small in comparison to its present size, was a bustling growing town, already possessing a vast trade territory stretching west to the Rockies. But as this well known city has been described by able writers far more effectively than I can, I shall make no further attempts at description.

We arrived in the city in late afternoon. The kind old gentleman directed me to a small hotel near the outskirts of the city, where the rates were reasonable. Here I got a room and my evening meal and shortly afterwards retired for my first night in what I imagined was the Wild and Wooly West.

I awakened the next morning with the sun, after a good nights sleep but found I had developed a touch of nostalgia that can best be described as plain old homesickness. I hadn't expected this but rather than set around and brood over it I pulled on my clothes, left the hotel and took a brisk walk. The early rays of the bright sun gave the town on the banks of the big Missouri a bright and clean look that morning and in spite of myself I commenced to feel more cheerful. Coming to a small restaurant I found my appetite was not impaired. After partaking of a hearty breakfast of ham and eggs I walked out on the street again, ready for anything the day had to offer. Returning to the hotel I procured some writing materials and penciled a letter to the homefolks. Having completed this chore I decided to spend the morning exploring this part of the city and see what I could find here at the gateway to the plains where I had come so far to find adventure and fortune. Unbeknown to me I was in for a busy day.

I suppose I spent hours walking up and down the streets of the business section, looking in store windows, speaking idly to passersby and generally acquainting myself with the town. Eventually I found myself in a store near the outskirts of the retail

3

section that was devoted almost entirely to firearms. Having always had a longing for a better gun than I had heretofore ever owned or even felt that I could afford, I browsed around the counters and displays with my mouth "literally watering." Here was displayed the latest model Sharps percussion cap rifle. The even newer Remington Rolling Block with its strong and fool-proof cartridge ejection system. These were both single-shot breech loaders of heavy caliber. Nearby was a display of Henry and Winchester Model "66" repeaters. I spent some time admiring these interesting hunting and sporting arms, and was about ready to leave, when I overheard a customer, good naturedly arguing with one of the clerks. He spoke in a pleasant voice, the plain vernacular of the outlands. "Nawsir, I don't reckon I would be happy with one of your fancy repeating irons. I calculate to stick with the ole Ballard for a spell and if she jams on me I'll only have one cartridge to dig out, not a whole hatfull like your purty 'Henry' pepperbox."

"But, she's not a pepperbox, Joe," remonstrated the clerk.

"Pepperbox or no pepperbox, them fancy repeaters may be all right for some. But for a fellar like me that uses em everyday in the sand and dust and mud, I reckon they wouldn't be much use only to look at."

"But Joe," persisted the clerk, "this rifle ain't nowise similar to the old revolving and pepperbox arms you're thinking of. The Henry, was well tested in the late war and was pretty well conceded by both them that used and them that fought agin it as the best shooting piece in the war."

My company had come into possesion of some captured Henry rifles in the area around Petersburg and I well remembered how they were admired. A little impulsively, I butted in, "Sir, that is correct, I had a little experience with captured Henrys myself and talked with officers who had much more and everyone was enthusiastic about the rifle.

"Joe" turned and I got my first look at his face. He was, I judged, in his early thirties, medium height, slender with a short scraggly black beard which came to a point on his chin like a goatee. His skin and hair was as dark as an Indian's. He gazed at me from a pair of black eyes as he enquired, "And who might you be stranger?"

"My name's Jack Reynolds, from North Carolina, Sir, and I spent a hard year or two with Lee in Virginia and thereabouts."

I think a trace of a grin appeared on his dark, and bearded face but it was gone before I could be sure. He gravely extended his hand, "My handle is Smith, Joe Smith, and I'm proud to know you, Reynolds. Who knows, sometime I might get full of red likker and develop a hankering to own one of them fancy guns you and the gent here recommend so high." He picked up his purchases, nodded to the clerk and left abruptly with quick, easy catlike steps.

"That's Smoky Joe Smith, he's part Cherokee and has a reputation as the best blamed hunter and trapper in the west," explained the clerk.

Fascinated by the display of firearms, I stayed on. The clerk scenting a customer handed me a Henry rifle and explained its features in detail. The particular gun I held had been slightly used and had been reworked by an expert gunsmith into a neat carbine by the simple matter of cutting about two inches off the end of the barrel and resetting the front sight. The work had been done so well that it couldn't be told from a completely new arm. As I held this fine rifle to my shoulder and looked down the sleek barrel, I forgot all about my homesickness and knew I must have one of these. The Henry at that time was made to sell in the neighborhood of twenty-five dollars. This particular arm, the clerk explained having been used, could be bought for that price and would include one hundred rounds of ammunition. My heart was set on owning one of these rifles, but twenty-five dollars was a lot of money in those days and especially, I reflected for myself, with no positive knowledge that I would be in that part of the country where an arm such as this would be of any use to me. I explained to the clerk that I was new to the country. While I wanted to go on to the frontier country at present I had no job nor knowledge of how to get there or what to do if I did. He suggested that I think it over until I got lined out on a job, agreeing to hold the rifle a couple of days for me. We shook hands on that agreement and I left the store.

By the spring of 1868, Kansas City's great overland freight business had already begun to decline, due to the building and partial completion of the Kansas Pacific and other railroads. However, the hustle and bustle of this industry seemed enormous to me, as my next tour of exploration led me to that section of the city's outskirts, monopolized by the freighters. By now it was past mid-morning and I found the freight yards filled with activity, preparing for the spring haul. After seeing this I could partly realize the immense amount of preparation and supplies it took for a journey of hundreds of miles across the uninhabited plains.

My friend of the journey up the river, a "Mr. Tyler" had given me the name of his firm and also that of his wagon boss, suggesting that I try there for a job. These names I had jotted down on a piece of paper and as I walked along dodging muleteams, Bullwhackers and mudholes, I kept an eye on the occasional signs identifying the firms in the area. After a time I noticed a large barnlike structure, sporting a faded sign which read "TYLER AND RANDALL, OVERLAND FREIGHT." I stopped and looked about me. The building appeared to be sort of blacksmith shop, livery stable and outfitting depot, all combined and all in a more or less rundown condition. A number of large freight wagons stood in the yard in various stages of repair, with a crew of seven or eight men working on them and perhaps that many loafers idling about.

Nearby, a couple of old-timers, seated on empty beerkegs, were chewing the fat. One of them a stubby old fellow with a short beard, heavily streaked with gray, kept up a constant chatter. He had a pair of sharp inquisitive eyes and a big quid of tobacco in the side of his cheek, which he maneuvered with a minimum of teeth and a maximum effort, apparently having some difficulty keeping the "chaw" in one side of his face where it wouldn't interfere with his conversation.

"Ie grannies," he was saying, "I sed to Jim, by jacks that consarned mare'll go lame afore we hit the Picket Wire . . ."*

There his sharp wandering eyes encountered me and with a wave of his hand he interupted himself long enough to point to a nearby box. "Set down young fellar, ie jacks iffen Clint sees you a standin around he'll put you'ns to work as sure as God made

---

* The Purgatoire River, a large tributary of the Arkansas which starts in the southern Colorado mountains and flows norheast to the Arkansas near Fort Lyon and "present" Las Animas.

6

little papoose'es." He slapped his thigh then and cackled as if that was a great joke.

I couldn't help grinning along with him as I accepted the proffered seat, but before I could say thanks or get a word in edgewise he resumed his story.

"Shore enough, I don't reckon we had made ten mile when I looked back and seed a passel of Kioways trailin along jist out of rifle reach and about that time Jim's mare commenced to limp, by gollies." He paused now to splatter a nearby wagon wheel with tobacco juice.

"Well Sir," he resumed, "we stopped right then and thar and had ourselves a little pow-wow. Jim, I sez, ie gollies, jist give us a few more mile and we'll be clos't enough to the stockade, them pesky red devils won't dare to pester us no more . . ."

We were interrupted by the appearance of the wagon boss.

"Zeekial," he ordered unceremoniously, "Tom Powers is down the road a piece, gabbin with Andy Cooper. I want you to run down there and tell him to bring his team up here, and be damn lively about it."

The listening "half" of the two old-timers, rose grumbling to his feet and went off muttering about all the tarnation senselessness of the hurry. As for myself I formed the opinion immediately that the wagon boss was indeed a forceful character. And as he was the man Mr. Tyler had advised me to enquire about a job, I commenced to wonder how such a hard-boiled fellow was going to respond to a request from an obvious greenhorn like myself, would he like to be interrupted at his work, for such a trivial thing as asking for a job? I could see him champing a cigar stub as he stamped from wagon to wagon barking orders, a big burly man with a red face and huge muscular arms.

I pondered the advisability of letting the job interview wait until a more opportune time.

"Is that *Clint Macanles, the wagon boss?" I asked, the old timer.

"Yep, thats him alright, Clint's a mighty rough fellar, rough

* McCanles or McCandless—the same.

7

as a cob, as a matter of fact, but a blamed good wagonmaster at that."

The old timer arose and with unsanitary precision, spat out his chaw, reached into his pouch and brought forth a fresh plug which he wiped carefully on his greasy pantleg and offered it to me. I declined his polite offer with thanks. He haggled off a chew for himself, looking me over with his sharp inquisitive eyes and I thought he was getting ready to resume his story, but for the moment that seemed to be forgotten.

"Who be you son, cain't seem to recollect seein yore face around these parts?"

"That's because I'm a new arrival, fresh from North Carolina," I told him, "My name is Jack Reynolds."

"Mighty pleased to meet you Jack. Balaam is my name, Bufflar, Barney Balaam I'm knowed as in these parts. I bin residin here and thar mostly on the plains and foothills for nigh unto forty-five year."

"You're just the man I want to talk to, then. I came here with the idea of making my way on west and I am anxious to learn all I can about the plains and western country."

"You're shore a talkin to the right fellar, Jack. I don't reckon thars another man twixt here and the mountings knows the country like old Barney Balaam, not even old Kit hisself. Why dad-blame it son I've hunted, fished and trapped in ever dog-blasted stream and holler atwixt here and the gold mines."

I smiled to myself as I listened to his preposterous talk, but there was a note of sincerity in his voice and that along with his rustic apparel and manner told me as plainly as "honest words" that the old man was the genuine article.

I suppose I talked to the old fellow for over an hour; or rather I listened. He told me that the past winter, he and his partner had trapped in the Solomon and Saline valleys and that was "the purtiest dad-blamed country he had ever seed" and had the most game. Probably his ideas of natural grandeur were based mostly on the amount of game a country would produce, however other men who were familiar with those areas before the time of settlement have described them in similar terms.

8

I became so interested in listening to his tales of hunting and trappng that I didn't realize how the morning had flown. The man, Powers, had already come with his team and hitched on to one of the wagons and on his way out stopped to visit with Barney.

I noticed the wagon boss standing by himself, apparently in a little better humor, so I screwed up my courage and walked over to where I "now" saw, he was gazing sourly at a partly repaired wagon.

"You are Clint Macanles, the wagon boss?" I enquired.

"That's me," he answered briefly, giving me an unfriendly look.

"I'm a tenderfoot from Carolina," I told him frankly, "And I am looking for a job with your outfit."

I could feel his critical eyes upon me as he measured my five feet eight and noted my modest build. Like many smaller men I was a little sensitive of my size and I felt myself flush under his steady stare.

"A Johnny Reb, hunh? Take the likes of you in the Reb Army did they?"

I commenced to bristle under his insolent stare. "I served in the Confederate Army in defense of the Southern Cause," I told him stiffly, and gave him stare for stare.

"I don't give a damn if you served in both armies. Half of em that fit on both sides was as worthless as tits on a boar, so's war experience don't cut no Gawddam ice in this outfit. I ain't hiring no one but them with plenty of jerk-line and jack-ass savvy and that takes men big enough to fill big britches." With that he turned and walked away.

Thus dismissed. I stood there swallowing. For a full minute, I could feel the hair rise on the back of my neck as I strove to control my temper. Finally I commenced to feel a little foolish standing there alone so I turned and walked back to old Barney.

Barney stopped talking and looked at me inquisitively, "How'dje come out son? Did Clint hire ye?"

"I didn't come out," I told him with a long face, "It seems like Clint judges men by their size and jack-ass savvy."

9

"Wal it don't matter nohow.   Jack meet Tom Powers hyar."

Powers, a large good natured fellow in his late thirties and just a little beefy around the middle, stepped forward and shook hands. "Glad to know you Jack. Looking for a job are you?"

I explained that I wanted to go west and had hoped to get a job on the wagon train.

"Handle a mule team can you?"

I assured him that I could handle an ordinary two-mule team and was willing to learn the larger teams.

"I got a little outfit of my own," Powers told me, "got a deal with Tyler and Randall to trail along with them as fur as Fort Dodge.   Safer that way, as I got my wife and fambly along with me as we aim to locate out that away.   I had a young fellar hired to drive my extra team but he got to believin all these wild Injun stories and took out on me, so you're welcome to the job if you want, I'll pay you the same wages that Macanles pays his men."

"Mr. Powers," I told him gratefully, "You have just hired yourself a hand, I am green and inexperienced in the freighting business I know but you will find I'm willing to do a days work."

"Fine," he looked at his watch, "it'll be dinner time afore long.   Jack, why don't you climb in and go over to our camp and have dinner with us?"

Of course the invitation appealed to me but I protested that as a stranger I wouldn't want to put Mrs. Powers to unnecessary trouble.

"No trouble at all, why Mamie and the kids will be plumb tickled to have company, as a matter of fact the missus will be right put out if she finds I've hired a new hand and hain't brought him to dinner."

So I shook hands with the old trapper, climbed up on the seat beside Powers, he clucked to the mules and we went clippity clop down the road and eventually across the wide *Kaw to the Wyandotte and Kansas side of the river. Here, Powers pulled his mules

---

* The Power's camp was a considerable distance from the main freighting headquarters and popular starting places for those taking the Santa Fe Trail.

to a stop in a small area taken over by immigrants on their way west.

"Mighty lucky finding a handy place like this to set up camp the way these towns are a grow'in nowdays, especially as this trip is on a new route fer me. Ain't never had no experience this side of the Kaw," he explained. "We bin here four days now a waitin and the kids and the woman, too, are a gettin restless. Its a bit too crowded here with people and bustle all around for country folks like us."

Tom Powers outfit consisted of three large wagons and as far as I could see three or four smaller rigs. (Attached to one of the large wagons, a crude though comfortable lean-to-tent had been erected, this served as kitchen and living quarters for part of the family.) About this modest abode was assembled or so I assumed, the Powers brood, nine or ten staring offspring.

"Ain't only four of em mine," Tom explained, evidently noting the consternation on my face. "Rest of em are neighbors but the Lord only knows whose."

"Sid," he commanded, and a lad about fourteen with black hair and freckled face came forward, "This is Jack Reynolds our new hand, go tell your maw to put an extra plate on the table, we're gonna have company for dinner."

We unhitched and fed the team and Tom showed me the rest of his mules and horses. I was familiar enough with the requirements of work animals that I could see he was equipped with better than average teams. He explained he had been farming about thirty miles east of here and had been engaged in freighting on the side for several yars, he had sold the farm for a good price about a month ago and had put part of the money in mules and equipment, intending to continue freighting until he found what he wanted in the way of a farm in the great western country.

"Only be a question of time," he told me, "Till the gov'nment cleans the Injuns out, mebee two, three years mebee longer but it'll be done sooner or later, and when it is the fellar thats there and waitin can have his pick of some of the best land as ever laid outdoors."

"But," I questioned, "Isn't it true that much of the plains country is desert or semi-desert."

11

"Yeah, I reckon it is more or less," agreed Tom, "But you take them crick and river valleys, they's as good a soil in them as there is any place in Missoury and a dam site less crowded. Besides there ain't no rocks and timber to clear. Anyway I aim to find out if it will grow stuff this summer, as I'm takin along a plow and some farmin tools."

"From what Barney Balaam told me this morning it would seem a shame to turn that country into farmland."

"You don't need to worry bout that," said Tom, "Why you can drive fer days west of Dodge and look off to the south and see a land that'll never be no good fer nothin but buffalo, antelope and wild horses."

"But right now, I reckon you and me could do with a bite to eat." So saying he led the way towards the tent.

After washing in a tin basin, outside, Tom drew aside the flap and motioned me in the tent. Inside a darkhaired woman was busily ladling noodles out of a kettle on a new iron cookstove.

"Mamie," said Tom, "This is Jack Reynolds from Caroliny, he's gonna drive a team for us."

"Mrs. Powers," I said as she shook hands, "I want to apologize for barging in on you this way but Mr. Powers insisted, and I just couldn't resist a good home cooked meal."

"Oh come now Mr. Reynolds, with your blarney," she said with a twinkle in her eyes. "I bet you tell that to everybody."

"Um'm," interrupted Tom, "I could eat the hind leg off a bear. Let's set down and get to work."

I gathered that whatever faults the Powers' might have, that unfriendliness and sophistication were not among them. Though next I saw their sober side. The family had just seated themselves when a sudden unexpected stillness fell around the table. Tom fixed his wife and kids with a stern and solemn glance, bowed his head abruptly and piously said grace. When Tom's head was lowered five others were lowered in nigh perfect time; as a matter of fact all but mine. Therefore, just as my slightly embarrassed head was going down the others were coming up; and the brief blessing was over. The solemn preliminaries

12

thus taken care of my host passed the bread and beans and in an easy-going careless manner was soon telling jokes picked up on some overland freighting trails he had traveled, some of them just a little "off-colour" considering his attentive family audience. His wife, Mamie, giggling a little in spite of herself, promptly called him down "for showin' off for Mister Reynolds," all of which Tom absorbed without a blink but right away I noticed the conversation changed to questions directed at myself. I explained briefly of my family and home in Carolina and of my trip out here. Mamie, then spoke up and explained how she was raised in Southern Indiany' and lived there until she was sixteen, when her folks got "to feelin' right crowded and moved to Illinoiy' where she met Tom. "He wasn't exactly no fairy prince," she giggled, "but to a silly seventeen year-old who didn't know no better he seemed like one and we up and got married, and there our eldest 'Sid' here, was born and then a spell later along came Mary. Then Tom took a notion to move out here to Missourv' a few years before the War, and this is where these two young'uns were born. After that I said to Tom, thats enough. With him gone on the road half the time and me having to look after the farm, it kept a body busy tryin' to raise four kids. But—I declare, here we are a fixin' to move on West again."

Having thus set me straight on the family history, we then settled down to enjoy the noon meal. The food was of the plain variety but was plentiful and well prepared, as I was soon to learn there were few who could bake bread quite like Mamie's or fix those ham-n-beans quite as tasty.

After finishing dinner, I followed Tom outside after expressing thanks to Mrs. Powers for the enjoyable meal. A change of weather was in progress, rolls of grayish clouds were in the sky partly obscuring the sun and a cool breeze was blowing from the northeast.

"Looks like we're gonna have some more weather." Tom observed, "let her come, better have it here than out on the road."

"When do you expect to start?" I asked.

"McCanles says Monday morning barring bad weather. Well, lets see—today is Thursday. That'll only leave two more workin' days. I got considerable loading to do but Fritz, my other driver

13

will be here tomorry so I don't reckon I'll need you before Sattidy."

That arrangement suited me fine as it would give me time to buy clothes and equipment for the journey, which reminded me of my pending deal at the gunstore. I then told Tom of it and asked his opinion of the Henry rifle.

"Never owned one," he answered, "but from what I've heard, they're a mighty fine weapon. They tell me when you start unloading that magazine at any varmint be he two-legged or four, he'll shore high-tail it for the tall timber. I don't reckon you'd be making any mistake buyin' at that price, goin' west as fur as Dodge there's generally plenty of chances to use a good gun, what with buffalo, antelope, wolves and such."

"That's about what I've been thinking," I told him, "but I wanted the advice of someone with experience in the western country."

"Well, as I sed before," he concluded, "it would be mighty handy to have along, especially as I don't have a rifle in my outfit."

Though a complete greenhorn, I was agast at the idea of a man starting a journey of hundreds of miles through Indian country without a rifle of some kind. Here was an example of carelessness I found to be typical of more than one frontiersman and one responsible for the loss of many a scalp. When I mentioned the risks of this attitude, Tom shrugged. "Oh I always aim to have my old Navy Colt handy, or a splattergun loaded with buckshot. Why I carried a .52 caliber Sharps with me three trips across the Plains and never once't got a shot at an Injun, so when I got a chance last summer to trade it for a fair to middlin' mule, I just naturally swapped and never seemed to get around to get another one."

Here was an insight to the character of "old" Tom Powers. He was in fact the salt of the earth, as true a friend and honest a fellow as I ever saw, but possessed of an easy-going, careless nature that more than once got him in hot water. At such times he usually came up with the lame excuse, "well I knowed better but just couldn't seem to get around to it."

Tom, true to his friendly accomodating nature insisted on

14

driving me back across the Kaw to the Tyler & Randall yards and as it was a long distance to "hoof it" I very graciously accepted. Riding on the wagon seat beside my benefactor a thought occurred to me that had been in my mind for some time, namely, "that it would be well to have a good riding horse of my own." Accordingly, I called on Tom again for his opinion.

"Well Sir, Jack, I think a good horse would be a mighty fine idee, if you kin afford it. I have got the old team of grays that I aim for the woman to drive, they're both broke to ride as well as some of the mules. But it would be handy to have a regular saddle horse along, in this busness you're liable to need one every once in a while. Shore would be glad to feed and take care of one if you want to spend your money that away."

As we pulled into the wagonyards he gave me this advice. "Beware of these horse traders, they're generally a pretty crafty lot. I never knowed one that was strictly honest and some of them are downright crooked. So keep your eyes open and let them do most of the talkin', 'remember', these fellars make their living a preying on the unwary."

CHAPTER II

My Money for a Horse

Tyler and Randall as an overland freighting concern had already seen their lush days. Though as a going business they would not yet admit they were on the decline, neverthless the "handwriting was on the wall." The construction of the railroad and inroads of settlers along the eastern environs of the Santa Fe Trail, had already sounded the beginnings of the death knell for the long distance commercial freighter. Hence Tyler & Randall, heeding the lessons of necessity were quietly liquidating unneeded equipment and work stock.

Barney Balaam, the old frontiersman, had told me earlier in the morning of the company's horse sale, but I had given it little thought at the time. Now, however as Tom's advice was fresh on my mind I decided to try there first for a horse rather than looking up a professional horse trader. Upon entering the wagonyard proper the first person I saw was the old "Bufflar" man himself with a blanket over his shoulders, squatting back against a pile of hay, in the language of the Spanish Southwest taking his afternoon "Siesta." I was about to turn away without awakening him when he spoke. "Ain't about to leave without sayin' howdy air ye Jack?"

Surprised, all I could say, was, "you're certainly a light sleeper."

"Shecks" the old man bragged, "they hain't nothin' goes on around here that I don't know about. Whut kin I do for you?"

I explained what I had in mind and asked for directions to the horses for sale. On receiving directions I left at once. Glancing back on leaving the yard I saw the old man huddled up against the hay apparently fast asleep again. A short way beyond I came to a wooden corral with shed attached, a freshly painted sign hung on a post which read "Work Stock For Sale." Seated on the ground and out of the wind a blackbearded citizen and a Mexican were leisurely playing cards. As I stepped closer neither of them looked up nor made any sign they knew I was about so I cleared

16

my throat, intent on their game they both continued to ignore me. Unable to get their attention I approached the fence and looked inside. I saw a motley collection of horses and mules numbering twenty-five or thirty head. They were shaggy, unkept and from all appearances underfed, though mostly heavy work stock there were a few lighter animals among them that were saddle or buggy broke. As I stood looking over the fence trying to locate one among the bunch that appealed to me, I turned to see the white man at my elbow. He was a short stocky fellow wearing a pair of blue jeans rolled to a neat cuff a third the way up his boot tops, and a dark, store bought coat. In his cheek was the inevitable "chaw." A hard looking citizen I thought, but his gaze was calm and unruffled, and his slow drawl was not unpleasant. "Wanta buy a hawse, Mistah?"

I admitted that such was my desire.

"Yore welcome to look." He turned to the Mexican, "Stir em up will you Jose."

Jose climbed the fence, took a rawhide reata off a post and proceeded to move the animals around to where I could view them better. I remembered Tom's advice so I watched closely and silently. The man beside me leaned on the fence gazing disinterestedly as the animals milled about, saying nothing. I watched just as silently for a long time but finally realizing that nothing was to be gained by further silence, I enquired as casually as I could make it sound about his prices, feeling self-consciously that my voice bespoke my inexperience more than my words.

"Mr. Randall said thutty-five apiece, fust come fust served." I could see him sizing me up. looking at my eastern clothes and generally giving me the once over.

"Any of them broke to ride?" I asked.

"Some of em air and some of em ain't. Rope the little sorrel, Jose."

The Mexican manuevered into position, expertly cast his rope and caught the sorrel slick as a whistle. As he led the horse towards the fence he flashed me a toothy grin.

"Ah she ees a good horse Meestair. I will show you," and he leaped on the sorrel's back and rode him around the corral guiding him with his knees as expertly as he had roped him.

17

I could see many good qualities in the sorrel. He seemed to be easy of gait, fairly gentle, yet with a certain amount of spirit, still he had the shabby look of age. As Jose rode him to a stop in front of me I thought of using the old horse traders "standby" of examining his mouth for age, but I knew that would be strictly bluff on my part as I was by no means sure of my ability to tell a horse's age by his teeth.

"How old is he?" I inquired.

The Mexican dismounted and examined the sorrel's mouth, head and feet, apparently satisfying himself before answering.

"She ees a eight, nine year," he hesitated, then finished cryptically in his sing-song accent, "I theenk."

I stole a glance at the other man but not a flicker of expression was in his eyes as he methodically picked his teeth with his pocket knife. Apparently these fellows motives were reasonably honest as far as they went but I saw now that I wasn't getting very far with either of them. Besides I had a distinct feeling of handicap in dealing with them. For it is sometimes a fact that he who has the cigarette to light, the plug of tobacco to chew and spit, or the stick to whittle has an advantage in that human element "composure." I reached down and picked up a piece of white pine and went to work on it with my pocket knife.

"Tell you what," I said making an effort to appear experienced and matter of fact, "I want to look around some more and if I decide to take the sorrel I'll come back and see you fellows."

"Suit yoreself," said my companion shifting his quid, "Might be gone though when you come back."

And that was as near as he ever came to a sales talk.

My next stop was at a popular livery barn, not far from the place I had just left and still in the freighters vicinity and undoubtedly catered to by that trade. In an office just inside the main entrance a small group of men were gathered, out of the weather. Immediately upon making my business known, an old gentleman arose and introduced himself, a southerner and a dyed in the wool "hoss" trader I soon learned.

"Yo'all want to buy a hoss? Well suh yo suttinly came to the right place. Glimp is mah name—Colonel Anthony J. Glimp, suh."

I introduced myself and thoughtfully added that I was from Carolina. He grabbed my hand and shook it and went on in a great fashion after the manner of overly friendly and overwindy salesman.

"I swan, a southern gentleman. I'm a southerner myself suh, bohn, bred, and raised in the bluegrass of old Kaintucky. As one southern gentleman to anothah I'm powerful proud to know you suh. Now I know you are anxious to see the hosses, so just step around the corner please suh, to the little white stockade and you can feast yo eyes on the best collection of hoss flesh that evah graced God's great outdoors."

All of this more or less in the voice and manner of an auctioneer at a country sale.

We stepped around the corner and I grinned to myself at the contrast of the Colonel to the two "wranglers" at the Tyler & Randall corral. With that experience in mind I stooped and picked up a piece of shingle before hitching myself to the top rail, partially ignoring the good Colonel's line. My attitude though never bothered him in the least as the rattle of his own voice was apparently a source of pleasure to him and came as natural as breathing. The only times he would interrupt his regular flow of words was to speak sharply to the stablehand accompanying us, a tall gangling colored boy named Mose.

I seated myself on the top rail and hooked my feet in the rail underneath and started the whittling operations, attempting to study each horse carefully yet not appear too interested. The Colonel had of course exaggerated considerable but he did have some good looking horses. One in particular "stood out." A dark, blaze-face, bay medium height and nimble of foot.

The Colonel having now seated himself beside me, breathing heavily from his exertion, waved his hand and started out anew. "Theah suh! they are. God's gift to the hossman. And I ask you confidentially suh, realizing that you'all is a true lover of hoss flesh, as well as a gentleman, did yo evah behold a noblah, higheh headed assotment of equine vusitality in all yo bohn days? Now, Mose! get in theah boy and put that haltah on the claybank dun.

19

Theah, mah friend, is a hoss as fast as a railway fliah and as gentle as a maiden's caress. No! no! not the gray, yo black jackass, the dun, the claybank dun, boy!"

But Mose was a little horse shy and required considerable urging. The dun was a fairly gentle horse and probably could have been easily caught by some men but he led the awkward Mose a merry chase, allowing him to almost get the rope around his neck and then throw up his head and trot away. It was amusing the way the Colonel's voice would change from his smooth horse traders line to one of sharp exasperation. Yet he never made the slightest move to assist other than bark commands and words of encouragement. But Mose never managed to get the halter on the dun, though he ran the gamut of the Colonel's displeasure from black despair to faint hope and back again. Finally the Colonel gave it up assuring me that he had no idea what in the world could have possessed the usually "placid natuh" of the beast.

I still had my eyes on the blaze-faced bay and was on the point of saying so when the Colonel ordered Mose, "catch the little pinto maih—No! no, the spotted pony. My God boy, don't yo know a pinto from a roan? Theah, theah, yo got her easy, easy! No! she won't kick. Confound yo're squeamish, blubbering soul, Mose, lay that rope around her neck and slip on the haltah."

And so after much encouragement from the sidelines, Mose finally led the little spotted mare over to the fence.

"Theah my boy, is a true Indian pony, puffect in every detail, sound of limb, body, and soul. Broke and trained suh as only the noble Redman can. I have a complete record of her ancestry supplied by the head man from whom I purchased her. The blood of chiefs flows in her veins and I give you my word of honah as a gentleman suh, that she's nevah been off the resuvation befoah I fetched her heah."

About that time an inquisitive mule poked his face near the pinto and the noble blood of the chiefs let go with both hind feet and Mose very nearly jumped the fence.

But the Colonel had a ready answer for that. "Fiah, fiah in her blood that what she's got."

I allowed to myself that a fiery disposition wasn't necessarily

20

one of my requirements. But the Colonel had no way of knowing my thoughts and I suppose he figured the time was ripe to talk turkey.

"Now, suh," he began confidently, "as one gentleman to ano-thah I'm going to sell yo'all this remarkable animal at a price yo nevah dreamed of, in fact suh, I stand to lose mah regulah commission . . ."

"All right," I interrupted just a little fed up with his palavar, "How much is it?"

He started out again on a longwinded build up but I cut him short. "See here Colonel, I'm quite a ways from my hotel and the weather is beginning to look pretty nasty. You don't need to break the news to me gently, I can stand the shock."

He gave me a quick look. "Alright suh I'm going to let you have this little filly foah just sixty-five dollahs."

"Fair enough," I said, "Now as one southern gentleman to another what'll you take for the blaze-faced bay?"

He paused and studied me sharply for a while. I suppose sizing me up for what I was worth. "Well suh, ah'll make yo just as good a deal on the bay hoss, in po'potion of co'se—One hundred dollahs, cash on the ball'el head."

That figure was in fifty dollars of my total cash. A little bit nettled I climbed slowly off the fence, closed my knife, and started to walk away.

"Wait a minute theah son," I thought his voice was a little wheedling. "Yo'all cain't walk out on an offer like this, why that gelding is only a five yeah old and as slick as a new dollah suh, not a blemish on him."

"As far as I am concerned a hundred dollars is enough blemish for me. I'll give you eighty." And I started to walk away again still a little peeved.

But the Colonel now laid his hand on my shoulder in a friendly fashion. "Ah'll tell you what I'll do. I'm a tradah fust, last and all the time suh, and I'll meet a gentleman half way though ah stand to lose money. The fact of the mattah is, I'm overstocked and hay and grain is eating up my profits."

21

"If you meet me half way thats ninety dollars and I'm afraid that is more money than I can spare."

"Now wait just a minute son, befoah you walk away, give this hoss a trial," begged the Colonel. "Besides suh, I want to show yo'all something."

He turned to the corral fence and whistled a plaintive whee-a-whee and the bayhorse instantly pricked up his ears. When the whistle was repeated he came prancing over to the fence, where with a little coaxing the Colonel got his fingers in his mane and held him firmly.

"Now," he invited, "Climb that fence and mount him and I'll gawantee he'll give you a ride as gentle and easy as though you had saddle and bridle suh."

I was a little hesitant at trying a strange horse in such a manner. But at the Colonel's insistence, I climbed on the bay's back, got a grip on his mane, touched him gently with my knees and away we went in a fast pacing walk, picking them up and putting them down as pretty as a drum major. I rode him around the enclosure a couple of times and brought him to a stop with a gentle whoa and an easy pull on the mane. I was more than pleased with his performance and partly to conceal my pleasure, I dismounted and examined him closely from head to foot. I could find no blemish save a faint old collar scar which showed he had been broke to work. For once the old horse trader was silent until he saw I had noticed this.

"He's been used slightly as a buggy hoss which is decidedly to his credit," he admitted.

This was probably true, at any rate the scar was not of a nature to affect his value. I wondered if the Colonel could be persuaded to lower his price another ten dollars, but in my experience, I felt that maybe I had already gotten the price down to "reason" considering the kind of horse the bay was.

"Alright," I finally said, "If you will hold him for me until tomorrow afternoon, I will take him providing I can scrape up enough money to buy a saddle and bridle."

To the old trader who knew enough about youth and was shrewd enough about horse customers in general to know that I was "hooked", this was agreeable so we shook hands on the bargain and parted until the morrow.

The afternoon was drawing to a close when I turned my steps toward the considerable distance separating me from the city proper and my hotel. The weather was getting gloomier all the time so I stepped out rapidly being anxious to get back to my room so that I could catalog the list of items and things that would need to be taken care of tomorrow. The day had been surprisingly eventful and as I walked along I couldn't help but feel it had been well spent.

My way led through the outskirts of the City which at that time had few if any improved roads. To add to this, recent wet weather had turned some areas into mudholes. I approached one of these covering a spot possibly forty feet across, and bridged for the pedestrian by a single long log. It was a precarious crossing at best, but now a slight mist was falling and it made even trickier footing. However I was intent on my thoughts and as has ever been the way of the young and agile, I started briskly across. It was with a start that I looked up from my feet and saw another man coming across from the other end of the log. It didn't appear practical to turn around and go back, besides the other fellow was as much, or more, obligated to do that as I had started first. With this attitude I continued on my way. As we approached each other I recognized the big wagon boss, bundled up from the weather in a heavy short coat and still champing a cigar. Apparently he was unconcerned that anyone else was in the vicinity. In the center of the mudhole a short log was laid crossways under the main log to support it, I spied this as I cast about for a place to pass. We were in a step of each other when I saw that he didn't intend to budge an inch though with proper cooperation we could have passed without mishap. I felt a little glow of anger as I saw the truculent stare on the wagon boss's face but in view of the difference in our size I deemed discretion the better part of valor and moved quickly to place my right foot on the short log and balance my body out of the way so that he could pass. While attempting the maneuver and murmering a slight apology at the same time, I was rudely jolted off balance by the deliberate impact of his hip. Down I went in the loblolly of mud

23

and water while Macanles continued on without so much as giving me a glance.

As I fell I managed to twist myself and hit the mud on my side missing the short log by inches and saving myself a nasty bruising, but that made me feel no better "temperwise." Down in the mud every atom and fiber in me called out for revenge. Like a drowning man grasping for straws I reached for anything to turn the tables. A broken limb, not over a few feet long thrust out from the main log. I grabbed this and twisted for all that I was worth. It caught Macanles in the middle of a step and off he went with his feet flying high and set down with a plop in the muck.

We must have made a pretty picture as we reached dry ground, covered with mud and eyeing each other like a pair of mastiffs. Macanles gave me as venomous a look as I ever saw but I was still mad enough that it tickled a freakish sense of humor in me and I couldn't help goading him, though a dangerous thing to do—more dangerous than I realized.

"I trust, Mr. MaCanles, that you have enjoyed your evening dip."

He said not a word at the moment but slowly unbuttoned his coat and laid it on the ground, then he unbuckled his heavy belt and slipped it out of his trouser loops and deliberately snapped it like a whip.

"Johnny, damn your rebel soul," he said, "You spil't me offa that log on purpose."

"Thats a brilliant deduction on your part," I mocked him, "same as you 'spil't' me."

"Don't back talk me young fellar cause I'm thinkin' already of flaying the hide offen you." He said savagely, and I saw by the cold determined look in his eyes, I wasn't dealing with an ordinary bully.

Appropriate words came to my mind but I kept my mouth shut and backed warily away a couple of steps hoping he was responsible enough person that he never intended to carry out his threats. But I was still too mad to be properly cowed and I had no intentions of backing away any further, when a dry voice

24

behind me spoke, "What's agoin' on here fellars, you two a fixin' to have a mud slingin' bee?"

There was something familiar about the voice, I turned and recognized my acquaintance at the gunstore, Smokey Joe Smith. McCanles stopped in his tracks, though he kept his eyes glued on me and made no answer.

Didn't know you went in for mud baths, Clint." Smith addressed the wagonboss. "Fact of the matter I didn't have the slightest idea you was addicted to the bath habit at all."

"Lots of things you don't know about me, Smith, most of which is none of your Gawdamn business." Returned the other.

"Well, thats right likely correct," agreed Smith, "but now, bein' as you've already snapped the mud offa that belt, wouldn't it be a good idee to put it back on before your drawers slip any further."

McCanles looked at him truculently. "You ain't putting that in the way of an order are you?" He enquired with an edge to his voice.

Smith shrugged. "Nope, I reckon just a friendly suggestion."
McCanles gave him a final disgusted look, turned his back and walked away. I walked over to Smith and offered my hand. You picked an opportune time to show up sir, the fur was about to fly here and in all probability I was in for the worst of it."

"Shucks, I was standin over agin that building a watching you fellars all the time." He said modestly. "Besides anyone a showin up when I did would've likely had the same effect on Clint. When a man's all set to do a meaness thinkin' there's nobody around, he's naturally gonna be some upset when a witness appears unexpected."

"Lots of fellows wouldn't have stood up to McCanles like you did though, and give him a gentle lecture. I sure appreciate it."

Smith dismissed this with a wave of his hand and a sly grin. "Forget it, forget it, it was worth a weeks pay for me to see the way you upset Clint off that log. I swear, I never saw a man leave his feet so sudden and set on his ass so hard in all my born days."

He watched me as I attempted ineffectively to clean the mud off myself and clothing. "Here Jack," he said with easy sociability, "let me clean off your back. You dasn't go in that fancy Ho'tel like a boar shoat fresh out of a hawg wallar."

He drew a butcher knife from a sheath under his coat and started scraping mud with the back of it. As the two of us worked at the well-nigh impossible job of making me presentable again I couldn't help notice that Smokey Joe went well armed; one of the few I noticed carrying hardware in the city. Under his carelessly opened coat hung a holstered pistol, one of the "lately converted cartridge" type, with a beltfull of gleaming copper shells. He carried his artillery with an unconcern, apparently so much a habit with him that he gave it no more thought than an article of clothing.

That night, I lay in my bed unable to sleep because of my trouble with McCanles and what effect that might jeopardize my job. True he wouldn't pay my wages, neither would I be directly responsible to him, yet he was the wagonmaster "the Captain" of the expedition and I had certainly got off on the wrong foot with him; especially (and I feared he was) if he was the type to hold a grudge. I had worked up so much enthusiasm for the trip west, in this one day alone, that I couldn't think of giving it up, yet it worried me, "when I as a very minor part of the freighting outfit would be under the command and prejudiced eye of the Wagon-boss."

When I finally dropped off to sleep, I dreamed I was behind a stone fortification, and unable to move because I was paralized with fear, when over the wall with a butcher knife in his teeth, came Smokey Joe Smith, his dark eyes flashing and a bloodthirsty leer on his face. I awoke in a cold sweat and staggered to the wash basin where I bathed my face in cold water. As full wakefulness returned I sat on the edge of the bed and told myself this would all be amusing in the morning, and came to the logical conclusion the nightmare was a direct result of the days events and the over-large serving of roast beef I had partaken of for supper.

26

CHAPTER III
Getting Ready

The next morning on awakening at about sunrise, I pulled on my trousers and walked to the window which opened on the backyard and alley of the two story brick hotel building. The somewhat shabby view was a typical example of the evolution process of a country town's gradual and sometimes painful change to a full fledged city. Below and to the right a dilapidated board privy leaned to one side with the door open and hanging from one hinge. Directly behind was a small weatherbeaten frame building with the door open and the hotels wood supply stacked against it, in front a dozen or so dominecker hens scratched and clucked industriously, while a red rooster perched on the woodpile welcomed the sun with a hearty crow. On the far side of a flimsy pen attached to one side of the building a black sow nursed a week old litter of pigs. Turning my eyes from this domestic an uncity like scene I was happy to observe the bright and sunny beginnings of another day.

As the weather had abated, so had my worries of the night before, especially after putting a brace of eggs and a generous portion of Missouri smoked ham under my belt. Of course, the thought of McCanles and his mental attitude toward me was too recent to disregard completely, so I resolved to talk to Tom Powers about it when we next met and in the meantime, quit worrying. After all I concluded, anyone responsible enough to hold the position of wagon boss for a large freighting concern was certain to have too many responsibilities and far too many greater problems, to harbor a grudge over such a trivial affair as ours.

As today was Friday, I had but one day to finish the tentative arrangements I had made the day before on gun and horse, besides make all the other purchases of clothes and equipment necessary to outfit myself for the trip west. I located a clothing store that featured reasonable prices, and purchased several sets of durable work clothing of a type much worn by freighters. I also laid in a supply of socks, underclothing, etc. Having settled for these purchases, I walked away with them in my arms mentally calculating my cash balance. As I figured it roughly, I now possessed approximately one hundred and twenty-one dollars.

With this money now, almost "burning a hole in my pockets," I spent the balance of the day in spending it, which included my tentative transactions of yesterday. When the day was over, I walked in my hotel, arms loaded with blankets and clothing, one Henry repeating rifle with several boxes of .44 caliber cartridges; a bill of sale for one bay horse, fifteen and one-half hands high and five years old.,—Know all men by these presents: The said seller hereby covenants with said buyer that he is the lawful owner of said horse,—signed Anthony J. Glimp. But last and not least a perfectly good McClellan saddle, straps, buckles, and all, with bridle thrown in.

Saturday morning arrived and 'ere the sun was hardly up, I was about arranging my belongings and making ready to vacate my hotel room. By the time I walked downstairs for breakfast everything was packed, bundled and ready to go.

After finishing breakfast I returned to my room and just for the record, reached in my pocket and pulled out the few coins that were all my remaining cash. It may be interesting to note that we have all heard old timers relate that they hit Kansas City, Denver or such and such a place with ten cents or so in their jeans. With me it was a little different. I left K. C. with twenty-five cents.

Sitting on my bed surveying my various bundles and such, I was strongly tempted to spend the "two-bits" and hire a colored boy to help carry my belongings to the Powers camp. But I decided to keep the small sum for emergency, probably more for sentimental than practical reasons.

How to carry everything at once was a problem soon solved, though it required some juggling and considerable muscular exertion. The bundles I fastened together and slung to my back with a piece of small rope, my traveler's bag. stuffed full, I held in my right hand, my rifle in my left and the McClellan which was mostly straps and stirrups under my left arm. Thus arrayed I stamped down stairs and out in the street two blocks before stopping to rest. Then only because my arms felt like they were being pulled from their sockets. Sittng there resting, passersby stared

28

at me and my paraphernalia, so as soon as I had rested a little I gathered up my load and made a few more blocks. After a number of similar stops for rest I eventually reached Colonel Glimp's establishment. Here the Colonel delegated his boy Mose to help me and after a time we had the saddle strapped on the bay's back and most of my loose equipment fastened on after one fashion or another. Never, I suppose has another animal ever been loaded in quite the same manner as a green easterner and an awkward colored boy loaded this one, and it certainly testified to the "placid natuh" of the beast.

I imagine I cut quite a figure as we went pacing down the road. Baggage to the front of me and baggage to the rear, tied on in whatever way was handy and possible, while under my leg tied securely fore and aft was the .44 rimfire repeating rifle. As I neared the vicinity of the Tyler & Randall Corrals I remembered the imperturbable stare of the stocky horse wrangler, and I suddenly had no desire to meet him again in my present get-up, so I steered my horse to the left and behind the corrals. While my "Blaze" horsed picked his way through this back way which was muddy and strewn with worn-out equipment, I heard the unexpected sound of music and a man's voice singing deep and pleasant. I pulled up in spite of myself and presently located the musician. The horse wrangler seated on the threshold of the stable's back door, picked and sawed with expert skill on an instrument, the likes of which I had never seen, while he sang the soft Latin jargon of a Spanish love song. To complete the duet, the Mexican wrangler danced, pivoted and swayed in perfect time to the music. For the minute or two I sat listening, I enjoyed their performance more than many a professional musicale I have paid to see, and I curbed an impulse to applaud when I remembered I was evesdropping, so I nudged old Blaze with my knee and we went on our way.

When finally, I rode into the Powers camp, I found everybody industriously preparing for the long trip ahead. Busy, but not too busy to stop and surround me, eager with questions of my horse and outfit. Questions, answers, commands and just plain palaver filled the air as I dismounted and started to unlimber my gear.

"Where d'je get the horse?" and before I could answer, "Sure

29

is a purty one," and "How fast kin he run?" "What d'je have to give for a horse like that? My, my, one of them fancy repeating guns, sure won't need no escort this trip." "Jeremiah! get out from under that horse this minnit and quit jerking his tail, my land, these young uns, I declare they wear body out, and Tommy don't you dast to touch that gun or I'll take a switch to both of you'ns right away . . ." and so on and so forth. There was rarely a dull moment in the Powers family.

After a while though things quieted down and I made the necessary answers and explanations. My bundles and gear were removed and placed in the wagon I was to drive, and Blaze was picketed out to graze with the other stock on the spring shoots of grass that was beginning to turn green.

Most of the actual work of loading and equipping the wagons had been finished days ago and all that now remained was the countless little things that go with any long journey. Among these were a multitude of chores like greasing the wagons, seeing the canvas covers or wagonsheets were in place and properly secured, repairing and rebuilding single trees, double trees, neck-yokes and harness. Work routine is almost constant in the life of a freighter.

I was only partially experienced in this type of work, but being fairly handy with tools I soon caught on and made myself useful, at least I pleased Tom Powers, partly I suspect, because it was not in his nature to be very particular. However, long years of freighting had instilled in him a dread of weak and unroad-worthy equipment. In this particularly, he didn't care much about the looks of things, but in the words of a popular saying he wanted it "Hell for strong."

Tasks of this sort kept us pretty well occupied until late in the afternoon when we were interrupted by the arrival of a large freight wagon loaded with sacked grain and other cargo. This was Power's final load and was handled by his other driver, Fritz Hemmermeyer. a heavy built, stolid but good natured Dutchman. In times to come he bore the brunt of many of Tom's jokes without losing his good humor. Where everyday hard work was to be done Fritz was worth his weight in gold. Where skill was required he had none whatsoever. His dumbness was sometimes monumental, yet occasionally he surprised us with an unexpected spark of mentality. So much for Fritz. I don't know how we could have got along without him and a few times I wonder how we got along with him.

Tom Powers little train consisted of six wagons or actually seven, the latter being a very light one with low sides and only partly loaded. Three of these rigs could be classed in the heavy category. Tom, old time freighter that he was, handled one of these trailing a medium sized one behind, the double layout was pulled by a six mule team and guided by a jerkline. Fritz drove a four mule team pulling one of the other wagons. All three of these wagons were loaded with Government freight for Fort Dodge. Fritz though experienced in years could never be considered expert enough to trust with a jerkline so his teams were equipped with regular lines as were mine and the other single team wagons.

The other heavy wagon was unique enough that it warrants a separate description. It was a little wider than standard tread and was equipped with a heavy home made bed of thick oak. Tom liked to brag of how he had picked this rig up for a "song" as nobody wanted a non-standard tread, and how he had hired a carpenter "out of a job" to build the special bed for thutty dollars. And this bed was special in particular for its extra width. It was built as wide "to the inch" as wheel clearance would permit, this was so that it could be used on the road as a sort of portable kitchen. After the arrival of Fritz, we three men with the able direction of Mamie loaded the kitchen stove in the wagon and cleated it securely to the floor near the rear where it would be handy for her to dispense the "vittles" to those on the ground. A homemade cabinet about three feet high was loaded and located just ahead of the stove. This had a flat table top and just about comprised the total furniture of the kitchen wagon. The rest of the space forward was used to store a supply of flour, sugar, molasses, potatoes and other eatables and served also as sleeping quarters for the two small boys. Altogether this didn't make a heavy load and was handled by a reliable old team of gray horses with Mamie at the reins.

Sid drove a gentle team of horses to a smaller wagon, lightly loaded with a little lumber on the bottom and other supplies and the light wagon already described was trailed behind.

My team, a pair of husky mules, pulled a wagon loaded with grain (corn and oats) in burlap bags, a few sacks of potatoes a few sweet potatoes and turnips and the balance bundled oats, carefully loaded. This latter for emergency feed and bedding. On one side was slung a plow and on the other a harrow, which just about made up the machinery for Tom's prospective farming venture.

My wagon served as sleeping quarters for Sid and myself. By shifting the grain sacks around and spreading some of the oats straw on top and laying our blankets overall we had a comfortable bed, especially for the young and hardy not used to present day pampering.

When I crawled between the blankets my first night with the Powers, it was with the feelings of well being and relaxed excitement. The cool damp breeze off the river bottom stirred under the wagon sheet and I could see the faint outlines of the hickory bows as the light from the dying campfire filtered through the canvas top and cast faint flickering shadows overhead. Pleasant sleep and the full blackness of night slowly came upon us. This was the beginning of a new life for me I felt then, and I know now a life and a privilege for which I shall never cease to thank our Divine Providence—the privilege to spend a period in the prime of my life in God's Great Domain, unspoiled, untamed and largely unnamed, "The Great Plains" in "68."

CHAPTER IV

We Hit The Trail

Sunday, before the start of our journey was largly uneventful except that I do remember we all went to church, the Powers family and crew complete, including Fritz Hemmermeyer and myself. "Church" was held in a barn which just a few hours earlier had served as a dancehall. This preceding affair, must have been quite lively as at least three freshly emptied beer kegs served as supports for planks seating the Sunday morning congregation. Services were conducted by a roaming Parson of the shouting variety who served us the promise of Hellfire and brimstone.

After the "preachin," and while visiting with others at the gathering, Tom learned McCanles intended to start the first leg of the journey, this afternoon. Supposedly, to take advantage of the fine weather and work some of the "kinks" out of his teams and equipment on the short afternoon haul. Understandably, Tom was a little upset that he hadn't been directly notified by the wagonboss of the change in plans. But not to be outdone he determined to get a head start on the main train before joining it tomorrow for whatever position in the caravan the wagonboss chose to allot us. Accordingly, we hurried back to the wagons, fed the teams well and harnessed them and Mamie prepared an early lunch. By two o'clock we had broke camp and were ready to roll. Tom decided that Fritz should go ahead as he was familar with the road and country having worked for his father-in-law, east of Tonganoxie during the war years. With Fritz at the reins of skittish and well rested teams, Tom knew there might be problems as the former was nervously pulling and jerking at his leaders heads before he had gone a couple of wagon lengths. Fortunately, however an acquaintance of Tom's, on a Sunday afternoon drive with his family, happened by. Noticing the commotion he pulled up and knowing Fritz. well, he climbed on the seat beside the Dutchman and took the reins for the first half mile until the lead team had settled down. From then Fritz managed the rest of the afternoon but not with a great deal of confidence. But, for that matter, myself and even Tom about had our hands full until the restive mules worked some of the surplus energy out of their systems. It was a quiet Sunday afternoon through a settled country with only light traffic and dry roads, after about eight miles Fritz led us off the trail to an open area where water was available, here we made camp. Although the afternoon haul was not long it helped that much and to Tom's satisfaction we stayed ahead of McCanles.

Monday morning, the real beginning of our journey, we were up long before the break of day and were soon gathered shivering around the kitchen wagon eating side-meat and eggs and sipping hot coffee. Breakfast soon finished, Mamie and the children were left to do the dishes and minor camp chores while we started harnessing and readying the teams for this first full day on the road. It was quite a chore as we had only the dim light from an oil lantern to work by. The main burden of course fell on Tom because the Freighter business was new to me and because Fritz was utterly useless for anything requiring the least mechanical ability. Naturally with a character of this kind underfoot and a green hand like myself it was quite a strain on Tom's patience and unfortunately that was a virtue with which he was not overly blessed. However, Tom held himself pretty well in check for a time. After a while the teams were harnessed. The hogs consisting of two sows, a gilt and young boar were manhandled in the crates in the low-wheeled cart trailed behind my wagon. The crates containing about three dozen chickens were loaded in the light wagon and the two milk cows were led up and tied to the rear of the kitchen wagon, where the rest of the cattle consisting of two calves and a yearling heifer, could be depended upon to trail along.

We were now ready to hitch up and here we soon had our

34

hands full. The mules having undergone a period of rest with good feed, now exhibited a lot of unnecessary friskiness. First we hitched the two teams of gentle horses, Mr. Power's and Sid's, without difficulty. Then we got my team of mules hitched and tethered to the wagon in front. Fritz's four mule team that had caused problems yesterday afternoon came next. The wheelers were hitched with little trouble but when the lead pair were led up under the bungling persuasion of Fritz, they promptly kicked out of their traces, got tangled up in the lines and we soon had a general mix-up on our hands. Tom had been gradually losing his calm, I could hear his muttered epithets and noticed his sharper language to Fritz who fumbled awkardly about, managing mostly to get in the way. Tom, about at the end of his endurance finally, bluntly ordered his driver to get out of the way and up on the wagon and see if he couldn't hold them mumbility-mumbility, mules.

Mamie then left her housewifely duties and took Fritz's place on the ground. This proved to be a big improvement. In fact, she and Tom would have probably done even better if I had not been in the way, as wrangling wild mules was a new experience for me—and an enlightening one. I remember thinking a time or two I would surely be trampled and how Tom escaped getting crippled must have been on account of his mule-whackers instinct, for he was in and out among the plunging animals, jerking and swearing in a whispering undertone. Suddenly one of the mules reversing from a vicious jerk on the head, brought his foot down on a weakened trace and snapped it. Powers grabbed the leader's lines, threw all patience to the winds, cut loose at the top of his lungs and fairly blistered the air. Mamie promptly possessed herself of the lantern and hustled the kids who had gathered to watch the excitement off to the kitchen saying she wasn't going to have no young uns of hers stand around and listen to sich language.

"I never knowed it to fail," bellowed Tom. "But when a body starts something like this if ever damn thing don't go wrong." And he added a few more choice superlatives, suddenly stopping in the middle of a jucy cussword to jerk some soberness into a raring mule. Strangely enough the mules quieted down somewhat after this verbal chastisement as though the thought had been conveyed to them better than soft words, that they had gone about far enough—mules are like that sometimes, especially the freighter variety.

Mamie still sore at Tom, refused to return the lantern so we had to patch the broken trace in the dark. We accomplished this without very much trouble and Tom regained some of his good humor and wound up confiding sheepishly to me that this trace ort to have been fixed long ago but he just naturally had never got around to it.

I supposed by now that everything was under control but abruptly Fritz was in trouble. The Dutchman by constantly pulling and jerking on the lines to hold the mules in check had caused them to back up and cramp the front wheels, thus putting the heavily loaded wagon in danger of turning over.

"Give em their heads, give em their heads," yelled Tom taking in the situation at a glance, "Or they'll turn the wagon over, you damn fool."

Thoroughly rattled, Fritz popped the wheelers on the back and loosened the reins on the leaders. The mules sprang forward with a jerk that nearly snapped the wagon tongue and took off down the muddy trail in the semi-darkness, raring and jumping with Fritz yelling "Whoa!" imploringly, as if his life depended on it; and he no doubt thought that it did.

Tom faced with a dilemma now, for which there appeared no alternative (save let Fritz take his chances and help himself as best he could) became surprisingly calm.

"Just have to let em go. I cain't leave these here ornery devils of mine. Maybe them critters of his'n'll calm down after a spell?" "Or," he added half hopefully, "Maybe the dumb bastard will fall off and break his fool neck."

During these morning preparations I had been trying manfully to do my part, though like poor Frtz I was no doubt at times more in the way than anything else. But when the four mule team and the loaded wagon went lurching down the trail, the wailing voice of the Dutchman imploring helplessly for his mules to "Whoa", was more than I could stand. I ran over quickly and untied the halter rope of my saddle horse, swung on his bare back

36

and neckreining him easily with the rope and without waiting for yea or nay from my boss, I swung out on the trail with a clatter of hooves, after the runaway wagon.

Down the trail perhaps a quarter of a mile, I made out in the morning light that Fritz's wagon had come to a halt, the narrow trail being quite simply blocked by an early-rising farmer with a load of hay. When I arrived on the scene the bearded farmer and his husky son had the frisky mules pretty well under control and were ineffectually trying to bring the scared Dutchman back to his senses. When the poor fellow recognized me, realizing by then that he and his cargo were safe, he soon came around although still visibly shaken. When the farmer moved his hay wagon we found a place where we could pull Fritz's load slightly off the trail. The accommodating farmer then volunteered that his son could stay with Fritz until we caught up with the other wagons. I thanked these two accommodating citizens sincerely and Fritz done the same (only profusely) and I mounted my horse and galloped back to Tom and the main wagons. Somewhere I had heard of a saying among muleskinners that to handle them you should know as much as the mules. If true, this left Fritz at considerable disadvantage. But I knew the Dutchman was not without experience as a teamster. Perhaps this little "baptism of fire" with these particular mules would bring out his better qualities on the trail.

Tom had things pretty well under control and was waiting a little impatiently for my return. But he quickly returned to good humor when I told him what happened and that everything was safe and in good hands.

Mamie gave the kids orders to set down and shut their mouths, and that she didn't want to hear "ary another squawk out of them." And they obeyed promptly for a change, as childlike, their minds were filled with excitement and awe for the big journey ahead. I tethered Blaze to the rear of my rig, and with the lines firmly in my hands, clambered up on the seat under the canvas canopy. Tom hollered, "Roll out." And I needed considerable strength to control even my gentle team and fall in line at my place in the rear.

Far to the east the coming of the sun commenced to change

the darkness of night to the morning light. As we moved out from the campgrounds and headed westerly we soon came to the spot where Fritz waited with his mules under the firm hands of the big farm boy. With little difficulty we pulled apart enough so that the Dutchman could pull in behind Tom where he would be less apt to get into any further difficulties. This maneuver soon accomplished, we pulled smoothly out on the trail again and were on our way.

Soon as the teams became accustomed to their loads and the trail, we were moving along at a steady pace, with only the lurch and clug of the wagons and the jangle of the chains and harness breaking the stillness of the morning. I felt the chill of the early air as the slowly rising sun promised a rising temperature. After a while we commenced to crawl slowly up a long grade. The mules began to buckle down in their collars and Tom yelled back at the top of his voice. "Keep em movin, till we get to the top."

By sun-up we had reached the crest of the ridge and pulled to a stop on level ground to let the teams blow. I stood up and looked back. Below in the glare of the early sun, stretched what appeared to be an endless train of white covered wagons. The lead ones just beginning the long climb up the ridge. This was the main Tyler and Randall train. Actually numbering only twenty-four wagons, it was not large as freighter trains went in those days. But watching as we did from the higher ground of the ridge, the line of heavy vehicles presented the appearance of a considerable procession.

Studying the slowly approaching wagons for a while, Tom finally dropped to the ground, pounded his hands lightly against his hips to get some of the morning chill out of them and then proceeded to carefully go over his harness and outfit. This was more or less habit, born of necessity with the experienced freighter and an example of how serious Powers considered the present undertaking, as his usual nature was inclined somewhat on the careless side. We carefully checked and made what adjustments seemed necessary and advisable as we waited. For this Tom decided would be a good place to wait and as "diplomatically as possible" join the main train under the leadership of Clint McCanles.

Presently the wagon boss appeared on horseback, well ahead of the lead wagon; chewing a cigar as usual. Recognizing him at a distance, I discreetly moved to the far side of my team and was busy adjusting a harness buckle as he rode by. Probably he didn't notice me nor never gave me a thought; as least he gave no sign that he did. I saw him nod casually as he rode by Mrs. Powers though he made no effort at politeness. "Howdy Powers," he said sourly as he rode up to Tom, "What you tryin to do, burn the Gawdamn trail up this mornin?"

Tom, wise in the ways of the times took no offense. "I reckon not Clint, just working a little of the vinegar out of my teams," he answered good humoredly.

After this, some men would have grinned and passed pleasantries of the day with a fellow traveler, but not McCanles, he came directly to the point. "By Gawd, Powers I reckon yore outfit better pull in behind and' take the drag for a spell."

"Just as you say Clint, anything to be agreeable," Tom of course knew it was common trail etiquette to take turns at the drag and reasoned he would as soon take his here where there was less chance for a dry dusty trail. Besides ". . . better humor Mc-Canles as long as possible."

Without further ado the wagon boss turned his horse and rode back toward his wagons. At Tom's suggestion we pulled our wagons off the main road and waited for the McCanles train to go by. As the wagons came over the brow of the rise, I got my first glimpse of the frontier freighter in his native element. The big Tyler and Randall wagons were pulled by six mule teams and controlled by jerk lines . Most of the drivers rode one of the wheelers and were as much at home on the back of a mule as they were on the ground. Some of these fellows were a pictuer-esque sort. Although they were generally dressed plainly, some of them had picked up a little apparel of the west; momentoes, I suppose of former trips which gave them an added touch of color. Without exception they were expert at their jobs and not a few showed they knew it with a devil-may-care manner.

The public has never known a great deal about the freighter. He has never been romanticized like the cowboy, yet in his own way his life was just as exciting. The skilled muleskinner was just as good and in many ways just as spectacular handling his particular job as the best of cowboys. Still, in the "storied annals" of the west, he is largely unsung.

As the first outfit went by, the driver astride the nigh wheeler, nodded and waved his hand. He was a big red-whiskered Missourian wearing an Army cap set cockily on his head. Sitting at the front, independent as if he owned the wagon, was our old acquaintance, Barney Balaam. The old timer, wearing a fringed buckskin shirt for the occasion was beaming with friendship and good humor. "How air ye Tom and Mis Powers and ie gollies Jack, how be you?"

As the train slowly passed by, some of the teamsters gave us a nod or greeting while others appeared not to notice us. Needless to say our entire group was an appreciative audience, taking in every detail as the big freighter outfit rumbled and clanked past. As the last wagon approached Tom and the driver hollered a friendly greeting to each other. "That's Andy Cooper," Powers explained, "Knowed him for years, a fine fellar, owns his own outfit and bringing up the drag as you might expect with Clint McCanles ramroddin."

Following Cooper s wagon came the "cavvyard' or remuda consisting of the spare stock, some forty or fifty head, mostly mules trailing docilely along, for the most part being veterans of many a road trip. The remuda was in the charge of two riders. As they came near I recognized them at once as the short, bearded fellow at Tyler and Randall's and his Mexican partner Jose. I started to speak as they went by lounging lazily in their saddles but as neither gave us more than a passing glance, I contented myself with a short nod remembering from my past experience that they were not a very demonstrative pair as far as the social graces were concerned. For some reason I had developed a curious interest in these two fellows. I suppose because in their manner there was sort of a mystery of adventure surrounding them, at least as far as I was concerned. The American was officially night wrangler and was known aptly enough as Mustang. The Mexican, a converted horse wrangler served part time as cook (and he was a good one). Jose was as villianous looking a fellow as I have ever seen though his actions as a wrangler and cook belied his appearance.

In time he proved to be as reliable a man as there was in the Tyler & Randall outfit despite his foreboding appearance.

Tom pulled the lead wagon in behind the remuda and again we were on our way. Our day that had started so brightly with sunshine soon changed as we again moved in to the lower lands. A light fog or mist soon enveloped us and cut visibility to a few hundred feet at the best. Because of this I was unable to tell much about the country we were passing through. We were held up at intervals for crossings, detours and such. At one of these Tom explained that this wasn't a regular route, but as soon as we got clear of the thicker settlement around the Kansas side or Wyandotte part of Kansas City, that we could really move out. Finally well past noon the sun came out and we pulled up for our midday rest and meal. The place picked was in a meadow near a small stream of clear water and in an apparently isolated spot. We had just finished unhitching the teams and were watering them, after having carried fresh water to the kitchen wagon and gathered a little dry wood for a cook fire, when a pair of strangers appeared and notified us we were trespassing on private lands and wanted to know who was in charge. Tom diplomatically directed them to the head of the train. These fellows were reasonable appearing and of course were well within their rights as the damage some two hundred head of livestock could do to the grass in the meadow was of some importance.

Presently they returned with the wagon boss, having been joined in the meantime by four more of their brethern. McCanles as expected was fuming and came right to the point. "These fellars want a dollar a wagon for us to noon here. You can do as you like Powers, but by God I ain't gonna pay tribute to no Goddamned brigands." And he put his heels to the side of his mount and galloped back to the head of the train.

Andy Cooper who had unhitched nearby came over and he and Tom held a little conference. From their remarks I could tell that they too were a little nettled at this unaccustomed charge for which as old freighters, they had always taken for granted. Still they were reasonable enough to see some justification in the demands made upon them. Besides it didn't

41

pay to push their teams too hard the first few days. The result was they came to terms with the owners by the payment of a few dollars and quietly settled the matter. But not so McCanles. It was apparent that he intended to stay put—and that he did. We could see him directing a number of his men to guard the stock while the rest ate. This consumed the better part of two hours during which time McCanles himself carried on an intermittent arguement with the landowner delegation which by this time had swelled to a crowd of about a dozen citizens of apparent Indian lineage. By now it began to look like there might be trouble. The wagon boss had buckled on his .44 Colts pistol, and the night wrangler also armed with a six-shooter took his place silently beside McCanles. Otherwise, the freighters remained unarmed but the very size and character of their force served to hold the other side in check.

We finished a square meal of fried potatoes, ham and gravy, apple butter and black coffee and were sitting around waiting for something to happen when we noticed the lead wagons of the main train pulling out. We quickly hitched our teams and were soon pulling in line and the train was under way again. The last we saw of our noon time callers, McCanles was standing in his stirrups shaking his fist at them.

Mile after mile we traveled that afternoon. To the north we could see intermittent hilly and prairie country, sprinkled at places with fairly heavy timber. Sometimes we saw well improved homes of finished lumber and stone, indicating a certain prosperity for the area. To the south lay the wide Kaw with its broad slow current some times in plain sight. It was an interesting afternoon's travel through mostly beautiful country. Only here and there scars on the landscape gave evidence of the inroads of a destructive civilization.

Interesting though it was, I felt a little disappointment. As we passed settlement after settlement, I reflected that this locality was practically uninhabited as little as twenty years ago. I had half expected to find a virgin land, instead I saw before me a modern farming country not too much unlike parts of Ohio and Illinois. Newer, it is true but settled and secure; while I had longed for the wild unsettled regions.

42

About an hour before dark McCanles came riding back and told Tom he had decided to split the train up for the night in about three or four divisions. As usual he gave his orders as one who expects to be obeyed and gave no reasons or details. We reasoned (and correctly it turned out) that the wagon boss didn't care for another squabble such as the one that had taken place at the noon camp. Accordingly, at the first likely looking place we pulled off the trail and made camp. We were careful to picket our stock close to the wagons and give them a good feed of shelled corn. The grass had been pretty well trampled around the place from numerous hooves ahead of us. So we could see little reason for complaint from the owner on that score. Tom figured we wouldn't have any difficulty that couldn't be settled with a little cold cash. Perhaps we were lucky, at least nobody bothered us.

When all the numerous chores of the camp had been completed, darkness was settling around us when we heard with pleasure the welcome call of supper. With another good hot meal tucked under our belts, we were ready to hit the hay without any further ceremony for though we had not made so many miles as we did many times afterward it had been a long hard day for all of us. I pulled the blankets up around my chin, snuggled down comfortably in the bed of oats straw and was asleep in a matter of minutes.

The next morning we were up long before daylight feeding and harnessing the teams by lantern light. Breakfast over, we had little difficulty hitching up, as our mules were pretty well tamed by yesterdays hard haul. Likewise myself and Fritz commenced to get the "hang" of our jobs and were able to contribute to a smooth and early start. Out on the road we moved right along and shortly after sun-up commenced to catch up with the remuda and drag of the main train.

It soon became apparent that this day we were not to be favored with the fine weather we had experienced the day before. Clouds commenced scudding across the sky and by mid-morning it was completely cloudy. A damp northeast breeze blew at our backs. Tom called a halt and we got spare pieces of canvas and made makeshift flaps to cover the rear of all the covered wagons except the kitchen wagon which was already so equipped.

43

Just in time too, because we had no sooner hit the trail again when big scattering flakes of snow commenced falling. These soon changed to a light drizzling rain. This was the kind of weather which made one realize the hardships of travel in the prairie schooner. Luckily for us the wind was directly behind us much of the time, thus giving us the protection of the canvas covers. Occasionally, however the trail would veer to the north and the driver would then get the brunt of the cold drizzle. Fortunately the temperature was slightly above freezing and we got cold only when we were partially exposed to the storm. I was dressed in warm clothing, though it lacked a lot of being waterproof. Tom had given me part of an old tarpaulin to cover my bedroll. I removed this from my bedding now and fastened it around the front opening of the wagon cover so as to serve as a windbreaker for the unprotected part of my body for I realized without the use of a little ingenuity I would soon be wet to the skin. Incidentally, I had gone through the rigors of this type of weather more than once during the war and I remember well the misery and discomforts of those experiences. Here with the temperature little above freezing I took advantage of every bit of protection from the cold drizzle.

I wondered how other members of our outfit were faring, especially Mrs. Powers and Sid. But both of those individuals knew enough to "come in out of the rain". With their gentle and trailwise horse teams, they simply tied up the lines, moved back under the full protection of the wagon sheets and let their teams follow the wagon ahead. Presently on the next turn I saw Tom "give it up" on the back of his off wheeler and crawl under the shelter of his wagon sheet. How Fritz was making out I couldn't tell but for his sake I hoped the instinct of self-preservation was stronger in him than his capacity for genuine intellect, or other wise he could be in for a long cold day.

This day we passed the "considerable" town of Lawrence. I had read and heard a great deal of this place and its importance in history during the violent pro-slavery versus free-state days prior to the war. But now as I strained my eyes through the drizzle and the distance, it appeared to be a modern and industrious town, albeit with a definite newer look than the towns back east.

The trail showed some improvement as we traveled west, there being evidence of much travel on it, though this dreary morning we met little traffic. As far as the road bed was concerned we found it in good shape except for the usual chugholes and muddy spots which by now we had grown used to and more or less expected. At intervals through the mist I could see the herder disconsolately, following the remuda. He wore the broad brimmed hat of his trade and a sort of a cape draped over his shoulders protecting his body. Nevertheless, I didn't envy him nor the majority of the muleskinners who continued to sit astride their mules. I wondered if they weren't prompted by the idea that it was a sign of weakness to try to seek a litte protection from the weather. Then again, under the wagon boss, they worked for a hard and tough taskmaster who had definite and outspoken opinions of how things should be done regardless of a little personal discomfort.

At noon we stopped on the east side of a small patch of timber. On the other side of this the rear section of the main train went into camp. I noticed they pulled a number of their wagons close together and overlapping each other, thus forming some protection from the drizzle before they lit their cook-fire. The cook with the main train carried a supply of dry wood for such an emergency as this. But Tom for no good reason at all had carelessly neglected to carry sufficient dry wood. Consequently, Mamie barely had enough to start a fire in the stove. After we had parked our wagons in a manner to protect the rear of the kitchen and give sort of an open court to light a fire on the ground, Tom and I grabbed the two axes and soon went to work on a likely looking log. After, of course, Mamie had given Tom a well-deserved lecture on allowing the wood supply to run so low. A lecture by the way, to which I fervently though silently agreed.

With Tom slinging his axe like a good fellow we soon had considerable wood cut. As for myself, the axe I was using was so dull it was impossible to do anything other than pound the wood to pieces, though I worked myself to the limit, and the axe was one tool with which I had a lot of experience and some skill.

After we had cut and "hacked" enough wood for a few

45

days' supply, Tom looked at me with a sheepish grin, "I reckon I knowed we ort to have had more wood along, but I just naturally never got around to cuttin it."

I turned the axe in my hand and ran a finger along the blade as dull and filled with nicks as an axe can get. I thought of all the long idle hours Tom and crew had spent in camp near Kansas City and said nothing.

With the help of Sid, we soon had the wood transferred to the wagons, putting the most inside for future use. The driest, we gave Mamie for the cookstove which was already going and appetizing smells were coming from it. With the help of coal oil and old newspapers, we soon had a roaring fire going on the ground. We stood around this cheery blaze out of the wind drying ourselves and awaiting the mess call. With time on our hands, I picked up the dull axe and asked Tom if he didn't think it would be a good time to sharpen it as I knew he carried a light grindstone in one of the wagons.

I got a typical Powers answer, "Oh shucks, we ain't likely to need it again for a spell. No sense wastin all our spare time a workin, nohow."

"Yes," I agreed, subduing an impluse to be sarcastic, "You're probably right."

Shortly Tom nudged me. "look at that Dutchman. He's been nigh an hour feedin them mules. I told him to be sure and give each one a level measure full and he is--down to the last grain. I swear this would be downright humorous if I wasn't the one payin his wages."

"Tell you what I'll do," continued Tom, "I'll bet you a dollar to a doughnut, and you kin keep the hole, if he does that one job regular for a week, he'll get to where it won't take him more'n twice as long as it would a regular human being. But you dass'nt tell him it ain't necessary to count each grain separate, or next time the dam fool's liable not to feed some of em at all. One thing about it though" Tom consoled himself, "Give him an axe or a shovel and plenty of room and he'll give you a full day's work."

How long Tom could have conversed on the peculiarities of

46

Fritz, I'll never know but he had to break off as that worthy approached with a good-natured grin on his broad face.

About that time Mamie called "come and get it". And with appetites sharpened by hard work and outdoor living, we broke off idle talk and proceeded to feed the inner man.

That afternoon the drizzle subsided somewhat and the road improved. We moved along at a lively gait considering our loads. As a matter of fact, we probably made the best mileage of our entire trip. Late in the evening we passed Topeka and continued on a mile or so west of the city before camping. Topeka, the capitol city of the comparitively new state of Kansas, like Lawrence, I would very much have liked to explore. But to the powers that controlled the pace of our train there was no thought of stopping or even slowing down so I had to content myself with the view we had of the outskirts from the high ground north of the river.

That evening when we pulled off the main trail for our night camp, we were near the Pottawatomie Reservation. This afternoon I had probably seen more Indians than I had all the rest of my life. To the Powers children, as well as myself, the novelty of seeing these dark-skinned natives had begun to wear off. To add to our disappointment, these Indians were of the so-called civilized tribes. To a great extent, they had adopted the white man's dress and customs, although we noticed some wrapped in the traditional blankets. The Power's offspring and I suppose to some extent myself, had expected to see them dressed in buckskin and feathers. In this respect we were disappointed. As we were unharnessing and taking care of the stock for the night. I heard Mamie repeating for the n'th time, "just to be patient, we will see plenty of wild Indians with bows and arrows, and feathers in their hair. before we get to Fort Dodge. if your paw knows what he's talkin about. "Me for one." she went on. "I ain't ever seen a wild Indian and I hope to high heaven I never do."

CHAPTER V

The Wagon-Boss and on to Abilene

Our stop this evening was not made until after sundown, apparently on account of the wagon boss's inability to find a suitable camping spot in this settled area. It had been a long and tiresome day, but the roads had generally been good, and this coupled with strong and comparitively fresh teams had enabled us to cover exceptional mileage. Tom speculated, roughly we had come twenty-five miles or more since our noon stop, which would ordinarily have been considered a good day's drive. At the rate we traveled the first two days, he predicted we would make it to Abilene "easy before the end of the week".

"Great guns," he said, "I never once't made this kinda time over on the Santa Fe Road."

But the long day had been tiring to both man and beast, even the Powers children appeared worn out and irritable and only waited for supper so they could go to bed, for once accepting without argument, their mother's assurances they would soon see "real wild Injuns". As soon as the tired teams were unharnessed, Sid was detailed to help Fritz with the watering and feeding, otherwise, with the Dutchman's natural slowness and unthinking penchant for exactness, the job wouldn't have been finished before it became too dark to see. Tom and I busied ourselves unloading the pigs from the cart into a temporary pen we had made by lashing boards and panels to the wheels of one of the larger wagons. We finished this chore and were standing around watching as these dumb critters, happy to be released from the close confines of their crates. pushed each other around and noisily crunched ear corn. Mamie's voice interrupted with the call for supper and Tom allowed, we'd better not keep her waitin.

The next morning we were greeted with bright sunshine, and a light frost gave assurance that the wet spell was over. We were a little delayed getting started due to difficulties loading the swine back to the cart. This was finally accomplished by main strength and awkwardness and considerable strain on Tom's patience, he expressed himself forcefully but without the slightest intention of carrying it through. "Them so and so hogs could rot in the crate afore he would be so kind and considerate as to even think of turning them out again."

The trail this morning ran fairly close to the Kansas Pacific Railway. Once a long worktrain loaded with rails, timbers and various equipment for the end of the line now under construction over three hundred miles to the west, passed us with the bell of the locomotive clanging and black clouds of smoke pouring from the smoke stack. Numerous free-riders or "construction workers" we were told, lined the cars and some of them gave us the hooraw as they sped past our slow moving caravan. The completion of this line to the west edge of the state now made it possible to travel from Kansas City and the eastern settlements to the raw frontier between suns . . . .

Like as has already been said of the frontier freighter; comparitively little has been written of the men who built and operated the early railways across the Great Plains. Lines like the Union Pacific, Kansas Pacific and the Santa Fe were built largely through as wild and unsettled a country as ever lay outdoors. It was a life of thrills and chills, hard work and opportunity, providing one had the good fortune to keep the hair on his head, and body and soul together.

Back to the business at hand—we continued on at a steady pace in what appeared to be a slight northwesterly direction, through a fine partially settled country. We crossed Vermillion Creek after dinner and continued on and crossed another sizeable creek near the town of Louisville. From there we commenced to bear to the southwest and soon were again close to the Kaw. The wide valley lined by rugged timber and brush-clad hills and bluffs, interspersed with the brownish green of scattering cedar and sharp rock outcroppings presented an interesting scenic picture somewhat different from our previous days of travel. Late that evening we crossed the Blue near the town of Manhattan and continued on regardless of the late hour and camped that night, after another exceptionally long day, not far from the eastern edge of the Fort Riley Military Reservation.

We had about completed the evening chores. The mules had been watered, fed, and tethered out to graze when we

49

were interrupted by the arrival of Barney Balaam and Andy Cooper bringing us disquieting news. It seems that between the big red-headed teamster who drove the lead wagon and McCanles, there had been bad blood, and tonight things had come to a head. What had started over a slight disagreement, led from one word to another and soon the two men were at it tooth and toe-nail. Our informants assured us that it was a "right good scrap" for a while, then the wagon boss commenced to get the better of it and he being the type without scruples in such a ruckus, proceeded to put his adversary out of commission while he had the opportunity. As a matter of fact, Big Red was in pretty bad shape, and needed the services of a doctor. Andy and Barney both looked at me. I thought of the long day behind me, and of the interest—yes—almost excitement that had held me as the landscape here on the edge of the frontier country had unfolded ahead of us. How pleasant that had been, but now I was shocked by the unnecessery brutality of the fracas that had just been described to me. Then it occurred to me that I had known all along that this was a hard and a rough country and "I had come west to find adventure." Many thoughts ran through my mind, of how long ago I had given up all ideas of following the medical profession. This was a decision I had come to after long and sober thought, simply because I had convinced myself that I had neither the desire nor the ability to become a successful doctor. Accordingly I had determined to make no mention of my experiences along that line, yet somehow it had apparently leaked out.

After a long period of musing I cleared my throught. "What ever gave you fellows the idea I know anything about doctoring?"

"Well, we heard that your paw was a doctor," said Andy, looking at Tom, "And that you spent considerable of the war on hospital duty."

"That may be, but I'm still not a doctor. I gave up all ideas of that long ago.

"Yeah, but with your experience, you know a dangsite more about treating the injured than ary one of us fellows do. And this fellow is bad hurt—mebee even'll kick the bucket if he don't get help."

"Look here," I said, "I don't want to get mixed up in this thing. McCanles and I have already had trouble. Ridiculous affair it was, but he made threats that maybe he meant, at least I don't mind telling you I've been staying clear of him ever since."

"There won't be ary trouble over this," Cooper assured me. "Barney and me and a dozen other fellar's will back you up. Me and some of the boys stood by and watched Clint work ole Red over and nary a one lifted a hand. But by God, that's the size of it. This affair ain't goin no further. Fact of the matter is Red was askin for some of what he got, but it pears to be only decent that we help him now considerin the shape he's in."

"All right, all right," I said, "You've convinced me. Besides I always was a damned fool. I have a small bag of medicine, drugs and so forth in my wagon and one of you fellows see if you can get hold of some whiskey."

"Got some in the buggy," Andy said, winking at Tom, "A quart I allus carry for snake bite."

"Wait a minute and I'll get my coat and go with you," Tom volunteered.

"Don't do it, Tom," I suggested, "No use of you getting mixed up in this. I can see the boys are gonna take good care of me."

We all climbed in the buggy. One of those two wheeled, one-hoss shay variety, pulled by a big freighter mule. This buggy, by the way, a convenience Andy always had around—usually trailing behind his freight wagon.

Nearly a mile down the trail we arrived at the head of the train. A cookfire was going with the Mexican cook in charge and ladling out the evening meal to the freighters, standing in line. As we alighted from the buggy, the wagon boss stepped out of the gloom. I could see by the light of the campfire that he packed a very black eye.

"What you fellars got on your minds?" He demanded suspiciously.

"We want to talk to you for a minute, Clint," requested Cooper, motioning McCanles to one side.

51

"Talk," he said as he followed us out of earshot of his men. "I'm listenin."

Cooper looked him square in the face and said bluntly, "Clint, Red is in bad shape and I reckon you know it. So Dad Balaam and me took it on ourselves and got a man here who's gonna doctor him up a bit."

"Doctor, Hell! Who in Hell amongst you is a doctor?"

Feeling a little bolder with the backing I had, I stepped forward. "I'm not a doctor at all," I said, "But under the circumstances I am qualified to examine the man and administer whatever treatment I can."

The wagon boss gave us a soul searching look. "Alright go ahead and look him over but remember, By Gawd, that Tyler & Randall and management ain't no wise responsible for any injuries incurred by any of their employees and won't pay ary Gawddam bills for the same." And he turned away and went off mumbling to himself about "passel of so and so, merciful old wimmen."

The injured freighter had been taken to his wagon and there we found him tossing and turning on a bed of gunny sacks and blankets. Old Barney lit a lantern and hung it on a hickory bow above the patient. One glance was enough to tell that Red was indeed in bad shape. He looked at us out of a semi-delirious stupor and gasped out "fer Gawds sake don't let him stomp on me again," and commenced to whimper and groan to himself.

"We're not going to hurt you," I soothed him as I opened the little bag of medical supplies and set it where I could reach it handy. "We came to help you. Do you understand?"

The man's face was a dirty, bloody mass of cuts and bruises. Andy got a pail of water and with he and Barney holding the patient down by main strength, I washed the blood and dirt off his head and face. I ran my fingers around his head and located a severe cut, possibly the dent of a bootheel. This had ceased to bleed but I knew it could be causing a concussion. It didn't seem likely though that this could be the cause of the severe pain the man was suffering.

Andy picked up the bottle. "Shall I give him a slug of whiskey?"

But I thought better. "Not yet. Let's get his shirt and underwear off and see what he looks like down there."

I felt along his ribs and instantly got a moan of pure anguish. I was as gentle as I could be but it took all Barney and Andy could do to handle him. In a few moments I had gotten enough of an examination to know where his main injuries were located. But to what extent and how serious, I had no way of telling. My two companions waited silently for my opinion.

"I hate to say so boys but there isn't a thing we can do for him other than give him something to kill the pain and let him rest. Otherwise, he needs hospital care and perhaps surgery. He has some broken ribs, one possibly bad enough to cause internal injury if it hasn't already. There's simply no two ways about it, he needs treatment that I can't give him. If this one rib should be injured less than I fear, he might recover in good shape if we could get him in a bed and keep him quiet, but if he rides in a wagon at the best, he would suffer the torments of Hell."

"That's fer daggone shore," agreed Old Barney. "Why I recollect once't I got a sneakin Pawnee arrer in my side. That was with Colonel Bents' train at the old Aubrey Crossin it t'was by gollies. Thar I was fer one whole day ridin in that wagon with that consarned arrer aticklin my gizzard. Why dad-blast it fellars, I was plumb prostate. Why I—"

"Yeah, we know," interrupted Cooper, impatient of the old man's chatter. "We might be able to get him down to Riley at the Post Hospital."

"How far is it to the Fort?" I asked.

"Tain't a very fur piece," volunteered Barney, from whom it was impossible to get an estimate in miles or linear measure.

"Not over four or five mile at the most," Andy surmised.

"If we could get in touch with the hospital authorities and have them send an ambulance and attendant down here our patient would certainly be better off than he is here."

53

"Give me three hours and I'll have one here or raise the biggest stink and holler they've heard since old Jown Brown took Harper's Arsenal," promised Andy. "Course it may take a detachment of the Seventh to quiet Clint down though."

"Don't worry none about Clint," bragged Barney, unexpectedly. "I reckon I kin quiet that rooster down ef I hev to."

"I didn't notice you quietin him down none a while ago," Andy said cuttingly. But the old plainsman ignored the "tenor" of the remark and never batted an eye.

Cooper stayed with us long enough to help administer a stiff dosage of drugs to the patient, then he left for his mule and buggy. We soon heard the fast clatter of hooves as he moved off down trail towards the Army Post. Shortly afterward, the drugs commenced to take effect and our patient quieted down so I could dress the cuts on his face and hands. Finally he settled down to a steady gasping snore.

For a while, even old Barney was quiet, apparently awed by the manner the strong medicine had quieted the big red-headed mule-skinner. I spent the time pondering the character of the wagon boss. I had seen enough of McCanles that I knew, in some respects he was a man to be admired. Particularly when you had once seen him handle men, mules and wagons. In that area he was a man among men. Iron willed and impatient, he knew the freighting game from one end to the other and there seemed no doubt of his loyalty to his employers and there was no question he was a born leader. His blunt commands and roaring rages won the begrudging respect of his men, though they were many times victims of his wrath. Strength and guts he had in abundance. But on the other side of the ledger were some varied and doubtful virtues. He was the most profane man I have ever known and maybe the most brutal. He was absolutely ruthless when he wanted to be and last but not least, his honesty was questionable. The man lying before me was the victim of such unnecessary brutality that it roused a desire to see justice done. Sitting there thinking about it made the hair rise on the back of my scalp. Yet my better judgement warned me not to meddle in this affair, only to see that the victim had a chance for proper and decent care. And this I resolved to do and this alone—regardless of my sense of justice. I had already aroused the ire of the wagon boss more than enough to do me for one trip.

I turned to the old man sitting crosslegged across the wagon from me. "Well, Barney we may as well break the news to McCanles. Something tells me he isn't gonna like it either, so I can sure use all the physical and moral support you can give me."

"Well, sir, Jack boy, ye kin sure count on me. But Clint ain't gonna do any more than raise considerable noise about this and I reckon you and me ain't dam fools enough to let ary thing he says offend our honor to the pint of doin sonthin foolish, air we?" The old man chuckled.

As we approached the fire, the cook was clearing away the cooking utensils. Apparently supper was over though a number of the men were still sitting and standing about. The wagon boss, seated with his back to a wagon wheel was sipping a cup of coffee. The coffee and the smell of fried spuds reminded me I was hungry.

"Mr. McCanles," I said, "I'd like to talk to you a minute— alone."

"Alone hell, By Gawd mister," he mimicked, "If you got anything to say to me, say it right here."

"Alright, I have this to say," and I gave him the first barrel. "I have examined your man 'Red', and treated him as best I could. But Andy Cooper was right, he is in bad shape, maybe seriously. So I am recommending that he be sent to the Post Hospital at Riley. In fact, Cooper has already gone to request an ambulance."

McCanles continued to sip his coffee and I was surprised at his apparent mildness. "Pears to me you're takin a heap for granted around here. I'm wagon master of this here train and as such I have the authority to say who the hell goes where, and what the hell, he goes for, By Gawd."

"In that case," and I gave him the other barrel, "If you refuse to allow this man to be transferred to a hospital, knowing full well the condition he is in and what the consequences may be if he rides any distance in a wagon, then I personally am

55

going to the Military and report this whole affair. If they don't take proper action, I'll go to the civil authorities. This is new country I know, but I take it there is law and order here."

McCanles came to his feet in a rage. "Why you sawed-off, two-bit, tin-horn quack, I could whittle a better doctor than you out of a cornstalk. Talk to me of law and order, I'm the law around here and I give the orders too. Do ye savy that?"

There was no use in arguing with the man but I told him again that I would report the whole affair if he refused to permit the transfer of the injured man.

"Don't stand there and threaten me young fellar."

"This is not a threat my friend," I assured him, "It's a promise."

"Mutiny eh! That's what it tis. You attempt to leave this train and I'll put you in irons."

This put a different complexion on things. I knew that he was not bluffing and was capable of doing just that and in all probability would if I made any attempt to carry out my promise. It looked like the only way out was to appeal to the better natures of the men listening, silent and poker-faced.

"Men," I started to say when the wagon boss drowned me out with a storm of profanity that smothered my words and numbed my senses. I looked around in helpless despair when suddenly old Barney jumped to his feet and let out the most unearthly war whoop that shook McCanles to a stop for an instant. Before he had a chance to get started again, the old man was addressing him in a conciliatory tone.

"Now by gollies, Clint, if you'll shet up and listen, might be you'd save yerself a heap of trouble. Jack hyar ain't no wise tryin to stir up no trouble. He's jest trying to save another fellars hide. And if yew get too tarnation set about this I'll turn yew in myself and so'll Andy Cooper and some of these other jaspers, too, I calculate."

McCanles leered mockingly at the whiskery old face. "Old man, whyn't you go crawl under yore wagon? If I need you I'll whistle."

"Kase I ain't yore yallar dog that's why. I hired on personal to Mr. Tyler." Then the old man's tone became a little ugly. "Clint I ain't one to carry tales acros't the road. I'm an ole, man, I know, but I ain't no complete dam fool or idjit, yet. Seems to me I recollect some Commissary stores delivered to Wallace a year or so ago, that had a powerful bad smell so they say. The Gineral at Riley would be mighty pleased to know some names on that deal. Pears to me they was some contraband whiskey got side tracked at Larned once't. Some say that was on purpose too. Course, they ain't only a few uv us fellars know fer shore is they Clint?"

I confess when the old man had talked of quieting McCanles, I figured it was some more of his idle talk (akin to the usual big yarns). But that is exactly what happened. I have never seen a man change from vile to good humor so sudden as the wagon boss did. The hard lines of his face changed to an expression of almost, admiration.

"Why you sneakin old son of-a-bitch you," he marveled, "I didn't 'low as how you had that much gumption in yore wrinkled old hide." And he went on to berate and insult Barney in the worst manner, but with a touch of humor to take the edge off his remarks.

This was another side of McCanles and one I had never seen. Actually I suppose it was mostly his way of saving face but he was the type of man who sometimes had a certain respect for anyone who had the fortitude to stand up to him.

With the change in the wagon boss's attitude the tension soon relaxed. Some of the men commenced to grin and crack jokes. One or two of them nodded guardedly to me and Jose, the cook, handed me a cup of coffee.

I returned to the wagon and found my patient still dead to the world. Pretty soon Barney showed up with plates of hot food and he and I put away a delayed, but satisfying, meal. Whatever McCanles faults, his men could never complain of not being fed well. In addition to the usual pork and potatoes, the meal consisted of tasty extras usually considered luxuries in those days.

We had just finished eating when Tom Powers came to the wagon. "Got kinda worried about you Jack, when you didn't show up after so long a time. Figgered I better come over and see what the trouble was."

"There's no trouble now but for a while, the sparks fairly flew." I went on with the irrepressable Barney cutting in, to tell him what had happened. We were still discussing the late affair and Tom was listening with a relish that made his eyes shine, when Andy arrived from the Post with an ambulance, complete with driver and hospital attendant.

The wagon boss never showed his face nor made any move to interfere. In a short time, we had transferred the injured man to the ambulance. After warning the attendant of his condition and seeing he was made comfortable as possible, we could only trust the rest to the two troopers. I had misgivings of the pair because the reek of whiskey on their breaths would almost make your head swim. Andy noticed my look and explained, "That's where my whiskey went." I wouldn't a got them two waddies here before midnight if I hadn't bribed em with that whiskey. Don't need to worry about them not getting him there safe, Jack. Them boys been weaned on that stuff. Why half the sojers at Riley don't draw a sober breath more'n twice't a week.

Next morning when the train pulled out on the trail another driver sat astride the off wheeler on the lead wagon. He was a character in his own right though a contrast to "Big Red", and for that matter, most other muleskinners. Tall, spare and past middle age, Pete Purdy was a God-fearin, Bible toting man of Scottish descent. Prayin Pete, as he was known by the other freighters (though not to his face) was an old and trusted employee of Tyler & Randall and owed his job directly to them. He was no favorite of the wagon boss who resented his out-spoken opinions and scripture-quoting piety. For this reason and not because he lacked qualifications, he was one of the two "extra hands" carried by the train to fill any emergency that might present itself. We would hear more of Prayin Pete before the trip was over.

After a little later start than usual our end of the train was again out on the road moving up the picturesque valley of the

Kaw. About ten o'clock we were stopped in Fort Riley, where I was required to report to the hospital authorities in regard to the "injured civilian" they had accepted as a patient last night. We cooled our heels for some time before anyone with the proper authority could see us. I spent my time while waiting, getting my first glimpse of a frontier Army Post. Actually Riley, at that time, could hardly be classed as frontier. For years this had been a military post of great importance. Thousands of dollars of Government money had been poured in to its construction and improvement with the result there were many fine and well constructed buildings. The hospital of long rambling style with wide verandas surrounding much of its exterior was eye-filling as well as practical.

After about an hours wait, I was ushered in to the presence of the medical officer in charge. I answered the usual routine questions and then came the "stumper."

"Why and how or by whom did he receive his injuries?"

Not about to be trapped into answering that one, I pleaded that "I hadn't seen the fracas and did not know the true facts." I was assured that all this was strictly confidential, but I knew that if the authorities gave McCanles any trouble over this he would know exactly who to blame and I had seen enough of his methods already that I had no desire to be the object of his displeasure again. True, he deserved punishment but for the benefit of the entire train as well as myself it was unthinkable that I should be reason for that.

"Surely," asked the Medical Officer, "You have some idea of why and how this happened and who the aggressor was?"

"Yes, I have" I told him, "But it is based purely on hearsay and it is for my own best interests and safety that I am not going to incriminate anyone by repeating that here."

The officer eyed me over the rims of his spectacles. "There seems to be a conspiracy afoot here to conceal evidence in this case. Nobody wants to say anything about anybody. So what can we do?" He shrugged his shoulders. "The Medical Department isn't attempting to prosecute anyone. As far as I am concerned that's strictly up to the Civil Authorities. All we want here is the facts so that we can make our reports."

59

"I am sorry, Sir, but what I have already said is all I can tell you."

"In that case, I'm wasting my time as well as yours. So I believe that is all." And with a brisk "good day sir," I was dismissed and I left hoping the matter was closed, for good.

Leaving Fort Riley, we came to the Republican River which joins the Smokey Hill at this place forming the Kaw as it is known from this point downstream. On up the road near Junction City we came in sight of high, rugged bluffs dotted with cedar. We stopped here for a brief lunch without unhitching the teams as the morning pull had been short. After eating we passed on through the town and in a short while were well in the broad valley of the Smokey.

So here at last was that stream with the picturesque name I had read so much of in the magazines back home. Ahead a blue haze lay over the valley which seemed to give reason for its name. For me it hinted of mystery and adventure to come.

By the middle of the afternoon by pushing our teams hard, we commenced to catch up with the drag of the main train. We learned later that while we were delayed at Riley, they were held up for a short time at Junction City where the "law" at that point made a feeble attempt to question McCanles. The wagon boss, rough and tough talking as usual, and armed with all the gall in the world brazened his way out of it without any more than an embarrassing little episode for the town officials. Thus the matter came to an end. But the Wagon Boss never forgot my part in it and continued to hold it against me adding to it imaginary grievances as time went on.

As we continued on that afternoon, I found the country more interesting as we progressed westward, gradually it seemed to me it was becoming less thickly settled. On the other side of the hills and bluffs that hemmed us in, I wondered if the frontier wasn't at last very near. At least, I hoped so.

We traveled a little later than usual being concerned with finding better grazing for our stock. Finally after dusk we pulled in to a little swale heading north from the main trail and made camp. Here we found better grass and plenty of stock water. Andy Cooper pulled in beside us saying he was tired of a bachelors life. He and Tom guessed we were in the neighborhood of nine or ten miles from the frontier cowtown of Abilene. Next morning after a leisurely start, we moved on to that town and after some inquiry, gained permission to camp about a mile out of town. Here we knew we were to be held up for a few days following the assembly and loading of additional wagons for the Tyler & Randall train. Needless to say this was a welcome stop for all of us. Though we had been on the trail less than five full days, we had made exceptionally good time. Naturally, the way our teams had been crowded there was physical wear and tear on our outfit to say nothing of the human element. We arranged our wagons in a manner to provide the most comfortable camp and settled down for a liesurely stay.

Abilene, the first of the famous western cowtowns, had made a name for itself the previous summer (1867) when the McCoy cattle shipping pens were built along side the Union Pacific Eastern Division (Kansas Pacific) Railway. This town then became the most popular "end of the trail" for the Texas cattle drovers who since the war had been seeking a Northern market for their herds. The rough little town on the edge of the Kansas settlements was said to have shipped over a thousand carloads of cattle to the eastern markets, that first fall after the shipping facilities had been completed. When we first saw Abilene early in the spring in "68", we were told it would be many weeks before the main influx of cattle from Texas would start moving into the shipping pens. But the business interests of the town in anticipations of the expected Eastern and Texas money to be made were busily making preparations to supply the demand for goods and in some cases "perhaps to fleece the unwary." Rumor had it that herds were being pastured in the Flint Hills to the south and of others which had been wintered in the "Nations" and were supposed to be already moving this way. Everywhere in town there was activity, the smell of sawdust and new lumber was a common one. A long string of railway cars stood on the siding, most of them loaded with freight for local distrbution. In other towns along the trail we had seen evidence of prosperity, but here it was more in the nature of a boom. New frame business buildings had been completed and others were in the process of construction. Most of these were simple affairs with the popular false fronts then in fashion especially in the new towns of the west. But one stood out as an imposing and substantial building, this was the town's leading lodging house, called the Drover's Cottage. The appearance of this structure standing more or less isolated from other business establishments, served to accenuate the newness of the town's prosperity. By itself, the "Drovers" was a symbol of the community's faith in the future of the cattle trade, and in the next two years helped to make Abilene one of the most widely known towns between the Gulf and the Missouri.

No description of Abilene, however brief, would be complete without mention of the "drover" who made the town possible. The first summer I spent in Kansas, I don't recall ever hearing the word cowboy used, trail drover or just drover was the accepted term. Possibly "cowboy" was in use at the time but it never became the popular monicker of the trail driving cowhands until a few years later. In 1868 the cattle business as a big and profitable business was just getting started in the west and as such, the methods used, the names and terms of description were sometimes different than those adopted later. This was true, some fiction to the contrary.

As it turned out, the first two days at our camp near Abilene I was occupied with other activities and didn't have a chance to explore the town, but then on the third day, my opportunity came and from then on, I had a "right lively time" and met a few characters I've never forgotten.

CHAPTER VI

In Camp Near Abilene

By the time we had finished our noon meal, the first in our new camp, we found ourselves with time on our hands for the first time since we had been on the road. For days, I had been itching to try my new rifle, at odd moments I had taken it out of the scabbard, held it to my shoulder and dry fired it many times. Like a kid with a new toy, I had loaded it and unloaded it so many times that I had worn the glitter off a handful of new cartridges. But so far, I had never fired the gun. That afternoon Tom and I determined to try it out. We proceeded a short distance from camp and set up an empty whiskey bottle as a target and stepped off about fifty paces. I took a long aim, then flinched as I pulled the trigger and missed the bottle completely. Tom insisted that I try again, this time I concentrated on squeezing the trigger and avoiding the jerk. The shot was closer this time, apparently just missing the neck of the bottle.

Tom chuckled, "Let me see that thing."

He tested the Henry to his shoulder a time or two for practice, levered in a shell, sighted for an instant and smashed the bottle in half. I walked over, a little chagrined now and set up the remaining half. This time I cut down on the target until the sights were in line perfectly and made my best shot. But still the piece of bottle sat upright, and untouched. Tom, confident as before, took a little longer aim this time and pieces of glass flew everyway. After that, Tom allowed he had better quit while he was ahead and suggesting also that there was no need to shoot up all my ammunition. But I wasn't worrying about a few cartridges as I had nearly a hundred rounds left and my shooting so far had convinced me that I needed more practice to get the feel of my rifle.

I knew Tom and the family planned to spend the balance of the afternoon in town. After they left, I saddled my horse, strapped on my rifle and scabbard and rode up the Smokey Hill trail until I came to a likely looking draw that headed in a northwesterly direction. The country around here was much less settled than around most of the towns we had come through further east. Here, there seemed to be no dwelling near nor sign of a regular trail, so I rode up this little valley for some distance. Suddenly Blaze shied, and a large jackrabbit bounded out of a clump of grass. I had heard of jackrabbits, of course, but never expected them to be the size of this one. I watched in amazement as he hopped off unconcernedly about fifty yards and stopped in the peculiar crouching position common to them. I dismounted carefully, rifle in hand expecting him to run, but he only hopped a little further and waited. I slipped my right arm through the reins and took aim, all the time talking soothingly to my horse. I fired a little hurriedly and the bullet struck to one side of the rabbit, which ran off a little further and stopped again. The next shot, I held on a perfect line but a little high and friend rabbit ducked his head for an instant then loped off a little further and sat down wriggling his ears. Blaze proving to be only slightly gunshy, hindered me very little and the jack offered me a beautiful broadside for my third shot which dropped him in his tracks. With this modest beginning, I bagged my first western game and possibly I got as much thrill and satisfaction out of this as I afterwards did from many a buffalo or antelope.

Deciding to pick up my game on the way back I rode on up the draw to where it broadened considerably. Here were a few scraggly trees and bushes, with still no sign of human habitation. It seemed like a good place and time to familiarize myself further with the rifle. I looked around for a suitable target. On the slope not far away lay the weathered and whitened skull of a buffalo. I stepped off about a hundred yards and placed the buffalo skull with the hillside as a background, and at about three-fourths that distance I placed a flat rock, maybe eight inches in diameter. In the course of the next two hours, I fired approximately forty rounds of ammunition. By the time it was over I had learned a lot about the Henry and a lot of my own shooting ability. What I learned gave me a new confidence. Unquestionably, the time and ammunition I spent that afternoon, laid the groundwork for a skill that later kept my belly full and the hair on my head—many times.

I used this Henry rifle for some time on the Plains. Generally, I found it to be a very good piece of life insurance. However, to clear up some overratings and legends that have developed over the years, in regard to this rifle, a brief description and evaluation are in order. The Henry was the forerunner of the Winchester. It was similar to the Winchester in both appearance and mechanism. The ammunition was a short rimfire cartridge loaded with a .44 caliber bullet of over 200 grains weight and propelled by a black powder charge of 25 to 30 grains. Clearly, it was not a long range gun even in its day. To the student of present ballistics, it was certainly not impressive, but in the hands of an experienced shot it was a good eighty yard arm and at fifty yards, it was capable of placing its shots closer than most men could hold it. Quoting an expert of the day, "Even with these limitations, the Henry was for practical purposes unbeatable in its class." This was true mostly to its good design, reliable fast repeating action and excellent medium range accuracy and killing power.

Returning to the events of the day, that afternoon I rode into camp with a big whitetail jack tied to my saddle. Hungry for fresh meat, we dressed him and that night dined for the first time on wild game. Contrary to the quality sometimes

65

experienced with the meat of full grown jack rabbits, this one was young, tender and very good eating.

ON THE SOLOMON

The next day, inspired perhaps by my experiences the day before, we decided to go hunting on the Solomon. Up as usual long before daylight, we located Barney Balaam and talked him into going with us. By sun-up Tom, Barney and myself were riding away from the Smokey Hill. Tom was astride a gentle gray horse of the team driven by Sid. Barney rode a small gray mule without benefit of saddle, only with a piece of buffalo robe, hair down, separated the old man's nether portions from the back of the mule—an arrangement which didn't appear overly comfortable—however, Barney didn't mind in the least and in truth, stood the day's ride better than either Tom or me. In addition to these and, of course, my mount, we led one of Tom's big work mules to pack in the meat—we hoped.

"Aw you fellars," gabbed old Barney as we rode along "Tain't likely we'll see nothin better'n a triflin antelope. Might be a few deer and elk left in these parts, but don't expaict to see no bufflar. Dad-blasted settlements are crowdin um out, ie-gollies. Tell ye boys, the country's going plum to the dogs."

Discounting considerable to cover the old scout's prejudices, it was true there were several settlements and isolated settlers along the Smokey and lower Solomon valleys. But as a whole, the country was undeveloped and certainly uncrowded. As we got on the higher ground above the main valley we were in practically a virgin area, covered by last summer's grayish native grass. This was the nearest open prairie we had yet seen, broken only by the rolling lay of the land and occasional high clumps of grass and brushy patches. As far as the eye could see there were no habitations. The only signs of civilization were a few grazing cattle and once or twice we came on the faint prints of wagon wheels on the prairie.

For some time the only game we saw were a few rabbits, quail and prairie chicken. As we were after larger game, we had no more than a passing interest in these. A black eagle hovered high above the prairie ahead of us.

66

"Likely a coyote down thar," explained the old plainsman, "Lot'sa times when ye see an eagle like that, he's a spottin a wolf or some other varmint."

Sure enough as we approached a wide shallow draw and started down the gentle slope, a coyote bounded out of the tall grass, took a slinking, backward look at us and moved off with the cautious gait of his kind. This was the first coyote I had ever seen and he left an impression of the wild and primeval, greater than his size and nature warranted.

We skirted a little patch of bushes, heard a sudden gobbling and a small flock of wild turkeys flew up about a stone's throw away. Tom carried a double barrel breech-loading shotgun, loaded with buckshot. He hauled this to his shoulder never minding the prancing of his horse, and let go wildly with both barrels. Old Barney pounded the back of his mule and cackled with laughter. About that time, one of the flock dropped wounded, to the ground. I started after him and soon turned him back towards my companions. I dismounted, dropped the reins to the ground and took after him on foot. Tom and Barney soon arrived and we had a merry chase before I finally caught the crippled bird.

"Wal I swan," panted old Barney, "That's shore nuff a horse on me. Fust time I ever seed a man down a gobble'r with a splatter gun at that fur a piece."

Tom grinned broadly from his horse where he had been well occupied with the pack mule he was leading. "Nothin' to it if you know how, ie gollies son," he mimicked, "Stick around me and you'll see a lot of things for the fust time."

Barney bristled at Tom's humor. "Accident ef I ever seed one. Ie gollies he musta been plumb skeered to death. Fust thing to do," he advised seriously, "Is cut off his haid and git rid of his dad-ratted craw. Spile the meat right sudden ef ye don't."

"Aw now, Barney," deviled Tom, "I don't reckon I ever heard that."

"Tis so, nohow," said the old man testily, "I reckon I orta know as I've killed and et thousands of turkeys."

So to humor Barney we removed the head and craw. Besides

67

it seemed like good advice. When the bird was dressed that evening, we found the reason for Tom's luck. One buckshot from the wild fusillade he fired had struck the main bone of the wing; otherwise, it never had a scratch.

The turkey taken care of and tied securely to the back of Tom's saddle, we continued on our way. After going about a mile further we topped a small rise and before us about a hundred and twenty yards, we saw a flock of perhaps a dozen antelope. Before either of us with rifles could dismount where we may have had a chance. Tom let fly with one barrel of his splatter gun and the antelope were soon out of sight and over the next ridge.

"Dad blast it, Tom," yelled Barney, "Twarn't no sense in that."

"I know it," apologized Tom ruefully, "I don't know what possessed me to do a fool thing like that."

After going some distance further, we approached a brushy thicket on the edge of quite a little valley. We dismounted and tied our animals. Barney and I with rifles in hand, worked around the edge of the thicket where we could see in the valley below. At first I could make out no sign of animal life. After a time Barney touched my arm, and instantly I realized we had been looking directly at a herd of antelope, perhaps two hundred yards away. We could make out the light spots on their rumps, but the rest of the animal blending so well with the surroundings to make them undistinguishable at that distance. Barney carried a late model Remington .50 caliber breech loader. One of the finest long range, hunting rifles made, and the old man was justly proud of it.

"They are too far off for my "44", I whispered. "Do you think you can reach them with your big "fifty?"

"I reckon, ef I kin git a decent bead drawed. Tell you what, tie yer hankerchief to the end of your gun barr'l and hold it up so they kin see it and wave it back and forth."

He lowered himself to a sitting position with his back against the bank, laid his right foot on top of his left shin, rested the long barrel of his rifle on his toes and in this unorthodox fashion took a long, careful aim. The lead antelope took about two steps and fell over. The rest of the flock, of course, took off as fast as they could run. For the sport of it, I took a couple of snap shots at the closest one being careful to hold extra high. I had the dubious satisfaction of seeing my bullets kick up dust close to their flying heels; and that was all. I turned to Barney who had his cleaning rod out and was unhurriedly swabbing his rifle barrel. I suggested that maybe I ought to run down and make sure of the kill.

"Tain't no hurry. I calculate he ain't goin nowhars. Fust thing ye wanta be sure and do after ye've made a kill," he advised me, "Is be shore and reload yore weapon. No tellin whut kin happen ef ye don't."

We mounted and rode down the declivity and located the dead antelope without any trouble.

Barney examined him and snorted with disgust. "Jest as well fergit about him boys. Thet consarned critter's half as old as Tom hyar."

Tom, anxious for fresh meat argued for some time. But the old man remained positive and unmoved. "Daggonit, fellars he's so tarnation old and tough ye couldn't stew his meat in a steambiler."

We continued on across this valley which turned out to be a dry tributary. Then on over a long stretch of prairie and presently to distinctly more rugged country that was dotted with scattered trees and brush.

"Fresh deer sign here," said Barney, "Might be a good idee to git off and scout this afoot."

He pointed out fresh deer dung which I had passed by thinking it was nothing more than rabbit pellets. We tied our mounts and spread out on foot. Not far to our left, we could see where the ground broke away sharply into a large canyon-like ravine the sides and edges of which were partially covered with timber and brush. We scouted along parallel with this and back a short distance from the edge. Before long, I spied a set of huge antlers, whitened and weathered with age. I told myself that not too many years ago a big buck had run here.

"This warn't no deer," said Barney as soon as he saw them,

"Them's elk horns. I run acrost some elk sign back thar. Not too old nuther—"

He was interrupted by the sound of some large animal crashing through the brush. Not waiting for the others, I spied sort of an open knob that stuck up above the surrounding country and gave a good view of the canyon. I reached this place easily and scanned the area about me. Shortly, I saw what was causing all the commotion; and got the thrill of a lifetime. Going rapidly up the opposite slope was a truly magnificent elk. Let me tell you, I know what buck fever is. I had experienced it before and I have had it since. But now, as my memory serves me, it never occurred to me that I might miss. I have never been surer or more confident as I caught the rear end of the elk in my sights and squeezed the trigger. He seemed to hesitate for an instant, then lost all sense of balance and went tumbling to the bottom end over end. I hastily levered another cartridge in the barrel, threw all caution to the wind and went jumping and sliding to the bottom of the brushy ravine. Once to the bottom and by now thoroughly excited, I thrashed around for some time before I located the wounded animal, trying to drag himself around by his front feet. I ran up not knowing whether to shoot him again or call for help to cut his throat. As I came close, he snorted and with eyes blazing defiance, he tried to strike and butt me.

"I got him down," I hollered at the top of my voice. "What'll I do? Shoot him again?"

"Don't let him git away," came Barney's voice from way down the canyon where he had evidently miscalculated.

Thus advised, I pulled up at twenty feet and missed the elk completely. Missing such a ridiciously easy shot, sobered me considerably. I realized then that he couldn't possibly get away, so I settled down to wait until Barney showed up with his butcher knife, preferring not to risk another shot as I was surrounded by timber and bush and feared another wild shot might endanger my companions. Frankly, my supreme confidence of a few moments ago had completely desserted me. Presently Barney came out of the timber and with his long hunting knife, the wounded elk was quickly dispatched.

Here I learned for the first time as does every successful hunter of big game, that is "after the kill", your troubles are just beginning. However, Barney was pretty adept at this trade and I was willing to learn. By the time Tom had located us, and coaxed his big pack mule through the trees and brush to our vicinity, we had the carcass about ready to be hung up. With Tom's horse pulling on the rope we soon had the big elk hanging from a limb, front quarters down, where Barney with a small axe razer-sharp, expertly split him in halves.

"No use trying to pack out any more than'll keep this time a year," Tom advised, judging correctly there was more meat than we could handily take out on one animal.

"Thet's fer shore," agreed Barney, "Might as well cut off all them thar ribs, reckon no one will eat them with all this good meat awastin."

Accordingly, the quarters were trimmed to the minimum. As the sky had become party cloudy, and the weather turned slightly chilly it was decided to let the meat hang and cool while we ate our midday lunch.

"Sides, it'll let thet mule of yourn get uset to the smell of fresh meat. Sumpin tells me Tom, he ain't gonna be none to pleased with the load he's gonna hev to carry."

"Don't you fret none about old Red," Tom said confidently, "Why two years ago I think it t'was, I rid him fifteen or twenty mile from the head of the Rattlesnake and across't the Arkansaw with the ham of a yearlin buffalo hind the saddle."

We located a trickle of clear water further down the canyon where we washed the blood and hair from our hands, and with our tincups got a cold drink. Tom produced a small coffee pot and soon we had coffee boiling over a campfire. We sat around the fire eating cold ham and blackberry jam sandwiches and drinking black coffee, with pure enjoyment, thanks to wholesome appetitites and the pleasant outdoor surroundings. The noon meal finished, old Barney being in a reminiscent mood, sat Indian style and regaled us with tall stories of his youth when he rode with Kit Carson and worked for the Bent boys.

71

"Why I tell you fellars," he wound up, "In all my yars in and out of Bent's Old Fort I hain't ever seed ary place ceptin one, thet was the equal of these here Solomon and Saline valleys fer good huntin. And thet one kentry I'm talkin about is the Middle Park in the Mountings. But nowadays the dad-gasted sod-buster and the miner has just about ruint both uv them."

Meditating this bit of trail-busters philosophy, we arose and busied ourselves with the business at hand. The mule was led up and the packsaddle adjusted. Tom unrolled a small piece of wagonsheet and we started the somewhat ticklish and laborsome job of loading the fresh elk meat on the unwilling mule. For a time it looked like Barney's prediction was to be realized. But Tom displayed more patience than usual, and after so long a time we had the meat loaded and securely in place. Barney went ahead, up the ravine to break trail and find an easier ascent, while I brought up the rear to see that everything was all right and incidentally urge the mule along if necessary. Tom took the lead rope and clucked reassuringly. The big red mule standing with legs solidlybraced to hold the heavy load, glanced around a little helplessly at his unaccustomed burden, dug his front feet in the ground and fell obediently in line. Soon amidst a shower of dirt and gravel we pulled up over the rim and were once more on the rolling flat.

Here, I experienced for the first time the feeling of being completely turned around. It seemed to me the direction Barney was taking was exactly the opposite the direction we should be going. I knew, of course, I was wrong. But the knowledge came to me "had I been alone I would surely be lost." For an instant I could imagine the helpless despair of being lost in an uninhabitated place such as this. Many times this is the worst danger that can befall a tenderfoot in the wild country and often the least expected. I realized that I had much to learn out here in the west. "Though I had done very well as a hunter, it was doubtful if I could find my way home with the meat."

With unerring instinct the old plainsman took an almost straight line for the Smokey Valley a few miles above Abilene. After several hours' ride, we covered many miles observing only two or three distant habitations and a few scattered plumes of

72

smoke far ahead of us in the distant valley. I rode up beside Barney.

He glanced at me shrewdly, guessing about what I had on my mind, "Whar do ye figger we air about now, Jack?"

"We-ll I can't say for sure," I admitted cautiously with a feeling of a returning sense of direction, yet not wishing to admit that I had been confused. I pointed to the largest wisp of smoke ahead and slightly to the left. "Abilene should be over there."

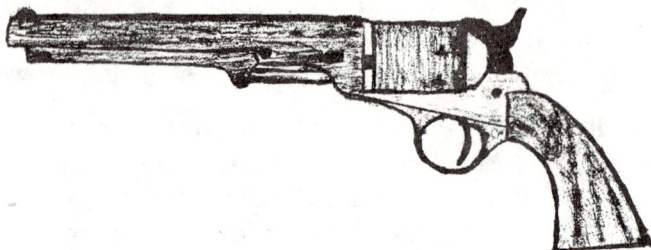

CHAPTER VII

A Night on the Town

The next day was Sunday and in recognition of that fact no wagon wheels were to roll today. Tom forsake his usual habits and we lay in our blankets until after day-break. After a late breakfast we watered all the livestock out of a little rivulet nearby and staked them out to graze on trampled dry grass a couple hundred yards from camp. Leaving Fritz in charge Tom and I returned to camp with time weighing heavily on our hands.

Sunday was apparently just another day in Abilene. There was a saying of the times; "there was no law west of Kansas City and no God west of Riley." Abilene may have had a church at that time, but if so, it was not overly advertised because Tom and Mamie were usually pretty quick to find out such things, for whenever the Sabbath arrived they were both prone to feel the need of Spiritual guidance.

Among the freighters with the main train was the extra hand, that exceptional character, Praying Pete Purdy, who in the absence of any qualified person could always be counted on to volunteers his services as substitute Parson. I am sure Pete Purdy was a sincerely religious man, but he was also naturally untalkative, poorly versed in grammar and in some respects ignorant. His remarks and mannerisms on Sunday were therefore apt to generate much amusement for the balance of the week, even from those who professed love of the Holy Spirit and good will toward their fellow-men. In fact, I suspect some of the Just as well as the Unjust went to hear him preach, mostly if not solely, for entertainment.

On this Sunday it was noised about camp, early, that Praying Pete would conduct church services at a little grove above the main camp. Accordingly, the Powers family were scrubbed, polished, dressed in their very best clothes and off to the "preachin." I felt little need for another sermon so soon, having had my fill of the "frontier variety" a week ago. I pleaded other things to do having in my mind a desire to see the town.

After yesterday's successful hunt we were supplied with more fresh meat than we could possible use. Rather than see the balance spoil, I determined to try peddling it downtown. I was sure that in one of the eatinghouses or stores I would find a ready market. My present destitute condition (money-wise) added to my determination even after being warned by old Barney. "Shecks, folks in these hyar parts don't know nawthin but beef, hawgmeat and bufflar."

Anyway about ten o'clock this fine sabbath morning I arrived at downtown Abilene in Tom's light, spare wagon with about eighty pounds of elk hind quarter. I stopped at the first store and accosted the proprietor behind the meat counter, somewhat timidly, stating my business.

"What kind of meat you say you got young fellar?"

"Why it's fresh elk, Sir, hind quarter, young and fat. Wouldn't you like to look at it?"

"Nope," said the owner positively, "Folks around here won't buy it. Now if it t'war bufflar . . . "

The next stop was at the Drover eating house. It was much the same. "Elk meat?" queried the red faced cook. "Not me mister, why I wuz raised in Illinois in the early days. We practically lived on deer meat and I kain't stand the stench of veniseen since."

"But, Sir, this is not to be confused with venison. I doubt if you can tell the difference between this and beef."

"Don't tell me my business young fellar, folks kin tell the difference and I got to cater to my customer's tastes. Then he added, a little apologetically, "Now if you had bufflar . . . . "

Somewhat disgustedly I approached the next establishment.

75

The door was locked, and I thought to myself, "What have we here—a citizen who observes the Sabbath?" On peering through the glass, however, I could see the owner poring over his books. I hesitated and then knocked on the door. After considerable time, the man appeared, irately unlocked the door, and gave me such a tongue lashing that I deemed it unwise to press my business.

"What do you mean, young fellow, by desecrating the day of the Lord by peddling and trading your wares?" Then he laid into me with a long and fanatical tirade of the wickedness of the town's citizens and the imposition of their sinful ways on those who only wished to spend a short time in solitary meditation on this day of rest.

After he had run down, and I had a chance to get a few words in; I expressed my regrets for bothering him in the first place. "However," I added pointedly, "Seeing you at work on your books I had no idea I was imposing on your religious principles."

Then he became a little more human and conversed on sociable terms. Explaining that he had always been dead set against transacting business on Sunday. And finally—if I would call the next day he would be glad to do business with me providing of course, I had some beef or buffalo.

By this time, I had my fill and in complete disgust, headed back toward camp. On the way home I concluded to stop by the main train. After carefully reconnoitering from a small rise to make sure the wagon boss was not about, I went into camp and gave the full quarter of elk to the Mexican cook. He accepted it so gratefully with so many "Gracias, gracias," that for the first time this morning, I felt a glow of brotherhood toward my fellow men.

"Jose, you are just about the finest fellow I've met all morning."

The cook grinned his appreciation and went on expressing, "Muchas gracias for the elk, she is a veree good. But me, I lak the meat of the buffaloah."

After getting back to camp, I busied myself cutting firewood and various chores. By the time the family had returned from the impromtu services I had heated water, shaved, taken a partial sponge bath, attired myself in clean shirt and socks and generally was ready for Sunday dinner and an afternoon on the town.

Seated around the table after listening to the usual discussion pro and con on the services, Tom and Mamie had chuckled over two or three particularly amusing "Purdy gems" and had promptly corrected the kids for showing a lack of respect, in doing exactly the same thing. I finally got around to telling of my futile experiences peddling elk meat.

"Well now, if that ain't a horse on me," commented Tom. "Why elk like that is as good as the best buffalo as ever walked. Doggone it, Jack, you done give away five or ten dollars worth of good meat to that ungrateful Mexican.

"Oh, he was grateful alright, and I don't regret that part a bit. It was much better than letting it spoil."

"Yeah, that's a fact, and the boys over there will appreciate it for sure, but Clint won't," he added grudgingly.

Both Tom and Mamie were properly sympathetic that I had been unable to make a sale. "Why," said Mamie shrewdly, "I bet you needed that money?"

"I certainly could have used it," I agreed, hopefully stealing a glance at Tom. For I was hesitant at coming right out and asking about my wages considering I had put in so few days at full time.

Soon Tom and I went to water the stock and after the last animal had again been picketed out to graze, I turned to him and told of my plans to spend the afternoon in town and that I needed a little money. He seemed a little taken aback but left for the kitchen wagon to get his wallet. While I waited, I could see he and Mamie in earnest conversation. Presently, he came back looking a little guilty and paid me. When I expressed some doubt as to whether I had actually earned the full amount. He assured me, "I ain't ever had a fellar that took a holt and done his share any better'n you. Why doggone it, I ort to paid you sooner, but seems like it never occurried to me."

As I cantered down the main drag of Abilene that Sunday

77

afternoon, almost a holiday air possessed the town. Apparently most of the stores, shops and so forth were open and doing a good business. A small band of Texas drovers jogged by me with spurs and bits jingling I caught a little of their yo'all southern lingo as they went by. In the proper costumes they would have appeared as a colorful group. Whereas in reality, their apparel and outfits showed the wear and tear of a trail much removed from the niceties and conveniences of civilization. They ranged in age from the fuzzy chinned boy in the rear to the fellow in Confederate coat with gray-tinged whiskers.

A small yellow dog ran out barking savagely. Encouraged by his own savagery he ran in closer as if to nip the heels of their horses. One of the drovers quickly whirled a rope about his head and cast expertly but the dog dodged just at the right time and came back carrying on worse than ever. A drunk holding on to a porch column to balance himself yelled derisively at the spectacle. Thus encouraged, two or three of the other Texans uncoiled their ropes and in good-natured rivalry attemped to lasso the dog. But no matter how skillful or how quick the men maneuvered their ponies the dog always managed to escape their loops. Now others of the bystanders took it up and added encouragement. I pulled my horse to one side and watched the fun. So far the contest was going one-sidedly in flavor of the dog. Then my attention was drawn to one of the drovers who had taken no part in the contest so far—a tall, dark bearded fellow astride a quick, well-handled pony. He maneuvered in position and cast his loop effortlessly and before the dog realized his predicament, a rope was around his neck.

I had just seen for the first time an expert roper at work (or rather play). Probably the greatest skill of the true cowhand. The bystanders yelled their approval of a job well done, and the Texan with a self-conscious grin on his face, rose in his stirrups and doffed his hat. One of the other riders rode up and slapped the roper on the back. "Now Bid, yo're like a cousin of mine who roped a bobcat. How in the hell yo'all gwine git loos'et from him?"

Bid made no answer but simply tightened the rope pulling the thoroughly frightened dog closer and suddenly lifted him off the ground and as his horse pranced and plunged and as the dog gurgled and tried to snap, he snatched the loop open and the dog was free.

This period of excitement now over, I rode on a bit further, tied my horse to a hitching post and made a few small purchases. Being somewhat in need of a haircut, I then entered a barbershop. Here two barbers were at work and a number of rough looking customers lolled about on benches awaiting their turn. A pair of half-drunk Mexicans carried on a loud conversation in Spanish. The larger of them was undoubtedly a mongrel mixture of many races, certainly Indian and Mexican and likely some Negro and White blood ran in his veins. He talked in a loud arrogant voice and when his companion sought to quiet him he only became louder. I saw the booted and spurred citizen across from me lower the battered Kansas City paper he was reading and give the loud mouth a quiet stare and unconcernedly resume his reading. The face I saw was that of the drover who had roped the dog.

Presently, the Mexicans became restless and got up and left. One of the barbers, a garrulous character, informed us the loud-mouthed one was called "Segundo". "Means real bad," he told us, thus expressing his ignorance of Spanish. He then went on at some length in expressing his opinion of those who were not of his own race. "Now take that little greaser there that didn't say much, he's a bad one too. I'll tell you for sure. Name's Gonzales, knifed a fellar over at Junction so I heard. But By Gawd boys, I'll tell you it ain't healthy fer no damn breeds to push their luck in this here town."

The barber went on and on but I soon lost interest in what he had to say as another customer entered. This fellow was undoubtedly from the city. A drummer, I took him to be, dressed in a loud, checkered suit and round top bowler hat. He smoked an expensive cigar and carried a number of spares in his breast pocket. He gave the impression of cocky self-confidence and clearly considered his present company a little "beneath" him.

"Just got in from Kansas City," he announced to all. "Plan to spend a little time in your community. And just to kill time, where could a man scare up a little game?" He took a deck of cards from his pocket and riffled them skillfully and favored the rest of us with a knowing grin.

"Saloon just down he street where they'll be happy to accomodate you," the talkative barber volunteered.

"Them tinhorns?" said the city slicker contemptuously. "I just want a nice friendly game where we can set down and be sociable and where the house don't take all the gravy. I understand," he continued. "There's some of them cattle rubes in town and loaded with money and ripe for picking. Now, no offense gentlemen." He grinned expansively as it evidently dawned on him that some of his listeners might be of the class he just mentioned. "I'm just a country boy myself. Just happen to love a little game of chance where one man's skill is pitted against another's. Yes sir, it's the sporting life for me, my friends."

He sat down beside the drover and nudged that worthy good-naturedly and proffered a fine cigar. "I say my friend, ever play cards for money?"

The Texan accepted the cigar and admitted with a slow drawl that he had held the pasteboards in games of chance a few times. The drummer apparently scenting a sucker, continued on in a long-winded devious method to bait his would-be victim. The drover, reticent and polite, only seemed casually interested at first but gradually he seemed to respond to the slicker's spiel.

"Tell you what my friend," wound up the drummer with a friendly grin, "Get some of your boys together and come over to Room 12 at the Drovers after supper."

"Next," said the barber, and as it was the Texan's turn, he nodded politely to the drummer and this little "confab" was over. I remember having a distinct curiosity as to the final outcome of this little by-play as the Texan, spurs clinking on the rough board floor, stepped over to the barber's chair.

After finishing at the barbershop, I mounted my horse and explored the town, eventually winding up at the cattle pens where I had hoped to see some cattle being loaded in the cars. But I was doomed for disappointment as there was nothing of that sort going on. The only cattle in the large corrals were some tame

80

native-looking stock in one pen. These appeared to have been there so long that they had established residence. An engine was puffing up and down the tracks switching cars and blowing off steam. Further down the tracks on the other side of the depot a number of heavy freight wagons were being unloaded from flat cars and a group of familiar Tyler & Randall hands were engaged leisurely in reassembling them on the ground.

These sight-seeing activities having taken care of the balance of the short afternoon, I returned to the downtown district and had supper at the restaurant. Supper finished and in no hurry to return to camp, I strolled down the main street intent on seeing a little of the night life in this salty little town. As I approached one of the saloons, the double doors suddenly swung open and a disheveled citizen was propelled into the street with the admonition to get out and stay out—"By Gawd." This fellow picked himself up after a while, rubbed his posterior ruefully, nodded gravely to me and went staggering down the street to the next grog shop. I had a curiosity to see the interior of one of these "dens of iniquity" so I swung the doors open and went inside. The bartender gave me a sharp look, but on seeing I was not his late departed guest, he nodded gruffly. The bar was lined with customers, the rumble of voices and the rattle of glasses filled the smokey room. Two or three card games were in progress and in the gloom of the far corner, some of the drovers I had seen that afternoon were playing a roulette wheel. Never being able to get much excited over this type of entertainment. I soon lost interest and was glad once agin to be in the fresh air of the street.

Near where I had tethered my horse, stood a new building in a still unfinished state. As I came near I heard the sound of music coming from this place. Something familiar stopped me, then I remember the stock wrangler and his strange instrument at the Tyler & Randall barn in Kansas City. The place I now entered was to be an eating house. Already the owner's sign hung in front and a long, new lumber lunch counter graced the interior though as yet no door or windows filled the unfinshed openings. Across the counter the proprietor and his wife dispensed hot tin cups of coffee and doughnuts at five cents apiece. As I entered, "Mustang" was sawing on his instrument to the accompaniment of a sandy-haired freighter with a mouth organ. Quite a crowd had gathered as the two musicians were in fine fettle. I hung around listening until they had more or less exhausted their repertoire and the gathering commenced to break up. The proprietor and wife thanked the entertainers very graciously and insisted they come back the next night. "Free coffee and doughnuts on the house," they promised.

Early Monday morning the word came that the main train would be loaded and ready to roll the next day. When we had pulled in to our present camp, many things on our wagons and equipment were beginning to need service and repairs. Typically, Tom had been putting these off until tomorrow. By now I knew him well enough to know unless someone showed some real determination we would move out in the morning with these things still undone. With these things in mind, as soon as breakfast was finished I hunted up the axle grease and was soon busily loosening wheel nuts, slipping the wheels out and greasing the axles. Fritz never needing encouragement when it came to hard work, quickly lent a hand. By the time Tom came out leisurely, smoking his pipe, Fritz and I had finished with the lighter rigs and were ready to start on the heavy wagons.

"What do you boys figger you're doin?" he grinned good-naturedly.

All Tom needed was a little encouragement once in a while, and he made a very good boss. Now he joined in and worked like a good fellow. Long before night, we had things in what appeared to be ship-shape order.

I told Tom of some of the events of the day before in town and he became interested at once. "Say Jack, let's you and me and Andy go in to town tonight. I ain't so doggone old, but what I like a little excitement once in a while. The woman and kids'll be safe here with Fritz."

After an early supper, Tom, Andy and I piled in the latter's one-hoss-shay. Mamie came out and said half seriously, "Now Andy don't you and Jack take Tom in no saloons or I sure won't let him go next time."

"Don't you worry or fret a mite, Mamie," Andy assured her. "We'll take care of him jist like he was our own."

So naturally the first thing Andy and Tom wanted to do after tying up the mule, was go in the first joint we came to. Inside we lined up at the bar and ordered a beer apiece. The brew turned out so strong and bitter, that for the life of me, I couldn't finish mine. Besides, the impromtu, unrehearsed, floor-show that went on behind us was infinitely more entertaining.

In the far end of the room two tables were occupied by card players. Among those grouped about were a pair of the opposite sex painted and dressed in the gaudy fashion of dance-hall girls. One of these, a rawboned redhead, with a hard face no amount of make-up could conceal, hung over the chair of one of the players and carried on in the ways of her kind while sipping intermittently from a glass of red-eye. When he raised his face, I made out that the object of her favoritism was none other than the loud-mouth of yesterday, "Segundo." Needless to say, this pair pretty well "drowned out" the noise made by the other players. But things came to a sudden quiet as the last cards were played and an unshaven freighter reached cross the table and gathered in the pot. When it dawned on the redhead's half-drunken senses what had happened, she let out an unearthly screech and commenced a vulgar tirade that would cause a pack mule to cringe with shame. The object of her displeasure lit a cigar and leaned back grinning insolently. I wasn't surprised to see that he was Clint McCanles, unperturbed and well pleased with himself. The woman continued to direct a stream of venom at McCanles and all others within range of her raw-edged voice. But apparently no one considered the matter worth making an "issue of". At least no one said anything until a rasping voice spoke suddenly from the back of the room, "Aw shet up! Why'nt you go lay down and let yer pups suck?"

The remark was by no means original but the implication was obvious and—fitting.

"Who said that?" shrieked the redhead, grasping a bottle and lunging around the room. "Speak up if ye air half a man."

Her swarthy friend jumped to his feet pulling his six-shooter and joined the search. Suddenly and undersized youth with a peculiarly mean face made a hurried exit toward the front doors with the half-breed in pursuit. To add impetus to the pursued, the latter aimed his pistol towards the ceiling and pulled the trigger. A series of deafening roars resulted and powder smoke half filled the room. What had happened was an unexpected multiple discharge of the loads in the cap-and-ball pistol, a not uncommon occurence where rough usuage and carelessness in loading were combined. To a sober man in full control of his senses one of these happenings can be a bit disconcerting. But to this half-drunken fellow, only a look of puzzlement at his unexpected prowess crossed his face before he thrust the still smoking "hawg-leg" in his belt and went swaggering back to the card table. Here he continued in a very ugly manner by pulling a knife and slamming it point down in the table and addressed the gathering in a mixture of Spanish and broken English to the effect "that any son-of-a-dog who cast a slur on thees' a fair flower of the prairies would have him to answer to, and that he personally would take pleasure in carving the hombre's liver out."

No one accepted his challenge. But McCanles, completely unintimidated, was still shaking from laughter at the shooting episode. Of course, this only infuriated the breed further, so to emphasize his remarks he kicked a spitoon spinning across the floor which caught the bartender—who had stepped around the bar to see what the trouble was—square in the shinns. This made the bartender mad, and without a word, he returned behind the bar and armed himself with one of those wooden mallets known in the beer trade as a "bungstarter".

Tom sensing real trouble, suggested, "We better get out of here."

Being well in the half-breed's line of fire—and not nearly as sure as the bartender appeared to be, that there wasn't another load or two left in the former's pistol—we edged quietly out the front doors.

As we walked down the street discussing the trouble in the saloon, we heard the strains of music coming from the new restaurant. As we came closer, we could hear the soft pleasant voice of Mustang bearing down on "Jim crack corn and I don't care." The singer had a God-given knack of bringing out all the melody and pathos there was in the old song.

84

"Well! I'll just be damned," said Andy in amazement, "I didn't know that no-account wrangler could sing like that."

We went to the counter, got ourselves a cup of coffee and a doughnut apiece and settled down to enjoy the concert. I noticed that a man helper took the place of the proprietor's wife tonight and perhaps for the lack of a lady's presence, the gathering seemed a little rougher than it had the previous evening.

Sitting near the windowless opening, the clack of bootheels and the jingle of spurs attracted my attention. Down the board walk, and out of the gloom, with his hat throwed back and a merry whistle coming from his lips, appeared a "spectacle". For an instant I was puzzled, then it dawned on me this was the drover who yesterday had roped the dog. He was shaved and shorn and dressed in the Kansas City drummers' raiment from head to foot. Only boots, spurs and six-shooter remained of his former get-up. It was readily apparent that the drummer had found his sociable little game.

When I realized the true import of what I beheld, I leaned back against the wall and laughed until the tears came to my eyes.

Tom nudged me, "What the dickens you laffin at?"

I pointed at the Texan who on hearing the "lamenting cry of Clementine," hesitated for an instant then strode abruptly through the open door where he stood grinning down on the singer. The music suddenly stopped and a look of pure astonishment came over Mustang's face. He shoved out his hand and grasped that of the drover.

"By Gawd! Bid McClaine!"

"I heard a turrible screeching and groanin," drawled the other, "figgered some one musta forgot to grease their wagon or else some soapweed troubadour was atrying out his tonsils."

The Mustang looked over his friend, sizing up his fancy clothes and the ludicrous appearance the drover made in garments obviously designed for a shorter man.

"Bid," he asked in horror, "Where in the hell did you get them clothes?"

"Well," admitted Bid looking around the crowd and grinning a little sheepishly, "I unexpectedly came into some good fortune last night."

The crowd roared enthusiastically. The proprietor set a cup of coffee in front of McClaine and someone yelled to strike up the music. The sandy-haired freighter started out on an old favorite with his harmonica, Mustang joined in and the show was on again. As the pair warmed and stirred by an approving audience, it became a regular hoedown. Someone passed around a bottle and things took on a festive air. McClaine and another drover joined hands in the middle of the floor. They promenaded swung, bowed and danced with all the trimmings.

A noisy commotion occurred at the door and unexpectedly the troublesome half-breed from the saloon strode in and roughly elbowed his way to the counter, followed in a somewhat quieter fashion by his "compadre" Gonzales.

"Whiskey," roared the larger of the two, pounding roughly on the counter top.

"We don't have no whiskey," returned the owner quietly but with a steely look in his eye.

The musicians had struck up a lively Spanish tune and McClaine, who had taken another nip at the bottle, started on a better than fair imitation of a Mexican dancing girl. I saw his sudden glance at the counter where the recent arrival was loudly demanding whiskey.

Gonzales, the most peaceful of the pair, grasped his companion by the shoulder and spun him around facing the crowd and at the same time, speaking earnestly to him. Segundo being foiled at making trouble at the counter, now turned his attention to another place. His eye immediately fell on the tall drover who was industriously kicking up his heels in the middle of the floor. He (Segundo) took one look and yelled a derisive insult in his native tongue. Of course, most of us there could only guess at the meaning, but the drover understood, though he gave no hint. Gonzales again grabbed his companion's arm and spoke excitedly to him, but to no avail. As the music ceased, Segundo again shouted an insult to the drover who had just turned his back.

For an instant there was absolute quiet in the room. When McClaine turned, his six-shooter was in his hand. It spun forward and then backward on his forefinger. He said one word sharply in Spanish, then in plain English, he spoke "his piece." I have never heard a man told off so well with as few words and with as little show of emotion. It was as a Sunday school teacher might remonstrate with an unruly student—that is, the manner was similar but the words were different.

"You saddle complected, son-of -a bitch, when yo'all are in the company of white folks, speak only when you're spoken to.— Savvy?"

But for once, the breed was unable to speak; even when spoken to. His mouth worked but the words wouldn't come. But Gonzales sensing the necessity of a quick decision grabbed his "compadre" by the arm. "Si, Si," he said to McClaine, "He savvy," and without any resistance he guided Segundo out in the night.

That climaxed the events of the evening. Most of the men present, knowing something of the two-day spree of the departed pair, particularly, Segundo, were pleased with the turn of events. Some of these fellows walked up to the drover, and in their rough fashion commended him for his actions. The proprietor announced to all. "Step up to the counter, boys, plenty of hot coffee, on the house."

Partly by design, I found myself by the side of McClaine. I introduced myself and went on saying that I had seen him the day before when he so expertly roped the dog. He shook hands politely, but without enthusiasm. Then I made the same mistake I had made at least once before. I went on explaining that I was a new-comer from North Carolina. When I mentioned Carolina, he perked up his ears.

"Noth Caroliny, sho nuff, now ain't thet where old Dan'el Boom come from?"

A little taken aback, I started to agree when he waved his hand affably, "See yo'all again sometime Caroliny." And he and Mustang moved off together to the far side of the room.

In this way, I came to know Bid McClaine and I gained "a nickname." In the days to come, I came to know Bid very well, perhaps better than I will ever know another man. This was no casual acquaintance. but a long experience wherein I saw his better nature and—I saw his worse. But a truer friend a man never had.

CHAPTER VIII

"Buffalo"

It was early Tuesday morning when the train moved out on the trail away from Abilene. Six more loaded wagons joined the train (or were added to it). Among the new drivers was Bid McClaine, handling one of the wagons picked up at the freight depot. In addition to these, necessary new men, we also acquired two other characters who did nothing to improve the efficiency or enchance the dignity of the crew in general. One of these was a cold-eyed, tinhorn gambler called Denver, who was a pure unadulterated scoundrel. His only virtues was a sour sense of humor and an air of good fellowship that he turned off and on as the occasion demanded. He had no visible means of support and he claimed none save that of his dubious profession, yet he drove a fine team of gray horses to a top buggy and dressed in expensive clothes. Just what hold this fellow had on the wagon boss, we didn't know, although it was through his courtesy the gambler was along. The other shady character was known as "Snird," who turned out to be the same mean-faced youth, the half-breed had ran out of the saloon the night before. If Snird had any virtues, he managed to hide them, but he did have a mean disposition and sticky fingers which he didn't hide. Accordingly, he was heartily disliked by all who came in contact with him. But enough of Denver and Snird, let us move on to more pleasant thoughts.

Though our stay at Abilene had been both exciting and eventful, we were all glad to be back on the road again heading up the valley of the Smokey Hill. By noon, we crossed the Solomon and camped briefly on the other side for dinner. Here, the valley was wide and level and partially wooded with stretches of fine timber. Moving several miles further, on a dry dusty afternoon, we crossed the Saline river, another stream similar to the Solomon. From the Saline, we continued on up the trail and camped for the evening south of the town of Salina. This was considered about the edge of civilization, so some of the boys got permission to go in the town that evening. Just how this was accomplished, it is difficult to say as the wagon master was usually a hard man to deal with on such matters. But at any rate, some of them did spend the evening in Salina and they must have enjoyed thmselves well, if not wisely.

We were awakened in the small hours of the next morning as they rode by our wagons on the way back to camp. A half-drunk freighter started to serenade us with an old rhyme "Ol Tom Powers is a merry old soul, with a buckskin belly and—", broke off lamely with unexpected decency, evidently remembering Mrs. Powers and the kids. As someone else guffawed loudly at the sudden interruption of the rhyme, I heard the voice of Bid McClaine clearly though a little thickly reciting to himself, solemnly, as one would a matter of great importance, "I'm Dan'el Boom from Nawth Caroliny. I am, By Gawd, I am."

I flushed to myself as I remembered my conversation with the drover the night before. As the noise of their passing receded, I wondered what kind of men were these who after a two-night's fling in Abilene, would waste another night's rest in riotous living.

Next morning at daybreak, however all hands were on the job. And it is a tribute to their physical condition that they were, for there must have been some headaches, and possibly some good resolutions made, as the whips cracked and the wagons pulled out on the trail.

At Salina, the train turned south on a little used trail and followed the line of the Smokey Hill, intending to cross that stream near the big bend and continue on south to the Santa Fe trail. This route was recommended by Scout Balaam as one of less travel thereby apt to furnish better grass and wood. The other and most commonly used trail continued on in a south-westerly direction from Salina and touched the Smokey again near Ft. Harker or the new railroad town of Ellsworth, thence across the river to the Arkansas and Santa Fe trail. This was known as the Ft. Larned road. Ft. Larned and beyond, was, of course, our destination, but we were assured we would reach it just as soon with our stock in better shape, by going south from Salina.

This day as we slowly progressed southward, we commenced to leave the main settlements and "civilization" behind. I think we all experienced an inner feeling of excitement as we moved over the thickly grassed hills and down across the thinly wooded tributaries. Just before noon, we ran into our first real trouble of the trip. Tom's double wagon rig mired down crossing a little stream that in dry weather would have been little more than a gully. In the plunging and raring of his teams, a double tree was snapped. Of course, Tom had no spare along so naturally, he lost his temper and cussed his teams, his wagons and so and so, and such and such, that sold him the outfit in the first place. He went on to say how he would enjoy seeing the blankety, blank fry in hell and how he wouldn't so much as give him a drop of water to cool his burning lips if the whole Arkansaw was his (Tom's) own private watering trough—and so on and so forth.

At first, I was a little shocked at Tom's violence, but before he was finished, I was amazed at his originality and lack of repeitition.

As his original subjects had been pretty well cussed and discussed, Tom happened to think of the pertinent fact that we had been forced to follow the drag for the entire trip. This fired him up anew and as we wrestled around in the mud getting the mules unhitched so that repairs could be made, he launched into a bitter tirade, dwelling on his opinion of McClanles. "Why", he concluded, applying a few particularly choice epithets to the wagon boss's name, "He druv his wagons through here and riled up the bottom so's the rest of us would git stuck and never givin a billy-be damn if we ever git out."

Regardless of where the fault lay, Tom had reason to be disturbed because we would have been in quite a prediciment if it had not been for "good neighbor" Andy Cooper. Andy, trailing along just ahead of Tom had managed to cross without difficulty but he recognized the crossing as a bad one and soon as he found a suitable spot, he pulled up to see how the rest of us made out. As soon as he saw that Tom was in trouble, he unhitched his lead team and came back to help us. Fortunately for Tom, he also carried a spare double tree and generously offered its us.

Tom having let off steam and naturally feeling very grateful towards Andy, quickly regained his good humor. Before long he was explaining he had ort to have carried a spare double tree but he just naturally hadn't got—. Andy spoke sharply to the mule he was hitching, and I glanced up quickly and met the grin on his face.

By hitching Andy's lead team on ahead and Fritz and I heaving on wheels we soon had the wagons extracted. By this time, Mamie who had discreetly taken her wagon and the younger children out of earshot, was starting dinner. We made the necessary arrangements for our noon stop, after inviting Andy to eat with us and gathered around the cook wagon.

After eating, and while the others were setting around swapping stories, I made a brief exploration of the little stream and located a better crossing a few hundred feet above our present location. We moved the other wagons to this crossing and pulled across without difficulty.

That afternoon we fell considerably behind the main train due to our unfortunate delay at the crossing. We had to cross one other tributary with a muddy ford that gave us some concern but got all the wagons across without much trouble. Continuing on we made good time as we approached the more rugged country at the big bend of the Smokey Hill. Some two hours before sundown we caught up with the main train, camped near a high hill or butte which towered above surrounding country.

As soon as the camp chores were completed, I saddled my horse, strapped on my rifle and taking my field glasses, I rode to the top of the butte. These field glasses were an exceptionally fine pair. They had been given to my father along with an expensive .36 caliber Colts revolver by a wounded Federal officer, as a token of his gratitude. On coming west, my brothers had generously agreed to let me take both articles with me. At the top of the butte I had a magnificent view of the surrounding country. Stretching as far as eye could see was a panorama of rolling hills, broad valleys sloping to narrow, irregular, patches of darkish, timber splotched here and there with the green of cedar. The day had been warm and sunny, now there was hardly a breath of air. The freighters scattered about the wagons below me seemed detached and out of this world. Though in the stillness I could hear the sound of an axe chopping wood and the rattle of tin pans and the murmur of distant voices. To the south I could see the night herders as they worked the "cavayard", slowly along in the grassy flats. To the northwest a long dark line of clouds obscured the horizon, "portending bad weather for tomorrow," I thought in my ignorance of the plains.

I dismounted and studied the country through the field glasses, distant objects became real and distinct. Below and at a probable distance of a mile at the most, nine or ten buffalo moved sluggishly along as they grazed near the edge of a small patch of timber which skirted the shallow, channel of a draw. A little thrill of excitement gripped me as I studied the animals, for these were the first buffalo I had ever seen and here they were just as I had hoped, only bigger, shaggier, and wilder looking than I had expected.

I thought of riding back to camp to break the news to Tom and Andy but a glance at the lowering sun told me if there was any chance to get a buffalo this day, I had better hurry. I mounted my horse, taking a quick survey of the vicinity, cataloging in my mind the landmarks so that I could be sure to find my way back to camp. Blaze picked his way downhill on the side of the butte opposite camp. From there I guided him on a beeline to a point below where I had seen the buffalo and came up on the far side of the patch of timber. On coming where I judged to be close, I rode with extreme caution until coming to the edge of the trees. I dismounted and tied the reins to a small sapling then taking my rifle, I moved carefully through the timber where sure enough as luck would have it, "there were my buffalo."

My heart was pounding like a trip hammer as I dropped to my knees and crawled quietly through the tall grass and brush until I came in about fifty yards of them. For several minutes I lay there taking in a picture of rare wonder as the shaggy beasts grazed placidly, nearer, unaware of their danger. I thought the elk I shot near the Solomon was a magnificent animal but the bull buffalo I was looking at now, far over-shadowed him. Tall and heavy of shoulders and head, his whole front portion was covered with a thick growth of almost jet black hair. As he raised his head and looked solemnly about, I was struck by his ominous and glowering appearance. For an instant I wondered if I hadn't crawled a little too close for my own safety but the sleek steel barrel of the Henry gave me confidence. I sized up the herd carefully and as my main interest was for meat, I passed the bull by and picked out a small, fat and young appearing cow. Carefully, taking plenty of time, I aimed behind her front flank and squeezed the trigger. Through the smoke she sank to the ground like she had been pole-axed. Though some of them jumped at the sound of the shot nothing else happened except they all stopped grazing and looked stupidly about. I levered another cartridge in the barrel and jumped to my feet and sent another forty-four slug into the cow nearest me. As soon as they saw me, the whole bunch took off as fast as they could go with their tails high and running like quarter horses. including the last cow I had just shot.

I ran back to my horse and took after them. The ground was fairly smooth and Blaze seemed to fly over the ground as I guided him in a line that cut across, thus giving me considerable advantage. But as we came nearer, I saw that we were actually gaining very slowly. The buffalo were moving unbelievably fast for such large and awkward looking animals. Only one which I rightly took to be the wounded cow, was unable to keep the pace. Gradually she began dropping behind the others. I urged Blaze to a little more speed and soon pulled along side where I pumped a couple more loads into her side at a range of only a few feet before she sank suddenly to the ground. I jumped off my horse and ran up with my butcher knife in hand only to have her raise unexpectedly to her feet and confront me with lowered head. She made a lunge at me blowing blood and foam from her nostrils. I leaped to one side and when she turned to make another pass she fell in a heap and was unable to get up, but still belligerently refusing to die. I finally was forced to get my rifle where with one well directed shot at close range I put her out of her misery.

I had been so absorbed in the hunt that I had hardly noticed an extreme change in the weather. The evening sun was obscured by dark clouds and a chill wind blew from the northeast. I realized that in a matter of an hour or so it would be dark; accordingly. I decided to return to the carcass of the first cow, and partially butcher her before returning to camp. I had no difficulty in relocating the first cow and working swiftly though awkwardly, I soon had the entrails removed and haggled off a portion of the hump. I put the meat in a gunny sack which I tied to the saddle, then mounting my horse, I started back to the wagons.

I was so positive of my directions, that I experienced no concern until after considerable distance, it became clear that instead of following down the draw as I thought I was actually going the opposite directon. When I realized what I had been doing I was struck by a chilling fear that left me colder on the inside than I was on the outside. As I was clad only in my shirt sleeves, that wasn't overly warm. I kicked old Blaze into a gallop and rode to the top of the ridge. In the gathering gloom, I studied the country. I was sure that at even this late hour, the big butte near camp would be plainly visible. But the familiar landmark was not where it should be. The only hill in sight was a strange looking one and far in the gathering darkness where no hill should be. "Surely," I told myself, "I couldn't mistake the home butte." I was just as sure

94

that there could be no other in the direction the strange appearing butte lay. Still there was a faint doubt in my mind and I cursed myself for not being more observant when we had gone into camp. I fumbled with the field glasses and tried to bring them to focus on the butte but due to the gloom and the fact I was shaking so much from the cold, etc. they were of little use.

When a man is lost in a strange country it is easy to lose confidence in one's own judgment. This was the state of emotion in which I now found myself and it only added to this feeling when I fully realized I was completely turned around. In spite of all the logic I could summon, that chill tingle of fear chased up and down my spine.

In a matter of minutes, perhaps seconds, the shock of my predicament commenced to wear off. I had rough enough knowledge of the geography of this area to know I had crossed no major divide, all draws, gullies and tributaries hereabouts drained, eventually, in the Smoky Hill. Therefore, I reasoned that I couldn't possibly have gotten over a few miles at the very most from the main stream. So why not ride down the nearby draw until it joined the river and then upstream until in time, I was bound to come in sight of camp. At least I hoped. . . . . .

Every instinct I possessed rebelled against this line of reasoning but common sense prodded me on. Besides, I told myself that I wouldn't be lost if I hadn't relied on my instinct so much.

As I turned, following the easy slope of the draw, with my back partly to the wind, I noticed snow flakes scudding by me. Darkness aided by the heavy cloud cover was coming fast. I hunkered forward on old Blaze as he stepped out in his fast pacing gait, guiding him along the edge of the little ravine that marked the dry watercourse. I tried singing an old mountain song to take my mind off the awful thought, "that I might be going the wrong way again." When dimly through the gloom and thickly falling snowflakes, I saw the thinly timbered gash that was the Smoky. I rode closer and made out the shallow current. Then I headed upstream, though in my sense of twisted direction, it seemed the wrong way. Before long Old Blaze needed no

95

guiding, he picked his way through the gathering darkness as if he knew exactly where he was going. I felt a definite surge of hope. Many times I had heard, "when lost give your horse his head." Why hadn't I done this sooner?"

By now it was getting quite dark and the snow driven by a rising wind was reaching blizzard tempo. Earlier I had been in such a state of emotion that I hadn't noticed the cold but now as the wet flakes melted against my shirt and soaked through into my long-handled underwear I commenced to feel discomfort. But Blaze stepping out in his best gait was fast "eating up" the distance. Gradually he commenced to pull away from the river. I started to rein him back when I noticed his ears were pointed forward so I let him have his head. We gradually turned partly into the storm. Presently I saw the dull glow of a lantern light shining through the canvas of the cook wagon. Tom, attired in his heavy coat, stepped out with a worried expression on his face, and I tossed him the sack of buffalo meat.

"This camp is the most beautiful sight I've seen in the whole state of Kansas," I told him with true sincerity.

Tom had proven himself a much better judge of prairie weather than I. In the interval since I had left camp, the wagons had been rearranged to furnish better protection against the storm. The wagon used by part of the family as sleeping quarters was moved back to back with the cook wagon, an interval of a few feet separating the two. A heavy spare wagon sheet, doubled and reaching the ground on the windward side and held down at the bottom by rocks, covered this space. My wagon had been backed in at a right angle and directly against the front of the cook wagon. The other rigs were arranged in a line with the two first mentioned wagons, crosswise to the wind and as close together as end to end positioning would permit, thus funishing a windbreak for the stock.

Tom insisted on putting up my horse and I retired to the cold darkness of my wagon and changed to dry underwear and outer clothing. Mamie handed me a pan of warm water and towel, and I washed the blood and stains of butchering from my hands. We ate our evening meal "finishing off" the last of the elk steaks, fried spuds, hot biscuits and coffee. We men folks standing in the little sheltered annex between the two wagons as the storm howled about us.

Supper over, the younger children were hustled off to bed under a pile of comforts in the adjoining wagon and Fritz retired to his private domicile. Tom and I climbed in the crowded cook wagon by the stove while Mamie and Sid did the dishes. Here I soaked up welcome warmth while I told my story.

I wouldn't have had to go into detail about being lost, but I saw no need of hiding the facts from my friends. Besides I was so relieved after my late experience that I wanted to get it off my chest. Afterwards Tom had considerable fun joshing me about the incident, but that night nobody thought it was very funny.

When Sid and I retired to our bed in my wagon that night we were supplied with an extra comforter and a tousled old buffalo robe. These were both welcome additions as the ordinary wagon bed was never designed to stop the cold of a blizzard. Though our bed on top the grain and straw was well insulated from the weather on the bottom, we found the extra coverings very helpful on top. Even then we huddled close together, fully clothed except for our boots and coats and spent the night without any great discomfort as the blizzard roared overhead and all around us. I remember breathing a prayer of thankfulness for the comforts I had.

Morning came, cold and windy, still snowing intermittently. There was only a few inches of snow on the ground, but it was wisely decided to stay in camp for the day. After dinner the storm abated, and Tom, Andy, Barney and I went out with horses and Andy's one mule shay to see if we could recover the meat of the buffalo I had partly dressed the day before. After some difficulty, I located the spot, but a number of large gray wolves had beaten us there. They beat a hasty retreat on seeing us approach without giving us a chance for a shot. However, we were able to save all of a hind quarter which was well worth the effort.

After the story of this hunt had been passed along among the freighters I acquired something of a reputation as a hunter which was mostly undeserved. So far, I had mainly, been lucky.

No doubt there were several men in the outfit with far more real hunter's ability than I, by reason of experience. What they probably did lack was my enthusiasm, and in my case, that covered a multitude of shortcomings.

At the camp of the main train, the storm had taken its toll. The wagon boss had failed to recognize the weather signs and had ordered the greater part of the stock out to graze, taking advantage of the good grass. Mustang and another herder with only the protection of their slickers, stayed with the herd until it drifted with the storm and they had to take shelter under the river bank. About daybreak, the herders came in with about twenty head and the bad news that the rest were gone. As soon as the men had breakfast, McCanles went out with a party of ten men to locate the strays. Shortly after we returned with the buffalo meat, they returned cold and hungry with the "remuda" and strayed stock all accounted for.

With little else to do, Tom, Andy and I went over to their camp to pass the time of day. A substitute cook had been recruited and the returned wranglers stood around a blazing fire with tin plates full of hot food and steaming cups of coffee. We joined them at the fire and as a gesture of good will presented them with what was left of the buffalo shank. This was accepted gratefully by the men, and even the wagon boss unbent a little and was the most sociable I had ever seen him. But not for long, however, the sight of buffalo meat caused a ripple among the freighters. They were interested in how, where and when we had gotten the buffalo. Soon some of the fellows were talking excitedly of when we would be in the main buffalo country. Then Clint raised his voice bruskly.

"Now by Gawd fellars, lookie here. Ain't no Goddamn use of you boys gettin any notions of makin a buffalo hunt out of this trip. We're in the freightin business. Remember that; and they'll be no tom-fool runnin around the country after buffalo whilst I'm in charge."

The subject of hunting buffalo was abruptly dropped and the genial air of neighborliness diminished along with it.

By now the storm had completely subsided and the light snow had commenced to thaw, though it remained partly cloudy and chilly. We returned to our camp and looked after our stock. We found to our saftisfaction they had weathered the storm in fine shape. Indeed we had been fortunate for the entire trip as all the stock had stood up well. Particularly this was so because we had no extra or spare animals save my saddle horse and Tom's old red mule. Tom trusting, as he was prone to do sometimes, in a just and benevolent providence. But to Tom's credit, it must be admitted that in some respects he did take good care of his stock. We carried an ample supply of corn and oats and the teams were grained three times a day.

The country we were passing through, (at least back a short distance from the trail) was covered with a heavy cover of grass. As our travels carried us slowly westward, we were gradually approaching the transition point where the tall eastern grasses (bluestems and their like) are mostly replace by the short grasses of the high plains, the blue gramma and the buffalo grass. Already, on the flat uplands these grasses had predominated for several days. Particularly the gramma which was similar in appearance to the buffalo grass only it was taller and more of a bunch grass. Although the country west of Salina supported in some areas all of these types of grasses by far the most important was the buffalo variety. For these reasons; it was far more drought resistant on the plains of the semi-arid country, and in the fall of the year after frost, it undergoes a curing process wherein it retains a greater proportion of its nutrition and thus furnishes satisfactory winter grazing. Largely on account of these two qualities, buffalo grass made the plains the vast year around grazing lands that they were. To the traveler of this area, though he might find many geographical and weather conditions that were not to his liking, he was usually assured of ample forage for his livestock. At least, we found this so, even with the light snow the animals continued to find fair gazing.

Next morning we were delayed by many minor details and it was long after sun-up before we were ready to roll. But it was soon apparent that the main train was even more delayed than ours. Pete Purdy who was already hitched and impatient of the delay, came over and enlightened us. It seems the wagon boss, Denver and some of the others had sat around the fire over half the night playing cards. According to Purdy, plenty of whiskey was available and he criticized McCanles bitterly for his part in the affair. "Card playin and drinkin is the work of the Devil," he said solemnly, "And many times tis' it so whin the wagon-master jines with his men in a night of sin, and tis I that will tell him so if it happens again."

Tom and I exchanged glances but made no comment. We remembered Clint's caustic remarks of yesterday in regard to buffalo hunting. We had heard some guarded talk of the wagon boss's drinking since the gambler Denver had joined the train. But it came as a surprise to learn that some of the men were drinking with him, as the rule of "no drinking" while in camp or with the train had been strictly enforced.

Earlier that morning as the wagon boss sat sourly around the fire drinking black coffee and contemplating the effects of a misspent night, he was approached by Bid McClaine. The Texan probably had no great opinion of McCanles, but he did posses in no small way, a certain respect for his employer. He spoke urgently though politely, "Mr. McCanles Sir, thet nigh wheeler of mine done lamed hisself over the storm."

"Lamed hisself did he?" growled the boss, "Now ain't that a hell of a note. You Gawdamn fellars don't need to come to me with your troubles, pick yourself another one out of the remuda and let me be."

As McClaine started to leave the wagon boss called him back. He had another idea, one which fitted his disposition better this morning. "Tell you what I want you to do, McClaine, is use that little roan mule* with the cross-eyes."

The Texan pondered the order, though he had been with the train but a few days, he well knew the reputation of the cross-eyed mule. He also knew that with the other good work animals available, there was no logical reason to use this one—save for the spite of the wagon boss.

"I've been told thet little mule is the most wuthless, Gawd-awful mean hawdtail this side of the boadah."

* Throughout this story the roan mule with the cross-eyes is referred to as little. Actually the mule was little only when compared with some of the large freighter-mules.

100

McCanles smirked, "Yeah, he's a mite mischievous alright. Course if you can't handle him?" he questioned wickedly.

At this barb, a trace of a flush ruffled McClaine's calm, though when he spoke his voice was still polite and deliberate. "Mr. McCanles, don't you worry none about me bein able to handle him. But I'll tell you this, I aim to do it my own way with no interference from yo'all. —That agreeable?"

"Go ahaid and do it your own way, Gawddammit, you will anyway," growled the boss again, disgruntled somewhat from the other man's manner. The gambler, Denver, and two or three others made up the group around the cook-fire listening to this little exchange. McCanles glared at them red-eyed and belligerent and continued authoritatively.

"But lookie here drover boy, whilst I'm in charge of this here train, I'll have no banging and cripplin of the livestock—. If that has to be done, I'll take keer of it myself, when and where the time comes. Is that clear?"

"It's clear to me, Sir," returned the other with an uncompromising stare, "The rest is strictly up to the Godamned mule."

As McClaine left, the gambler smirked audibly, but McCanles ignored him and spat in the fire, and remarked after the departing back of the Texan, "Perlite son-of-a-bitch ain't he."

The gambler who, so far, had enjoyed a life of indolent ease while with the train; being privileged to the point of having his own team harnessed, hitched and looked after by the help, was not inclined to give his benefactor even a "thank thee kindly". Now he settled back against his bedroll, spread his feet luxuriously toward the dying fire, and twisting his face in sort of a snarl which passed for a smile, he spoke for the benefit of all, "Kinda rankles you, don't he Clint?"

The wagon boss continued to ignore the gambler, but glancing around, he noticed the shabby Snird standing idly by, "Hyar you no account Saint Louie gutter puke, see if you caint find something to do around here, afore I take a hank of hide offen your lazv ass. And now the rest of you men get things to movin. We got this damned river to cross, so let's don't stand around here all morning and palavar."

A place had been located the day before where the banks of the stream were sloping and work had been done with shovels for a crossing. In time, the lead wagon crossed and soon a solid line was splashing across the shallow stream and up the opposite side. The teams urged on by the crack of whips and the sharp yells of the mule-skinners. We were delayed slightly by McClaine who had trouble with the replacement for his nigh wheeler. Finally his wagon pulled in line with the drover astride the cross-eyed mule, kicking him in the sides and guiding the leaders expertly, while voicing words like the cracking of a pistol.

CHAPTER IX

"The Big Domain"

After crossing the Smoky, we followed a little used trail which appeared to veer to the southwest. More rolling prairie, with heavy grass cover stretched as far as eye could see. Literally thousands of wild ducks and geese flew overhead and settled wherever there was water or streams. Prairie chicken and quail were plentiful. The whole area seemed a hunters' paradise.

The appeal of the country made me wonder, "Why go on west?" What was wrong with it here? Surely it was sufficiently unpopulated to satisfy the most outdoor minded. An unlimited domain lay before us, apparently for the taking of any who cared to settle on it. To one used to the populated areas of the east, the immense proportions of this rich country seemed unbelievable. As far as I could see it was practically uninhabited, yet only a day's drive separated us from the settlements.

Absorbed in these thoughts, I was interrupted by old Barney,

"How be ye this morning, Jack? Mind if I tie my mount along-side and ride with you fur a piece?"

When the old man was seated comfortably beside me I plied him with questions.

"Why dad-blame it son," he finally said, "You hain't seed nothin yet. Iffen we'ud come the old trail through Burlingame and Council Grove, you would've seed some of the finest springs and streams as ever laid outdoors. Yessir purtier than a young squaw's laig."

"How long before we strike the old Trail?"

"Oh, tain't a very fur piece, likely afore noon tomorry."

"It's a wonder to me," I said as we rode along, "Why there isn't more timber here. Along all the streams there are fine trees and scattered groves, but most of the country is nothing but a sea of grass."

"Ain't no wonder to it, the reason is 'far'—prairie far. Why long about this time a year, on a dry day this kentry'll burn like tinder. Tech a match to that grass thar and it'll go swoosh faster'n you kin say Bill Robins. That there Jack, is what keeps the timber from agrowin here ceptin a few places "far" cain't git to."

One word led to another and eventually the conversation got around to Indians. I asked him if we were likely to see any soon. For a little while, he didn't answer, when he did his voice was sober.

"That I kain't rightly say, but thars Injuns about I reckon, kase I cut thar sign this mornin. Kain't tell how old, made afore the snow, mebbie two, three day, mebbie nearer a week, but I'm abettin thars redskins in a day's ride of hyar right now."

At these words I felt a shiver of excitement. "What do you mean by sign and how can you be sure?"

He looked a little disgusted, "Injuns is fellars same as you and me Jack. They eat, drink, sleep and build campfires and empty thar bellies same as white folks, only mebbe not so regular and careless like. When they do all these things, onless they air mighty keerful they leave sign—fer them as knows how to read it."

"Maybe these were white men," I suggested for the sake of argument.

"Fiddle ta diddle, Jack, do you take me fer a tarnation fool, why I'd a lost my "har" long ago ef it twasn't I could tell Injun sign from white."

"Just how do you tell?" I persisted, enjoying every word of the old man's answer.

"Well Sir, in the fust place ef these fellars had been white thar would most likely been no reason to hide thar sign. Thar would've been boot and heel marks and thar hosses would likely been shod and a swarm of other things. Now whin the redskins are out with thar squaws and young uns yu'll find plenty uv sign, from footprints likely to throwed away moccasins and a heap o' tother things, mebbee some that will nigh turn yer stummick. But a huntin, or wuss yet, a war party, they'll hide everything that can be hid and not do anything that cain't be. And whin you read that kind uv sign ye gotta be as smart as the tother fellar, and I hain't lived on the plains and mountings forty year for nothin. No siree," and his eyes flashed, "Ain't no dad-blamed Injun any smarter on a trail than old Barney Balaam."

"With Indians near," I inquired, surprised a little at the calmness of my voice, "Aren't we in some danger, and what can we do about it?"

"Tain't nothin to git worked up about, course thars alurs danger now-a-days whin redskins air about. Most likely they'll try to steal yer hosses or shoot arrers in them. Or ef they ketch a man out by hisself—'adios amigo'." Barney slipped his finger across his throat with a near perfect Mexican accent.

Shortly after this the old man mounted his mule and left with the explanation he, "aimed to scout on ahaid a piece." I had been so engrossed in thoughts of wild Indians, that I was unaware of what was going on only a few wagons ahead of me. Bid McClaine was having all kinds of trouble with his replacement (nigh wheeler). For a while, he had managed through super-human effort with spur, whip and voice to keep in line. But now

105

the cross-eyed mule commenced to live up to his reputation. Unable to unseat his driver, he commenced to bite savagely at the off wheeler and at the mule ahead of him. More or less foiled at this by the efforts of the driver and the rigging of the harness, he eventually got sulky and tried balking. McClaine urged the rest of the team along with all of his might and the balky mule was dragged along whether he liked it or not. But this was a delaying action that slowed down the rest of the team, and in time, forced the Texan to pull out of line and let the rest of us go past. Tom offered his assistance as he went by but got only a curt, "I'll make it," from McClaine. So about all the rest of us could do was give him a sympathetic look as we pulled by.

A little later, Sid who had turned his gentle team over to his sister Mary for a spell, was riding on the seat beside me. The boy kept looking back, fascinated by the troubles of the driver behind us. Every once in a while, partly from Sid's insistence I would pull up and allow the wagon behind to close some of the gap. In this way, we both dropped considerable behind the rest of the wagons. I remembered too vividly, old Barney's talk of Indians and commenced to wonder if it might be a little dangerous to drop too far behind. I felt an urge to lend a hand to the troubled mule-skinner but I figured he had a stubborn pride and would resent any direct offer of assistance. Besides, I recalled his sarcastic "Dan'l Boom from Nawth Caroliny", and decided it was none of my business.

Finally Sid could stand it no longer. "Say Jack why can't we help that drover fellow? I bet Paw would loan him his old Red mule if I was to ride your horse on ahead and ask him?"

I pulled up and looked back at the drover's wagon. "No, Sid, I'm afraid there's not much we can do. If your Paw loaned him a mule that wuld put your Paw in bad with the wagon boss. Besides this man McClaine is a stiff-necked sort of a fellow and that kind don't always appreciate an outright favor."

Ahead of us some joker at the front of the column had discarded a ragged old coat. For some prankish reason it had been draped on the overhanging branch of a spreading cottonwood tree that grew on the brink of a small ravine that crossed the trail. I think every team in the train snorted or shied when they came unexpectedly on the old garment hanging in the breeze. The prankster who had concieved this bright idea got many a good cussing that day. But apparently, it never occured to anyone to remove it. I had to ply the whip and shout to get my gentle team under the tree and across the ravine. I pulled to level ground on the other side and looked back.

McClaine had at last got his teams strung out and for the time being was coming briskly down grade about a hundred yards behind. On sudden impluse, I handed the reins to Sid, ran back to the tree, climbed the short trunk and out on the long overhanging limb, I plucked the coat from the branches and dropped lightly to the ground before McClaine reached the place. But he was close enough I could almost see the brooding glare in his eyes as he guided his leaders down the trail.

"There," I said as I climbed back on the seat beside the boy, "We've done our good deed for your friend the drover, and I doubt very much if he even noticed it."

The day's drive was a short one, about two hours before sundown we stopped near a little stream in a shallow valley and prepared to make camp for the night. For the first time of the trip, on orders from McCanles, the wagons were pulled in a huge circle and a corral was formed.

"Ain't no reason to get worked up about Indians at all now folks," the wagon boss told us. "Nobody in his right mind would even look for em this near the settlements. But this old Tomcat," he went on casually, referring to Balaam," was out prowling around in his sleep last night and he stumbled on some last year's Injun sign. Like to skeered the hell plumb out of him, and he come aridin back to camp apoundin' that old she mule of his'n up one side and down the other and a blabbin at the mouth about Injuns."

"Twarn't nothin like that Clint, and you know it," the old scout spoke up, sober as a judge. "That wuz tolerable fresh sign that I cut, and not a fur piece from here and I didn't come arunnin."

"Why you Gawdamned, old rooster," jeered the boss profanely, "I knowed long time ago they had ort to turned you out on clover. But I didn't know you had lost your wits complete. Time was when you were a fair to middlin' scout. Why when I first knowed you, years ago, you could foller Injun spoor blindfold, in the dark, and through a sandstorm, by your nose alone. Now you cain't foller a wagon rut a foot deep in broad daylight."

The old man sat still and was unusally quiet for him. When he spoke, it was with sober deliberation.

"Hev yer fun Clint, time'll tell whether thars Injuns about or not but I reckon it might be a good idee to keep yer primin nigh yer powder dry."

Some comment was heard in regard to making camp earlier than usual. McCanles was in rare humor and explained with a relish.

"It appears that Texican fellar ain't able to keep his team up with the rest of us today, so I figgered we just as well stop a mite early and give him a chance to ketch up. Wouldn't want him to be caught out after dark." And the wagon boss favored us with a broad grin.

Soon McClaine came in sight with his teams reduced to five and the cross-eyed mule following dociley along as if nothing had happened. The drover swung his wagon in place, dismounted and unhitched, tacturnly offering no explanation or comment. His arrival stirred some interest but tactfully no questions were asked, not even by McCanles.

After supper as Fritz and I were returning from outside the corral after checking our stock, McClaine stepped out of the shadows near his wagon and spoke, "Caroliny, I want to say much obliged for taking thet garment off thet tree, back there on the trail. I'm right beholden to you'all."

Next morning as breakfast was over and the rising sun reddened the sky in the east, the wagon boss was hunkered down by the fire like a baseball catcher, finishing his last cup of coffee. The tall drover approached him with a determined look. McCanles saw him coming and greeted him sourly.

"Now what in the hell ails you this morning?"

"Nothing ails me," said the other is his deliberate Texas

108

brogue, without his usual politeness, "But 'I EXPAICT' a suitable replacement for thet nigh wheeler on my team."

"Well now, I jist figgered you had something like that on your mind when I saw you stampin up here like a bull goat. So go pick somethin that suits you out of the 'cavvy' and see if 'you'all' caint keep up with the train today. It appears you Texicans cain't cut the mustard around here onless you got the best stock," he add pointedly.

McClaine answered him not, but turned on his heel and strode away. Denver, the only man near with the temerity to speak, took the occasion to needle the boss again.

"That fellar sure meant business this morning, didn't he, Clint?"

The wagon boss had enough. "I don't see as that's any damn concern of your'n. Besides it appears to me you ain't proper beholden to this here outfit for the favors you've received and the benefits that's been lavished on you. So I reckon you better take that fancy rig of yours and fetch up the drag for a spell."

And that's the way it was, when Clint spoke his orders were obeyed, and this time the gambler was no exception.

This day was one of those especially calm and pleasant spring days, and we traveled through more rolling grassland. About the middle of the forenoon, we came to a little stream, the name of which I have forgotten, but nearby was a corral and a cabin with stable, called a ranche. Here, we came to the famous Santa Fe Trail. We pulled out on this venerable frontier highway and made a few miles more, before making noon camp at a small buffalo wallow of clear water .

After lunch I mounted Blaze bareback and rode down trail a short distance. From the top of a little promotory, I could see for miles in a westerly direction, there were three distinct trails running almost perfectly parallel with one another. The center one apparently being the original and main trail. The ruts here were deep and wide, worn by thousands of wheels and hooves. The explanation of the road's dimensions was plain, when one set of ruts became deep, they would be straddled and a new set started, and so on until it had reached a width many times that of a wagon's gauge. "And why not," I recalled, "This trail had been in use forty perhaps fifty years, since away back in the twenty's when ours was a new nation."

As I bemused myself with these nostalgic thoughts, I saw a dusty commotion, far down the road. The faint outlines of a stage coach appeared and rolled along at a fast trot towards me. This came as a surprise to me as no one had mentioned a stage line on the Santa Fe Trail and I had not expected such a link with civilization. I hurried back to camp and quickly scrawled an address on a letter, to the homefolks, I had been writing at intervals since leaving Abilene. Just before we pulled out, I stopped the stage and mailed it.

While we were stopped at this noon camp, an interesting incident took place at the main camp which I will relate. This morning, the latter half of the train being delayed somewhat in starting, the lead wagons went on ahead in charge of Pete Purdy. With the result, Purdy's men reached the waterhole an hour and a half ahead of the rest of the train. Now Purdy, among other qualities he possessed not common among freighters, was that of being scrupulously clean. So naturally as plenty of water was available, Pete heated a couple of kettles and proceeded to do his washing. Accordingly, when the main train hove into camp, two pairs of ludicrously patched underwear and various and sundry other articles of clothing greeted them from an improvised line hooked to the rear of Purdy's wagon.

The sight caused some merriment at first, but the men had their laugh and had forgotten pretty well about it by the time grub was served. McCanles, who had been otherwise occupied, squatted down with tin plate and coffee and for the first time, noticed the resplendent clothesline. Purdy being a special thorn in his side, had to do but little to rouse the wagon boss to sarcasm and ridicule.

"Well, by Gawd," he said, "I see spring is done hyar. Grandma Moses has washed her drawers aready."

This sally brought forth another chuckle from the men which soon died down as they occupied themselves with the business of eating. Snird, the outcast, having already had one helping, including one of dried prunes, which was a special treat

110

for the day; was waiting idly near the fire for the cook to turn his back so that he could steal another helping. He nervously occupied his time tossing pebbles. Denver watching him, was struck by an idea that appealed to his warped sense of humor.

"Here, Snird," he said, tossing a twenty-five cent piece in the air and catching it, "I'll bet you two-bits to a boot in the tail that you can't belt a pair of them drawers offen that line."

"Who say's I can't?" said the boy jumping up and letting fly with a rock the size of his fist.

Of course, at a range of about ten paces, he soon had both pairs of old Purdy's underwear on the ground. Whereupon he loudly demanded his money from the gambler. Denver, playing it coy, pretended he couldn't see the carnage. He figured Purdy would catch Snird if the boy attempted to get away with his clothes, knowing the old man had already had a "run in" with Snird; and in all probability was laying for him. But Snird, tantalized by the silver piece, dodged under the line, grabbed the drawers and was back quick as a flash. As he started to give a triumphant yell, he noticed his way was barred by Bid McClaine.

"Gimmie them drawers," said the drover.

The gutter-snipe started to say a very nasty word but thought better of it. Suddenly he dodged, but quicker than he, a long leg shot out and knocked his pins from under him. Bid reached down and retrieved the clothing. Snird got up retreating, and started to mouth an ugly insult, but again the look in the tall man's eyes stopped him and he backed silently away showing his teeth.

Bid with Purdy's drawers in one hand and his plate in the other carefully balanced the latter on a wagon wheel and commenced brushing the particles of grass and grime from the formerly spotless wash. Then he walked over calmly as a Chinese launderer and started hanging them back on the line. Praying Pete stepped around from the other side of the wagon and accosted him.

"Mr. Purdy," explained McClaine in his best drawl, "Some

of the boys sorta took some liberties with your undergarments and I taken it on myself to put them back in their rightful place."

"Thank ye, thank ye, kindly, McClaine," said the old freighter with real sincerity, "I saw the whole thing from the back of me wagon and it t'was a noble thing for you to do and I'm downright beholden to you. The Scriptures say . . . .

The younger man, now a little embarrassed by the other's thanks, murmured some slight acknowledgement and backed warily away. He got his plate and without a word or glance resumed his meal.

A wide-eyed silence followed. Men looked at one another but no one spoke, only a faint snicker by the gambler and the rattle of cutlery on tin plates broke the quiet. Opinion of the rank and file of the crew approved McClaine's actions. Though Prayin Pete was considered a little 'peculiar' he was known to be an able and honest man and held enough respect from his fellow freighters that a prank of this type was considered a little beyond good 'trail etiquette'. The wagon boss had taken no part in this little episode, yet he realized it hadn't improved his image. "Image", at least that he himself cast, was usually one of Clint's least worries, nevertheless with all his bluster and roughshod ways, he did value the esteem of his men and it rankled to see where he had lost some of that because the Texan had the fortitude to stand up for old Purdy while he had merely sat and leered at the spectacle. He digested these thoughts over a last cup of coffee as the rest of the men arose and went about their work.

McClaine, delayed a little on account of his good Samaritan deed, was finishing the last of his meal when the wagonboss walked up to him.

"You're a kind of a high an mighty sort of a fellar," Grumbled the boss, "Seems to me for an outfit that lost the War, you Texicans kinda take it on your selves to show us 'Nawtheners' in a bad light. Now fer some time I managed to git along without your personality and I figger I could hold out a spell longer if had to, but, you are a right smart muleskinner and I see no reason for us to be always buttin' heads. The point

I'm gitting at is if we could see our way to work together there might be somethin in it for both of us. There's money to be made in the freightin' game, for them that knows the ropes and right men at these Army Posts. I kin always use a good man who knows how to keep his mouth shet and foller orders. Take this card-sharp now, folks think he's got a holt on me, but I got no use for the tin-horn bastard—personally. We got a "business arrangement"—savvy? Tell me what you think of something like that my friend?"

McClaine laid aside his eating utensils and rose to his full height. "Mister McCanles," he said with finalty, "when I hired on to skin hawdtails for y'all I wasn't expecting any "business arrangements"—And I still ain't".

CHAPTER X

Indians

That afternoon we moved on down the Santa Fe Trail and through the great grass country. Well before stopping time we struck the Little Arkansas, here a picturesque ranche and a large stone corral was located. But as forage had been heavily pastured in the vicinity, we turned upstream for several miles and camped where the grass was very good. The wagons were formed into a corral in sort of a horseshoe shaped circle, with the open end facing the meadow and some low bluffs to our backs. Precautions were taken against Indians though no one appeared to take the thought of danger seriously. The wagon boss showed his lack of concern by ordering most of the stock turned out with the remuda on account of the good grass in the meadow. But Tom, I think was a little concerned for he chose to picket our stock behind the wagons and next to the bluffs where grass was plentiful enough for our purposes.

For the first time of the trip, some semblance of military order was maintained. McCanles assigned eight men in shifts of four each to guard the stock in the meadow. In addition, four men in two shifts were stationed on the bluffs behind our wagons. I volunteered for this duty and was promptly aroused from a warm bed at midnight by Barney Balaam, whom I relieved.

Perfectly comfortable in the blissful land of nod, I can honestly say, I have never felt less like guard duty in my entire life. But I dutifully though sluggishly pulled on my clothes and took my assigned place at the top of the bluffs about a hundred yards from the home wagons. I picked my way stumbling and groping in the dark, to my place. From the first I felt the cool night air, though I was dressed warmly and had a blanket wrapped about my shoulders. The still and loneliness of the place at that hour affected me. I felt like a little boy afraid of the dark, only my grip of the Henry rifle gave me assurance. I remembered the first time I had drawn night watch during the war. I was scared that night on Wilderness Run, too. For a young soldier with little but hospital duty behind him, I had felt like I had jumped from the frying pan into the fire. In my mind's eye I could almost see again, the flashes of gunfire and hear the faraway rumble of the cannons. A far cry, I thought, from this quiet place on the endless prairie. I wondered if perhaps as dangerous a foe waited out there in the beyond as had faced me that night of the war. "Probably nothing at all to worry about," I told myself, "We are here only as a precaution." I now took some satisfaction that I had volunteered. "Somebody has to do it," I reasoned, "And the experience will do me good."

After a long time, my eyes became accustomed to the dark and I made out the other sentry, perhaps a long stone's throw to my left. I stood up looking towards him and he arose also. Then I knew he saw me. I threw up my arm and waved and he instantly waved back. I chuckled, "He's lonesome, too, I bet." When I sat down, he sat down and before long he commenced coming slowly towards me.

"Golly, it's creepy out here," He said and his voice shook. "I kin stand about anything except being by myself in a dark skeery place."

"If it bothers you that much, how come you volunteered?"

"Volunteer! heck, Clint ordered me out here, said it would be the makin of me."

My fellow sentry was Joe Nevers, only nineteen years old, yet this was his third year on the trail, so he told me. Joe was a friendly, sociable fellow of the type that craves and needs companionship. After visiting some time, I suggested that perhaps he should return to his post, but he allowed "it twarn't necessary." Finally I saw that he didn't intend to go back to his solitary place so I suggested that we trade posts every half hour, and that is the way we spent the balance of the night. Each time as we passed each other, Joe insisted on stopping and visiting. Thus the time passed quickly, and I suppose we performed our duties about as well as if we had used the solitary method, as ordered.

Over an hour before daybreak, I noticed a lantern light in one of our wagons and I knew Tom was up. At the same time I noticed one of our mules had pulled his picket pin. I called Joe and asked him to watch my post while I clambered down the slope and retrieved the loose mule's picket rope. While I was at it, I pulled three more pins and led those mules down to the corral. Tom lowered a wagon tongue for me and I led them inside. Tom and I then went out at once and got the other stock. Leaving him to grain them, I returned to the top of the bluffs· By this time, the sky had commenced to redden in the east and distant objects began to take shape. Joe came over and we stood with our rifles loosely in our arms and commented on the beauty of the sunrise. Suddenly, he grasped my arm and I felt the tremor of his body.

"Oh, Lordy! Look yonder!"

Below us on the other side of the creek, perhaps three-quarters of a mile away, yet distinct enough in the early light, was a large band of mounted Indians. They were strung out in a line forty or fifty strong, sitting quietly facing us. I suppose studying the situation and planning their attack.

My first sensation was one half way between thrill and chill. Then the full realization of our predicament hit, something I thought I had been prepared for had now become reality. I raised my rifle and fired three quick shots as fast as I could lever in the shells. Then Joe and I went slithering down the slope yelling Indians at the top of our voices.

Down among the wagons, the alarm spread instantly. The wagon boss mounted a wagon and took in the situation at a glance. Of course, his main concern was the stock for therein was the greatest danger, and he knew enough about Indians to know that would be their first objective. Like a good commander, it only took a minute for him to decide on a course of action. Names came to his lips like the crack of a whip and men came running and took their places. Quickly seven or eight men with rifles were posted in positions at the ends of each prong of the horseshoe-shaped corral.

Now he ordered, "Cooper, I'm putting you in charge of the rest of these men. Man every other wagon and every man see that his piece is in firin order loaded and primed! Purdy, you take Denver and break out the extra ammunition and six-shooters and pass 'em around as fur as they'll go. And Purdy! Tell Powers and his men to stay with his wagons and tell him to put his Goddamned woman and kids inside, and keep 'em there!—Now where in the hell is that old man! Somebody wake Balaam and tell the old summabitch to git out hyar pronto. These may jist be some frisky Osages off their reservation and tryin to give us a scare. Anyway, the old man ort to know."

The fellow that went to wake Balaam, met the old scout pulling his galluses over a soiled undershirt and trailing the stock of his long breechloader, with a packet of long cartridges protruding from a hip pocket.

"Clint says they's most likely a passel of Osages," the freighter said, misquoting the wagon master somewhat.

The old man picked up his rifle and perked up his gait and like an overaged tomcat lit on a wagonwheel, where he took one look.

"Osages hell! Boys, them's Cheyennes!"

The wagon train was armed with 52 caliber Sharps carbines, using fixed ammunition in paper or linen cartridges. They packed a slug of lead capable of downing a man or horse at several hundred yards; (providing you could hit him) but they habitually leaked fire so badly at the breech that the distraction to the shooter was never helpful to their accuracy. These guns were, however, much faster loading than muzzle-loaders and men inured to their peculiarities, sometimes swore by them.

In a matter of minutes McCanles had deployed his men in a manner calculated to provide a defense for the wagons. At the same time, the men who had been posted at the ends of the corral were placed in such a way that it was hoped they could prevent the Indians from getting between the cavvyard and the corral. The boss had no doubts that we could hold our own if only we could get the stock back safe in the corral. The real danger was to the mule herd and the four men who were risking their lives to bring it in.

Bid McClaine was one of the four men with the herd and in this emergency took charge. The wranglers had just started to gather the stock in a compact bunch preparatory to bringing them in, when my warning shots were fired. The men busied in

117

this manner had not noticed the Indians, though the latter were not over a quarter of a mile away. As soon as McClaine saw the raiders, he knew what had to be done and the risks that had to be taken. If the herd had been bunched it would have been fairly simple, "pound them on the tails and strike out hell for breakfast and beat the redskins to the corral." However, the herd, this morning was much larger than usual because most of the working stock had been turned out to graze with the regular "cavvy".

"Move em up! Move em up!" Bid yelled to his companions, "And bunch em, easy now, easy, don't spook em."

He estimated how long it would be before the Indians were upon them, and he worked himself and the others as fast as he dared, steeling himself to not look around for the last thing he wanted to do was quit the herd and run for it. That was the one thing for which he could never face up to McCanles.

The animals were already restless, knowing instinctively something unusual was brewing. But despite this, the skittish stock were quickly rounded up and brought together is some sort of order with Mustang in the lead as was his custom in bringing the herd in. Bid, bringing up the rear would have liked just a little more time, but he heard the yells of the Indians as they crossed the creek below the herd and he figured it was now or never if he kept them from getting between him and the corral. He cracked his trailing rope like a bullwhip and gave his drover's yell, "Take 'em out boys!"

With the pounding of hooves and the yells of the riders, the herd swung towards the creek, crossing. Mustang leaning low on his pony swung down the bank and out of sight at a dead run, followed closely by the old bell mare and the mean little cross-eyed mule. McClaine could see the Indians on his right as they lurched their ponies up the steep creek bank. The band was smaller than at first and he wondered why. He glanced back half expecting to be hit from the rear but no Indians were in sight and for an instant, he was puzzled, then he saw the reason. The band had split and part of them were moving from behind him to his left, as fast as their ponies could go with the evident intention of flanking the herd from that side as well as the other. "How slow do they thing we are," he muttered grimly. Then with a dead sinking feeling he realized the first band (the Indians on the right) had too much head start and for the time being, the "cavvy" was effectively cut off from the corral. He spurred his horse and cut an angle towards downstream, waving frantically to bunch the herd in the creek bottom. Mustang had already crossed the creek and reached the flat above when he saw the Indians racing their ponies to cut him off. He quickly whirled his horse to a halt, waving his hat and yelling with all his might, at the same time he saw Bid and recognized his signals. The other herders on the flanks responded instantly and like a well-trained team the remuda was swung into the creek bed and came to a slithering and panting halt between the high banks. Bid slid his pony down the steep incline, splashed fetlock deep in the stream and blocked the channel at the lower end.

At almost this same instant, the rattle of rifle fire came from the corral. The wagon boss had his men ready and when he saw the Indians had gained the lead and were about to cut in front of the herd, he ordered the men on his left to hold high and fire. The range was long but the bullets struck among the redskins and surprised and slowed them as they had not expected to be fired on at that distance. Then the freighters on the right, let go a volley that crippled a couple of ponies and scattered the attackers like quail, only to regroup in a hurry. By this time the men who had opened the "ball" reloaded and let go with another volley, followed immediately by the group on the other side. Old Balaam taking part this time with his long range Remington. The old Scout was probably the best shot in the outfit and without a doubt the best armed. At this last fusilade a pony was seen to go down and others were hit. The Indians pulled back, more out of range and regrouped for a pow-wow.

McClaine, recconoitering from the creek bank, felt for the first time since he had been with the train, a real glow of brotherhood towards his fellow freighters. But it was no time for sentiment. Now was the time to make an all-out break for the safety of the corral. He waved to Mustang.

"Take 'em out and haid for the wagons!"

The drover couldn't be sure of the Indians above them, but

he gambled that if he made his move at once, they couldn't stop him; it would be mostly a matter of outrunning the first group of hostiles and he knew that would take all the speed and skill his men possessed to prevent a sizeable loss to the remuda.

Along with McClaine, the other riders recognized it was "now or never." With hoarse yells and cracks of their whips, up out of the creek bed they came in a wild neck-stretching race for the corral. The Indians accepted the challenge with blood curdling "ki-yi's", pushing their ponies to the limit and for the time being throwing all caution to the winds.

In the meantime, back at our wagons near the loop of the corral, all of our stock had been secured behind the wagons. Mamie and the kids had scurried to the shelter of the kitchen wagon which had a wider than standard bed and was double lined with Missouri oak. Tom handed Mamie his six-shooter "in case of emergency" and we never doubted that she had the courage to use it on any redskin foolish enough to venture near. Tom had his double-barrel loaded for bear and his pockets crammed with shells, big copper, ten-gauge center-fires. Last but not least, Purdy had equipped Fritz with a loaded six-shooter. With such a weapon the bewildered Dutchman was a bigger menace to himself and the rest of us than to the Indians. Fortunately, Fritz realized this and accordingly he handled the big pistol like a red hot iron.

Owing to our position, we didn't always have a clear view of the action going on below us. Unable to get a clear idea of what was going on I told Tom I would go up on the bluff and take a look. He thought it might be a little dangerous, but I assured him I could be back to the wagons in less than a minute if necessary. Perhaps some hidden instinct urged me to go out there. At any rate with my field glasses dangling from my neck and rifle in hand, I was up the steep slope in a hurry.

With the glasses, I saw the remuda driven into the creek and completely disappear. I could see the dust and the fast maneuver of the band of Indians trying to encircle them from the north (above). Then the heavy firing broke out at the far end of the corral and I got a good view of the attackers scurrying to get out of rifle range. Soon the gunfire died down and I looked to the north for the other Indians and they had disappeared. I suppose they had gone into the creek or else ridden in some brush and scattering timber that grew in the valley above us.

The action having quieted down, I casually turned my glasses on the sloping hillside. Beyond the bench-like bluff where I was standing, a small ravine cut through the bluff and came out on the flatter ground, two or three wagons below where Tom stood guard, it ran on up the hillside becoming shallower as it ascended the slope. At the edge of this ravine at the top of the bluff a patch of tall bunchgrass grew. Here had been my sentry position the night before. As I swept the hillside with the glasses, eight or ten Indians suddenly appeared coming down the ravine less than two hundred yards away. I dodged behind the tall grass and motioned frantically to Tom and the other men, making signs with my hands indicating the Indians. Tom waved for me to come on down but I pretended I didn't see him for I wasn't about to leave leave this position, well-armed as I was. Besides my rifle which was fully loaded, I carried the Colts 36 caliber, cap and ball revolver.

I parted the tall grass and took a peek. The Indians had now come out in the open where they halted and held a brief parley. Then they kicked their ponies in the sides and came down the gentle slope at a dead run. I made a quick motion warning the men below to be ready and got myself in a shooting position, resting mostly on a pulled up knee and forearm. I slid the Henry barrel through the grass and worked out a peek-hole through which I could see very well, and waited. It didn't take long. They came down the slope without a yell or sound save the pounding of their hooves. Closer and closer, until the lead brave, riding well ahead of the others, was forty—maybe thirty yards away. I didn't see the whites of his eyes but I did see the lone eagle feather that drooped over his right ear, the daubs of paint on his savage face, and the ready six-shooter he held in his hand.

It is amazing how the human reflexes work when one is keyed to the right emotional pitch. The rifle hammer came back with a reassuring click. The sights lined up almost effortlessly and zeroed in on the redskin's mid-section at just the right angle to miss his horse's head, and the curve of the trigger had just the right comforting feel.

121

The Indian never knew what had hit him—as he suddenly stiffened and slid sideways off his pony. Fascinated for an instant, at what had happened, I watched slack mouthed, as his pony never stopped but came on down the mouth of the ravine, shied away from the sudden sight of the canvas sheeted wagons, darted in between them and the bluffs, still at a dead run and out in the open and away. The other Indians pulled to a sudden stop, laid low over their ponies and high-tailed it back up the slope. I came alive now and sent a couple of parting shots over their heads. A rifle boomed below on the slope of the bluff and Andy Cooper stood with legs braced, a whisk of smoke curling from the barrel of his Sharps.

He gave a short strained laugh. "Tom sent me up here. Said to go get that damn fool before he gets hisself killed. Guess there warn't much danger." And he laughed again.

Below us, Tom could be seen perched on a wheel of the kitchen wagon, looking anxiously toward us, with his gun barrels resting on the canvas cover next to the stove pipe. At opposite ends, Mamie's and Sid's heads protruded.

"It's all over here," I waved, "They've left." And I held up a forefinger indicating we had downed one.

Our Indians fled up the hill and didn't halt until they were well out of range, evidently believing they had charged into a large force of defenders. Andy and I thought it wise to stay in our present positions for a while as we were located well defensively from an attack above and had an excellent view of the action below. While waiting, we saw the remuda come out of the creek bed and make their desperate attempt to reach the corral.

No motion picture could have portrayed the scene any more dramatically than it happened. It seemed that blooded racing animals could have run no faster than the some one-hundred and eighty mules and horses when they made their head long dash for the safety of the corral. The herders sudden decision caught the Indians off guard and the seconds the redmen lost then cost them the battle. For a while the issue was in doubt as the warriors pulled in bullet and arrow range to the rear and to the right of the remuda. We could see the puffs of smoke as they fired at the herders. McClaine bringing up the rear, hung low on the side of his horse like a trick rider, firing his six-shooter under his horse's neck. At the same time giving his loud staccato wrangler's yell for the benefit of the herd. If an animal stumbled or fell it was too bad for there could be no stopping or slowing in this wild rush for safety.

The men at the lower end of the wagon corral fired as fast as they could load and aim. On the other side of the open end of the corral the defenders were forced to hold their fire somewhat on account of the oncoming remuda. These men however served to discourage that small band of Indians who had circled above intending to strike the train from that side; though as it turned out this band was a little too far away to be a menace.

As the herd raced pell mell through the short thick stubble of the meadow grass, we on the bluff got a clear dust-free picture of their charge. A mule hit in the head by a bullet, reared high on his hind feet and plunged crazily away from the others square in the path of an oncoming rider. Down went the pony and crippled mule in a thudding collision. The rider was thrown completely over both animals but fortunately fell in a soft place. He got to his feet drunkenly running and staggering for his life. An Indian riding close with musket empty, and reckless of his own safety, attempted to ride him down. Old man Balaam, perched high in the lead wagon a good hundred and twenty yards away slipped a fresh cartridge in his rolling-block and dropped the redman's pony with a clean shot through the head. It was now the Indian's turn to run for it and he did—as fast as he could make his feet fly, the only thing that saved him from the happy hunting grounds was Barney's inability to locate another cartridge immediately. One of the other men emptied his six-shooter ineffectively but the Indian escaped and was picked up by one of his companions. For practical purposes, that ended the Indians' charge, as the head of the remuda, led by Mustang, with the old bell mare and the little cross-eyed mule right on her tail, dashed into the corral.

For a few minutes there was bedlam as the stock poured in the comparatively limited space of the wagon-lined enclosure. Andy and I dashed down to help control our own animals. For a while we had our hands full but in time a semblance of order was restored and we took stock of the damage the train had sustained. The Indians by now having drawn off completely out of range, apparently having no desire for another taste of hot led.

The injured rider had been helped inside and McClaine who had been under the hottest fire was the last man in. The drover came through the attack without a scratch though his horse dripped blood from a slight wound in the leg and an arrow stuck in the cantle of his saddle. Altogether, counting the animals wounded so badly they had to be shot, the train lost four head and had no serious injuries to the men. As for the Indians, they had lost one warrior for sure and probably two or three others wounded besides having several ponies killed and disabled.

The feeling among the crew and shared by the wagon boss, was one of exultation. By the time things had quieted down and the cook had prepared a delayed breakfast, McCanles addressed the crew in rare words of praise.

"Men," he said without a smile or any show of sentiment, "I had begun to think you fellars was about the sorriest bunch of inept, oxgaddin, plowboys that I ever hired to skin mules, but this morning you took aholt and done yourselves proud. You men with the cavvyard in particular, you done earned your salt for once. As a reward, after you've et, we're gonna open a keg of whiskey. They'll be no roistering or carry'ns on—understand, just hang unto your tincups after breakfast and there'll be a helpin of whiskey for everybody."

Pete Purdy stepped up beside the wagon boss, he was one of the few who remembered this was the Sabbath. "Aye men since ye'll soon be drinkin of the dregs of sin, me thinks tis only fitten and proper we thank the Almighty for the blessings he's lavished on us this Sunday mornin."

The injured rider who had survived a brief glimpse down "The deep, dark valley" echoed a fervent, "Amen."

"Alright!" said the wagon boss with his usual lack of grace. "Say yore prayers and count yore beads for all I care but don't git the idee this is gonna be a regular ritual around here of a

124

morning. This is a freightin outfit not a Gawdamn camp-meetin."

Accordingly, Praying Pete conducted a prayer and said grace. No man snickered and there were few who did not bow their heads humbly this morning.

Though the attack had actually lasted but a short time, the speed and violence of the thing, plus the unexpectedness, threw the train in a state of excitement and turmoil. Accordingly, it was decided to stay in camp for the balance of the day, repair all damage and have everything shipshape for an early start the next morning. It being the prevailing concensus that we had given the "Injuns" a good lacin and they warn't apt to bother us no more fer a spell."

In rehashing the events of the morning, due to the rapidity and turmoil of the happenings, some of the men were not aware the train had been attacked from the rear. They, of course, had only to see the dead Indian to be convinced. It was a little distressing to observe the callousness displayed toward the body of our late foe. The freighters helped themselves to every bit of decoration and accouterment. One man, Denver it was, even removed a forefinger. Frankly, I wouldn't have been surprised to see someone help himself to the scalp. Fortunately, to my relief, this didn't happen. When somebody suggested maybe "they ort to bury the varmint." He was promptly ridiculed by a bearded and veteran freighter. "Bury an Injun? Naw, let him lay thar to be fit over by the wolves and buzzards as an example fer the rest of the theivin scalawags."

However, the wagon boss took a hand, deciding the proximity of the deceased was nearer the wagons than necessary. A loop was put around an ankle and Mustang with the other end of the rope snubbed to his saddle horn dragged the dead raider up the ravine a ways further, where the body was left in the hopes his brethern would try to recover it; thus, giving the freighters a chance to down some more of the hated redskins.*

For myself, I was accorded the possession of the savages's six-shooter, a somewhat battered, war issue, cap and ball, 44

* In those days when the two races collided in a shooting affray, the redman's and the whiteman's feelings were anything but congenial.

125

caliber Starr. The weapon seemed to be in good shooting condition, however, so I gave it to Tom as an addition to our limited armament. That old six-shooter by the way, is still in the possession of the Power's family and the explanation given now is that it was taken from a dead Indian.

McCanles, came across Barney Balaam cleaning and oiling his rifle. "Well, now old man, I reckon you figger you have something to crow about, with yore harpin Injuns all the time and that redskin aridin his pony square into a slug from old Betsy here," he jeered.

"Ie doggies yes, and I'll tell ye for shore I'ud downed that hay-hoppin Ki-yi too if it hadn't been for them boys of yourn a jostlin the wagon whilst they was atakin kiver, causin me to spill my dad-blamed cartridges."

For the balance of the day, sentries were placed at vantage points surrounding the wagons. And old Barney took a sashay to the top of the ridge and scouted around a bit. The rest of the crew, Tom and I, included spent the morning going over our team and equipment. In the afternoon, Scout Balaam reported no sign of hostiles and the stock were moved out to graze again, this time under heavy guard. Late in the day, Tom and I took our teams down to the creek for water and fetched water for camp use.

The weather had been fine and as the evening sun set the wagon train camped at the foot of the bluffs made a pretty picture of the rugged outdoors. The campfires glowing and sending up thin wisps of smoke scented with cedar and hardwood, along with the remuda grazing contentedly, gave an appearance of peace and serenity completely the opposite of the violence that had gripped the valley just a short sun away.

Before complete darkness, the stock were all brought in and the corral was closed up tight for the night. I hadn't intended doing sentry duty this night, feeling I had done my share for the present. Having lost half a night's sleep and finished a harder than usual day I found myself looking forward to a pleasant night's shut-eye under a canvas cover. However, this feeling wasn't shared by the wagon boss. Just as we finished supper he came along making his rounds.

"Well, Reynolds," he said and I noticed it was the first time he had bothered to call me by my right name, "You appear to have a pair of right sharp eyes, so's I reckon you'd best shinny right back to your old stand on that bluff and take the first watch. I'm posting a man about every hundred paces around the whole corral and I expect every man to be damn particular and keep his eyes peeled whils't he's on duty. If them red sons-a-bitches come back tonight, they're gonna be a sight cuter than they was last night."

"Sure," I agreed with a vigor I didn't altogether feel, "I'll be glad to do my part." Admittedly, I had lost enthusiasm for sentry duty this particular night. For one thing the thought of the dead Indian lying just a few hundred feet up the ravine—"a victim of my own hand," gave me an uncomfortable feeling. For a man of my war experiences, I realized I had no call to be so squemish, still this was different and under circumstances new to me. I couldn't put the thought from my mind. During the day I had experienced a sort of a heady pleasure at being pointed out as "that Caroliny fellar, that got the Injun." Now, I would have felt better if someone else had held this dubious honor.

On the bluff, later on that night when faced with the reality of the situation (as usually happens) I managed to banish these thoughts and my share of the night's watch was uneventful, as was the entire night.

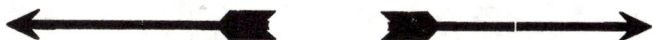

In the late Sixties and early Seventies, there was a continuous controversy over the Indian question. The War Department and the Bureau of Indians Affairs, as well as the State and Territorial governments, quite often held different views. Consequently, official action usually reflected the views of those who were able to exert the most authority and was sure to draw the criticism of the opposition. This state of affairs aroused suspicions and caused so much bitterness that it undoubtedly prevented a fair and proper settlement of the whole ticklish question.

The much publicized Medicine Lodge Peace Treaty had been made in the fall of "67". This treaty was with the "wild tribes" which included the Cheyennes, Arapahoes, Kiowas, Commanches and some of the Apaches. The Indians were given goods and supplies (and promised annuties) as well as certain privileges and concessions. Supposedly, they in turn as their part of the agreement, promised to stay south of the Arkansas and to not molest the construction and operation of the Kansas Pacific Railway. But before the winter was over the Indians were known to be roaming as far north as the Platte; sometimes in a trouble-making manner. By the same token, some of the whites regularly violated their part of the bargain whenever it suited their convenience. In some cases these violations were committed by those who were no doubt ignorant of the terms of the treaty, though the majority never considered them binding upon themselves whether they were familiar with the terms or not. It being a common attitude of those whites who were always pushing westward, that the Public Domain was one vast hunting ground specifically created for their use and to be exploited in any manner they chose. On the other hand, the policy of the Government appears to have been at first, a sincere attempt to deal with the Redman fairly according to the treaty. But conflicting opinions of the Military and the Peace Commission, plus the actions of the Indians themselves served to destroy much that should have been accomplished by the Medicine Lodge Treaty.

CHAPTER XI

Wagonboss Diplomacy

On the morning following the Indian raid, we were up early preparing our teams and wagons for a long days pull, hopefully to partly make up for the day lost. Shortly after sunrise the wagontrain was strung out and headed down the valley of the stream. When we reached the Stone Ranche we paused long enough to leave a few head of crippled stock, casualities of the raid. These animals were found to be too stiff and sore to keep up with the wagons and arrangements were made to have them cared for until the return trip. Tom and Andy counted their lucky stars that their stock were pastured near our wagons the night of the raid and came through completely unmolested. Yesterday spent idle in camp had given Tom's milkcows a brief respite from the rigors of the trail, particularly the one known as old Roanie who had some trouble keeping the pace of the train on some of those first days when the long drives were made. Both cows had fallen off in milk and now never gave enough for their calves. At least that eliminated the chore of milking.

The people at the ranche were much interested in our story of the attack, acknowledging they had heard the distant sounds of gunfire. But the ranche had not been bothered nor had anyone seen any of the hostiles except one herder who had been out at the time. He reported he saw part of the Indians passing to the west after the rucus.

Near the Ranche we crossed the stream on a rustic bridge, paying toll for the privilege. McCanles, as was his way kicked like a bay steer at the toll cost, but the keeper was a hardened veteran and listened to the wagon boss's exaggerated complaints with little sympathy.

"If it tain't bad enough to be attacked by a couple hundred thievin, murderin, savages. With our stock shot full of bullets and arrows, the crew all crippled up and the women and children skeered half to death and then come down here and be held up by yore own kind for the paltry privilege of drivin our wagons over a few loose and rotten planks that ain't more'n half safe to start with. Why I've half a mind to slip out the banks a bit and cross at the old ford."

"Go right ahaid," said the unimpressed keeper, "It's a free country, but I'll tell you right now it'll cost you a damn sight more to fix up that old ford and it's a whale of a lot unsafer too."

So—after much argument and dickering, an agreement was reached with slightly reduced costs. McCanles still insisting we were being robbed. The freighting firm of Tyler & Randall should have been pleased with Clint's bargaining power as anything that required the outlay of a little cold cash was always attacked by him with the zeal of one who was paying out of his own pocket. At any rate that bridge was finally crossed and quite safely, too. We found instead of a few loose and rotten planks as had been intimated, it was actually a substantial structure.

Continuing on, we came to the Difficult Branch of Cow Creek which was somewhat miry, but the train crossed without any serious trouble. After crossing here, we made our noon stop. A few miles further and we came to Chavez Creek. It was named

130

for a wealthy Mexican trader who had been robbed and murdered by outlaws, here, many years before the war. We found a rather pretty little timbered stream with good water. Tom stopped our wagons for a short time and Sid and I took the light wagon downstream a ways and gathered a supply of firewood. Tom had warned us we were approaching country where wood was scarce. We continued onward at a good gait some miles westward we crossed the main fork of Cow Creek, another stream with timber along its banks. We never paused as we found the ford to be shallow with a firm roadbed. We knew now we were approaching the vicinity of the Arkansaw and as we plodded on we noticed more and more the sandy nature of the country. Low grass-covered sandhills became common with scrubby plum bushes covering the little hollows and sometimes the summits of the hills themselves.

All day long scouts had been kept about a quarter of a mile on each side of the train and old Balaam had kept in advance as a precaution. Although no one including Tom and myself, really expected to see any Indians and indeed that day we did not. For which it goes without saying we were grateful.

We moved on that afternoon until nearly sundown, when unexpectedly on my part at least, the broad, water covered, channel of the Arkansas appeared. We picked our way off the beaten path across the level bottoms and at a place where the grass appeared a little less trampled, we formed the usual corral, with our wagons. The stock of the main train was turned out to graze under the care of herders. We staked ours out in the narrow grassy strip separating the wagons from the river. When the camp chores were completed and our evening meal completed, I accepted the inevitable and presented myself for lookout duty. No one seemed to feel there was much likelihood of Indians; nevertheless, a guard was mounted. The memory of the night before last being fresh in our minds.

I spent my watch directly behind our wagons and to be explicit, I braced my back against a wagon wheel. By now I had become somewhat inured to sentry duty especially under such comfortable conditions as these. With a blanket draped over my shoulders and my knees pulled up I leaned back against the rim of a wheel, and listened to the low gurgle of the broad prairie stream. I sat there for a couple of hours, alone with my thoughts, only the occasional and lonesome call of nightbirds breaking the monotony. When suddenly, there came a terrible, mournful, screaming cry that defies description. In spite of myself, I sat up tense with prickles running up and down my spine. With eyes accustomed to the dark, I peered in the gloom across the stream from where the sound seemed to come. While I waited, it was repeated—this time more terrible and mournful than before, when abruptly it dropped off into howls and sharp yaps. I knew then it was the cry of wolves, probably coyotes at that. Harmless, to be sure, but more terrible in its unearthliness than the war cry of the Cheyennes we had heard the other morning.

The sound had hardly died away when old Balaam was beside me. "Mighty peculiar, coyotes ahowlin that away this time a year, but coyotes it t'was fer shore. No human throat coulda sung that song, that away—not even an Injun."

Prior to this interruption, the stock had just quieted down for the night, now some of them were restless and one of the horses became tangled in his picket rope. Barney and I walked out and untangled his rope and calmed the others. Blaze, grazing near the river pricked up his ears and lost interest in his appetite for a while and then settled down hipshot, for his night's rest.

The old Scout who possessed nocturnal habits and normally done much of his sleeping by catching catnaps during the day, seemed to have no interest in returning to his blankets. He now settled himself down beside me for a period of reminiscing.

"Recollect, sunthin that happened a few year back. Me and a fellar by the name of Attorbee was a huntin wolves on a dry crick, nigh a day's ride nawth of Aubrey Station. Now this is a kinda wild little crick with steep dirt banks and bluffs at places, that cuts across that big flat country out thar, and finally runs in a big shallor valley and peters out complete. I have heerd this called Lost Crick but anymores its knowed as White Woman and some times Punished Woman,* on account of a pore white

* White Woman Creek—Ladder Creek, a branch of the Smokey was the stream usually known as Punished Woman.

132

woman who had escaped from the Injuns and perished thar many years ago. They say she done lost her mind and went on in a turrible fashion afore she died. Anyway to this very day, no Injun will go near them parts at a certain time of year. They say this White Woman comes out on the bluffs and screams to punish them that tormented her."

The old man paused in his superstitious tale and let it soak in for awhile.—"Fust night me an this tother fellar was camped thar, we was waked about two hour afore sunrise by the most horrible screechin scream you ever heerd, that it done stampeded our stock and we spent half the next day aroundin them up. Well, Sir, we figgered we was brave fellars and told one atother that it t'warn't nawthin but wolves ahowlin, though I reckon we both knowed better. So's naturally we went right back to the same gol-blamed place and made camp the next night. And shore enough, that night, right plumb squar on the minnit, that same awful scream rant the air—twarn't no animal made that noise, nor human nuther. I'll tell you son, we saddled our mounts, broke camp and lit a shuck out of thar. Why dagnap it Jack, I wouldn't spend a nother night on that crick, that time of year fer all the blamed wolf pelts west of the Big Bend."

And so the old man rambled on until past midnight when my 'guard' was up, and then one o'clock by my father's watch, before I managed to break away and turn in. I was young and full of energy but certainly needed the sleep, if this garralous old codger didn't.

In relating the experiences of this trip perhaps I have tended to neglect how it all effected Mrs. Powers and the kids. To properly dwell on that subject would take a fairly large volume in itself, for that reason I will attempt a very brief resume. Mamie herself though all female was not exactly the swooning delicate type. Her children could be described in a similar vein, normally they were inclined towards misbehavior but were fairly easily cowed by events and environment, from which of course they could be expected to make a rapid recovery. Our recent affray with the Indians had filled them as well as their mother with fear, but Mamie wasn't the hysterical kind, besides she had faith in 'Tom' and the rest of us to defend them along with the help of the Almighty.

Of course the wagonboss viewed anything in the nature of a family as a hindrance and rarely lost an oppurtunity to gripe about it. But time proved him mostly wrong. Possibly at times, McCanles recognized this fact—at least his actions on leaving camp the next morning, would indicate that he did or else he was enjoying one of his rare periods of good humor. At any rate as we were getting hitched and ready to roll, he rode up on his big brown horse with his usual morning cigar in the side of his face. "Ie Gawd, Powers, knowing the nature of this Gaw— this danged country through here, we're gonna do things different this mornin'. We're gonna strike out four abreast, you and Cooper hev had your share of the drag so I reckon you pull your wagons out and keep to the right of my rigs." And he rode on down the line giving instructions.

So it was, we pulled out and traveled a mile or two when a half dozen horsemen were observed approaching us from the west. As they came closer we made out their blue jackets and trousers and recognized them to be a detachment of U. S. Troopers, a Captain and five enlisted men. This was our first contact with the military since leaving Fort Riley and what we were about to hear and see, done little to enhance our image of Uncle Sam's boys.

The officer in charge, though possibly not a bad fellow in many ways, was nevertheless of that military stripe that civilians find a little hard to stomach. During the war (we learned later) he had held a much higher rank but had suffered the common demotion of the times, plus an unwanted transfer to this "God forsaken west". Here he had acquired a fondness for hard liquor, taken at first to lighten the boredom of his life, but later as a daily stimulant. No doubt this accumulation of factors had tended to curdle the small remnant of human kindness still remaining in his soul. Add to this his training and life as, a whole, had long ago convinced him that he as an officer and gentleman was far superior to the majority of his fellowmen and you have a fair picture of the officer who greeted our wagon train.

The soldiers rode up directly in front of our lead wagons where the Captain held up his hand and ordered a halt. "Whose in charge here?" He demanded bruskly.

McCanles had served his time with the Army and had a multitude of dealings with the military; besides he knew an arrogant officer when he saw one. He took his time about answering and when he did, his manner wasn't overly cordial. "I'm Clint McCanles, wagon master in charge of Tyler & Randall's Overland Freight Wagons carrying Government supplies for Fort Lyon and points west."

The Captain turned to one of his men who carried a note-book and pencil. "Take down this man's name and statement, Corporal. Now Sir," he said, turning to the wagon boss, "I am Captain B——, Company——, United States Army, operating out of Fort Larned in conjunction with Agents Wyncoop and Leavenworth of the Department of Indian Affairs. I understand Sir," he said fixing McCanles with an icy stare, "That your men, made an unprovoked attack upon a party of friendly Cheyennes about two days ago in the vicinity of the Little Arkansas. Also I have information that one of these Indians was killed and a number suffered wounds in this totally unnecessary action."

For an instant, the wagon boss looked like he might have apoplexy, but long experience and a prejudiced nature had taught him you could expect anything from the Army or more particularly the Indian Department. He rose to the occasion and when he spoke his manner wasn't mild.

"That's a Gawddamned, dirty, malicious lie," he said loud and clear, "And there ain't ary man in this outfit but what'll back me up on this statement. The truth of the matter is we was set upon by a pack of thievin, murderin, savages that attempted to run off my stock, kill my herders and murder our wimmen and children."

"It will do you no good to Goddamn me, Sir," said the Captain, his voice cold with fury, obviously not used to being answered in this manner. "You are aware of course, or you would be aware if you would take the trouble to come down off your high horse and look about; that there are no hostiles in this area and have not been since the Medicine Lodge Treaty, last fall."

"That's another Gawddamned lie," retorted McCanles, "And don't try to cram that kinda bull down me. I wasn't born yestiddy.

135

I ain't ever seen the Cheyenne or the Kiowa yet that ain't hostile enough to steal a hoss, take a scalp or ravish a white woman."

The Captain was no panty-waist and with eyes blazing, he came right back at McCanles. "Be that as it may, but By God Sir! do you deny that your men fired on these Indians and killed one of them?—Contrary to General Orders that have been issued in this area for some time."

"Hell No! I don't deny it, of course, we fired on the horse, thievin sons-a bitches. And furthermore, I don't consider myself or my men bound by no crack-pot General Order that lays a man and his property wide open to attack by thievin, murderin, redskins."

"All right," spat the Captain, a little slowed but still pressing his point, "I demand that you produce the party or parties that committed this crime. so that he or they may be taken in my custody to Larned where the case may be studied and proper disciplinary action taken if found justifiable."

"Disciplinary action Hell! If I knowed who the man was that downed that red bastard, I'd give him a medal. God amighty hisself couldn't tell who killed who, with thirty or so men shootin as fast they could load their pieces. But all that is beside the point, I wouldn't tell you who done it if I knowed. Furthermore, Captain, let me say right now that no brass button, bluecoat with a yaller stripe down his laig is gonna take custody of ary man in this outfit, General Orders or not. I'm a citizen and a taxpayer and I know my rights—By Gawd."

The Captain, by now sensing the uselessness of further argument, murmured a few uncomplimentary remarks concerning the brazen gall and insolence of some contemptible and uncooperative civilians. Turning his back stiffly, he went his way with his troop jangling along behind.

I had a ringside seat to this little episode and listened with particular interest when the Captain spoke of disciplining those who had killed the Indian. Innocently, I had heard of no General Orders (though it was said to be true that orders had been issued to the effect that a white man under no circumstances was to shoot at an Indian.) But even to those who were familiar

136

with the orders, they were usually disregarded on the grounds that they were entirely unfair and unenforceable. For that matter, I doubt if they were ever strickly adhered to except, possibly in a few cases near some of the Military Posts where special attempts were made to keep the peace. Everyone with the wagon train was amazed that anyone with official status could suggest that it was a crime to shoot an Indian in defense of life and property. As far as we were concerned, the wagon boss was not one bit too blunt and emphatic in his answer to the officer on these charges. In fact, for once, there was a general feeling of gratitude towards McCanles and for the manner which he had handled the situation.

Even, Mamie Powers, who had always looked upon the boss as a blustering, blowhard and evil, man, changed her opinion to the point that for a day or two she sang his praises. She claimed though, that she never heard all he said because when she thought he was going to swear she put her hands over her ears. Probably the most amazing reaction was that of Bid McClaine who had stopped his wagon next to mine. When the wagon boss had reached his "peak", Bid who had hardly smiled for days due to his and McCanles' difficulties, now allowed himself a broad grin of approval. "Caroliny," he said afterward, "If you would've told me yesterday that anything 'McCanles ever said' would tickle my funnybone, I would a said you was crazy as hell. But No Suh, I was mistaken for the old boy was certainly riled up right sharp this mawnin."

Following the departure of the soldiers, there was little immediate discussion of that which had just taken place. This would take place later in the privacy of small groups and away from the wrathful eye of McCanles, though sentiment was for once in his favor.

We moved on at a steady clip, striving to make up for the time we had lost at our unscheduled stop. Well before noon, we came to the Walnut, a sizeable stream timbered with ash, elm and perhaps hackberry and cottonwood, but the hand of the woodsman was evident and about all that was left near the crossing was stumps and saplings. This would have been an ideal place for our noon stop except that the grass had been trampled and grazed too short by too many before us. Near here were some substantial stone buildings known as Fort Zarah. But I am not sure the post had any military use at the time as the only people we saw about the place were in civilian dress. But the fact of its presence suggested to us as well as words, that we were entering an area of Military importance. This feeling grew stronger as we moved on meeting more and more traffic and at one time catching up with a slowmoving ox-train. A few miles after leaving the Walnut, our trail veered gradually to the southwest as we had passed the apex of the Big Bend of the Arkansas River.

Toward the middle of the afternoon, the pace of the wagons became too much for Tom's old roan cow, as she had been becoming more and more footsore for days. We had been in the habit of tieing the calves in the tail wagon the last few days to rest their feet, and trusting to the mothering instinct of the cows to keep them moving. But today, old Roanie simply could not keep up. We stopped and held a pow-wow. Rather than abandon the poor critter to the mercy of wild animals or perhaps Indians, we decided for Sid to drive my team while I, on my horse would coax the old bossy along as best I could.

I started this late afternoon venture with some misgivings as we knew the country was full of Indians, gathering in this area in the hopes of collecting Government annuities at Fort Larned. Of course, these Indians were supposed to be peaceful, but no one placed much faith in them (especially we with the Tyler & Randall train) as they represented three of the wildest tribes in the country. Cheyennes, Commanches and Kiowas. The last wagons had commenced to pull out of sight over a low ridge when I looked up with pleasure and greeted Barney Balaam. The old scout astride his mule, rode out of the tall grass from nowhere and gave me a welcome moral uplift. I had commenced to feel sort of a nervous frustration as the wagon train continued to pull further ahead while the sore-footed cow plodded along at a snail's pace. This time, Barney tarried only a short while as in his capacity as scout, he was supposed to be on ahead of the train to locate the evening campground. Before he left he gave me a bit of advice.

"Jack, thars Injuns a lurkin nigh, no big bands; jist two or three to a bunch I reckon but more'n likely they's Kioways which cain't be trusted atall. Yore well-heeled so if any comes clos't jest show them yer shootin iron and make em keep thar distance. Remember an Injun's got a power of respect for a good repeatin iron in a pair likely lookin hands." Barney kicked his heels in the side of his mule and left at a gallop and again I was left alone with my problem.

The afternoon passed until the sun seemed to be just inches above the slightly rolling prairie. By now I thought, "the train had already pulled into camp. Probably the stock were being put out to graze and supper was being prepared somewhere in that distance ahead." I noticed the low wind that had blown all afternoon had gradually subsided into nothing and no sound could be heard except the slow shuffle of the old cow beside me. Then I heard it! Low and mournful like the call of a hoot owl! I thought that a little strange as that bird was usually only found near timber, in a little while the call came again only this time distinct and nearer. I felt a sudden loneliness that had been building in me. Then a horseman appeared out of a gully ahead and to my right. As I watched another rode out the grass on the other side and they met in the trail ahead of me. I will admit I was a little scared but thankfully a slow anger boiled under my skin, too, triggered by the arrogance of the two Indians sitting on their ponies blocking the trail I remembered what Barney had told me and I kept urging the old cow along as fast as she would move. Even that poor critter seemed to realize the urgency of the situation and moved out briskly until we approached within a stone's throw of the two Indians whom I could see now were each armed with a muzzle-loading musket. Old Roanie stopped abruptly and turned facing me with a low disconsolate bawl as if she recognized this was the end. I didn't feel too well either and my actions were based more on common sense than sheer nerve. It seemed clear that my best chance for safety was straight ahead down the trail. I could plainly see that I had the Redskins outgunned and I was just as sure, "outhorsed" and those two advantages could mean more than half the battle, in "Injun country."

With a quick effortless motion, I slipped my carbine out of the scabbard and waved it motioning them to be on their way. They jumped their ponies apart with the trail between them, at the same time one making an arrogant motion with his thumb to his nose. By now I was scared enough to be dangerous. A determined, confident sort of fear. I jerked the carbine up and levered a shell in the barrel and brought it to bear on the cocky one as old Blaze side-stepped soft as a cat. keeping me facing the Indians, with only a slight pressure of the reins.

"Move, I yelled and they both got the idea pronto and moved back as I swung the Henry back and forth and kept them going.

"Now Bossy," I said, "You better move too. If you get contrary, I'll sacrifice you to the wolves as I aim to save my own hide first."

I rode up close an nudged her in the tail-end with the toe of my boot. Blaze seemed to get the idea, too, and laid back his ears and nipped her a time or two as the poor old cow moved on in kind of a limping, lurching gait covering the ground at a more rapid rate than she had all afternoon. But I could soon see we were not yet out of trouble as the two Indians merely pulled back out of close rifle range and continued to threaten me by their very presence. By now the dusk of past, sunset already dimmed the distance and full darkness would soon be upon us, and I had little idea how far ahead the wagon train was camped. As the early night settled about me the pace of the old cow slowed in spite of all I could do to keep her at a gait I figured the urgency of the situation demanded. I commenced to feel uncomfortable again and pondered the advisability of abandoning her. but the thought struck me of how hard to explain. that would be in camp. I knew Tom well enough to know he would understand, but there was sure to be some doubting Thomases who would figure I simply didn't have the guts to face the dark by myself in Injun country.

Someone hollered in the semi-darkness ahead, followed by a sharp whistle. Then Tom and Bid McClaine rode up bareback on a pair of mules. "Figgered you might be having some trouble," said Tom, "So's soon as we got the stock out of the way, me and Bid here who was kind enough to come along, come right on out."

After the arrival of these reinforcements, we saw no more of the Indians. A couple of miles up the trail from where I was

140

met by my companions, the wagon train was camped in the shelter of Pawnee Rock. Sentries were posted on the rock itself as we could see their figures against the sky as we rode into camp. We had McClaine as a supper guest that night and Mamie outdid herself at the cookstove. After supper by the light of a lantern we fashioned some shoes, made from rawhide and leather, for the old roan cow. Tom said, "he knowed the old critter was gettin a mite sore-footed and had ort to have done sunthing about it afore this, but just seemed like he never got around to it."

A little after sunrise the next morning the lead wagons commenced pulling out of camp. But as we were still saddled with the problem of the sore-footed cow, Tom choose to bring up the rear. I had wanted to explore this rocky point known as Pawnee Rock, but had to content myself with the close view we had from camp. Pawnee Rock was probably the most famous landmark and one of the most interesting on the entire Santa Fe Trail, arising as it did out of the comparitively level country surrounding it. In those old trail days before the country was settled and before it was used as a quarry for building and construction stone. the Rock was a pretty impressive piece of nature's handiwork. The names of hundreds of travelers were carved on its face. Some of them dating back to the 1820's, the very early days of the trail. Among those names were famous people like General (Captain) Fremont, Kit Carson, William Bent and—Barney Balaam—, so the old scout told me. The latter he never explained and I accepted with some skepticism as the old man was completely illiterate.

As we were waiting to pull in line, the wagon boss approached the dying campfire, which was in our vicinity, for a last cup of coffee. It was the first time I had an opportunity to express my gratitude to him for what I considered his defense of me in yesterday's argument with the Military. I tied up my lines and walked over and spoke to him.

"Mr. McCanles, I want to say I appreciate the manner in which you stood up for me yesterday. I realize you could have turned me over to the Authorities, though I feel what I did justified no investigation."

He looked me over cold-eyed and unfriendly and I felt a

141

sudden foreboding and wished I had stayed on my wagon. "Reynolds git this straight, I didn't say a damn word for your sake. What I did say I woulda said fer a yaller dog. No two-bit soldier brass can stop my train and try to pull a hawse on me. I'd seen him in Hell first. As fer you, I ain't forgot how you run tattle-tailin agin me, to the Authorities at Riley. So don't expect any favors from me—ever."

I protested in vain that I hadn't made any statement at all, against him and that I hadn't tattle-tailed in any sense, but that I had been officially questioned against my wishes and I had refused to implicate anyone. But it was no use. McCanles was so prejudiced in his thinking that no amount of truth and logic would change his views.

"Gawddamn it," he said, "Git on back to yore wagon, no sense in argeein. I know you're back-bitin kind from way back."

So I went angry, frustrated and bewildered. With all his faults and nail-hard, disposition, McCanles had admirable qualities and in many ways I could have liked him. But through no fault of my own, it appeared we would always be at swords points.

Back to the trail, it soon became apparent that old Roanie would never to able to keep up with the wagons. She would either have to be abandoned or else some means of hauling her be devised. Bid McClaine and Andy Cooper both sympathized with us in this predicament and managed to keep their wagons towards the end of the train near us, where they could be of assistance if needed. Tom called a halt and it was decided to transfer the pig crates and chickens to one of the wagons and load the cow in the cart which was a low-wheeled vehicle and obviously the only thing available that she could be carried on. Accordingly, with the use of mainstrength and McClaine's talents with a rope, we soon had her loaded in the cart and tied in a manner that she couldn't get out. We had just finished the job and were congratulating ourselves on how simple it had been when the wagon boss came riding up to see what the "Defugalty" was all about.

"Taixas Man," he said addressing McClaine with biting sarcasm, "who the hell do yo' all figger you're workin fer, me or

Powers here? I'd be mighty obliged if you would plant your ass on that red mule and guide them hardtails and that load of freight, to hell and out of here and down the road like you was done hired to do."

The Texan had the capacity for silence, when necessary, and now he used it. For an instant the fire blazed in his eyes and the dark tan of his cheeks changed shade. Then with set jaw and stern lips, he mounted his wheeler and cracked his whip without a word.

Tom, however, was riled to the point he spoke out, "Clint if you figger your firm kain't afford to let one of your men accomodate a fellar in trouble, I'll jist be more'n glad to pay you for his time."

"Aw go on you," growled McCanles, I ain't got time to stay here and palavar with you over trifles. Git yore damn teams to movin afore you git picked up by some band of redskins for loiterin along here by yourselves."

The latter remark (or order) caught Tom where he was vulnerable, as he well knew the advisability of keeping up with the main train. So the discussion was carried no further and we moved briskly on our way, unhindered now by the lame cow.

At Ash Creek we stopped long enough to fill the two small barrels we carried for drinking water. Tom remembered the previous summer there had been a cholera outbreak at Ft. Larned on the Pawnee, and this probable unnecessary precaution was taken so we wouldn't have to drink from that stream. The trail from here though heavily traveled was in good condition outside of the disagreeable dust that was especially annoying to our crew on the end of the drag. But we were soon favored by a brisk wind from the south that gave us some relief and near mid-day we saw the Stars and Stripes waving high above the low stone buildings of Fort Larned. We made our noon stop on the Pawnee a half mile below the Post. Here, we were greeted just after eating, by a small body of troops who escorted us well above this busy Military Establishment, where we made permanent camp. We were informed that we would be detained here a few days until official clearance was given for us to continue on our way, as the whole area was full of Indians, "all friendly of course."

Our experience the last few days had developed in us a cynical attitude toward all offical remarks stressing the friendly nature of the Indians and we viewed with some skepticism anyone voicing such opinions. Consequently, we never completely relaxed our guard even when under the wing of the Government. But like all good citizens, we felt a sense of relief and appreciation for the sanctuary of the Army Post though it was apparent the soldiers and Indian Bureau about had their hands full keeping the Indians in a partial state of contentment.

We had known of the probability of a lenghty stay here and were prepared for it. We were allowed to camp where we had convenient access to water and fair grazing. A loose corral was formed with the wagons and the stock were turned out to graze under the supervision of herders during the daytime and preparations were made to corral them of a night. Although we were assured there was no need of the latter, McCanles and the crew in general placed little reliance on the assurances of the authorities and none at all on the trustworthiness of the Indians. I rode bareback to the top of a low ridge less than a mile from camp and could see through the field glasses a clutter of tee-pees along the creek only a few miles above us.

"Fort Larned"

From a physical standpoint, the prolonged stop at Larned was a welcome break. Since the fight at the Little Arkansas, ours had been a journey of hurry and worry, with a consequent strain on man, beast and equipment. For once Tom didn't relapse into his usually easy-going nature and we spent the afternoon greasing, repairing and looking after the livestock, things that needed to be done. As plenty of wood and water were available, and the weather was mild, a large iron kettle was unloaded, a couple of wooden washtubs were unlimbered and we had our first baths since leaving Abilene.

I had longed for the luxury of a shave, but on surveying myself in the mirror, I was so pleased with the luxuriance and blackness of my whiskers that I settled for a little trimming around the edges with my razor and assured myself that at least one mark of a tenderfoot was covered.

I was interrupted from my musings by the voice of Mamie informing us with authority that "tomorry would be wash day, that she wanted plenty of wood and water provided and the big kettle set to boil early."

The crew of the main train, with the exceptions of those who pulled herd duty, were busied much the same during the afternoon as we were, with one exception. One wagon was pulled out to some undisclosed spot with the gambler, Denver, in charge. This wagon had been trailed behind a heavy freight wagon since Abilene and was rumored to contain whiskey and gambling paraphenalia. When the men gathered for their evening meal, the wagon boss gave them a little talk.

"Now men, I want you to listen to what I have to say, so's there won't be nothin come up that might delay this train when its time to roll again. Its being whispered around camp," he paused now with a knowing grin, "that there's contraband whiskey bein sold in these parts. Now if any of you fellars figger you know yore limits go ahaid and spend yore money and drink the gawddamned rotgut, its no hide off my tail. But hear this; ary mother's son of you that don't show up ready and able to handle a jerkline when we get our clearance papers whether that be tomorry, the next day or the next, I personally am gonna nail his hide on the side of his wagon. And you men know that By Gawd, I'll do it-—Now that's all."

That evening Bid McClaine and his friend Mustang, strolled by our camp. Bid stopped to visit and told us of McCanles' warning to the crew. "I ain't right sure," he wound up, "That he can nail my hide on his wagon. Course he certainly told me off right smart this mawnin and I stood right there and taken it like a Christian too. I reckon I never wanted to speak my mind more in my life than I did then. But thet wasn't the time or place for a ruckus."

"McCanles has been in a bad mood all day," I agreed, and I told them of my run-in with him this morning.

"Well I'll be damned," sympathized the Texan, "If he kain't be the orneriest, most evil dispositioned wagon boss I ever run acrost."

"Yeah, he's thet for shore," spoke up Mustang (a fairly rough citizen in his own right). "But me, I ain't about to cross him if I kin help it. I made one trip acrost these plains with him and I'll take his cussins any day rather than his fists and his bootheels."

The next morning, bright and early the duties of washday commenced, and we were all occupied for a time until Mamie dismissed us all except Tom with the good-natured explanation that she couldn't get anything done for walking around us. I, with Sid who insisted on going along, walked down to the corral with the intention of looking up McClaine. Having gotten on a friendly status with this unusual character I thought it would be a pleasant way to pass the time, listening to his southern drawl and homey humor. I would have preferred to have left Sid with his parents because the Southerner's habitual choice of language was not the best atmosphere for an impressionable lad of Sid's caliber. However as it turned out, McClaine wasn't available having pulled herd duty but we did run across Barney Balaam.

146

"Shore, Jack, ef you and Sid wanta see the Fort, I'll taken you down thar as I know the place right well, and a right smart place it tis too, now that they've got her nigh unto finished."

So Sid riding a gentle old work plug and Barney and I mounted on our respective mounts, jogged down the banks of the creek and entered the hollow square of the Fort. When viewed from close in, I was impressed at the solid substantial appearance of the native stone buildings. Certainly a lot of hard work and good workmanship had gone in their construction. It struck me the Government had advanced its thinking in the construction of Military Posts, over the log and stockade idea I had always connected with frontier forts. Of course, timber suitable for heavy log buildings was not readily available in this region although streams like the Pawnee were timbered to some extent for many miles back, it wasn't material adaptable to heavy construction uses.

Barney led the way to an outside wall of one of the buildings and showed the gunslits that had been carved in the thick stone wall.

"Mighty powerful, idee them thar," surmised the old man. "Tain't likely no inimy could withstand a stiddy far from them walls. Right smart little fort alright. Course it ain't to be likened to the place the Bent boys had on the upper river, thutty year ago. Why daggone it, I reckon Bent's Old Fort was the stoutest dad-blame stockade as man ever built. Twarn't no man, beast or cannon could breech them walls."

The old man was in one of his talking moods and he told the following tale—, the truth of which I can't vouch for. At intervals while he talked several bystanders gathered round, drawn by the fervor of his oratory—and he expanded to fit the occasion.

"Why fellars I don't rightly know why I ort to belittle this place—fur as a matter ofact, I could be called the daddy uv it. Ie doggies, I recollect, fer years when I was a freightin supplies to the Old Fort on the upper river with Will Bent's wagons, we was continually plagued by the daggoned Kioways and Commanches allurs a wantin "wahow" or "chucka-way", ef they warn't down-right tryin to steal our stock or wuss, acommitin war on us. So's one day I rid in from a scout and met Will alookin powerful

147

worried kase we had been a hevin a heap of trouble from them Ki-yi's. So I says to him, Will, I says, you and Charlie allurs seem to hev a pile of power with the Gov'nment. Now why in tarnation don't you hev em build a Post and garrison it with Dragoons along the mouth of the Pawnee hyar somewheres. And Will says to me, Barney, if you ain't a plumb hum-dinger, you know I never once't thought uv anything like that, but fust thing I'm a gonna do whin we get to Westport is take yer advice and ketch a boat for Leavenworth and proposition them Ginerals. And he did jist that and hyar we air today with a right fitten Post whar I tole Will Bent years ago there ort to be one."

The old man finished his heroic tale and reached in his pocket for a fresh chaw, when a man in buckskin coat clapped him on the shoulder and remarked with a grin. "Ie gollies, if it ain't Barney Balaam, the Whisperin He Wolf of the Picketwire. I knowed you plowed the furrie that laid off this trail and a heap of other powerful things but it certainly comes as a surprise to find you're the pappy of this here post."

I looked for the old man to flare up like a banty rooster at this sarcasm, but a look of pleasure spread over his face as he grasped the other's hand. "Ie gollies, if it ain't Smoky Joe."

So again, we met Smoky Joe Smith of my Kansas City acquaintance. The three of us spent the next few minutes renewing acquaintances. We learned from Smith that he was employed by the Stage Company in the capacity of sort of a trouble shooter whose duties ranged from extra driver and riding guard, to scout with emergency authority answerable only to the division manager. Smith and Barney were old friends, having once spent months together trapping in the Solomon and Saline valleys. To be expected the conversation soon turned to Indians, particularly Cheyennes as Barney claimed to have lived with them for a time. "Yes Siree, afore the war and the Sand Creek Massacree, the Cheyenne was a powerful admiring set of people and I was right proud to be called thar brother. I've sed it afore and I'll say it agin that if it hadn't been for sartin land grabbin and hawgish whites they ud be on our side today."

"That's for sure," agreed Smith. "And speakin of Cheyennes, you likely remember Red Bear. Well Sir, he is camped below here and the old Devil don't appear to have changed a bit since I knowed him in '58."

Presently, one word led to another and soon sight seeing at the Fort was forgotten and we were mounted and on our way to the Indian camp where Red Bear was some sort of a lesser chief. With these two redoubtable companions I "jumped" at the chance to meet a real wild Indian face to face in a peaceful venture. We arrived at the Indian camp of nine or ten skin lodges and were greeted by a pack of barking and yapping dogs. Three male figures wrapped in blankets with their backs to a wigwam sat silently sunning themselves and paid little heed to us. Four women, busily engaged fleshing buffalo hides, gave us unfriendly stares. Finally, a powerfully built squaw grabbed a stick and went among the dogs striking right and left and sent them fleeing with a harsh "vamose". An old man emerged from one of the lodges to see what all the commotion was about. He wore a white-man's hat, flat on his head without crease or shape with a long feather stuck in the brim, a Government overcoat and Injun britches completed his apparel and to top it all off, his face was set with a melancholy homliness.

Balaam and Smith greeted him with the universal "How" and Barney continued in a guttural gibberish with much hand waving. As he spoke, the old Indian's face lit with pleasure and I, for one, was surprised to discover that despite his doleful appearance the old boy actually possessed a personality. Abruptly, Barney dismounted and the two shook hands and gleefully popped each other on the backs.

Grinning broadly, Smith turned to me and explained, "Barney just said to Red Bear in 'Injun' that his face was purtier to him than the back end of a mare mule after a long day's walk."

These preliminary pleasantries having been exchanged by the two old codgers, Smith shook hands with Red Bear and introduced me as "Coyotie Jack" and Sid as "Little Whiteman", inventing Indian appelations without a stutter. Sid had been a very quiet boy since leaving the Fort, obviously scared at the prospect of meeting real Injuns. Now with eyes popping and a dubious expression on his face, he didn't know whether to blush or snicker so he did both as the old Indian shook hands with the utmost gravity.

To show his sociability and knowledge of the whiteman's tongue, Red Bear spoke to us in a mixture of broken English and bad Spanish.

"Yeah," explained Smith with tongue in cheek, "Red Bear is sure quite a conversationalist, when we can't get a regular interpreter around hyar, we can always count on him. Ain't that right Red Bear, you make whiteman—talk—heap good?"

The old Indian grinned his pleasure at this compliment and proceeded to further enlighten us with his linquistic talents. "Uhg! Red Bear, she talk heap, whiteman's savvy, lak wan big godam."

In our ignorance, Sid and I could hardly hold our laughter. But what Red Bear really meant, translated literally, was he could speak the whiteman's language good like a big wagon driver. The last word Red Bear used being a very natural nickname for wagon driver, from the Indian's point of view, because of the habitual use of the word by Muleskinners and ox-drivers. Yes, Red Bear, had been around a bit.

The conversation continued along this line for some time, Barney and Red Bear ressurecting old recollections and plying each other with goodnatured insults—some of them too salty to appear on a printed page. Both Barney and Smith taking advantage of the old Indian's limited knowledge of the English language and thoroughly enjoying the effect it had on Sid and me. Red Bear a little at a loss at times for words, nevertheless, entered into the spirit of the game with vigor and enjoyment equaling theirs.

Before long, we were joined by the other red brethern and it became apparent they thought we had come as traders and wanted to "make swap". Smith turned to me.

"These fellars want to trade. If you happen to be interested in a bufflar robe, Injun leggins, moccasins or ary thing along that line, I'll sure be glad to help you arrange a swap that'll be fair to both of you."

Red Bear clapped his hands and shouted authoritatively in the

Indian tongue and presently his squaw appeared, staggering under the weight of a heavy robe. The woman, a squatty young squaw was in an advanced stage of pregnancy though her condition was apparently of no more concern to her husband than if she had been a beast of burden. The robe was of fine quality, tanned smooth and amost as pliable as a deerskin but was too large and heavy for my wants. Smith made this known to Red Bear and the old "despot" ordered his helpmate to bring out a smaller and lighter one, though of the same quality. According to Balaam and Smith, both of whom were partial to the Cheyennes, the women of this tribe tanned the best robes available. When I showed an interest in the fine robe before me, Red Bear's manner changed from good humor to a look of craftiness. He noticed I carried the gold watch which had been my fathers. Now he made signs that he wished to see the watch. I took it from my pocket leaving the chain attached to my clothing, explaining that I couldn't possibly swap this as it was a gift from my father. Smith had to come to my rescue and explain to the old man's satisfaction why I couldn't trade. But that I would trade silver coins for the robe. Red Bear had been around Whitemen most of his long life and in that time he had learned to some extent the value of money but still his Indian instinct tended towards the glitter and the shine of certain coins rather than their value. I wound up buying the robe for five silver dollars and ten copper cents, despite all that Smith and I could do to persuade him that five dollars and a half was of more value. Encouraged by Red Bear's sharp bargaining, the other Indians crowded around with all sorts of articles to trade or swap. Sid carried a pocket knife attached to his waistband with a chain. It was one of those inexpensive ones with a quality look similar to that now known as a Barlow. This caught the eye of a young brave who pressed forward and reached for it, causing the boy to nervously pull back and in the process, he lost his knife. Smith whose roving eye missed nothing addressed the young savage sternly in Injun and at the same time whipping aside his coat and laying a hand on his revolver butt. The young Indian returned the knife at once to the grateful and frightened boy. After that, there was no more promiscus grabbing as Smith was a man well-known to those Indians.

After things had quieted down again, I selected a pair of

plain moccasins for myself and a similar pair with fancy beadwork, for Sid. The price asked for the plain ones was very little but they placed a high value on the beaded ones. "Two—dree—dollar". I didn't feel able to afford such luxuries so I picked another plain pair. But the Indian still had his head set on "two—dree—dollar" and the dickering continued. Smith took me aside and advised me the Indian was trying to hold me up. He reached in his pocket and produced a handful of shiny change, mostly new pennies. The redskin's eyes lit up when he saw these and I was able to buy both pair of moccasins for two dollars and thirty cents. As I was out of silver dollars, I started to pay him with paper. "No! No!" he shook his head and waved his hands. So again Smith reached in his pocket and produced two silver cartwheels in exchange for my greenback and our red brother was perfectly satisfied.

Before leaving, Smith unbuckled his saddle pouch and took out a fresh plug of tobbacco which he presented to the chief and Barney gave each of the Indians some little trinket, a number of which he usually kept for this purpose. Not to be outdone, I gave Red Bear a bag of candy I had bought at the Fort for the Power's kids, and we took our leave in an atmosphere of good will.

On our way back to the Fort, we were discussing the Indians we had just left and I brought up the question whether some of these same Cheyennes may have been in the band that had attacked us a few days earlier on the Little Arkansas. Both of my companions thought it very unlikely as the Cheyennes were a large tribe composed of many divisions.

We then told Smith of the battle of words between the Captain and the wagon boss. He grinned, "Yeah, I know that Captain. He's a Hancock man and ain't admired much in these parts. And I doubt like Hell if Col. Leavenworth or Wyncoop ever gave him the authority to raise thunder with McCanles like you say he did. I know these two, and right respectable gentlemen they are."

Back at the Fort, we took our leave of Smoky Joe Smith with the assurance that he would look us up at Ft. Dodge. We stopped at the store which had just recently been restocked with

152

goods from the east. I purchased another bag of candy, coffee and a few other articles Mamie had asked me to get. Then Sid and I rode back to camp, well laden with goods and short of money.

We spent the balance of that day in camp and all of the next during which we saw more Indians, Soldiers and Freighters. And became much better acquainted with Larned. Then with little advance notice the word got around that we were to leave just after noon on the third day. It was known McCanles was in bad humor. The story was that he had fallen out with the Authorities over his alleged connection with the whiskey peddling. Rumor had it that Denver had sold whiskey to the Indians but it is hard for me to believe that McCanles had knowledge of such a thing considering his experience with the Indians and lack of trust in them, even when they were unpolluted with red-eye. But there was one among us who believed the wagon boss was as guilty as Denver and continued to believe it. That man was Bid McClaine.

When the time came to pull out the men showed they had heeded well the admonition of McCanles. That is all had heeded save my friend McClaine, and that much to the consternation of Tom Powers and I.

The wagons had already started to roll when the wagon boss rode up to McClaine's wagon with a glare in his eye. The Drover's team stood hitched and waiting, thanks to the night-herder and the Mexican cook. McClaine stood spraddle-legged and loaded to the gills, and by the way, a rare condition for him as he could usually carry more liquor than two ordinary men. For a minute McCanles sat on his horse glaring at him deciding what steps to take, for the Texan was no ordinary skinner and the boss knew this case would take special treatment. McClaine drunk enough to be completely unpreturbed as to the size of the occasion balanced himself and started to speak in a calm, even, polite voice, though his tongue was a bit thick.

"Mr. McCanles, I'm drunk, and I know thet y'all know, thet I know I am drunk, and I'm a standin heah———." By now Mustang, who was cold sober and had a powerful respect for the temper of McCanles, shook Bid roughly and tried to get him to quiet down. But Bid would have none of it and pushed the wrangler aside and continued.

"I'm a standin heah ready willin and able for yo'all to nail my hide to your Goddamn wagon. And Mister McCanles, I've done come to the conclusion thet you're a hawse beatin, man drivin, miscreant, with morals lower than a snakes feet and habits of consortin with polecats and reptyles and—". The wagon boss had enough but with unusual restraint for him, interrupted the Texan's lecture. "Put the Gawdamn, pot-likker on his mule," he ordered the other men. "And Mustang, the Mexican here, and the other wrangler kin handle the "cavvy", so's you climb on that other mule aside yore drunken Texican friend and see that he stays on the top side even if you have to tie him there. If he does fall off, that's his hard luck; and mebbie yourn."

Accordingly, Mustang and a couple of the other freighters grabbed McClaine and attempted to soothe and coax him on his mule. This failing, they eventually lifted the unwilling driver on his mule where he exhibited a surprising sense of balance while his plunging team pulled out and down the trail. The last we saw of them McClaine was kicking his mount in the sides with his boot heels and waving his hat like a bronc buster and yelling loud "yip-pee's" from sheer delight. While Mustang beside him on the other wheeler handled the lead team and at the same time, kept a firm grip on the halter rope of Bid's plunging, bucking mule. And needless to say, the tense set expression on the night wrangler's face displayed no amusement for his partner's antics. In some way they managed to close the gap between the next wagon without a mishap, which was probably accomplished by the combined efforts of Mustang, the pair of wise old leader mules at the front and—pure luck.

Our part of the caravan was somewhat delayed by Tom's last-minute decision to go on without the sore-footed cow as it was apparent her feet hadn't healed well enough for her to go on. Tom made arrangements with the Sutler at the Fort to keep the cow until he could return for her later on. The other cow and the two calves seemed well able to make the balance of the journey. Tom had always claimed the latter cow was a "real go'er and could keep up with ary mule he had." We were thankful now that she was, as we were already looking forward to the end of the trail when a little milk and butter would be mighty welcome.

A small train of eight wagons, headed for the mountains, joined us at Larned, having placed themselves under McCanles' leadership for protection. This outfit was led by a man named Jones and consisted of nine fairly well-armed and experienced men. As we pulled out, they strung out behind us. Altogether, we hoped to be formidable enough force to discourage any redskins we might encounter, hopefully strong enough to completely protect our livestock as well as ourselves.

CHAPTER XIII

On Towards Dodge

From Fort Larned we took the branch of the Santa Fe Trail known as the dry route or also called the stage route. This trail being shorter and easier pulling than the route that more nearly followed the river. We left the Pawnee creek area with plenty of fresh water for drinking and kitchen use and anticipated no difficulties on that score as we planned to reach Ft. Dodge in about two days.

Since leaving Abilene, we had steadily moved into more remote and wilder country, though geographically becoming flatter and more barren of significant vegetation, each day. As we progressed westward, Mamie and the kids occasionally exhibited traces of discouragement and homesickness. When this occurred Tom proved himself a true pioneer. He would cheer us up with expressions of, "Jest wait till we get to Dodge and settled down fer the summer and what great times we will have." But when pressed for details, he was never very explicit, passing those questions off with a wave of his hand, "Aw never mind that, we'll sure find plenty to do."

At the beginning of the trip, I had supposed we would live at Fort Dodge, but as time went on, I found that was not Tom's intention. The previous fall, Tom and a small party of freighters on their way home from Ft. Garland in the mountains of Colorado Territory had stopped at Ft. Dodge to rest their stock. While there, they had gone buffalo hunting and finding buffalo so plentiful and a ready market for the meat, to the Military, they had conceived the idea of going in the business in a commercial way. They had located a likely looking place a few hours' drive from the Military Post and errected a sturdy sod structure for their headquarters. Four men made up the partnership including Tom and Andy Cooper and each partner had a hired muleskinner. With that much willing help available the construction was completed in a matter of a little over two weeks. Tom claimed he had never been sold altogether on the project, as he was too much of a family man and a farmer at heart. He said he had mostly just gone along with the others to be agreeable and admitted he became homesick about the time the place was completed. About that time an ox-train came along on their way back to the settlements and "he just naturally jined up and went back to Missoury with them, leaving his part of the venture to his erstwhile partners. Tom said the other fellows had stuck around for a couple of weeks but finding buffalo hunting not as enjoyable nor as profitable as they had anticipated, the whole project had been abandoned. "As a matter of fact," Tom admitted, "I tole myself when we was buildin the place that it would make a danged good place for a man and his family to try to make a go of it. Why we had a fellar with us that was a stone mason and he laid them walls off with corners as square and door and winder openings as true as a Government building. We hauled poles for the roof beams and the roof itself from a little creek several miles north, and straight cottonwood poles twenty-five feet long for the lookout tower that raises right out of the roof. Yes sir, jest wait till you see it."

Tom had "dreamed up" the idea of bringing his family west, during the winter when there was strong belief that the Medicine Lodge Treaty had settled the Indian troubles once and for all. Subsequent developments had failed to daunt him, in particular because there had been no large scale outbreaks. Still he was experienced enough in frontier ways that the events of this trip alone were enough to weaken his convictions. To keep his spirits up and those of the rest of us, particularly Mamie's, he went out of his way to belittle the Indian troubles, insisting that he looked for a quiet summer. He would talk to me freely of these matters, always exhibiting an air of optimism. But with Mamie, he was reluctant to discuss the subject at all, holding the opinion that any discussion would only be distressing to her and would serve to put himself and his own actions in a very bad light. "Shucks tain't no use gettin the woman worked up about sunthin that ain't likely to happen nohow."

"Why," he told me more than once, "How in tarnation are the Injuns gonna get loose to cause trouble this year? The Gov'nment's got strong Posts now on the Arkansaw at Larned, Dodge and Lyons and Fort Garland out in the aidge of the Ute country, and mebbie even better protection up on the Smoky, like Fort Harker, Hays and Wallace all as good and stout as Larned, and on up north on the Platte, God only knows how many soldiers they have got. They've done laid rails clear across Nebrasky and pert nigh across this state, along the Smoky. Only be a question of time till the good part of this country settles up and I aim to get there ahead of the rush. If I don't like it out there in the short grass country along the South Bend of the Arkansaw, I reckon I kin pack up and go somewheres else."

Few others seemed to share Tom's optimism on these matters, nor his faith in the future settlement and agriculture prospects of this western plains country. I remember mentioning Tom's farming plans, specifically his talk of raising corn, to Barney Balaam, one day after we had left Fort Larned. The old man exploded in a tirade of ridicule. "Why that tarnation idjit, raise corn in this kentry, why dad-blame it, you kain't raise cane here abouts with a jug of whiskey."

And so it was with Tom's optimism cheering us and raising hopes for the future. With an inherent interest and curiosity as to what lay ahead, we moved out on the last leg of our journey. As we clunked along that afternoon, I found my thoughts going back to the first days of our trip. It seemed almost ages since I had first met the Power's family, Barney Balaam, McCanles and the other members of the train. I found I had lost track of time and when trying to count the days I had to resort to my little pocket memorandum in which I had penciled a few lines each day, outlining the highlights. On adding up these days, I was surprised at the comparitively short time which had elapsed since my arrival in Kansas City. This time had been filled with experiences that not only were enlightening and instructive but had also matured me somewhat to frontier life. I no longer felt like a tenderfoot though as compared to my companions, I still lacked a lot of being an experienced freighter or plainsman.

That evening we made camp with our usual loose corral next to a small, flat, grass banked, gully that contained a shallow pond of clear surface water. It was probably a dry tributary of Coon Creek though as a water course, it was too insignificant to mention. Here for the first time, I saw buffalo chips used to fuel the campfires. Our outfit, thanks to Fritz and myself, carried plenty of wood from Pawnee Creek for another camp or two. But the help with the main train had not taken this precaution and had to resort to gathering some of the prairie fuel.

After supper I strolled down by the main cook fire where some of the men were finishing their evening meal. I wondered how my friend, McClaine, had survived the afternoon, but Bid was not among the freighters around the fire. And I was told with knowing grins that the Texan hadn't showed up for supper as he didn't feel "right well". His physical condition this evening invoked no sympathy from his fellow freighters nor from me—he had earned his hangover. But I did feel a kind of sneaking admiration for the manner he had told off the wagon boss. Moved by that feeling, I walked by his wagon and was greeted by the sound of snores, I beheld his long form stretched flat on his back underneath the wagon partially covered by a disheveled blanket with his booted legs protruding. I took one look at his blissful pose and went on my way to take my regular turn at the night's watch.

Next day as we moved on, more evidence of gradual change in the physical appearance of the landscape became noticeable, or perhaps the change had been so gradual that we were just beginning to notice it. The tall bluestem and pleasant little timbered streams of eastern and central Kansas were left behind. Now an interminable carpet of buffalo grass lay around us, with only an occasional soapweed (yucca) or clump of tall bunchgrass to break the monotony of the rolling prairie swells. To the south, covered with a light haze, the valley of the Arkansas lay with its irregular extremities marked here and there with draws and ravines. On the rolling sandy stretches sagebrush became more common and the sandhill plum bush less plentiful. Which all bespoke as well as words that we were now approaching the Great American Desert or to be more correct, the High Plains.

Barney Balaam rode out of a little draw and climbed aboard to chat. I motioned toward the wide horizon, "I take it Barney, this is the wide, wild west. Where now, are your buffalo, antelope and wild game? We haven't even see an Indian since yesterday noon."

"Jes keep yer shirt on, Jack, thars aplenty of game and not

159

a fur piece from hyar nuther. Tother side of that low ridge thar I seen a right smart herd of antelope not more'n an hour ago. These hyar wild critters ain't so dumb, they know when to keep out of sight with all these wagons agoin helter-skelter up and down the trail."

"That sounds reasonable," I agreed, having made my remarks mostly to get a rise out of the old man and incidentally gather information.

"You called this kentry the wide, wild west," Barney reflected, after a short silence. "Don't ever recollect havin heered it spoken of jist like that afore but shore is right fitten. Why dad-blame it, the nearest civilization to our north is the Smoky and that's right sparse. And to the south thar ain't nothin from hyar to Texas, but buffalo, Injuns and wild kentry down to the Canadian. Take jist over tother side of the Arkansaw and aforelong you'll strike the heads of the Rattlesnake, the Ninnesquaw, the Medicine, Chickaskia, Bluff and Crooked Cricks and so on down to the Nations to the Cimmaron, all apowerful wide and lonesome kentry with plenty of game jist awaiting to be taken." He paused and sighed resignedly. "But tother side that river thar is Injun Land nowadays and a whiteman's har ain't safe once't he crosses over it."

I felt a shiver of excitement because I could tell the old man was not romancing. What he had told me was basically facts. As I had him in a truthful mood, I asked him about the country south of the river. Whether it was as barren of tree and bush as that we were now passing through. "Some of it tis and some of it tain't, them cricks has got right smart timber at places. Take down on the Medicine, she's a right purty country with timber of many kinds with steep red dirt canyons and cedar brakes. Why I reckon thars timber hyar and thar all over this wide kentry if you know whar and got the time to find it. But hits a gittin scarcer and scarcer. Ever time a passel of sojers pass nigh a few trees they take some farwood, usually more'n they need, the consarned hunter and trapper takes his bit to cook his grub and build his hut and the Injun figgers these white fellars air a ruining the kentry. They claim the wood will grow back faster'n they use it and the whiteman plumb destroys more between moons than growed in a lifetime. Likely they air purt nigh right."

160

At Little Coon Creek, we found good water so made our noon stop there. Where we stopped, it was a flat little prairie stream without tree or bush but had plenty of clear fresh water. Accordingly, the stock were watered well and all containers were filled as the possibility of a dry camp was likely tonight. And it turned out we did camp that night, on the high and dry. After an uneventful afternoon, during which we were buffeted by an annoying side wind from the south, we made camp on the high shortgrass country less than half day's drive from Fort Dodge. We had been told to expect much the same Indian problem as had beset Larned. That is, the gathering of the tribes for their handout from Uncle Sam. So it was with an anticipation of something new to come and perhaps a little fear of the unknown that we of the Power's train pulled our wagons into place in our section of the loose corral, that last night on the trail. The loose corral, as I like to call it, was simply this—the wagons were pulled up one directly behind another with the end of the tongue almost touching the rear of the wagon ahead. The tongue was then usually propped up with a neck-yoke and doubletrees and harness was hung there. The whole layout making a fairly stock-tight enclosure.

As a precaution against Indians, the stock were kept inside the corral and the resultant dust and confusion caused by the milling of about three hundred head of horses and mules in that limited space, prompted us to rope off our end of the enclosure to keep our stock separate from the main herd. Andy Cooper joined us in this venture and it appeared it would work out very well for all concerned as our respective rigs pretty well formed the east end of the oblong shaped corral. After the stock had quieted down and the dust had settled so that we could finish the supper Mamie had prepared for us inside the protection of the kitchen wagon, Andy and I went out and checked our rope corral and set a few extra stakes to tighten the rope fence.

About that time Bid McClaine strolled up, sober and reticent. He stood around without uttering a half-dozen words and I knew he had something on his mind, but he waited until Andy was out of sight before he mentioned it. "Caroliny, you and Tom and Mis Powers have been mighty obliging to me, and I've come over to apologize to yo'all for gettin drunk and raising Hell like

I done yestiddy. I've drunk considerable whiskey in my time and will likely drink considerable more but I sho' don't want yo'all to get the idee, I'm just a common damn drunk. I don't much care what these other yay-hoo's around heah think, cause I reckon barrin Mustang, yo'all are the only friends I got and I certainly value your opinions."

He was so sincere that I assured him that we appreciated his consideration and accepted his apology in the same spirit it was made. And partly to cheer him up, as he was down in the dumps, and to let him know that my own moral attitude was aware of the weaknesses of human nature and for that matter, capable of some deviation from the straight and narrow paths attributed to some of my ancestors, I reminded him that he had put on a pretty good show besides done a pretty smooth job of telling McCanles off.

"Thet was just the wiskey talkin," he grinned ruefully, "And me trying to tree them mules like I did, thet was certainly a tom fool trick. Why McCanles would a been plumb justified in trompin hell out of me for thet alone————."

Tom, seeing the two of us in the gloom at the corral fence came out smoking his pipe and we stood there visiting until we were interrupted by the tramp of heavy boots and the glow of a cigar. The figure of the wagon boss appeared. He never brothered to even nod at us but focused his attention on the rope enclosure.

"Now what in the G—d—Hell! have we got hyar?"

No one answered as we were all stunned at his temper. He, having never before objected to any contrivance we had used for our own stock.

"Answer me," he roared with an oath that would have made a freight mule quiver, "You —— ——— ——— Nannies, don't jist stand there."

Tom started to speak in a voice choked with shock and rage, "By Gawd, Clint, we was only trying to keep our stuff separate from your'n."

"Don't back talk me Powers, I've put up with yore harebrained contrivances and yore G—d——woman and scrawny pack of whelps, till I'm sick to my guts with the whole kit and kaboodle

162

of you." Now he grabbed the rope fence and jerked on it until a stake snapped. "Git this damn cobbled up mess out of hyar and them ropes coiled and in yer wagons afore the break of day—I mean it By Gawd."

As he turned and strode off in the darkness, I caught the strong smell of raw whiskey on his breath. Tom left abruptly too, for his wagon and returned at once with his .36 navy Colt in his waistband and his face pale with rage. "That so and so cain't talk to me of my family like that." Bid and I both detained him and talked him out of his homicidal intentions. Pretty soon. he handed me his six-hooter and returned to his wagon, calmed somewhat but still visibly shaken.

Bid and I replaced the broken stake and restretched the rope corral. "Don't take this rope down in the mawnin til you're damn good and ready," Bid advised me, "McCanles is a mean one all right, but I reckon 'like me' his whiskey was doin most of the talkin here. But if he makes any more trouble over this I'm with you and Tom all the way. I don't know as I ever told you Caroliny, but the only reason I hired on with McCanles was cause his wagons was haided towards the mountains and it seemed a likely way to see my first of kin thet have settled nawthwest of the little settlement of Trinidad about a year ago. But I reckon I about got my bellyfull of him and his ways and I doubt if I can stand another hundred and fifty mile with the overbearing son-of-a-bitch."

Then he left with a calm, "see yo'all in the mawnin."

About then Andy came out of his wagon in his sock-feet, wanting to know what all the fracas was about, though he had heard most of it and guessed pretty well at the rest. "Whew," he said, "I wish now I was as footloose as McClaine, but I reckon I'm stuck with McCanles whether I like it or not. My consignments are billed for Lyon same as most of his'n and I'll have to put up with his company for protection and keep on takin his orders too."

"I understand that Andy." I agreed, "But I think Tom and I can make out even if we have to cut loose from the main train; as near Fort Dodge as we now are. If we can't, I don't know how we ever expected to make it through the summer here."

163

"That's what kinda worries me about Tom's thinkin," mused Andy, If the Indians turn out as peaceful as he seems to think they will, then everything will likely be fine. But, if they cut up and raise old Ned like they did last year, it sure ain't gonna be any safe place for women and kids. Not even in that stout sod-house."

No arrangements had been made at our end of the corral for guard duty so Andy and I agreed to handle that chore ourselves. I took the first watch as I was still so riled up, I could'nt sleep anyway. Taking my rifle and a blanket I sat down outside the corral with my back to a wagon wheel. For once I spent little time worrying about Indians or dangers that might be out there in the night. My mind was on the recent events of the evening and the problems that might arise on the morrow. As the scattered campfires died down to an occasional glow or flickering spark and the mules ceased their shifting and stamping, the fresh night air cleared my head and I made one calm decision that seemed perfectly rational at the time. I told myself that never again would McCanles speak to Tom or me as he had done tonight—drunk or sober."

Fort Dodge

CHAPTER XIV

Tom, having feelings similar to mine only more so, and not being able to sleep on account of them, was up and stirring the next morning an hour before anyone from the main train. I was awakened by the glow of his lantern through the wagon sheet. I pulled on my clothes and joined him. We talked things over and agreed that McCanles had became intolerable and that to continue on under his leadership was out of the question. We decided to have everything ready to move and pull in behind the main train and make every effort to avoid McCanles and trouble. But one thing we agreed as a matter of principal, that the rope corral should stay up until the last. I told Tom of Bid's advice and we both felt we had a dependable ally in him. On the other hand, our friendship with Andy Cooper could present a problem. Because of his freighting committments, he couldn't afford to sever his ties with McCanles. So Tom and I insisted on taking full responsibility for the rope corral if that issue came to a showdown.

Before the break of day, our teams had been harnessed, grained and tethered to the wagons where they could be hitched in a hurry. Breakfast a little earlier than usual, was a sober affair. Tom had told Mamie only a mild version of our troubles and the kids knew even less. But I think they all guessed that a grave decision had been made and perhaps trouble lay ahead. The meal finished, we spent some time puttering around the wagons, taking more care than usual in loading the pigs, chickens and similar chores. As a matter of fact, we were partly killing time. Every so often I would steal a glance toward the main camp, half expecting to see the wagon boss headed our way. Soon I saw the teams were being hitched and the day wrangler bunching the spare stock. Andy had his rig ready to move and sat on the seat with his foot on the brake pole. With a wry grin I gave him a half-way salute that he returned with a sober nod. I glanced the other way and sure enough, McCanles mounted on his big horse was headed our way giving orders as he passed each wagon. He rode up to the rope fence where I pretended not to notice him, feigning interest in adjusting my wagon sheet.

"Thought I tole you fellars last night to take this Gawdamn rope down."

He rasped.

I continued to ignore him and out of the corner of my eye I saw McClaine strolling our way with his six-shooter strapped prominently to his waist.

"Reynolds," the wagon boss said loudly, "You rebel son-of-a-bitch! I'm atalkin to you."

I reached behind me and got my blacksnake. Having been prepared for this eventuality, I was cool as a cucumber and when I spoke, it was with more confidence than wisdom. "When you speak to me, McCanles, I'll thank you to keep a civil tongue in your head."

In answer, he spurred his horse into the stretched rope directly at me. As his horse hit the rope stretching it to the breaking point, I let him have it with the whip, managing a tolerable snap of the popper with force enough to raise a welt on his tough chest. Instinctively, he pulled back on the reins causing his horse to rear. While his horse was in this position, I, thinking attack was my best defense, brought the leash across the exposed belly of the horse with all the strength I could muster. For an instant, McCanles had his hands full keeping his seat, but soon he was able to dismount where he handed the reins to a gaping muleskinner who had stepped around his wagon to see what all the commotion was about. With a vile oath, he told the surprised driver to hold his horse. As he turned his attention toward me again, McClaine stepped determinedly over the rope barrier.

"Go on back to yore wagon Taixas man, I aim to reconstruct a Johnny Reb hyar, and I don't figger its none of your Gawddam concern."

"I'm making it my concern," said Bid authoratively. "This business' has done gone fur enough. Ain't no need for trouble atall and I'd jist feel right obliged if I don't heah anymore swearin and loud talk from yo'all. I've heard you mention concern for wimmen and children more'n once't the past week Mister McCanles and I don't want to hev to remind yo'all agin that they're in earshot right now."

"Well now, By Gawd, McClaine, you-all seem to forgit who's givin orders to who around here. Remember you're workin for me—now."

"Was a workin for yo'all—you mean. I quit, effective this mawnin——. At present ah'm employed by Mister Powers, heah."

McCanles digested this piece of news and his face got a little redder. "What in the Hell, kind of a Gaw——".

"Careful, careful, now," cautioned McClaine, "No more swearin, I reckon you and me and our kind are more at home among'st the cavvyard, but it ain't no reason we cain't discuss this like civilized folk."

"You talk mighty big this mawning," mimicked McCanles, but impressed in spite of himself. "I notice you're packing hardware, figger on pullin a gun on me are you?"

"You're heeled too, I see," But there ain't gonna be any gun play or trouble of any kind unless you start it."

"Jes take off your shootin iron, McClaine, and I'll peg your hide out to dry in short order."

"Nope, we ain't gonna do it that way neighter, much as I would like to accommodate yo'all," said the Texan common sensibly. "It ain't the time nor the place to settle personal differences and you ain't gonna take your personal spite out on anyone herabouts. I'm heah to see to thet. It's done reached the point where decent folks cain't get along with you any mores. So whatever Mr. Powers sees fit to do after last night and this mawnin is none of your business so long as we don't interfere

167

none with your wagons. Thet's about the size of it and I don't see no sense of arguin any futher."

The wagon boss stood awhile studing the logic of McClaine's remarks. When he did move, it proved again the only way to impress his type was with a show of strength. Not that he could be cowed into doing anything but he did have a shrewd sense of caution in his makeup. And occasionally, perhaps, even a little propriety.

"Alright McClaine, if you and Powers (apparently he thought I was not worth mentioning) figger you kin make it by yoreselves, well I reckon that ain't no hide off'n my tail. But By Gawd, McClaine, if it ain't a hell of a thing fer you to do, leavin a man in the lurch like this. I spose I'll have to break in some sorry, son-of-a-bitch to take yore place. In the old days they'd called a council and tied a man to a wagon wheel fer sich as this. And as fer you—Powers, this may jist be the longest forenoon of the trip for you without old Clint to keep you out of the clutches of Satanta and his band of hawse thieves, which I know fera fact, hang around Dodge here so's they can pester unprotected Pilgrims and thumb their noses at the Sojers.

McClaine made no reply, even though the other had reverted to his usual rough language which he had warned him of. After all the, Texan had won his point without resorting to violence and he knew enough to not push McCanles too far, for the sake of mere insignificant principles. Tom managed an unsociable, "we'll git along somehow," as the wagon boss mounted his horse and rode off.

So it was that we split up with the main train after traveling well over three hundred miles together. But I think we all had mixed emotions. On the one hand, the present crisis was over but on the other hand, we knew there was a real possibility of danger from Indians, even though we were near the Government Post of Ft. Dodge. Tom about summed it up. "It's a blame shame we couldn't have got along together fur ten, twelve more mile after travelin together this fur."

Of course, Tom was pleasantly surprised to learn the resourceful Texan was now in his "employ" as he figured Bid about doubled our odds against danger. As Bid had his own

168

horse, saddle and late model repeating carbine, it was agreed that he would ride guard or scout for our little train. We shook hands and bade farewell to Andy Cooper. While McClaine left to get his horse and personal belongings, Tom and I dismantled the rope corral, that "contrivance" having served its purpose as a symbol of our independence. Our teams were soon hitched and the McCanles train had already commenced to roll out when McClaine returned. He rode up and tossed his bedroll and belongings in my wagon, reaching in his pocket, he brought forth a small sheaf of bills and riffled the edges with a knowing grin.

"Mr. McCanles was a mite obstinate about partin with these heah greenbacks, but he finally came around to my point of view." Typically Bid never explained how he had persuaded the wagon boss to pay him his wages.

After pulling out on the trail, we purposely held back a distance of a quarter of a mile from the rear wagons of the McCanles train so there would be no reason for further friction with the wagon boss. The morning drive proved uneventful and as the excitement of the earlier hour died away, we settled down in a partially relaxed manner. About mid-morning we observed in the distance a few light wisps of smoke and soon we came to where we could see a great flat spread before us miles away. We guessed the smokes came from Fort Dodge and in an hour the lead wagons ahead of us commenced slowly sinking out of sight. Then we started the slight gradual descent, towards the southwest and next we came in sight of the wide glistening channel of the Arkansas with its broad flat valley stretching east, west and south. Before long, the frontier army post of Fort Dodge lay before us.

Fort Dodge was situated on the north bank of the Arkansas, at the foot of a line of thinly grassed and limestone speckled bluffs. The river meadows were wide, level and covered with a thick stand of heavy grasses which in places was grazed and trampled to a short stubble. No mentionable timber was in sight, occasional clumps of willows and brush along the river banks being the only sizeable vegetation worth mentioning. Nevertheless, the view was a pleasant one and with the knowledge our journey was over and our new home near, brought a welcome relief and optimistic thoughts of the time to come.

169

In my day, I have seen many of the old frontier forts and in most of them there was a similarity, though no two were alike. Fort Dodge was no exception to this rule. The better and more substantial buildings were of the native light yellowish stone so common in the plains country and so similar to what we had already seen at Larned. Some of the barracks, large storehouses, the hospital and smaller buildings were built of this sturdy material. The other buildings were adobe and sod with a few of lumber construction. The corrals had high sod walls on the outside for protection from the Indians and the elements. Attached to these walls were sheds sometimes running the full length. The inside corral fences were mostly of post and rail and cottonwood poles. In contrast to Fort Larned a stockade of cottonwood poles, sharpened at the top protected part of the area. Plainly considerable work and a lot of ingenuity in the use of the materials available, had gone into strengthening the defenses of this Indian Fort.

As we approached the outskirts, we were met by an officer and two troopers, who inquired as to our destination. On learning the Fort was it, they politely suggested we go on up the river where the grass had not been grazed and make camp. Moving by the Sutler's store, the proprietor and a clerk stood on the step and waved at us. I heard the former and Tom greet each other by name. It being a fine Sunday morning, several of the inhabitants were out, drawn by curiosity I suppose, as the complete train of McCanles, Jones and ours made an impressive number of wagons. Three or four women and as many children greeted us with waving hands. The Power's children were all eyes and strangely quiet—in the manner of country kids just came to town. I heard a woman say as my wagon clunked past, "Good Heavens, a woman and children, in this country. I wonder?"

We pulled into camp above the fort and picketed our stock out to graze. Tom, allowed we would camp here until the next morning then we would move out and downstream to where our new home was located. This afternoon we would move the wagons carrying Government freight back to the fort to be unloaded and checked off. The fact the day was Sunday not being considered a reason for not performing essential business in this lattitude.

The kettle was set to boil on a fire of chips and dead willow branches. Then everybody indulged in another good scrubbing and cleaning up. Afterwards, Tom dug out a fine Missouri cured ham which Mamie sliced and fried to perfection. We dined on this with warmed over sour-dough biscuits, saved from breakfast, and washed down with steaming black coffee.

In the afternoon, the big six-mule team was hitched to the double wagon, with Bid and I perched on the driver's seat. Tom, Mamie and all the kids in the wagon Fritz had handled, and we were ready to make an afternoon of it down at the Fort. Fritz was left at camp to guard the stock or rather look after them as this portion of the trail was under constant military surveilance that day. Indians were in evidence, but seemed to be well controlled. Across the river a few miles away appeared to be quite a large encampment and others were said to be on the streams a few miles north of the Fort, but without the sanction of the authorities. But whatever the number and character of these, they were probably held in check by a show of force by the Soldiers and a promise of Government Annuities.

Bid and I were just pulling out from camp with the heavy wagons when we were hailed by Barney Balaam, astride his faithful mule, with a Sharps carbine across his saddle. "Te doggies, I didn't notice you fellars had left the main train till nigh noon as I ketched myself a mite of a nap, a fur piece back thar."

Bid, who always got a terrific kick out of Barney's outspoken backcountry lingo and semi-belligerant manner, allowed himself a sly grin. I could see the deviltry in his eyes and knew it portended no good, so I answered quickly, "Yes, Barney, seemed like we couldn't get along with McCanles any more so we decided we would rather take our chances with Satanta and the Indians."

"Wall, cain't say as I blame you, seems like Clint wuz allurs a pickin on you and Bid, hyar. But boys I'm in a turrible hurry. Andy done sent me back with this Sharps smoker, fer Tom and you fellars. Sed he reckoned you'uns would likely need it a right smart more'n him."

"Well, I'll be damned," said Bid ruefully as the old scout rode away. "here, I was all set to devil that old man, just for the hell of it. Makes me feel about as low as a snake's belly."

At the Fort, Tom was waiting for us, and we proceeded to a large storehouse, where a Lieutenant and Sergeant in charge, and a pair of Irish troopers to do the work, assisted us in unloading the bags of corn from the wagons. The loads were checked off and everything accounted for. Freight bills and receipts were signed and exchanged and all red tape taken care of.

As it turned out, Tom and the Sergeant were old acquaintances and more or less spoke the same language. The Lieutenant was young and obviously not too long from the East. Though courteous and polite, it was plain to see that he was a little over filled with military-bull but interestingly, he relied mostly on the Sergeant to handle the freight papers. During the course of the unloading, Tom and the Sergeant indulged in some kidding and joshing and as one subject led to another Tom told of his intention to locate near here for the summer. In time that led to the question that was uppermost in Tom's mind, "What about the Indian situation? This was the inevitable question of the time. Every wagon master, freighter, traveler, cook and bottlewasher, asked this same question. The Lieutenant had probobly heard it a hundred times and yet he had devised no straight forward answer—likely. because he knew none. He started out in a devious large-worded official tone. used since time immemorial by some public servants, to evade the question by attempting to talk over the interrogator's head.

"Well sir, Mr. Powers, it has been the policy of the War Department and particularly the Department of Missouri to maintain a firm hand on the activities of the Indians. Especially this is true where their activities encroach upon the normal and valid commerce of the Santa Fe Road. However, considering the numerous and sometimes necessary activities of all the tribes involved, over which we have jurisdiction and perhaps also, to some extent jurisprudence, all adds up to insurmountable problems for which there is no direct and forthright answer. In conclusion I would like to emphasize that it behooves we of the military to exercise extreme caution lest we work against the best interests of the Government and the citizenry. Now Mr. Powers, as to your question pertaining to settling and making a home here, I certainly am not in a position to give you a direct answer. Officially, though this area has not been recommended

172

for settlement. Now Sergeant, do you have anything further to add."

The Sergeant looked up with a perfect poker face and admitted the Lieutenant had just about covered everything.

"Well Sir," asked the young Lieutenant, "Does that answer your question?"

Tom's face was a blank of bewilderment. "I ain't right sure I know as much as I did to start with."

The Sergeant, an old hand at buck passing, and beating round the bush, was also experienced in the more direct methods of the common man. He now cleared his throat. "With the Lieutenants permission. What the Lieutenant means is since the treaty last fall we believe the Indians, at least most of em are trying to keep the peace and we aim to keep them that way. But they are pretty well armed, so's they can hunt buffalo and make their own livin and there is a real danger that they can use these same arms to attack you civilians and maybe even us soliders in spite of all we can do."

"Well," grumbled Tom now slightly nettled, "Why in Hell didn't he say so in the first place."

The Lieutenant's face got a little red, as he was actually a rather nice fellow, though given to grandiose language. "Now Sir, you must recognize its a little difficult to make a simple and responsible statement on the Indian question. I think though, the Sergeant summed it up pretty well and I might add to his remarks—from here it doesn't look good."

Tom commenced to get pretty warm. "In that case, are you soldiers gonna be able to give us citizens the protection we deserve? If you ain't, how about issuing me two or three Springfield rifles and a hundred rounds of bullets."

"We're making an effort to protect all citizens. But you must understand we are too thinly spread to cover every hill and hollow in these parts. Besides to put it bluntly, Sir, no one with authority recognizes this area as being sufficiently civilized to warrant settlement, especially with women and children. And Mr. Powers we have no authority to issue arms and ammunition to civilians at this time. It has been the Government's position that it isn't in the best interests of peace to indiscriminately distribute arms to the citizenry. You may want to consult the Major about that but I think he will give you the same answer."

Tom was adamant, "Well, *Bob Wright fetched his family out here a year or so ago. I know that for a fact, and that was when the Indians were the worst ever. And here I am now with mine on my hands, partly cause I had faith the Gov'nment, "since this damned treaty," aimed to keep the Injuns in their place. And I'll tell you right now Lieutenant, if you soldiers won't give us protection, we'll take care of ourselves. I've got two good men, both of em with repeatin rifles, a working for me and any redskin as shows his face around my layout is gonna git a right warm reception."

The Lieutenant's face got a little redder, not having yet gotten used to irate citizens demanding protection. "Now Mr. Powers, don't misunderstand me, the Army recognizes its responsibility to the settlers and we are particularly concerned when it comes to women and children. But there is something else I should point out to you Sir, regardless of what you may have heard, there have been no serious depredations lately, in this immediate area. So now I trust Mr. Powers, and you other gentlemen won't be too hard on the "soldiers." With these remarks, he nodded "good day" and retired as gracefully as he could.

"Well now Tom," the Sergeant said, "I don't blame you for bein worried some, but like the Lieutenant says the soldiers will be here if and when you need us. I think I'm safe in saying all you gotta do is get the word to us. And as far as that goes, we are continually sending out patrols to smell around for one thing or another. So likely one of em will be droppin in on you once in a while. I know where that sod ranche of yourn is. Some of our boys got caught in a blizzard last winter, while bringin in some strayed stock and spent the night there. Mighty welcome place it t'was and one they ain't likely to forget."

The Sergeant's words soothed Tom considerably and I must admit they restored some of my own sagging faith in our armed forces. After a short time spent in cordial small talk, we left

* Bob Wright, one of the true pioneers of the Dodge area.

the soldiers and drove over to the Sutler's store, where Mamie and the kids were waiting. Here we purchased a few needed supplies and groceries most of the latter in the knick-knack line as the store was surprisingly well supplied, having been restocked with merchandise the last few days. Of course, prices were high, but not unreasonable considering everything had to be freighted in by wagons. In recent months, the freight route to Hays City on the new railroad had been established and the cost of transportation reduced accordingly. Already the importance of the Santa Fe Trail had lessened somewhat. Its usefullness in the future, east of Dodge would be more as a military road and stage route than as a freight road. We absorbed these facts after talking with the personnel at the store. Tom renewed acquaintances with two or three fellows he had known the previous summer and introduced Bid and I. Then we climbed in our wagons and left for our camp.

At our camp that evening, we bid farewell to our fellow teamster, Fritz. His and Tom's agreement had been for the former to remain in Tom's employ until our destination was reached and leave on the first opportunity to catch an eastbound train. Tom had talked to a freighter at the Sutler's store who was going to Hays City. This suited Fritz fine as his family lived in Salina and he could easily afford to ride the cars that distance as he was anxious to get back to civilization, having had enough of the "wild country" to suit his unimaginative nature for a long time. After supper, Bid and I, in the light rig, drove him down to the Fort. We hung around the place a while hoping to amuse ourselves with a little excitement but we found most of the place out of bounds for "unknown civilians," so soon returned to camp.

PART II

At the Sod Ranche

CHAPTER I

Days at the Soddy

To the traveler of 1868, the journey along the Santa Fe Trail from the last scattered settlements west of Council Grove to Fort Lyon, seemed through a land of rough semi-civilization. The occasional trading store, ranche or rustic stage station tended to give the impression of settlement and security that was deceiving. At best, you might say there was a narrow band of frontier civilization a half mile wide and over four hundred miles long. In that day, if you were to wander a mile or two from the trail, you were out of the effective bounds of law and order and, definitely, in the wilds. If you were rash enough to venture across the Arkansas, you were beyond the realm of the white man and God have mercy on you,—because the Indians and the elements were not likely to.

At the time of our arrival at Ft. Dodge, I was beginning to realize these facts, though not fully. But in the following days of spring and summer, they became more and more apparent, as we experienced the excitement, curiosity and thrills that life in this wild land had to offer.

To the north lay a hundred miles of unsettled prairie and brakes, before the new-made grade of the Kansas Pacific was reached; and there, again, was a narrow band of "only" semi-civilization. But to the south was where the long, wild reaches stretched endlessly to the scattered frontier of mid-Texas. One of the few scratches on the face of this whole vast wilderness was the southwest branch, or the "Dry Route of the Santa Fe Trail," known to the Mexicans as the "Jornado Del Muerti". But this year, even this famous road was not as popular as in the past, due to the inability of the military to effectively police the area south of the river.

"First Days at the Soddy"

Next morning, we hitched our teams for the last time of the journey, loaded up the equipment and headed back downstream toward our new home. A number of miles east of the Fort, we pulled out of the river bottom toward the north and started the ascent of a broad draw. Before long we saw the solid outlines of the sodhouse built in the side of the hill. Probably we all viewed this with mixed emotions, the strongest of which was likely disappointment. For no matter how practical a sodhouse might actually be, at first sight it was never attractive, least of all to the "uninitiated". The structure before us, however, did have the appearance of sturdiness. In size it was about eighteen by thirty-four feet (outside dimensions). It was built in sort of a "happen-so" Spanish style, with the front, or southeasterly wall, nine or ten feet high and the opposite wall a little over six feet inside, and actually dug a little into the hill to strike a proper level, or rather pitch, for the roof. The shed style roof was supported lengthways by two log beams placed about equal distance apart between the walls and running the length of the building and held from sagging by sturdy logs set upright in the center. The roof proper was made of cottonwood poles laid side by side as close together as their straightness would permit. Over these, old canvas wagonsheets had been spread, then a layer of tall meadow grass, finally heavy buffalo grass sod. On top of this, a layer of black dirt was worked into the crevices and smoothed on top. Then coarse river gravel had been spread to retard the surface from washing and blowing away. This type of roof, while not the best to withstand a long, wet spell, was actually strong enough to support a man on horseback and from the more practical standpoint had natural insulation qualities that were effective against both heat and cold. The walls were of buffalo grass sod over a foot thick, with one door and four window openings. The door was heavy, made of two thicknesses of rough lumber (pine) and swung on home-made iron hinges. The windows were little more than rough openings fitted with pine shutters that swung upward on leather hinges from the outside. These opening were designed with the object of defense in mind, as well as ventilation and light. They were placed about four feet from the floor, and were about twenty inches in heights and thirty inches long; making them ideal for a man to prop the shutter open with a stick, rest his rifle barrel on the sill, and effectively cover the countryside. They were framed or boxed with the rough lumber and supported from sagging in the middle by a single upright, sawed from a four inch cottonwood trunk. We brought with us from the east, glass paned sashes, which we fitted to the interior of these with a crude, but serviceable slide arrangement made of narrow boards nailed to the opening frames. Those glass windows were one of the few niceties the homely soddy possessed; and Mamie gave us little rest until they were properly installed.

Perhaps the most interesting feature of the whole structure was the lookout tower. This was a simple affair of four long cottonwood poles, placed about five feet apart in the extreme southwest corner, and rising through the roof. A boxed opening with board cover provided a manhole exit and entry. Above the roof the poles were held in place and proper alignment by rough one-by-sixes, spaced about four feet apart, except on one side where they were close enough together to serve as rungs of a ladder to reach the top.

As the reader has probably guessed, the interior of the building was not of the type to please the fastidious or luxury loving. However, by reason of circumstances, none of us fitted that category. I think, though, the first sight of the rough sod interior and the dirt floor was a bit of a shock to a hardy Missouri farm woman like Mamie, but she was enough of a realist that she took it in stride.

Her first reaction was, "My gracious to Heaven, nary a one gets a bite to eat around here 'til this dump is cleaned up so's a body can live in it."

Accordingly, everyone pitched in and the sod abode was cleaned out and made livable. The interior was simply one large room, though it was divided in the center by two upright logs which supported the roof. These made an ideal framework for a partition. As soon as one of the wagons was unloaded, the canvas cover was removed and hung at this point, thus dividing the interior in two equal sized rooms. The front room was fitted up as kitchen and living room. We backed the "kitchen wagon" to

179

the front door and unloaded Mamie's heavy range and set it in the corner opposite the lookout poles, installed stovepipe through the roof, and were ready for housekeeping.

A heavy home-made table and wooden bench were the only furniture left by the builders of the house. As these were quite serviceable, we put them to good use. In the far corner of the part partitioned off for family sleeping quarters was a small mud, doby and rock fireplace with a chimney built through the low roof. But since Mamie had her modern range, she had no use for this old-fashioned device. Accordingly, it was not used that first summer.

Upon entering the sod house for the first time that morning, we were surprised to see a pile of rough sawed pine lumber stacked against the far wall. Lumber of any kind was a luxury in this frontier plains country. The fact that we had this did much to add to our comfort and convenience. Tom explained how this supply of material had come about. On his way home from disposing of government freight the previous fall, on the upper Arkansas River, he had come upon an unfortunate freighter who had wrecked his wagon and spilled his load of fresh sawed lumber. The unlucky freighter had been happy to dispose of the lumber at cost. Tom had bought it, knowing he would have no trouble making a profit at any of the lower army posts. After helping to construct the sod house and utilizing a little of the lumber there, the rest had been stored inside. Tom, being suddenly motivated by a desire to get home in a hurry regardless of the modest investment he had in the pile of rough lumber.

Outside of the soddy itself, the only improvements on the place was a large sod corral. This was a sod wall about five feet high, connected to the northwest corner of the house and running straight westerly for about a hundred and twenty feet, where it turned south at a right angle for about sixty feet thence east for a short distance. Here the builders had evidently lost enthusiasm for their job and dropped the project. Nevertheless, they had partly completed a well-designed and practical corral for both protection from weather and raids from the Indians. The sod for much of the corral had been taken from inside the north wall, thus lowering the height necessary to protect man and beast. This wall was built into the slope of the hill, which rose to the north. Interestingly enough, by either luck or design, there was enough slope left to properly drain the entire layout.

Bid examined the layout with the eye of one who knows what he is doing, and nodded with approval, noting that the first thing we should do was finish the south wall for fifty or sixty feet and complete the rest of the corral with poles if such were available. Tom, always open to ideas that would strengthen our defences, agreed readily. It was decided that as soon as we were settled, Bid and I should finish this job. Tom allowed "as fur himself, the first thing he would do was build a backhouse* for the women and kids."

For the next two days we were occupied with finishing the corral and the many other chores that went with adjusting ourselves and our livestock to our new home. Bid and I, with plow and spade, cut buffalo sod and finished laying the south wall for fifty feet or more from the southwest corner. By then we were getting pretty confident in our new-found skill, so we looked around for something more on which to vent our energies. That was in a day when a man young and strong, with all he needed to eat and drink, found a pleasure in working with his hands. Our day's work was from sunup until dark, with an hour off for noon. Although much of this was hard physical labor, it was in a way, rewarding. We all realized that in our present state, we were more or less at the mercy of the Indians, if they should choose to attack, and anything that could be done to improve our defenses gave us a lot of satisfaction and greater peace of mind.

During these first few days, while keeping busy improving the layout around the soddy, we nevertheless kept a sharp lookout for Redskins. Sid took a special delight at the top of the lookout tower. Whenever he reported anything that appeared suspicious, Bid or I would go to the top and check it out with the field glasses. From the top of the tower, we could see for miles in the country below us. But due to our location in the wide draw, there was an area above us in a northerly direction where we could not see over the ridge. Twice a day one of us

* "Backhouse" for the information of the present generation and those who have not shared the experiences of the "pre-electric" age, was a privy or more explicitly a toilet.

would ride to the top of this ridge, where we had a clear view of much of the countryside for miles. The slope above us was covered with the usual thick stand of short buffalo and gramma grass, with only an occasional soapweed or tall clump of grass large enough to offer the slightest concealment.

From a defensive standpoint, the proximity of the ridge above the soddy was the weakest part of our location. An attack from this direction, if well carried out, would at best give us only a few minutes warning. On the other hand, the soddy and corral had been built with defense in mind. If given time for everyone to get inside, a few well-armed defenders could conceivably hold off a large force of attackers. For examples, from the roof of the house, the entire premises could be covered, and all except the far side of the corral could be protected from inside the house.

Luckily, during our early occupancy of the soddy, we saw no Indians and began to feel more secure each day. After all, we felt we had a strong abode for ourselves, as well as protection for the livestock. We had reason to believe, with some logic, that three well-armed men such as ourselves could make it very warm for any ordinary band of raiders that might be reckless enough to attack us. Our proximity to the military garrison at Fort Dodge would, we felt, surely bring us help from that direction.

After all, though, on looking back on that first year on the Plains, I wonder that we survived as well as we did, because before the snow fell, it was a period of almost constant Indian trouble somewhere in the area. The fact that we did survive without any great loss, I can only attribute to these reasons: we were almost constantly alert and prepared; also, our location was such that we could be said to be in sort of an out-of-the-way place as far as usual Indian travel was concerned, but mostly, I think, it was pure, unadulterated luck. Perhaps Almightly Providence's way of taking care of those with the courage, or rather "rashness" to venture into the unknown.

Outside of danger from Indians, probably our greatest problem was that of water supply. The nearest water was at the river, well over a mile to the south. We discussed digging a well, but put that off for the reasons that we were entirely ignorant of ground water supplies, and of course, had no idea at what depth water could be found, if at all. More important, the need for water was urgent; so at present it must be hauled. On Monday, when coming from our camp above Dodge, we had all available barrels and containers filled. Besides this, a small pool of clear surface water, which had collected from winter-spring moisture, greeted us in the draw below the soddy. This supplied the livestock for the first three days, then it became necessary to obtain more water for them, as well as for household use.

CHAPTER II

"Nothin' Much Happened A'Tall"

By Thursday, Bid and I had pretty well caught up on the work we could do on the corral. Tom had finished his carpenter work; and an appropriate "two-holer" made of the rough lumber graced the hillside just northeast of the house. This, and other jobs taken care of, Tom, farmer that he was, had been going since daylight with his best mules hitched to the plow, and was busily turning black furrows of buffalo sod on a comparitively level spot below the house that was to be the garden.

This was the day water supplies had become short in the house, and the small pond where the stock had been watering had become little more than a puddle. We had first talked of hauling water for the stock, as well as ourselves; but to McClaine, who would rather drive a horse a mile to water than lead him out of the stable, "this was unthinkable."

"Hell, Caroliny," he said, "We can trail this damn stuff down to water a sight easier than we can haul it up heah for 'em."

So—we mounted our ponies and drove the stock to the river. Sid followed along behind with a gentle old team hooked to a wagon loaded with barrels and everything available that would hold water, and trailing the cart loaded "likewise."

The Arkansas, (or Arkansaw) as it was generally called, was quite a stream in the old days. This was long before irrigation of any consequence was practiced on the upper reaches of the stream, and the normal spring flow was considerable. This increased a great amount later in the season when the main snow pack commenced to let go in the mountains. But now it was well below its banks, flowing a moderately clear stream of water, which with a few exceptions, was not over a few feet deep. It was a little roilly with sand, particularly around the edges; but as Tom said, "That'll settle to the bottom of the barr'l in an hour or so and no one need be the wiser."

Upon arriving at the river we watered the loose stock along with our mounts, then unhitched the team from the wagon and led them to water. We hitched them up again and drove upstream a short distance, looking for a good place to fill the barrels. We soon found a likely looking spot where the water appeared to be clear and deep in close to a grassy bank. It seemed an ideal place to load our containers except when we approached the bank, the sides commenced caving in. We discussed driving the wagon in the river and dipping the water out as it swirled by the wagon bed, a method that later that summer we sometimes used. But now we were unfamiliar with the stream at this place, and Bid cautioned about quicksand. Besides, here, the banks were too steep.

Nearby, a couple of long cottonwood saplings had washed ashore from some recent flood.

Bid had an idea. "Hand me that axe on the side of the wagon, will you, Sid?"

He took the axe and chopped off the roots at the base of the trunk; then we lopped off the limbs.

"Tell you what," he said with a grin, "one of you fellows wade out in the river and locate the fur end, whil'st I stay here and stiddy this end."

Bid was a great hand to play practical jokes, and I "smelled a mouse" immediately. I had been the victim of his jokes too many times in the last few days to relish the prospect of another one. It wasn't that I didn't enjoy a good joke at the "other fellow's expense"; but the drover was an expert along this line, and no matter how I tried, I usually found myself on the losing or receiving end. Besides, although it was a pleasant spring day, it was not overly warm, and I wasn't about to go in that cold water if I could help it.

"To the Devil with you, Bid," I said, "I had a bath Sunday in camp."

"Hell, a little water never hurt nobody," he said seriously. "Let's flip a coin. Heads I go in; tails you go in."

I was still suspicious, although his manner was dead serious; for, Bid was one who could be solemn as a judge when he was up to one of his tricks. This morning I wasn't in the mood for this type of "horseplay." I was only interested in filling the water barrels and heading for home. But some faint sense of sportsmanship prompted me to go along with his game, whatever it

185

was. But I was determined to come out on top this time, even if I had to fudge a little. I pulled a half-dollar from my pocket, which I flipped in the air and caught. I saw the American Eagle staring me in the face, but I made like I had won.

"Heads it is," I lied like a trooper.

Surprisingly, Bid put up no argument. He remarked something about lucky so and so, commenced pulling off his boots and gun belt, and promptly slipped off into the water, which was waist deep. I knew Bid would sometimes go to about any lengths to prove his toughness. Seeing him wading around in the cold water, trying to appear unconcerned, knowing how easily I had tricked him this time struck me as so funny, I could hardly keep my face straight as Sid and I wrestled our end of the poles into position. Finally, we got them in place and lashed together where they protruded about six feet over the water, providing a platform to dip water from the stream. I deliberately took as much time as possible so that Bid would have longer to enjoy the water. Finally, I could endure it no longer and burst out laughing.

From his place in the "drink", Bid looked at me with good-natured disgust. He appeared to be no more uncomfortable than if he had gone in the stream to get away from the heat. But I knew all that was an act for Sid's and my benefit.

"Gimme your hand, will you Caroliny, and I'll get out of here," he said matter-of-factly.

I sat the water pail I held on the end of the logs and offered him my hand, making a manful effort to keep my face straight.

"Goddamn you, Caroliny," he grinned, as he grasped my hand. "I saw the eagle's tail on that silver piece of yourn."

The next thing I knew I was head first in the water. I came up squirting water and hunting my headgear. The Texan was leaning over, beside himself with laughter. While he was enjoying himself so much, I reached up and got the water pail and splashed a bucket of water over his upper portions, which was the only dry part of him. Then we both had something to laugh about.

It was noon that day when we got in with the stock and water, and neither of us was completely dry. But we never

186

indulged in that particular kind of horseplay again until the weather warmed up.

To return again to the matter of the overall water problem, we later found the garrison at the Fort dumped their sewage in the river; however, this wasn't of any grave concern of ours, as the volume of flow was great enough to fear little danger of pollution as far downstream as our watering place. However, at times, especially during flood periods, muddy water was a serious problem. Eventually, we located a small spring near this watering place, which we dug out and curbed with boards and from that time on, we got most of our drinking water from there.

Back to the more serious business at hand. As has been mentioned, we had finished the sod walls for the corral and had made ambitious plans for a shed-like stable to be built in the northwest corner, utilizing the north and west walls of the corral for those of the stable, with both the south and east sides to be open. Thus, about all required to complete the thing was a roof. The only materials available for such a job were poles to be covered with hay and that would take a bit of doing. Tom knew of a sizeable grove of young cottonwood timber several miles downstream. It was decided that we take two wagons and get all the poles we could haul, since besides the stable we needed more poles to finish the corral.

So far, since moving to the sod stronghold, we had seen no signs of Indians, although we knew there were many in the area of the Fort. But we had been assured there had been no recent outbreakes of trouble; so accepting to some extent the optimism of the times, we felt fairly safe in splitting up our little force and two of us making the short trip necessary to procure the poles.

Friday morning we left before sun-up with two mule teams and two wagons stripped to the running gears, leaving Tom to continue his plowing and hold down the ranch. Tom, by now, had started on his plowing for cropland, which he hoped to be as much as ten or twelve acres when completed.

On this trip we took the better teams, but purposely used single teams to each rig because most of the way was comparatively level with no bad hills or sand to be encountered.

187

Naturally, we went well armed; Bid with his rifle, a seven shot Spencer carbine, and, of course, six shooter. As for myself, I never ventured out without rifle and pistol. Bid took along his saddle horse and at intervals along the way, tied his team to the rear of my wagon and scouted on ahead. We hoped to get some meat on this trip, as the meat supply at the soddy had dwindled to a couple of cured pork shoulders and a few slabs of side meat. About half way down to the timbers we sighted a small herd of buffalo. We reluctantly passed them up; hoping for another chance on our way back, knowing that any meat we might get this season of the year would need to be taken care of at once or it would spoil.

By noon we had set up camp in the middle of the timbered bottom, put the mules out to graze, and had already cut and lopped a number of saplings. This cottonwood-covered bottom was one typical of the Arkansas and similar streams of the early days. Not large in extent, it consisted mostly of young trees that had come up and flourished in the rich soil in fairly recent years. These trees, in places, stood thick and tall and straight; ideal for our purposes. We selected mostly trees that were small in diameter at the base and would trim out over twenty feet in length.

In discussing the Great Plains, today, one most common description is "treeless plains" and one of the truest. Yet, this is not a complete literal fact, many good people to the contrary. *I believe that I can safely say that in the very earliest days of settlement of this vast country, from the Dakotas to the Caprock in the Panhandle, there were few areas as much as twenty miles square that did not have timber of some kind. Somewhere every so often, in a hidden canyon, some rocky draw, some spring-fed creek or river bottom, where there was sufficient moisture and protection from prairie fires, trees were likely to grow. Usually you needed to have a good idea of where to look or you might have a long and very tiresome search to find it. Nevertheless, every so often on these monotonous plains, there was one of these welcome little patches of timber. When the main stream of settlement occurred in the eighties, many of these trees were gone, and the reasons are obvious. Too many

* References: Robert M. Wright's "Dodge City Cowboy Capital"; "Annals of Kansas" and many others.

188

fellows like Bid and I had been there first with our "axes". I remember our conversation that day as we ate our lunch. We agreed that it seemed a shame to destroy what little timber there was in a country like this. Bid perched his tincup of steaming coffee on a fresh cut stump and summed it up philosophically. "We're just thinnin' these trees out, Caroliny, so's them that's left will do good. It's the feller that comes along and cuts the last of 'em, that is the real Pole-cat."

We chopped trees like good fellows that afternoon and by the time the sun was sinking low, we had felled about all we needed for ordinary poles. However, we did need a few heavier ones for roof supports, gate posts and so forth. Bid threw the saddle on his horse; we mounted "double"; and, with axes in hand, we moved on about a quarter of a mile and nearer the river where some older and larger trees grew. We rode in among them, talking and joshing one another. Bid was complaining that my axe was "gigging" him in the rear, and I was telling him that if his butt wasn't so prominent he wouldn't notice such trivial things. All of a sudden a loud crashing in the underbrush ahead interrupted us. Then, out of the scattering cottonwoods dashed two large elk. Frightened by the sudden appearance of the animals, Bid's horse started rearing and prancing. I didn't have much to hang on to, so I promptly dropped my axe and slid off after it. Bid jerked and cursed his pony to partial quiet. He carried his Spencer in a scabbard under his leg, but his axe had been struck down beside it in such a manner that he couldn't remove it in a hurry, so he pulled six-shooter and steadied his horse for a shot. By that time the elk had splashed into the river and were half way across. Bid fired once; but the shot only added to their speed; and we watched in disappointment as they cleared the water and ran over a ridge on the other side. We were about to turn away when they reappeared, running towards us. They suddenly cut downstream just before they reached the riverbank and went out of sight as fast as they could go. We looked at one another.

Bid spoke for both of us. "Somethin' on the other side of thet ridge spooked them critters."

"Suppose it could have been a wolf or such?" I surmised hopefully.

"Yeah, I reckon—could have—could have been anything." He dismissed the whole thing with an unconcern I sensed he didn't feel.

We turned then to the business at hand. We picked a likely looking tree and went to work with our axes, each keeping a wary eye on the other side of the river, and each making a pretence of careless unconcern. We swung our axes with unconscious rhythm, making deep and true cuts almost effortlessly, as if our energies had received some magic boost. Actually, though, I think both of us commenced to wonder how badly we needed these extra logs.

In a short time we had the first tree felled and trimmed of branches.

"D'you suppose another one about like this will fill the bill?" I ventured with elaborate casualness, but with one eye cocked on the other side of the river.

"We—ll," the Texan glanced at the lowering sun, scrutinizing it carefully as though it was all a matter of daylight, "that sun is a droppin' right smart—I reckon one more ought to do it."

By the time we had selected another tree, felled and trimmed it, nothing had occured to change the tranquility of the situation. When we stopped to look and listen, the landscape before us was as still as a picture, and only the low sigh of the branches and the gurgle of the stream broke the silence of a perfect evening. Still, I felt an uneasiness in the air that gave me an urge to return to the wagons.

I have mentioned setting up camp when we first arrived at the main grove that morning. Actually, that may have been an overstatement. We had parked our wagons side by side about twenty feet apart in a little clearing near the edge of the grove. Camp consisted merely of unloading our bedrolls, frying pan, coffee pot, grub box and water jug next to a wagon wheel and covering the whole lot with a small canvas wagonsheet.

Now, as we rode into camp, Bid's horse nickered a greeting as he recognized the grazing mules; and I, for one, felt a homey lift.

Bid was never one to shirk his share of the camp chores.

190

He spoke with his usual easy and unconscious profanity. "Tell you what, I'll take the goddam mules down to water if you'll light a fire and start supper."

I offered to help, but he insisted it was only a one man job. Anyway, I got the halters and helped remove the hobbles, then handed him the halter ropes. He expertly gathered them in, nudged his horse with his heel, and led off at a trot for the river about a hundred and fifty yards away. The first thing I did was go to my bedroll and get my rifle. I checked to see that the magazine was full and slipped a fresh box of cartridges in my pocket. As I set some rocks to cook on, and gathered dry wood for a fire, I kept a nervous eye on Bid as he led the mules through the scattering of cottonwoods. The Texan appeared calm and unconcerned; but as he approached the river, I noticed he loosened his rifle in the scabbard.

I fought an uncomfortable feeling until Bid rode back among the trees. By that time I had the fire going and was slicing spuds and sidemeat. He rode in without speaking, dropped his reins to the ground, tied the mules to the propped up tongue of the far wagon, and fed them some oats. By the time he had finished with the teams and saddle horse, I had forked the fried pork in tin plates which were set beside the fire to keep warm, and had just put the sliced potatoes in the hot skillet. The coffee simmered merrily and the mixed aroma of wood smoke and hot "vittles" filled the air. To the west the sun had sunk, and darkness with an evening chill was settling over the flat valley of the Arkansas.

The Texan approached the fire appreciatively. "By Gawd, Caroliny, you sure as hell will make some woman a fine little cook."

I made some sarcastic rejoiner and started to turn the potatoes that sizzled in the pan—when from the distance came the mournful cry of a hoot owl. Far away, apparently from the distant timber, came an answer, almost like an echo. Bid and I looked at each other and neither of us batted and eye; but I felt a chill run up my spine. For awhile neither of us spoke; then, suddenly, came the same cry, with an answer as before.

I spoke, partly to break the silence, and partly what was on my mind. "Tell me, Bid, is this a normal thing for owls to call this time of year?"

"I wish to hell you hadn't said that," the Texan responded with a wry grin, "I was thinkin' the same blame thing—, but I reckon the time of year don't matter much to a tarnation owl."

"How about Indians, then? Does it matter to them?" I persisted, determined to bring the discussion out in the open.

"How about them vittles?" returned the other, "we gonna stand around heah like a couple of old wimmen scared of the dark and tell witch stories? What we need is somethin' to fill thet empty place in our bellies."

We had about finished eating and were sopping blackstrap molasses out of our plates with some of Mamie's good bread, when the owl calls were repeated. This time I thought one had a different tone; but as Bid didn't appear to notice, I didn't press the subject and we went ahead and finished eating and washed up our few dishes. We were just straightening up when the cry came again: this time closer and with an eerie shrillness. We froze in our tracks and neither spoke, but I felt an awful chill grip my being.

Bid finally broke the silence. His voice was calm as ever.

"Thet last screech would chill the soul of a she-catamount, but I reckon it wa'nt nothin' but a damn owl. Sure ain't no use of lettin' it give us the "willies". But it's a cinch, it won't hurt to take a few precautions around heah."

We busied ourselves taking those precautions. We led one team of the mules to the rear of the wagons and tethered them to the hind wheels, leaving the other team tethered to the tongue; then Bid tied his horse to the inward side of the wagon opposite our campfire. That afternoon we had piled a large stack of poles against the outside wheels of the wagon nearest the fire. We now took some of these poles and laid them on the ground at right angles, and about ten feet behind the wagons. Then we did the same thing in front, thus forming a light barricade, both for our protection and designed to trip up any unwary intruder. we pushed the balance of the pole pile directly against the wagon wheels and loaded enough of them on the wagon to form a layer from bolster to bolster. We each got our bedroll; and wrapping ourselves in blankets under the pole-covered wagon with our backs to the pole pile, we settled down to wait, rifles in hand.

I felt a childish inclination to whisper when conversing but thankfully I didn't.

Bid kept an eye on the mules. "It ain't thet I have any love for the ornery devils, but a mule has a better sense of self-preservation when there's danger about than a hawse. If there's anything a'movin' out yonder, them hawdtails'll give us some warning."

"Take thet old crowbait of mine," he went on, mostly I suppose to relieve the tension, "when he's settled for the night on three laigs, a brace of U and P engines pulling a quarter mile of cattle cars past him on a sidin' wouldn't more'n cause him to flitch an ear."

"Most animals have some of their senses better developed than man," I opined, entering the spirit of the thing. "I knew an old cavalry sargeant during the war, who claimed any war horse worth his salt could smell trouble a mile away."

*"Not old Joker heah. Why, thet stupid cayuse couldn't smell blackeyed peas aburnin' directly under his nose. But them mules there, they'll kick you, bite you, buck you off and tromp all over you for pure cussedness, but the contrary bastards always got their eyes and ears peeled for unexpected trouble."

We sat there fully clothed; boots and all, with our blankets wrapped about us and rifles in hand, carrying on a desultory conversation. But our minds were alert to the situation at hand and our senses were strained for whatever might be in the surrounding darkness. The idea had occurred to me that my companion might be taking advantage of the situation to pull another of his practical jokes. But I dismissed this at once; for in the year of '68', the Indian menace on the High Plains was too real to joke about, particularly in a position such as our present one. Besides, although Bid displayed an outer calm, I knew he nursed an inner worry the same as I.

* Bid's horse. Rather than express the sentiment he really felt for his horse he was apt to refer to him in insulting terms.

I reflected how we had planned this little trip with the cocksure assumption of broad daylight and in a safe place; that we were well equipped to take care of ourselves. Now, with imagination running riot it was easy to guess at the chances we had taken and the danger from some unknown that could befall us.

Finally, as the early hours of the night wore on, the cries of the hoot owls ceased altogether. But that failed to give us any real sense of relief. Our eyes still searched the darkness and our ears strained for sounds. Most of the time we were able to observe the outlines of the mules. Occasionally, they would arouse and cock their ears as if they had heard some sound beyond our limits, then, they would lapse back into their former unconcern. As for ourselves, we heard no definite sounds save that caused by the movements of our own stock. We soon tired of our attempts at conversation and lapsed into a silence of our own.

Time went on and Bid was so still I wondered if he had gone to sleep. Abruptly, he roused and crawled out from under the wagon, stood up and stretched himself. I could see him dimly as he moved quietly around our little enclosure. Soon he returned to his place under the wagon.

A match flickered as he lit his pipe and glanced at his watch.

"Caroliny, yo'all might as well get some sleep. I'll take the first watch and rouse you later on." He said.

That sounded reasonable; besides, the normal tone of his voice made me feel a little better. We had put in a long hard day; and ordinarily I would have been 'long gone in sleep'—for that matter, both of us would. But now, I felt little in the mood for it. I shifted myself in a more comfortable position and tried to relax and get some rest. Eventually, I dozed off in a light intermittent sleep. After seemingly ages, I fully awoke and checked my watch by the light of a match. It was one-thirty; time to relieve Bid, and in a little while that worthy was breathing heavily in deep sleep. In time, I commenced to feel drowsy and was debating on whether to get up and move around to rouse myself, when the Texan started murmuring in his sleep.

"T'ain't so", he said plaintively. And then in a sudden rougher

194

tone, "t'ain't, by Gawd, it ain't!" I grinned to myself, thinking of the joke I would have in the morning, exaggerating the things he had said. But then I remembered the seriousness of our position and the close-mouthed sacredness which the Texan seemed to have for certain segments of his past life, and suddenly it wasn't funny. He mumbled a few unintelligible words and then dropped off in a quiet sleep.

I spent the balance of the night wondering what the morning would bring. But strangely, it brought with it a certain sense of relief. When the first faint traces of light appeared in the east, I glanced at Bid and saw that he was already awake.

"I reckon it's about thet time of day and we ought to be a fixin' to stir about heah, directly."

We took our time and as a faint color commenced to warn of sunrise, we began cautiously, studying the immediate country-side around our little bulwark, halfway expecting the sudden cry of a war-whoop. Gradually, as it became more light, we could see no change nor did anything appear to be out of place in the entire area around us. By the time it was broad daylight, we still could detect no danger. We grained the stock and prepared breakfast, keeping our eyes peeled for anything suspicious. After eating breakfast, we hung around camp carefully scanning the countryside for half an hour before we were sure it was safe to venture out. By then it had become apparent there were no Indians about; nor had there been.

We, having had our big scare all for nothing, were greatly relieved but didn't see anything funny about the whole affair until we were loaded and well on our way back to the ranche.

It took us until noon to cut and trim some more poles and load those we had cut the day before. We also loaded on all the small branches we had room for, as these would come in handy around the place. We watered our teams, cooked the balance of the sidemeat and fried a few spuds which we topped off with a pot of coffee. Then we climbed aboard our heavily loaded wagons and headed for home.

About halfway to the ranche we stopped to rest our teams as we had found the going pretty heavy at times. This was near where we had seen the buffalo the morning before. While the mules were resting we decided for Bid to take his horse and ride up on the flats and see if he could locate the herd. Pretty soon he came riding back with the news he had located the herd about a mile and a half away. He generously offered to toss for the privilege of the hunt, but I insisted that he go as the horse was his and he had the heavier gun, the Spencer, which used the "56" caliber government cartridge. We tethered his team to the poles that protruded from the rear of my wagon. I pulled out, following him, picking my way slowly up the grass covered slope, feeling confident we would soon have some meat to load. Just about the time I reached the top with the wagons, I heard a shot followed by two others. Pretty soon I located dust and saw the herd running northeasterly where they disappeared over a slight ridge. Nearly half a mile away, Bid waved his hat, beckoning me on. When I got there I saw two dead buffalo, and Bid. with his butcher knife was busily engaged on the nearer, a fat young cow.

"The other's an old sister with a broken laig. I don't reckon we'll want her. I shot her mostly to put her out of her misery when the rest of the herd run off. She's got a calf too; looks like it's nigh starved, as likely it ain't sucked since its mammy got hurt."

We gutted the young cow and skinned her out and propped open the carcass to cool a little.

"Many's the steer and cow critter I've butchered," admitted the Texan, "but this is the first buffalo I ever tackled."

We now decided to capture the buffalo calf, a poor little half-starved creature standing mournfully by his dead mother.

I wiped my bloody hands on the grass, removed my pistol and belt and advanced expectantly on the baby calf. I heard the dry voice of my companion as he coiled his rope and prepared to mount his horse. "Go ahaid and catch him afoot if you kin, but I reckon this calls for a hawse and a rope."

I ignored his remarks and continued stalking the calf, "cat-footedly" detouring around the dead cow and with hands out-stretched, was just about to pounce on the little fellow, when

196

he suddenly jumped up and ran off a short distance, where he stood brace-legged, looking at me with a puzzled expression. By no means disheartened, I continued with all the stealth I could muster, and was getting closer all the time. I stole a backward glance at the Texan and saw he was mounted and waiting with an expectant grin on his face.

I thought, "Bid, old boy, you don't get the laugh on me this time. I'm gonna show you how to capture a live buffalo."

Suddenly, I saw my chance and quick as a cat, I sprang. All I got was a handful of grass and a solid jolt when I hit the ground. Again, the calf only ran a little ways and stopped. By now I was about ready to admit that he was too quick for me, but on studying his frail appearance and, incidentally, guessing about how my partner must be enjoying the show, I suddenly changed my tactics and charged the calf as fast as I could go. This evidently convinced him that I meant business and away he went like a jackrabbit and I after him as fast as I could make my feet fly. I was in good condition and I think I must have covered that first hundred yards in ten seconds flat, but I never came close enough to get my hands on the calf. While I pulled up to get my breath, he ran a little further and commenced to circle, evidently reluctant to leave his mother. By now, realizing the futility of chasing him further, I waved to Bid to go get him with his horse, and ruefully sat down to watch the proceedings.

Old Joker had his shortcomings, as Bid was free to admit, but he was a trained cow-pony and for a short distance it took a pretty good fourlegged animal to outrun him. Bid carefully bided his time until he had gotten close to the buffalo, then he gave his horse the spur and the weakened condition of the calf began to tell and in a matter of seconds, Bid's sure rope was tightening about his neck. In an instant, the drover had dismounted and tied the calf's legs together and came riding back with the calf before him on the saddle.

"Why the pore little critter don't weigh more'n a handful." he said half-ashamedly, as we went back to the wagons.

And there I had learned a lesson again—never underestimate the speed of a buffalo.

We laid the little fellow in the shade of a wagon and gave him some water. Of course, he was too wild and frightened to drink normally, but we managed to get some water down him.

Then we returned to the business at hand, that of getting the buffalo loaded and started on our way home. Our axes came in handy when we were ready to cut the carcass into quarters. This soon accomplished, we loaded the meat on top my load by main strength and awkwardness and covered it with the wagon sheet. We put the calf on a bed of cottonwood branches on top of Bid's load and once more were on our homeward way.

The afternoon sun was slowly sinking towards the horizon by now, and we knew we would be hard pressed to reach the ranche before dark. We had pulled pretty well up on the flats to get the buffalo, so now we continued across country in a bee-line for the soddy. On the course we now took, there was no trail at all, but the country wasn't overly rough and we made tolerable progress without difficulty. We started down the slope of a small draw and surprised a band of wild horses. They ran out ahead of us toward the river and we fired over their heads with our revolvers just to see them run.

At the sight of these, the Texan's eyes glistened for an instant.

"Mustangs!" he said, "I've heard this country was full of 'em. Man, how I'd like to be among'st 'em with a rope."

At dusk we came to the home draw and as darkness was settling, we pulled our wagons up to the sod corral. Tom greeted us from the kitchen door where the family had been awaiting our arrival. Upon learning we had brought fresh meat, Tom and the boys were out in a hurry to help and to hinder. After unhitching and turning the stock in the corral, we quickly improvised a pole, supported on one end by the sod roof and the other by a pair of crossed poles, set "A" fashion. On this we hung the buffalo meat.

Then we pulled the surprise. Bid clambered to the top of his load and stepped to the ground with the buffalo calf in his arms. He was instantly surrounded by the Powers family and beseiged by a barrage of questions. He laid the still hog-tied calf on the ground and threw up his hands in mock horror.

"Whoa now, just a minute heah afore I answer all them questions. We need a place to put this feller as he's had a right hawd day. Now, as soon as me and Caroliny get them chains loose from this pile of poles, we'll set up a little pen yonder agin thet sod corral." With the eager help of the boys from Sid on down, we quickly criss-crossed poles into a small triangular pen and turned the young buffalo loose inside it.

By then we had answered a few of their questions and things had quieted down somewhat. Mamie and the girl came out and it was all to be told over again. For Bid, this was a little disconcerting, as he was the type who, when he did talk was inclined to be deliberate and take one subject at a time. So this left me with the balance of the explaining to do. In time, I was about to catch up when someone suggested the poor little orphan ought to be named. Names flew thick and fast for a while, but the kids just couldn't seem to agree and tempers were beginning to flare, when Tom put a stop to it.

"Now lookie here, if you young'uns cain't get along we'll just let Caroliny and Bid name him. After all, they was the ones that catch't him."

I looked at Bid and he looked back, then again I looked at him.

Bid found his voice. "Well," he drawled in his best manner, I would surmise, the way this fellow done run from this here pursuing force from the fair and sovereign state of North Caroliny, thet 'Bull Run' would be a right proper name for him."

And so it was, the buffalo calf was christened Bull Run.

Mamie called supper and we needed no second urging to wash up and gather around the table. The family, still curious as to what had happened on our trip, continued to fire questions. I took my cue from the Texan, we admitted it had been a pretty uneventful excursion, "cut a couple loads of poles, butchered out a buffalo and nothin' much happened a'tall."

CHAPTER III
Living It Up

The next day was Sunday but it was no day of rest for us at the Power's soddy, at least until the buffalo meat was taken care of. It was decided to make jerky by the process of smoking and drying. We were fortunate in having a supply of firewood as the original builders of the place had hauled a large wagon-load of elm and hackberry from Sawlog Creek, several miles north.* Racks were built next to the outside wall of the soddy from some of our green poles. Then the meat was cut in long thin strips, salted and spread evenly over the racks, with a slow smoky fire going for twenty-four hours or more. Both Tom and his spouse were adept at this work and their finished product was better tasting and more sanitary than ordinary sun-dried jerky.

By noon, we finished cutting the meat and had trimmed the woodpile of branches and smaller pieces, for the slow fires which were lighted and fed carefully until they were going to Mamie's 'particular satisfaction'. Finally, the strips of buffalo beef were spread over the racks soaking up wood smoke. Tom then took charge, armed with a pitchfork to turn the strips if and when needed to suit his 'particular satisfaction' until everything was deemed to be in ship-shape order for the long smoking and drying process.

Thus, it was a little later than usual when we dined, but we fared well on roast hump, after it had been appropriately and piously blessed by Tom who was at his Sunday Best. Following the meal, we adults sat around the table a little longer than usual in respect for the sabbath, and feeling a real but unvoiced thankfulness for our providential blessings.

Later, the afternoon turned quite warm. Bid and I stirred ourselves from the shade of the corral, saddled our horses and hitched Sid's team to the wagon with the cart hooked behind, and prepared for our daily trip to the river. Today we took along a bar of soap and a clean change of clothing. After the stock were watered and turned loose to graze for a spell, and the water was loaded, we shucked our clothing and jumped into the cold

* References: R. M. Wright; Kansas Historical Quarterlies; and many others. According to all references the Sawlog was well blessed with timber of several varieties in the early days of Fort Dodge.

water of the stream. To say the water was fine wouldn't be a proper discription, but it was fresh and invigorating, to say the least. If one kept all but his head submerged and threshed around vigorously enough on the sand bottom, he could bear it and that was about all. Needless-to-say, it didn't take long to convince us that we were properly cleansed; so we got out and chased one another up and down the grassy meadow, clad only in our birthday attire. Tiring of this rather suddenly after stepping on a few sharp sticks, burrs, gravel, and so forth we dried ourselves as best we could with clean gunnysacks and donned fresh clothing for another week in the wild.

On the way back we started Sid on ahead with the water wagon and followed leisurely behind with the stock, allowing them to graze as we went along.

Bid had one of his rare, reminiscent moods. Suddenly, out of nowhere he spoke of Tom's "Sunday" religion.

"You know," he said, "Mister Powers reminds me considerable of my own paw. I can recollect when the 'Old Gentleman' would spend the whole week a'cussin' and a'swearin', schemin', swappin, tradin, and dealin' with the best of 'em. And come Sattidy afternoon he was sure to be right in the thick of the hawse racin' and Sattidy night, he would sometimes be a settin' at cards with a bottle at his elbow til' mid night. But Sunday mawnin' at services time, the 'Old Gentleman' would be at the haid of the line in collar, necktie, and his best clothes with a Bible under his arm." He paused and looked at me as if he expected my opinion.

"Well," I said, for want of something better to say, "at least he was setting a good example on Sunday, same as Tom always does."

"Yeah, but it appears to me a man with a family to raise, and a "example" to set, be he so almighty pious and God-fearin' on Sunday, ought to spread a little of it over the week days too."

I was surprised at the Texan's moral tone, but I had learned before that his character was more than surface deep. While I couldn't help but agree with his sentiments, I went on loyally, "If you're referring to Tom, I think he pretty well lives up to

201

his beliefs and sets a tolerable fair example for his family outside of when he loses his temper and raises old Ned.

"I wasn't referring to Tom," Bid drawled firmly, "I was thinkin' about the example thet was set for me and my brothers and sisters. Ain't much wonder we grew up such a wilful haidstrong and hell-raisin' outfit."

I had known Bid intimately the last two weeks; much of the time we had been together, yet all I knew of his family life was that his father had died as a result of an accident a year ago and that he had a number of brothers and sisters.

I thought now is the time to satisfy some of my curiosity, so I started out subtly, "Bid, I can't imagine your family being strictly a bunch of headstrong, hellraisers. I would guess them to be just the opposite."

"Well—-I reckon we got our share of decency and dignity, too, though sometimes it ain't right apparent. But 'right now', Caroliny, we better get these hawdtail sonsabitches to movin' or Miz Powers'll be waitin' supper on us."

The next week our time at the ranche was spent in making various improvements, most of them necessary to the liveability of the place. Besides these jobs, the regular daily chores like watering the stock had to be taken care of. Bid and I often managed to make sort of a lark out of this chore. We were usually glad to drop our tools and mount our horses to drive the stock to water, this generally consuming a couple of hours at the close of the day. Tom was nearly always pretty well "tuckered" following his plow by four-thirty in the afternoon. So by the time he had unharnessed his team and allowed them to roll and rest a bit, Bid and I would be mounted and ready for the trek to the river. We usually made the drive down to water at a pretty good clip, as the "remuda" as the Texan liked to call them, had done nothing all day but graze, and were rarin' to go. The tired work team and the cattle could be depended upon to follow, but at a more leisurely pace. Of course, on these daily chores, we always kept on the lookout for Indians, but once at the river we relaxed a little and let the stock take their time while we lay in the grass or lolled in our saddles taking it easy. On the return trip, unless there were reasons otherwise, we set a fairly slow pace, as our only concern was to get them in and corraled or hobbled before complete darkness set in. At the Powers" domicile, it was regular custom to eat supper by lamplight; by the same token we usually ate by lamplight in the morning.

I remember on one of these trips to the river this second week, we saw a herd of antelope upstream about a half mile. We left our horses and reconoitered on foot and belly and slipped up on them from down-wind. We separated and I, being smaller, was able to find better cover. I was anxious to get the first shot, as Bid thought he had quite a "hawse on me", referring to to the buffalo calf episode; and I was determined to even the score one way or another. As I crawled within a hundred and fifty paces of the herd, I glanced around for Bid and saw he had reached an "impasse". He had taken a route further from the river than I and gotten in short grass where it was necessary for him to crawl on his belly. But it appeared he was as anxious to get in range first as I, for he had tightened his gun belt and swung his six-gun around behind him to get it out of the way. I could see the glint of the hammer and breech about his rump every time he hunched forward. But Bid was an active man and was making a good stalk in spite of his lack of cover. Though by now I was so sure of my advantage that I was laughing to myself at the sporadic glimpses I caught of his nether regions bobbing up and down, I had no time to linger and enjoy his maneuverings as in easy rifle range of a clump of willows which grew next to the river fifty yards in front of me, the antelope grazed, completely unware of their danger. From behind the cover of the willows, I arose and bending low, I ran quietly forward and knelt at their edge. Peering through the branches, I could see the herd still grazing. I picked out a nice one broadside to me, quietly levered in a shell and down went the antelope. I rose to my feet and dropped another on the dead run and the whole herd was gone in a flurry of legs and a flash of flags.

The Texan came up out of the grass and approached me with a look of good-natured disgust. "Hell, Caroliny, you might as well'a got a mess whils't yo'all was about it."

That evening we pushed the "remuda" home at a faster gait than usual, for we both longed for fresh antelope steaks. When

203

we came in sight of the soddy we were astonished to see four strange horses picketed out on the slope above the house. On coming closer we observed four men in uniform, in conversation with Tom and draped in various poses over the pole fence.

"Well, I'll be damned," said Bid, "I figured thet was jist some more of thet old army bull when the sergeant back there at the Post said they wuld be droppin' in on us. I sure as Hell never expected to see none of them boys in blue around heah, come Injuns or high-water."

We rode in, corraled our stock and unloaded the antelope and found the boys in blue were, indeed, a small patrol from Fort Dodge on a scouting mission and led by none other than the young Lieutenant we had met at the Fort. In contrast to their first meeting, he and Tom were getting along famously. He was telling Tom they had just come from the Sawlog, north of us and had seen no fresh signs of Indians and in his opinion, which he expressed quite assuredly, there were none in our area along the Arkansas. "And I am confident there are no concentrations of hostiles along the Mulberry nor in the canyon country south of there."

Of course, Tom was pleased to hear such optimistic reports, but Bid and I, though hopeful, were quietly skeptical. Too many times in our daily treks to the river we observed distant smokes in the south and southwest that bespoke of Indians and their smoke signals. The Lieutenant went on to say the Indians were scattered along the river above the Fort and on above the Cimarron Crossings and were rumored to be along the brakes of the Upper Buckner and Pawnee,* well to the north and northwest of us.

Bid and I, with Sid's willing assistance soon had the two antelope dressed and hanging from a pole where we cut choice steaks for Mamie. Shortly after dark, we, along with the four soldiers, were treated to a fine frontier meal. The Lieutenant and his men were loud in their praises of Tom's hospitality and Mamie's fine cooking, and those two were so pleased that they outdid themselves as host and hostess, with the result that every-

---

* The Pawnee, a fine prairie stream that starts northwest of the Cimarron Crossings and joins the Arkansas near Fort Larned. The Buckner a branch of the Pawnee.

body unbent a little and before the evening was over, even the Lieutenant and Bid were conversing on common ground. I looked up from where I had been discussing the battle of Five Forks with the Lieutenant and was surprised to see a big, bearded trooper, with one of the small Powers boys on each knee, telling them big cock and bull tales of chasing Injuns across the prairies. His stories were colored to fit the minds of the listeners, but in spite of that, I found myself absorbed in what he was saying, for now he had switched from Injuns to wild horses. He told of a magnificent black horse, the leader of a wild horse band, that ran in these parts and south of the Arkansas. According to the story teller, no white man but himself had ever beheld this marvelous animal at close range. But the Injuns had chased him for days at a time and only succeeded on running their horses down. The Kiowas, in particular, had worn out so many of their own animals in fruitless efforts to catch him that they no longer tried to run him down, hoping now to entice him in some kind of trap.

As the trooper embelished on his tall tale, I noticed Bid, too, was listening and the Lieutenant was grinning with a wry expression on his face. "How about this Lieutenant," I asked, sensing something deeper, "what do you know about this wonderful horse?"

"Oh, Corporal Driscol is apt to get carried away when he gets on the subject of that horse. Indeed there is quite a legend being built up about "Old Nigger Horse" as he is sometimes called, particularly among the Indians and some of my men too, I'm afraid."

I saw the cautious look of interest in Bid's eyes. "Is there really such a horse, Lieutenant?" I asked. "Or are you fellows just pulling our legs?"

"Oh, there's such a horse alright, or if there isn't some of our fellows have certainly been fooled. But the wild horse business is a fascinating subject for some men and in an untamed country such as this, where mustangs are exceeded only by the buffalo in numbers, there's bound to be some fine animals and incidently, some exaggerated stories to go with them."

CHAPTER IV

Playing Second Fiddle

The next day Tom and Mamie took advantage of the military escort and drove into the Fort for a day of shopping and catching up on the news. We sent one of the dressed antelope along to dispose as they saw fit, as usually any kind of fresh meat was appreciated around the military posts. Bid and I left in charge of the ranche (and the boys), decided to start work on a lean-to addition to the west side of the sod-house. Already this week, we had finished the pole part of the corral and the hay-roofed shed (or barn) and now we looked forward to utilizing Tom's rough lumber to make things more convenient around our somewhat primitive abode. The extra space was needed for storage as well as for sleeping quarters for Bid and myself and for any other of those occasional wayfarers of this unsettled land, who might expect shelter under a christian roof. Though Bid and I were toughened to sleeping in wagons, on the ground or what have you, we were by no means adverse to having a roof over our heads, especially during those spells of bad weather that can move in suddenly across the broad plains. We checked our lumber inventory and found we had more than enough rough Colorado Pine 1x12's for the three walls of a room ten by fifteen. We found we were a little short of 2x4's and dimension stuff, but that was in a day when one made out with what he had, so we figured we could trim up some cottonwood poles with hatchet and drawknife and get by very well. We knew nails would have to be used sparingly until Tom got back as he had vowed to beg, borrow or steal enough to complete the job. About all the carpenter or wood working tools Tom possessed was hammer, rasp, brace and augers, drawknife, hatchet, and saw, all of the latter exceedingly dull. But we found a good file and Bid went to work manfully on the saw, and I applied myself to the grindstone sharpening the other tools. Bid was a handy fellow with tools and when there wasn't any riding or roping to do, he rather enjoyed it. I had always liked to putter around with saw and hammer and was looking forward to my part in the venture.

We eventually got our tools in good shape, then we selected the best of the poles and trimmed them with hatchet and drawknife until they were fairly true. This accomplished, we were ready to lay out the dimensions, when we remembered we were without a carpenter's square or any other means of accurate measurement. Bid was going ahead by sighting through as best we could. But I happened to remember an old math or geometry rule about the square of the hypotenuse of a right angle triangle being equal to the square of the other two sides and I told him we could rig up a square out of some straight lath Tom had in one of the wagons. Bid was mildly skepticial and said so, which only urged me to greater effort. I found a long nail and laid my lath out on the smooth floor of the wagon bed and measured eight lengths of the nail on one side of a triangle and six on the other, then ten for the hypotenuse and came up with a perfect right angle triangle. I tacked the lath together carefully with some small nails and looked at my pardner with self-satisfaction.

"Well, I'll be damned," Bid said at my elbow, "yo'all done thet with a triangle."

My ego swelled a little in spite of myself, but I assumed an air of modesty. "There's nothing to it at all, Bid, if you know the theorem or rule. Anybody who can add two and two together and get four can do the same," and I explained the theorem to him briefly.

"Well, it sure does beat all what a man can do with angles and figures if he knows how to use 'em. I worked for an engineer fellah once't down theh in Texas, a layin' off lines. And he got to tellin' me about triangulation. Know anythin' about triangulation, Caroliny?"

I had to admit that I knew little of the science of surveying at all, particularly triangulation. I said, "I've heard of it and that's about all."

"Well, sir," I would certainly admire to know all thet engineer knowed about thet "science". It seems there was this Virginian, a Dr. Claybourne, who really developed the system of triangulation, so's he told me. It seems this Dr. Claybourne learned the surveyin' trade when he was a boy carrying a chain for old George Washington hisself. Later on, he came into a big inheritance and went to England, and traveled all over Europe and got hisself a strictly high class edication with all the trimmin's. As a matter of fact, he developed into a regulah damn genius and when he came back to Virginny, he done had a Doctor's degree in medicine and surgery and brought with him one of them Stradivarious vi-o-lins and an ear for opery music to go with it; and besides all thet, he was a he-wolf at math and all them theorems and such. Then he writ this textbook on triangulation thet all surveyors use today, so I was told by this heah engineer. Ever read of Dr. Claybourne, Caroliny?"

I was thinking more of the job at hand and wasn't as alert as usual, besides the name struck some chord of memory and I admitted that some way the Claybourne name was familiar.

"Yes, sir, I'll bet yo'all have. Tain't likely now adays thet many fellahs with college edication but what has heard of Dr. Claybourne. My folks come from Virginny and for thet reason, I reckon I took an interest in this Gazabo from the start. So last fall when I went to Chicago in the cars with them steers from Abilene and worked for Mr. McCoy in the yards there for a spell, I run across't a story about him in one of them Harper's magazines. It sho' was a powerful story. 'Course, I reckon not more'n half true, like them newspaper fellers usually write. But it t'was mighty interesting and I set right down and read her from beginning to end and what an "ending it had", 'though I 'spose it was mostly pure fabrication."

By now the whole story was beginning to sound like one of Bid's tricks, as he was monopolizing the conversation, which wasn't the rule for him. So I decided to give him no encouragement. Besides, I was a little piqued that he would go on and on with this story, when there was so much about himself that I would have much preferred to hear. After all, during the last few weeks we had become the best of friends, yet about all I knew of him was his name and where he came from; and he was even a little indefinite about the latter as Texas covered considerable territory. But Bid appeared not to notice my lack of interest and after a short pause, while he sawed the end off a board, continued with his story.

"Well sir, after comin' back to Virginny with a Doctor's degree and all thet European culture, you would've thought he would settle down, hang out his shingle and start carin' for the sick and unfo'tunate. But there appeared to bo no record thet he ever had much of a practice as a doctor a'tall, preferrin', instead, the transit and note book of his surveyin' days. 'Course, along this line he finally developed the art of measuring by triangulation better'n ary man before him ever had. Then he wrote a passel of books about surveyin', fiddleplayin' and one thing and t'other. So the story goes, his life went on like this 'til he was a man of forty years or older and had never married. Along about then. there was a fine lookin' young widow in the neighborhood and the doctor done took a fancy to her right off. She really must've been somethin' cause he had never took a second look at ary females before in his life. 'Course, the upshot of the whole thing is they wound up a'marryin'."

Bid paused now and favored me with a half grin. "Naturally, yo'all know these writer fellahs got to have a woman and some romance. According to this writer, they got along fine. Claybourne, naturally, as any man with a woman like thet would, and she, because he lavished her with attentions and had all thet wealth with a big house and servants and such. But as time went on, he relapsed into his old interests with transit and notebook. Whil'st still thinkin' the world and all of his young wife, he started agin on his Goddamned experiments and studies and spent most of his time up in the hills with his instruments and papers. About thet time he started workin' on his "Theory of Relativity": thet is the famous 'Claybourne Theory'."

Now the Texan paused long enough to take the board I had just marked with my improvised square and I noticed a look of honest skepticism on his face. "Thet part is mostly a big yarn, I reckon, probably cooked up by this writer to make a big story. But anyway, about this time something happened thet shows what a genius Dr. Claybourne really was. It seems the Doctor had a nephew thet had carried the rod and chain for him for years; the Doctor havin' taken him as an apprentice aiming to teach him the surveyor's trade. But said nephew turned out to be a triflin' sort; not mean, mind you, but no will to git ahaid, and a weakness for cards and likker and unprincipled women, too, I reckon. But he did stick to his job well enough thet the doctor come to depend on him when he was out with his transit and

209

theod-o-lite, which was most of the time in summer. In winter, the nephew was turned loose to his own devices; the old gentleman always payin' him a small sum to get him through 'til grass come. For 'though the doctor was generous to a fault in most ways, he was a trifle stingy with his wages, usually payin' the nephew little more'n a pittance when he was a'workin'. Anyway, come spring about a month after the doctor's marriage, and him already a yearnin' for the outdoors and his surveyin' instruments, he brung the nephew to his big fancy place and let him lay around a few days, a'soberin' up. But the young man didn't respond as usual, havin' lost two front teeth in a brawl over some trollop, I reckon; and he was right despondent over what the loss of them teeth would do to his looks, as he was a vain sort of a fellar. So Doc Claybourne sets down and puts his genius to work and pretty soon comes up with a pair of gold teeth for his nephew. Whereupon, nephew was so doggoned pleased that he promised his uncle to stick with him to the "end".

By now, I was convinced that Bid was without guile in telling his longwinded tale. I suppose the story fascinated him because it was of a setting and way of life so different from his own, which had been spent largely near the frontier. He was, in fact, I realized then, little more than a backwoodsman as far as knowledge of the outside world was concerned. So; secure in my own superior education and eastern culture, I allowed myself a condescending smile, without comment. But frankly I was a little amazed at the knowing manner in which he spoke of technical things, which I had supposed he had never heard. Although you could tell he relished the sound of the unfamiliar words as he drawled them out with special emphasis.

Yet, all the while he told his story, he never missed a nail or relaxed his vigilance of the countryside. For example, the two young Powers boys had climbed the sod wall to the new shed roof and were busily engaged in jumping up and down on the springy hay, and brush cover, having the time of their lives. Bid noticed them sooner than I.

"Them ornery little devils! Heah! Yo'all git down from thet roof," he rebuked them gently but firmly, "now me and Caroliny don't wanta ketch you boys on thet barn again—savvy?"

The boys clambered quickly down and scampered out of sight with red faces and we didn't have to call them down again. Bid looked at me with a grin and resumed his story.

"So t'was back to the hills for the doctor. He would set his instruments up high on the hill above the big house, early in the mawnin' an likely be there all day, a sightin' and figurin' and a jottin' down notes. Whil'st the nephew would be down by the place with flag and rod awaitin' his uncle's signals. They had worked together for so long, they had worked out a system of talkin' back and forth by hand signals and when the doctor was busy with his calculations, mebee it would be two or three hours between sightings which just suited thet triflin' nephew to a tee. Sometimes he would lay down and take a nap or slip around to the back door and talk the cook out of a nip of his uncle's favorite brandy and flirt a bit with the chambermaid, or even try to get on a better footin' with the widder herself, if he got half a chance. But he knowed he was always to be alert for a signal from the hill. Thet is the way the 'Claybourne Theory' was born—the doctor takin' his sightin's at the house and the heavens with his instruments and a lookin' at the sky through his high-powered glass, then aworkin' out his problems and theorems on paper. All of which bein' way over my haid, of course, and I reckon thet of the story writer too. But anyway, this was how it was all worked out and in the end he had figured out his complicated theory."

By now, Sid, who was supposed to be herding stock on the slope north of the house, rode in on the gentle old mule, where he dismounted and stood with gaping mouth listening to the story. Curiosity, a Powers family weakness, got the better of him. "Is that the end?" he inquired with disappointment.

"Just keep your shirt on," said Bid soothingly, "I'm a'gettin' to thet directly—. Now whil'st the doctor was enjoying hisself a workin' long hours at his confounded theory, his new wife felt herself neglected. Cause by the time he got in of a night, he would be so downright tuckered he would just eat a little bit for supper and set around and play his Stradivarious for a spell, then go right off to his side of the bed without ary a thought of any tom-foolishness——.

"What d'ya mean?" Sid interrupted again, giggling with curious impatience.

Bid looked at him with disgust. "Them mules yondeh," he drawled pointedly, "are liable to stray off directly if yo'all don't look after 'em."

Sid had been told emphatically by his father to not leave the stock for a minute, until he was relieved for dinner by Bid or I. Well, knowing that is where he belonged, he regretfully climbed aboard his gentle old mule and returned to his duties.

"Now, as I was sayin'," Bid resumed, "the widder, bein' a woman, expected all thet lovin' and caressin' she had got used to when they was first hitched, and she naturally felt now that she was aplayin' second fiddle to the damn Stradivarious. But she stayed right in the harness and went out of her way to wait on her husband hand and foot. Every night she would be a waitin' in her fanciest low-cut night gown, with a bowl of hot soup and a glass of brandy. But it didn't appear to do no good for the doctor was done past his prime and no amount of tantalizin' could seem to rejuvinate his vitality. So, usually no sooner'n he'd et his bite and sawed out a few tender tunes on thet fancy fiddle, then he was off in the arms of "Morpheus" aleavin' his young wife afeelin' as lonesome as a hawse thief at a necktie party. I reckon this went on most of thet summer, her a hopin' and contrivin' to get his mind off them tarnation instruments and studies, 'til finally the good doctor got to havin' other troubles. He had reached the point in his calculations where it required more and more carefulness in his observations on the hill. Sometimes he would go hours between signals to his nephew; in time thet feller got so lazy, or he was off 'fiddlin' around some'eres else'. thet he wouldn't even respond to his uncle's signals. Now this really upset the older man and he gave the nephew such a chewin' about it, thet the young fellah got mad and said he would just quit; as the pay he got didn't amount to a hill of beans nohow.— It sho' looked like the 'aind'."

I was interested in spite of myself. "But, if I am any judge of your story telling, Bid, I take it, it isn't the end."

"Well, sir, you take it correctly, then," he grinned. "In spite of all the troubles he was havin' the doctor wasn't about to give up his work, 'cause by now it meant too much to him. So he got one of his darkey boys and started trainin' him to take his nephew's place. In the meantime, the nephew went back to his old ways, a hangin' around the taverns. But things didn't go too well for the doctor either, as his darkey boy couldn't read and write nor count too well; and a'course this threw more burden on the doctor hisself, who became more and more let down. One night he came in from work, had his meal, and was just settlin' down with his Stradivarious, when a messenger came tellin' him thet his nephew was turrible sick with belly pains and appeared about to cash in his chips. As the nephew was his only sister's boy, the doctor had them bring him to his house, where he determined right quick thet the trouble was in the appendix, brought on, I reckon, by riotous livin'. Well, the doctor saw right off the only chance the man had was for him to operate and the nephew bein' in so much pain, he figgered he was a gonner nohow, so's he told him to go ahaid. So Doc called a couple of his black boys in to hold the patient in bed and then he got his scalpel, or whatever you call it, and made a slit in the nephew's belly and snipped that little old appendix off. Then he sacrificed some of the strings of his beloved vi-o-lin and sewed the feller up neat as a seamstress. Strange to say, in a few days the nephew was up and about and he was so grateful he promised the doctor to stay with him 'til the end. According to the story thet was the first successful appendix operation. And even today it's considered pretty risky business to tamper with a man's innards thet away, which just goes to show what a genius Dr. Claybourne was. But in the end, the doctor and his nephew went back to work with more teamwork than ever and in time the job was finished and "Claybourne's Theory" was a real thing."

The Texan brought his story to an end with the proper ring to his voice; and with a little sigh of finality reached in his breast pocket for his tobacco.

"You don't mean," I said increduously, "that is the end?" Before the words were out of my mouth, I knew I had stumbled. I saw the little half-shadow of a grin on his face. But it was too late to take back my words.

"No, Caroliny, not until after the widder's first born came.

The doctor delivered the young gentleman 'hisself'; and when he arrived, he had two gold teeth and fiddle strings on his belly, and thet was the 'aind'."

By the time Tom, Mamie and Mary drove in from the Fort, we had the frame work of the leanto about completed and several of the rough 1x12's nailed on for siding. But it was then time to drive the stock to water and we had to leave our work until the next day.

Tom brought with him the news that numerous Indians were camped along the river above the Fort and that it was common talk there were more along the streams to the north. There were rumors of trouble in the area but so far as he could see, everything seemed to be under control at the Fort. I suspect to some extent Tom was talking what he wanted to believe and was being careful not to say anything that might alarm Mamie. A detail of four men had encorted them on their way home until they were in sight of the soddy. Bid and I were in agreement that the Indian situation must be worse than Tom talked or the Post Commander wouldn't have given them an escort.

On the more pleasant side, Tom had been able to make some needed purchases that would make life a little easier at the ranche. For example, he had been able to buy some wooden barrels, two of these being of the large hogshead size. This would enable us in case of necessity to water the stock at home for perhaps one day. As now we had barrels and casks enough to transport four hundred gallons on one trip to the river. Tom admitted getting these barrels hadn't been easy, but that a little bribe of fresh antelope had helped. He had given the rest of the antelope away too, but in a way to do us most good. In the line of groceries, Mamie had purchased flour, corn meal, coffee and a little sugar and last but not least, some cheese and a long stick of bologna sausage. After a pretty steady diet of pork and buffalo jerky it was surprising how welcome these store products were.

The next day, while Bid and I worked on the lean-to, Tom and Mamie had the whole family out in the freshly prepared plot in front of the house planting the garden. The garden patch, perhaps over half an acre in area, had been harrowed and dragged since plowing, and now was as smooth and level as a floor. Row after row of potatoes were planted, mostly from the peelings saved from cooking. A similar amount of onions were planted from sets brought from Missouri; and from seed, radishes, turnips, carrots, lettuce and peas were planted in smaller quantities to be followed later in the spring with cucumbers, beans, squash, and melons. Tomatoes and cabbage now growing in boxes would be added when these became large enough to transplant. In fact, almost anything in the vegetable line that had grown well in Missouri, Tom and Mamie had the seed and the optimism to try in the buffalo grass soil of Western Kansas.

On the next day, Bid and I finished the lean-to, complete with one canvas covered window and a real swinging door with leather hinges fashioned from an old harness tug. Upon completion we carefully smoothed and swept out the dirt floor and constructed us each a bunk about three and a half feet wide in opposite corners of the south wall, one on each side of the door which was located in the center of that wall. These bunks were simply wide boards set on edge on the dirt floor and cleated together at right angles and thence to the walls. On our trip for water that evening we took along an extra wagon and brought it back piled with last year's meadow grass which we had cut with Tom's scythe. We stuffed our boxlike bunks with this and spread bedrolls on top; and for the first time since leaving Abilene we slept under a roof. And it couldn't have happened at a better time. At bedtime it commenced raining; all night long and most of the next day, it kept up a slow drizzle. We spend most of that day inside, going out only long enough at noon to feed the stock of our dwindling supply of sacked oats. As Bid and I sloshed among the dejected animals, separating them so that each could get their fair share of oats, Tom joined us in his shirt sleeves, ignoring the cold drizzle and rubbing his hands with satisfaction. "I tell you, boys, this is jist what we need. I told the woman yestiddy when we was plantin' that blame garden that we sure needed a good rain and this will bring the grass too. Won't have to worry 'cause we're runnin' out of grain, fer long. Might even plant some corn afore long, too, after this spell lets up."

With Tom's help we moved the gear and supplies, including the grain and seed corn, from the wagon where they had been stored to our new abode in the dry. There, after dinner, Bid and I settled down to let it rain. I dug out a pencil and paper from my belongings and started a long letter to my folks in Carolina. Seeing me occupied in this way, reminded Bid of a long tardy duty. "Yo'all got some more of thet paper, have you, Caroliny? I reckon I ought to pencil a few lines to the homefolks as I ain't writ since I left Chicago, the first of last Novembeh."

I took the liberty to chide him a little for this. "Bid, don't you think your folks would appreciate hearing from you oftener? Take your mother, now, don't you suppose she worries when she doesn't hear from you only once in a blue moon? Don't you ever get a little homesick?"

"Hell no," he said, "I was never homesick but twic't in my life. Onc't when my folks sent me off to school in Austin when I was fifteen years old and when I went in the war in '63! But I surmise yo're right, I should write oftener than I do."

We finished our letters and still the rain continued, so Bid dug out a tattered deck of cards from his gear and we spent most of the afternoon with Bid teaching me some of the finer points of poker. We played for modest stakes and I wound up losing twenty-five cents. The game finally broke up when Sid interrupted us with his presence and insisted on sticking around displaying too much interest to suit me, as well as Bid, who before long scooped up the cards and addressed the youth bluntly "Sid, if yo'all wants to learn cards, you will have to get someone besides me to teach you, as I don't aim to have your maw mad at me for teachin' you my sinful ways."

The rain came to an end that night and for the next few days we had fine spring weather. The waterholes in the draw had been replenished and the stock water problems were solved for a few days at least. For the first time since coming to the Sod Ranche we had idle time on our hands.

CHAPTER V

On the Trail of the Nigger Horse

The wonder and excitement of spring was too much for Bid and I. Although we well knew the risks involved, we planned a scout or exploratory jaunt south of the river. On Sunday morning we packed a lunch, with canteen and coffee pot, and left at daybreak. We started following the route of our pole hauling trip, planning to go to the mouth of Mulberry Creek* near where we had been told was one of the old crossings to the "Famous Dry Route". But on coming in sight of the Timbers of our previous visit, we saw two or three light wisps of smoke that appeared to come from the other side of the trees and suggested very strongly the presence of campfires. We had no desire for company, especially when they were likely to be red, so we promptly pulled off the trace of the trail and rode back upstream this time near the river where there was some scant cover. After about a mile in this direction we found a shallow appearing place and urged our ponies in the stream; but even here the water was, in places, belly deep to our mounts and we had to take our feet out of the stirrups and hold our rifles in our hands to keep them from getting wet. Although the river was probably over three hundred feet wide here, it proved to have a solid bottom and we crossed without trouble.

From the crossing we moved south bearing a little to the east and in time was out of the flat valley of the Arkansas and in a few miles came to a little creek. At this place we disturbed a pair of fat, white-tailed deer that bounded down the creek and disappeared in the brush and cover that grew along the bank. They gave us a little thrill, but we made no effort to shoot them as we were not after meat at that early hour. Besides, the possibility of an Indian camp on the river to the north had warned us well of the need for caution in this immediate area. Continuing on, we were soon on the divide between the creeks which were open flatlands, gradually becoming more rolling as we moved south. And eventually we started down a draw which in

---

* Mulberry Creek flows into the Arkansas on the south side several miles below Ft. Dodge.

time led to the Mulberry. This creek flowed a little trickle of clear water between deep ponds or pools and, interestingly, there was timber along its banks. Some of it already showed the ravages of civilized man as axe-hewn stumps were to be seen, a few of them blackened with age.

We crossed where the water was only inches deep and lurched our ponies up the bank and continued in a southerly way following an old buffalo trail and soon we were once again on the open flats. We stopped at the top of a slight rise and scanned the whole area about us, first with the naked eye and then with the field glasses. Not a living object was in sight, only an occasional soapweed or tall clump of grass broke the monotony of the slightly rolling plain. Far to the south through a faint haze, appeared to be the outlines of rougher country. We continued in a trot in that direction, both of us feeling a sense of disappointment that we had seen no more wildlife, as ordinarily we had to ride but a few miles to see antelope or buffalo. But this morning, outside of the two deer, we had seen nothing more exciting than a few jackrabbits. Of course, game was not our particular object this morning; we were hoping to locate a band of wild horses. At least, that was uppermost in the Texan's mind. Me, I was thrilled to be along just for the ride, but there was no question that the soldiers' tales of the black stallion had fascinated us both more than we would admit.

After nearly another hour's ride, we spied a dark ragged line to our right, which on examination proved to be an immense herd of buffalo. We stayed well clear of them, missing the fringes of the herd by over half a mile. Soon after, we started the descent of a grassy valley, taking care to scan the country ahead of us, not knowing what to expect. We drew up quickly when we saw a band of horses grazing on the flat less than half a mile away.

"Thet's the same bunch we saw nawth of the river t'other day," Bid said positively after looking at them through the glasses.

"How can you tell that?" I asked.

"Hell, you'd never see two paint hawses thet near alike in different herds," he said, calling my attention to spotted ponies

218

that grazed on opposite sides of the herd, "what bothers me now is what to do about 'em. It's a daid cinch we can't run 'em down with our own hawses half jaded already."

"You're not speaking of my horse," I said half seriously, "why, old Blaze here isn't half warmed up."

"By Gawd, he is right perky yet, ain't he," Bid acknowledged grudgingly, "course, he ain't carrying no load, with thet Yankee contraption of straps and buckles yo'all call a saddle."

We cautiously dismounted and carefully led our horses back a little way from the edge of the declivity, the animals below not having noticed us yet. I suggested that Bid lighten the load for his horse by transferring his rifle and canteen to mine. This we did immediately, as we both knew the only chance we had to capture one of the mustangs was for Bid to get close enough to use his rope. Even then he warned me, "this is likely gonna be a wild goose chase and I reckon we're a pair of damn fools for even tryin', but I didn't ride this far just to pick mawnin' glories."

Actually, both our horses were in good shape, although we had probably already ridden nearly twenty miles. We decided our best plan would be to circle the herd and try to turn them if we could, back into the brakes of the Mulberry. But it didn't work out that way, as we no sooner showed ourselves than the entire bunch left in a dead run and headed due south. We followed at a careful gait, keeping out of sight as much as possible in hopes they would stop in a draw of some sort where we could come up on them unseen. In a way, our strategy worked after we had dropped a mile or more behind, for the herd came abruptly to a halt. We could see the leaders and a few of the more frisky ones kicking up their heels and putting on quite a little show, while the main herd circled and became more or less stationary. As soon as they stopped, we drew to a walk and approached very slowly, at times even stopping altogether. But when we came within a few hundred yards, they took off again only not as fast as before. This time we only tried to keep them in sight and after running about a mile they stopped near a small buffalo wallow about half full of clear water. We pulled up behind some scattering soapweeds half a mile away, where Bid leisurely dismounted, removed the saddle and blanket and bridle from his horse and turned him loose to graze. I followed suit, tethering Blaze with a light rope I carried, and sat down in the grass beside Bid to await the next development.

"Might s well set down and take it easy for a spell. I gotta hunch if we don't crowd 'em, they'll fill up from thet water hole yonder."

Any hopes we may have had that they would gorge themselves with water were soon dispelled. Although most of the herd drank, it was plain to see they were not driven by any great thirst and after a short time they strung out behind the leaders and trotted away. We got our mounts ready and soon were trailing patiently along behind. We had gradually been working into slightly rougher country, some of the draws we crossed now becoming quite deep. But the herd ahead of us seemed to prefer the more open prairie and they eventually came out on a flat level stretch. Here they came to a stop, but apparently assuring themselves they were still being pursued, they moved on; when suddenly the lead horses commenced dropping out of sight and in just a little while the herd was completely swallowed up in the plain. We urged our horses on at a faster trot and soon came to where the prairie ended spectacularly in a steep precipice. We approached the edge and looked down in a beautiful valley with a little creek meandering lazily in the bottom that was covered with heavy grass and dotted here and there with scattered trees. We were both so surprised at the sudden change of scenery, we forgot the mustangs for a minute. Whether this was the headwaters of the Rattlesnake, or more probably a tributary of Bluff Creek, of the Cimarron, we could only guess, as we had become so absorbed in following the wild horses we had failed to keep a clear sense of direction.

I commented on the wonder of the place and the Texan agreed. "What a place for a cow ranch," he allowed.

At first, we couldn't locate the horse herd and then we saw them spread out grazing, apparently under the impression they had given us the slip. "Well sir." said Bid, glancing at the sun, "let's just rest our hawses a spell and eat a bite ourselves. There's likely some little canyons thet lead down in the valley from up heah and if we can find one thet'll take us down out of sight, maybe we can circle 'em, then we'll try to box 'em in someplace where I can git clo'st enough to use my rope.

As soon as we had finished our lunch of bread, jerky and cheese sandwiches, we squatted down on the edge of the precipice and watched the horse herd through the field glasses. We looked down on a conglomeration of about every color that ever marked horseflesh, but mostly bays and brown. The true mustang was a cayuse of wild parentage, rough in appearance and hard to tame and usually of little value on the horse market. But the wild horse herds of the High Plains country were usually well-sprinkled with strays of domesticated horses and their progeny, these being sometimes fine animals. The herd we studied through the glasses ran true to form. The one we took to be the leader was an old brown stud of anything but pleasing appearance; and, for that matter, the majority of the herd would list in that same category. However, there were several fine looking animals, "mostly fillies and young mares", Bid reckoned.

After another long look, Bid handed me the glasses. I sensed the excitement in his voice. "There's your Goddamned black hawse! He's directly between here and thet tree, a'standin' there by hisself. Notice the way he holds his tail, ain't no mustang in his make-up."

I focused my view on the black horse; and, at first, felt a little disappointed at his rough coat and unkept mane and general shaggy appearance. Bid spoke again at my elbow, "bet you're thinkin' the same as me, before I took a good look. But—take him in a couple of months when he's fully shed and trim about a foot off his tail and he'd put some of them fancy show hawses to shame."

"I suppose you're right, Bid. Probably not much doubt this is the horse the soldiers were talking about. I don't know what I was expecting as I really didn't believe their stories anyway."

Bid grinned, "By Gawd, I know how you 'did'nt believe'. You was suckered same as me, or we wouldn't a'rode all this distance just to chase some broomtails."

We put the bridles on our horses and went over our gear carefully, Bid spending considerable time adjusting his cinch and rigging to suit him. I threw the "Yankee contraption" on Blaze and tightened the cinch and tied the carbines securely, one on each side and buckled the other paraphanelia on tightly so that it wouldn't interfere with my ride nor jostle loose. Soon we were riding along the rim of the valley looking for a suitable way down. After passing by two or three rugged breaks in the wall, we came to where the ground dropped off less steeply in a deep ravine with rock and brush dotted-walls. We found a faint seldom used trail and promptly started our skidding and sliding descent. When we reached bottom, we looked around for the horse herd and found they had spotted us first and were on their way again at a dead run. We recognized the futility of trying to circle them now and grudgingly dropped in behind where we followed at a moderate pace. In descending to the valley floor and in the melee that followed, I lost what little sense of direction I had possessed and could never say exactly which way we went. But anyway after some time, we came to a fairly easy slope and soon were again on the open prairie less than a mile behind the mustangs. I got my bearings from the sun and ascertained we were heading in a southwesterly direction. By now I commenced to wonder at the wisdom of continuing this apparently fruitless chase. But I saw the hunter's gleam in my companion's eye and said nothing. As we rode on maintaining our distance behind the herd, we soon noticed the lead animals dropping down in another canyon. We reconnoitered from the rim and located them in the bottom where they had halted again and appeared to be somewhat winded from their last run. After observing them for some time, from the rim, they commenced to spread out and started grazing evidently not being too much concerned by our pursuit. We decided this was probably one of their familiar retreats. Bid thought we ought to make one more try; and this time we were in luck. We located a break in the canyon wall that came out in a bend above the horse herd and downwind from them. We descended cautiously and when we reached bottom we were ready. We rounded the bluff hiding us from their view and came up on them for the first time with the odds in our favor. Our mounts had been spared as much as possible and they were still in good shape. Now, when we gave them their heads, they responded from the excitement of the chase as much as ourselves.

We charged the mustangs, waving our hats and yelling like Indians, attempting to force them in the mouth of a steep little canyon that cut in the main wall. But, as to be expected, most of the herd escaped around us, although we managed to hold about a dozen which we drove rearing and squealing in the steep natural pocket. Bid's favorite rope was in his hand and the light of battle was in his eyes. "Hold 'em heah if you kin, Caroliny," he yelled, "I'm going in and pick me out one."

He spurred his horse and was in the midst of them; in a minute he had cut out a sleek little blue mare. Frantic, she plunged up the steep slope, tearing the gravel and rocks with her forefeet. But Bid's old Joker, neck stretched to the limit and surefooted as a cat, was right after her. The rest of the horses came dashing down on me and in spite of all Biaze and I could do. They crowded by us in a shower of gravel and dirt. I turned to see Bid whirling his rope and the loop settle around the mare's neck. Quickly, he took a double dally around his saddle horn and old Joker braced his feet. The mare, caught in the middle of a lurch upward, came over backward and landed on her back; but before Bid could take up the slack in his rope, she rolled half way over again and twisting herself to her feet, she dashed by old Joker like the wild thing she was and hit the end of the rope on a downhill pull. Down went Bid and his horse and I spurred forward, afraid that he would be hurt. But the Texan was an old hand at wrangling wild ones and was out of the saddle and on his feet in a jiffy; but, of course, had to release his rope from around the horn and the mare dashed down the canyon as fast as she could go, dragging some thirty feet of good Texas rope.

"Hell, I figgered I as good as had my saddle on thet little buckskin," Bid complained, "when there she went, rope and all. Why, dammit, I wouldn't have took ten dollars for thet rope."

He led his horse who was limping slightly, to level ground, where we looked him over. Old Joker seemed to be all right, so we mounted and rode out where we could see down the canyon. There we located the mare limping along a considerable distance behind the other horses.

"Why, she's hurt," I told Bid, "we might be able to get your rope back after all."

"Yeah, as bad as she's limpin' now, give her a little time to cool off and she'll be as stiff as a board." He hopefully surmised.

We decided our best course would be to go back on top, gambling the herd would stop again as soon as they saw no further signs of our pursuit. We led our horses up the same ravine we had come down, scrambling and puffing all the way up. On top again, we adjusted our saddles and equipment. Bid switched his spare rope to the right hand side of his saddle, remarking with the proper expletives that he would be willing to bet that he wouldn't turn loose of his rope if he got another "chanc't at thet little mare."

We mounted and rode at a gallop for about a mile; then we pulled up at the edge of the canyon where the top of the opposite bluffs could be seen. As both horses could be trusted to stand, we dropped our reins and walked to a point where we could see into the canyon. Below, we saw the thin and clear channel of Bluff Creek as it bent its crooked way through the grassy bottoms. And then we saw more than we had bargained for! A number of skin tee-pees were clustered near a few trees; and above them in a little meadow, a flock of Indian ponies grazed. As we watched, the herd of mustangs approached the Indian herd apparently frightened from something above. They ran directly through the meadow. scattering the Indian horses right and left amid a pounding of hooves and nickering and squealing of both bands. Incidentally, frightening the wits out of a couple of "Injun" boys (herders) who had been lying half asleep on the sunny side of the bluffs. At the sound of the ruckus, we saw the Indians bound out of their camp towards their ponies. waving ropes and blankets and gesticulating wildly. From our view and in spite of our predicament. it was funny the way the redskins carried on: but considering the circumstances we managed to control our merriment. Upon approaching the look-out where we now crouched. taking in the circus that went on below, Bid had continued to "grouch" about losing his rope. After a while I called his attention to the buckskin mare who had just hove. limping into sight. trying to catch up with the rest of the herd.

"Bid. I see your lariat dragging down there across the meadow. Do you want to run down and fetch it while I hold your horse?" I suggested sarcastically.

"To hell with the rope and to hell with the mare! I don't

224

know about yo'all, but, me, I aim to light out of here and haid for the ranche. If them Ki-Yi's happen to get curious about what spooked them mustangs through their herd, you and me are liable to be in a heap of trouble if we tarry too long in this place."

I didn't argue the matter with him and in a few minutes we were mounted and on our way. We kept our horses in a mile-eating trot, careful not to push them too hard, because we estimated we were over twenty-five miles from home. I rode along side Bid and handed him his Spencer. He was of the opinion the Indians were Kiowas, "likely some of old Satanta's boys, restin' up after stealin' themselves a bunch of hawses."

The afternoon was now over half gone and the day's fun was finished. We applied ourselves to covering as many miles as possible without exerting our horses, for we well knew the danger if the Indians should strike our trail. We had the disadvantage of being deep in their hunting grounds. It being common talk around Fort Dodge at that time that it wasn't healthy to venture south of the river unless you had plenty of protection. We stayed pretty well on the open prairie, making a bee-line for home, reasoning that for awhile at least the Indians would be occupied in the canyons.

Mile after mile we covered; and as we scanned the country behind us, we could see no signs of pursuit. After an hour and a half's ride we pulled up to rest our horses. Bid's horse had developed a slight limp, no doubt, as a result of the spill he had taken in the canyon. We examined him carefully and decided there was nothing of a serious nature ailing him; but any injury, however slight, could be a handicap under our present circumstances. My horse, on the other hand, was holding up remarkably well. He seemed to realize we were headed home and had been stepping out at such a pace I had been forced to hold him up. Bid looked at him with grudging admiration.

"Never saw a gaited hawse befoah, thet was wuth a damn, 'ceptin' for show, but thet blaze-faced cayuse of yourn has certainly got a stout set of laigs."

"They are plenty stout so far," I admitted, "and I wonder if he couldn't carry both of us easier than old Joker is making out

225

with you alone—providing you're not too proud to ride double on a gaited 'hawse.'"

Knowing Bid's "stiffneckness" about accepting a favor, even from a close friend, I had deliberately put it to him bluntly and sarcastically. He looked at me sharply and then grinned with good humor. "Ya know, I may just take you up on thet offer, bein' as yo'all are so Goddamned charitable about it."

We proceeded on, both of us astride my horse and leading his. As the sun gradually lowered in the west, we reached the rolling brakes of the Mulberry. We rode down a wide draw and followed it to the creek. This was considerable above where we had crossed in the morning and the channel was less distinct; but there was a deep pool of clear water fed from a trickle in the main channel. The day had been warm and our canteens had long been emptied. We let our horses drink from the pool; and stretching ourselves flat on the ground, we drank from the stream and filled our canteens. We led our horses across the Mulberry and well up the slope towards the flats before we mounted again, each on his own horse. By the time we had gotten up on the level, the sun was just going out of sight. When we approached the next little creek, it was getting quite dark. Before us we could make out a multitude of dark forms. We slowed up and carefully scanned the area ahead of us, then we discovered the shallow valley was covered with buffalo. Our horses were tired and unexcited so we decided to ride right on through them. Most of the shaggy animals were either grazing or lying down and didn't pay much attention to us until we were well among them. We continued on at a slow pace, most of the herd exhibiting no more alarm than an occasional cow jumping to her feet and running off stiff-legged with short tail in the air. It was amazing how tame the majority of the herd was. We could have fired almost point blank into them and killed any number; but we didn't for some very good reasons. We still had a healthy fear of the Indians, especially as long as we were on the wrong side of the river and plagued with a lame horse. Besides, we knew any sudden disturbance could embroil the whole herd and catch us right in the middle of it. And lastly, as far as game and meat was concerned, we could get it any time we had a few hours to spare under more sporting and exciting circumstances than our present one.

As we picked our way slowly through the herd, a frisky young cow suddenly jumped to her feet in front of us, snorted, and ran off in the peculiar buffalo fashion. This alarmed a gruff old cow who looked at us belligerently and started rattling and grunting, which started sort of a chain reaction and that part of the herd took off amid a clamor of grunts and clacking of hooves with the old cow, her tail in the air, disdainfully bringing up the rear. We both laughed at the comical picture she made.

"You know, thet old sister 'minds me of my Aint Amandy," Bid chuckled, "the way she used to stamp off with her haid in the air, when Uncle Zack would come home from one of his gallivantin' spells with some big Jackson tale of why he had been delayed."

"Uncle Zack," he explained with a grin, "is said to be the black sheep among'st us McClains."

I thought, now I had Bid in one of his moods when he would talk about himself and his family. So I started out in a subtle manner as I had, more than once before, to pump him. But as usual, I never got far. Instead, he entertained me with antecdotes of Uncle Zack. whom he said was notable mostly for his habitual use of strong stimulants, wagerin' on hawses, and as 'aint' Amandy, always suspected, a "weakness for wimmen of doubtful virtue."

The time passed quickly and before we knew it we were near the river. It was fully dark but one of those nights when there was light enough to see some distance ahead. We stopped near the edge of the stream and took our bearings. We guessed we were not far below our regular watering place. Exploring along the water's edge we found a sloping bank and I rode Blaze in first and Bid followed on his horse. The water was belly deep but unlike our morning crossing, the bottom was none too good and Bid's horse especially had a rough time of it as we struggled across the wide channel. But we made it without getting more than our feet wet. Once on the north side we both breathed a sigh of relief for we had crossed the Border into whiteman's country.

A couple of miles further, as we rode along in the dark, the faint outlines of the sod ranche showed up in the gloom. Our

227

horses nickered a greeting that was answered from the corral. The door of the house opened a crack and we could see Tom's face peering anxiously into the dark from the dimly lighted room. In his hand was his trusty double-barrel splatter-gun.

"It's all right, Tom," I yelled, "this is me and Bid, in at last."

"Well, It's about time, I reckon," he grumbled, having obviously been worried, "I had jest about commenced to wonder."

"Well Sir, Tom," apologized Bid, as we unsaddled our horses, "I don't blame y'all for bein' a mite upset. We bin on a regular wild goose chase with not a damn thing to show for it but a lame hawse and a pair of saddle-sore asses; and beside thet, I done lost my best rope."

Tom, his good humor quickly restored, now that his wandering hired-help had returned safely to the fold, insisted we come in for supper. "Cold beans and corn bread awarmin' in the oven. The woman's been asavin' it for you." He assured us.

So, with appetites sharpened by many hours in the saddle since we had last eaten, we finished the cold beans and cornbread off in short order. Then we retired to our hay-lined bunks where we slept the sleep of the weary and the just.

CHAPTER VI

Hang on to Your Hair

The next few days found us at last caught up with the main work of building and equipping the sod ranche; then, our labors were directed at repairing the wagons, harness, and what have you, of Tom's freighting outfit. Bid was adept at all this work, particularly repairing harness and leather goods. Give him sufficient rawhide or "whang" leather and he could repair leather equipment as good as new and enjoyed doing it too. One day we spent, thusly engaged, in and round the shade of a wagon. The Texas drover, head bare, pocket knife and awl in hand, plied the leather deft as a seamstress. It was one of those days when conversation came easily and Bid had one of his talkative moods. I told of some of my life and Bid, for the first time, unburdened a little of his. For some reason, he had always been reticent on subjects relating to his family life; but, today, he was frank and confidential, expressing himself in no uncertain terms on intimate matters such as his own next of kin—. As he told it, he came from a proud and hidebound family.

Long before today he had mentioned some of his droving days. "Of thet bunch we had trailed nawth." And this time he had gathered steers to fill "thet government contract". And how he had ramrodded the drive of steers and she-stuff from "down home" to the mountains of Southern Colorado where his folks were now located. All this he mentioned casually in the course of our acquaintance. Never going into detail on any of them or any of the other vague references he had made as to countless other things he had done and witnessed. To me, not only at this day, but for a long time to come, it was somewhat confusing. More so perhaps, because I knew he was telling the truth. For Bid, whatever his other faults, was not one to blow and bluster. But in time, as I came to know more and more of his past, happenings fell into place like the parts of a puzzle; and I realized he had led an eventful and remarkable life, particularly in the last few years.

Today, he spoke of some of those experiences. "Well, sir,

229

when the war was over, I reckon we was as pore as most folks in Taixas. Sho' now, we had cattle runnin' all over hell, but no money market for 'em. But the 'Old Gentleman' always had his ear to the ground and was never one to let his stiff-neckness interfeah with turnin' an honest dollar, so when any little beef deal came up, he most usually had his hand in it. In this way, he kinda got a few licks in at poverty and by the time I got home from the war, the folks had done raised their living some above the common level of corn-pone and 'lasses. Well, I stuck around for a spell, gettin' acquainted agin and fillin' up on home cookin'." He paused here and I knew there was something he didn't want to discuss. "But before long I concluded there was nothin' in the old life for me—; besides, they was too many bosses and I'd had enough of thet in the war. I heerd about this Gov'nment beef herd they was a fixin' to gather and drive up Arkansas way, so I hired on for twenty-five a month, U.S. money. Whilst I was on thet drive, some of them Nawtheners started showin up down home, wantin' to buy cheap steers and pay for them with Federal Paper. Now, most of them mossy-backs down home wouldn't lend an ear to no 'damn Yankee', let alone take their paper money. But the 'Old Gentleman' had spent his life swappin' and makin' deals, so he poked around a spell and found them Nawthe'n hombres was on the level and it wasn't long 'til he was dealin' with them and naturally came out all right. Accordingly, when I came home from this Gov'nment drive in the spring of '66'. I found the folks plannin' a drive of their own, havin' got word of a market at Sedalia, Missouri. We left early in May and hit the country around Baxter Springs around the fourth of July where we was held up on first one pretext and then another for nigh a week and finally wound up a sellin' to them Jawhawkin' thieves for about half what the critters would a brought at the railroau. But as the 'Old Gentleman' said, 'anything we got out of them was pure gravy', for they warn't wuth nothin' down home. Thet was, I reckon, Caroliny, one of the first successful drives to the Nawth; and considerin' the steers we sold, and them as was stole outright, we still didn't do too bad."

He let up now, as we got another batch of harness and spread it on the ground before us.

"Bid," I asked, giving in to a curiousity that had long puzzled me. "How come you 'drovers' were in Abilene so early in the spring, when we first met? We were told that the cattle drives wouldn't arrive before summer."

"And you was certainly told right, too, as far as the main rush is concerned. But me bein' in Abilene at that time is a right long story and I'm just a mind to tell it to yo'all now. Well sir, last fall when I got my belly full of city life, a workin' for Mr. McCoy* in the 'Yards' there at Chicago, I left in the 'Cars'; and, eventually, by muleback, ferry boat, wagon and sometimes plain old mare's shank, I worked my way back to Texas. I hadn't got settled there, 'til I done up and signed on for a winter's drive. I'll never do thet fool thing again. Although we got along right well for a spell, by the middle of December we passed Fort Wuth and was in the brakes of the Red River before winter really struck. But luck was with us and we found shelter and weathered out the storm and never lost a Goddamn haid. We crossed the Red and was well up in the Nations before we had to hole up agin on account of the weather. We had protection there and plenty of tall grass, but they warn't no "body"** in it at that time of year. We dug caves and built brush and log shelters and grazed the herd there for nigh a month before we decided to trail on in hopes of findin' better grazin'. From then on, it was drive a spell and hole up a spell, with the steers getting thinner all the time. We never hit any 'nawtheners' or any specially bad weather, but but it was just plain disagreeable. Finally in February we got in to some of the better Bluestem country and from then on we just kinda let 'em drag along and fill up. By the fust week in March, we was near a little creek at the haid of the Cottonwood; and the boss concluded to graze the herd there 'til summer and fatten 'em out. Well, by this time we was gettin' short of grub and supplies, as the only places we had been able to buy anything after leaving Fort Wuth, was at the scatterin' little backcountry tradin' posts. So havin' been at Abilene last summer, I talked the boss into lettin' a bunch of us go there for supplies. I told the boss before we left if I found something that suited me better, I wasn't comin' back, as he'd done lied to me when I signed on about thet a'gonna be a straight through drive, 'not

* Joseph McCoy, the founder of Abilene as a cattle market.

** "body" in it—sustenance, nutrition.

stoppin' for nothin'. And I went off with him a'owin' me three months wages, but I'll run acros't him someday. For the time bein', I was damn glad to get shut of that Godforsaken job and them mangy steers."

"And," he wound up with a grin, as he reached in his breast pocket for his tobacco, "there was where I met 'Mister' McCanles and yo'all and Tom Powers."

The last days of April passed at the Sod Ranche and the first week of May was well along. Row on row of light green vegetables graced the well-cared-for garden in front of the house. Next to them the darker green of the potato leaves punched their way through the virgin soil. On the hillsides and on the flats where last year's grass had been grazed short, the new grass showed a greenish cast. With the exception of a few days of strong southerly winds the spring weather had been ideal. About the time those few windy days (so common to the high plains) would become exasperating, we would be favored with a beneficial shower and a period of calm warm sunshine. It was no wonder that during these spells, Tom and Mamie beamed with pleasure at nature's promise. In fact, Tom could hold his patience no longer and announced one morning that it was time to plant corn. With two small poles lashed to the bottom of his harrow and parallel with each other and about forty inches apart, he started laying off the rows for his corn field. Bid, Sid, and I, armed with plenty of seed, fell in behind and after a few long days the planting was "laid by".

After planting the weather continued fine and growing conditions were well nigh perfect. The grass coming on the prairie, and the little black field of sprouting corn gave the Sod Ranche a look of civilization, an oasis in a vast wilderness of rolling grass-covered flats. To all of us now, it was home—the Powers' kids no longer complained, "I wish't we'ud stayed in Missoury". Even Bid showed enthusiasm for what he considered a "hoe-man's" life, but a few days after completing the planting, I noticed a restlessness in him. One day he said to me.

"Caroliny, I sorta reckon I had ought to be on my way. It looks now like the Injuns ain't apt to bother yo'all for a spell 'anyhow', and it don't seem right for me to hang around and sponge off Tom and Mrs. Powers no longer. Besides, if I stick around much longer, there won't be nothin' for me to do but ride herd on them chickens due to hatch around heah directly."

He broke off then to bring a wandering mule back in line and didn't get back on the subject again until on our way home from the river. "As I was sayin'," he remarked, as one who had come to a definite decision, "I reckon I'll just break the news gently to Tom and tie my bedroll and plunder on Old Joker heah and be on my way one of these fine mawnings."

After supper Bid had broken the news gently to Tom; and he and I sat around in our lean-to quarters by lantern light, dolefully contemplating the weeks we had been together. We realized we had become close friends and as our time of parting drew near we could think of little to talk about. Bid got up and busied himself, gathering up the odds and ends of his few personal belongings. He repacked the small valise where he kept his clean socks, white shirt and "Sunday go t' meetin' clothes. Then he dug out some more duffle and without any explanation suddenly unrolled a soiled and wrinkled suit of fancy checked clothes. As soon as I recognized them as the fancy duds he had won from the drummer in Abilene, I started laughing. He grinned along with me.

"You know, Caroliny, I'm just a gonna donate these glad-rags as a farewell gift to yo'all and the Powers family. Might make a Hell of a good scarecrow to keep the varmits out of Tom's corn patch.

Strangely, we had never spoken of that night in Abilene; but as the ice was broken, I joked and quizzed him about it.

"Well sir, I'll tell you," he said seriously, "thet son-of-a-bitch tried to trim me good and proper; like I figured he would from the start. But I never learned to play cards from my no-account Uncle Zack for nothin'. I acted dumb 'til I figgered out his game and from then on he played right into my hands. Funny thing, though, he squawked so loud that I give him back his gold watch and more'n half the money I'd won. But I told myself then and there, 'this is the first chanc't I ever had to pluck one of them smart roosters and I aim to keep his tail feathers'."

While I had Bid in a talkative mood I kept him on the subject and soon we were discussing the affair he had with the mixed-breed "badman".

"Thet was a kind of coltish damn stunt thet I sure wouldn't a'tried on no real gun-slinger;" he explained, "but I'd listened to him shoot off his mouth for two days and then thet night he said the wrong thing, when I just happened to have enough whiskey under my belt I figgered the time was ripe to put him in his proper place."

Next morning we sat around the breakfast table a little later than usual as this was to be Bid's last meal with us. With a habit born of caution, I walked to the door for a glance around the country side; one look stopped me in my tracks. The landscape was black with buffalo less than a mile away, gradually grazing their way toward the little field of week-old corn. The thrill at the sight of the great herd was more than offset by the look on Tom's face.

"Oh my Gawd!" he groaned, "if we can't get them critters turned, our spring work will be all shot to tarnation."

Bid and I grabbed our guns and quickly saddled our horses while Tom and Sid rushed out above the corral and brought in the mules that had been picketed out to graze, along with the milk cow and loose stock and hustled them all safely behind the corral fence.

We rode at a gallop until we were within a hundred yards of the outskirts of the herd, then we separated and slowed to a walk until the leading buffalo commenced to raise their heads and take alarm. We waved our hats and gave the rebel yell. The leaders turned with tails in the air and charged directly into the main herd. For a while there was utter confusion as the herd milled about; and we were not sure which way they would go. We raised our rifles and commenced firing at the ground directly in front of them. The bullets kicked up spurts of dust and whined and ricocheted, eventually putting the bewildered beasts to flight in an easterly direction and away from the ranche. This accomplished; and by now feeling the excitement of the moment, we spurred our horses to top speed with the idea of downing an animal or two for meat while they were still near the soddy. With rifle in hand and the reins in my teeth, I guided old Blaze mostly with my knees towards a young cow that was trying to push her way through a wall of slower animals. My horse was soon nose-to-rump with the herd and I could almost touch with my left boot the young buffalo beside me. Two quick shots from my .44 dropped her. To my right I heard the dull boom of Bid's Spencer and spied him circling a wounded bull, holding his rifle with one hand as he steadied his horse for a finishing shot. I pulled Blaze to a halt and grabbed my butcher knife which I had learned to carry in a sheath by my side and quickly bled the cow. Bid rode over just as I was straightening up.

"By Gawd, Yo'all got a young one, didn't you? Mine was a regular damn Methuslah. As soon as I saw how old he was, I didn't even bother to get off."

"No use," I agreed, "this one appears to be fat and tender and will likely be more meat than we can take care of before it spoils."

From our horses-backs' we watched as the herd raced away from us, gathering speed amid thin clouds of dust and particles of flying grass. A roar and rumble and clattering of their hooves reached us that was undescribably different from anything I had ever heard. Bid yelled in my ear, "We'd best keep 'em movin' for a spell, even if we have to run 'em clean outa the country or in no time a'tall they'll be right back again."

We chased them at a dead run for close to a mile before we saw the futility of trying to catch them as they had gained too much head start while we were stopped.

"Hells afire!" Bid exploded, "I thought some of them old bresh-bred longhorns from down home could run, but I never saw the cow critter yet thet could move like these buffalo when they once't get strung out."

We followed the herd at a trot for several miles until we observed them far ahead of us, gradually slowing their pace near the head of some draws and ravines that ran toward the river. We agreed there was no point in following them further, besides we had a buffalo to butcher back near the ranche.

235

On our way back, I was riding ahead; and as Bid had stopped to tighten his cinch, which I hadn't noticed, some little distance separated us. I had topped a slight rise and started across a draw with a deep ravine running down the middle when suddenly on the edge of the ravine, I noticed, amid a group of large soapweed, a small wagon stripped of its bed and pulled by a team of off-colored ponies. In some way, it seemed sort of a strange rig; but I put that from my mind and continued on my way, thinking that after weeks on the uninhabited prairie, it would be a pleasure to meet a new face again. I pulled up short at a shrill whistle from Bid. His frontiersman instinct had caught something I hadn't noticed. When he spoke there was an urgency in his words.

"Whoa there, Caroliny! Watch that feller! He's a Goddamned Injun!"

Sure enough a figure emerged from the ravine, carrying a rifle and headed toward the wagon in the fast shuffling gait of an Indian in a hurry; and with one last agile leap landed on the running gears where he popped his ponies on the back and headed them easterly at a dead run.

"Golly, Bid," I breathed, "it's a good thing you whistled when you did or I would've rode right on top that redskin. I never thought but what it was a white man when I saw the wagon."

"Caroliny," he chided me, gently sarcactic, "I was thinkin' you had got to be a regular bred-in-the-cactus trail hand; but one thing you've got to learn tis, it ain't proper to rush up and shake the hand of every Goddamn stranger you see out here in this wild country."

"I know that," I lamely defended my poor judgment, "but as I said when I saw that wagon, I never had the least idea but what 'there was a white man'; I never expected to see an Indian in a rig like that, especially way out here."

"You never can tell nowadays how them red devils'll be gettin' about. I noticed right off them hawses was considerable off-color and they didn't appear to be harnessed with no regular collars and hames and such—. But I'm a wondering now if he ain't got some company some'eres clos't? Likely on the other side of thet ridge the way he's pourin' on the leather to git there."

We rode back to the higher ground avoiding the ravine by circling the head of the draw. A mile below us, we could see the Indian's wagon still traveling as if he was being pursued. Away on below, in the edge of the brakes, we could make out numerous black dots which we knew were remnants of the buffalo herd, quieted down after their long run. We studied the distant objects until our eyes became better adjusted to the distance, soon ant-like figures became visible crawling swiftly over a ridge toward the buffalo. We watched this panorama with straining eyes until it was a jumble of haze; but one thing was clear, the buffalo were being attacked again, this time by Indians. We concluded the Indians had been somewhere in the area of the brakes when the buffalo had ran themselves out. They had simply bided their time until the herd was settled and then moved in for the kill.

The thought of what might have happened made me ponder. "Bid, old chap, its not that I don't appreciate your instinct for danger, but it appears to me that we've had an even greater power on our side this morning. If something hadn't prompted us to turn back when we did, we would have ridden square into those redskins."

"Yeah, haidlong with eyes open too. But they're a gonna be a sight too busy now to worry us none and it's safe to say thet rapid one in the wagon is the only one that has the least idee we was anywheres around here."

We retraced our way homeward and when we came in sight of the two dead buffalo, we found Tom and Sid already there with a light wagon. They had already gutted and skinned the smaller one and were preparing to quarter the carcass and load the meat in the wagon.

"We was watchin' you fellers from the house all the time with Jack's field glasses," explained Tom, "and when we saw you had downed two of 'em we hitched a team and came right on out."

Tom was filled with exuberance and good humor at the happy turn of events. The buffalo had been chased out of the country and his cornfield had been saved. And besides, we had fresh meat "more than a'plenty". But when we told him about the Indians, he quieted down considerably. Although we stressed the facts that none of them had seen us save the one; and "that one" could have no idea where we came from; and all of them were seen a good many miles from the ranche, we still failed to bring him out of the dumps. Tom had allowed himself to be convinced, partly by the soldiers and partly by his own wishful thinking that there was really little about the Indians that need give us any cause for worry. On the other hand, Bid and I had been out and around too many times during our stay at the soddy to harbour any such optimistic allusions.

As the last of the meat was loaded on the wagon, Sid was cautioned explicitly by his father not to say a word about "this Indian business" around his mother. "You know how she stews and carries on; sure ain't no use gettin' her all stirred up about some fool Injuns seen maybe six-eight mile from here."

Bid and I knew the words were directed for our ears as well, **lest we drop some careless word that might upset Mamie.** However, we had seen enough of Mamie's reaction to danger to be **convinced of her fortitude in any crisis, real or imaginary. Our** concern, at present, was more with Tom; but we knew that given time he would soon come around to his old careless optimism.

By late evening, having spent the balance of the day cutting, smoking, and salting meat, Tom commenced to perk up. Bid took him aside and explained that "he reckoned he had better hit the trail in the mawnin' as he had planned to do today." Sometimes the Texan had a tactful use of words that was persuasive; now he was at his best, and Tom accepted his decision in the best of spirits that was possibly partly accounted for by the fact Bid refused to accept any pay, save for the first week, insisting that he hadn't done enough to earn his board and keep and "didn't never recollect havin' so much fun since he was a kid."

I think Bid had some misgivings about leaving on account of our always possible danger from Indians, but he was careful not to voice them, not even to me. That night just after supper he stepped outside and over to the leanto and presently came back with his seven-shot Spencer and saddle scabbard and stood them in the corner beside Andy's Sharps. "It's likely yo'all have more use for this than I will, with all the buffalo, antelope, wolves, and sich, as yo'all have around here."

If Bid had misgivings about leaving, you can imagine the

feelings of the rest of us. It was like losing a member of the family and at that, a most important one, for in any emergency we had come to depend on the resourceful Texan. Although, somewhat inclined to recklessness in the conduct of his own personal life, his good judgment and physical skills while at the ranche had been of the greatest help in getting us settled in our new home in a wild and unsettled land.

Next morning at sunrise Bid and I on the seat of the light wagon, with old Joker led behind, waited in front of the soddy as the Powers family gathered to say their last farewells. Bid, who was never a sentimental fellow, managed to show his appreciation in a quiet natural manner, rather than a lot of flowery words. "Well, so long folks. I reckon I'll be a droppin' in on you'all again, later this summer on my way back to Abilene. As I told you, I got a job awaitin' for me with Mr. McCoy, so I'll see yo'all then."

I popped the mules on the backs and we were off down the trace of a trail towards Ft. Dodge. Besides Bid and his belongings, I was entrusted with two barrels of buffalo meat packed in brine that was to be traded for groceries and supplies. We arrived at the Army Post to find it bustling with activity. Soldiers, freighters and citizens on their way west conducted their separate businesses between headquarters and the Sutler's store. Even a few Indians stood in a group by themselves near the wall of a stone building. They appeared sullen and unglamorous, a little out of their natural element. Only one of them seemed given to conversation. He, undoubtedly, was a chief and was draped in a colorful blanket with a ridiculous hat on his head and heavy black hair falling almost to his shoulders. He strode up and down, speaking forcefully in his native language. We pulled up to allow a loaded ox wagon to cross in front of us. As we waited, the Indian turned; his face was hard and arrogant with the most burning hawklike eyes I have ever seen.

Aside to Bid I said, half jokingly, "I would sure hate to greet that face across a campfire on a dark night. From the descriptions I've heard, he could well be old Satanta himself."

"No, he sure ain't Satanta. That old Devil always has a goody-goody expression on his trap, in public at least. Of course, all the time figgerin' where would be the best place to slip a knife in your back. But this feller here, he's an honest cuss, you can see the hate a blazin' right out of his eyes."

"That's true all right, but what motivates a man like him? Sure he's an untutored and uncivilized savage, but you can see he is intelligent, how can he justify such a hatred? As far as I've been able to see, the Injun is treated as well by the whites as he deserves, if not by the ordinary citizen, certainly by the Government."

"It appears that way to us," Bid said, suddenly broadminded on the subject, "but they got their side of the story too. You and me both know white fellers we wouldn't trust as fur as I kin throw this here wagon by the tongue; but mostly I reckon what's ailin' thet Injin there and his likes is us whites have crowded in and upset his way of life, and fur thet he'll never forgive us as long as the grass grows and the rivers run."

I brought the team to a stop as our way was barred by a soldier with a rifle. "Sorry, sirs, but no unauthorized wagons permitted passed here. If you have business with Headquarters, you will have to see the Lieutenant."

I explained that we had no business with the command, but my friend was interested in joining a caravan or train which was headed west to the mountains. He directed us to the camp-grounds above the fort; here, on further inquiry we located the wagon boss of a small train which was headed for New Mexico. The boss took one look at the rugged drover and promptly hired him and his horse for as long as he cared to stay. Bid's last words as we shook hands were, "Caroliny, yo'all hang onto your hair." I forced a grin as I turned the team back towards the trading store.

After leaving the freighter's camp following the casual farewells I suddenly felt a little lonesome and let-down and temporarily lost some of the interest I had felt in Ft. Dodge. For the first time I saw the little military post as an overcrowded somewhat shabby collection of buildings and sodwalls set in the middle of nowhere with a wide, bare and sandy river snuggled up to its south side. But being of a temperment that could never stay long 'in the dumps', I remembered I had been trusted with the responsibility of swapping buffalo meat for certain 'shipped in' staples for our daily diet at the Sod Ranche. That would require some sharp bargaining, otherwise the fare might become pretty common in the next few days. So, rousing myself out of gloomy thoughts, I managed a sharp whistle at the team and shortly brought the wagon to a stop in front of the Trader's Store. Then the appearance of that somewhat rude building, constructed mostly of sturdy local materials, reminded me once again this was the raw frontier. To the 'adventurous soul' that gave a certain aura to Ft. Dodge that was totally lacking in more developed settlements further east.

CHAPTER VII

Big Chief Red Bear

Buffalo meat, though in demand this time of year, seldom brought high prices due to its plentifulness, but I was able to dispose of the some two hundred pounds at five cents a pound, I immediately traded the entire amount for groceries and supplies. Besides the usual staples such as bacon, flour, cornmeal, sugar, and coffee, I splurged a little and paid twenty cents a pound for ten pounds of dried apples. Further east in the more settled and sedate sections of our country, such a price for a common grocery item would have been considered outrageous; but out here where everything had to be freighted in by wagon a hundred miles or more; and Lord only knows how far by rail or other means, such an item was, indeed, a luxury and you were lucky to buy it at any price.

Early that morning when we had first arrived at the fort, I left a portion of fresh buffalo hump with the proprietor of the store, which he placed in his sawdust packed ice chest, to be divided later between himself and the Sergeant, both of whom were old acquaintances of Tom's. I was surprised to find that ice was available in an outpost such as this. But it was—due to the hard work and initiative of the storekeeper who had the foresight to cut river ice and store it in a dugout cave packed in hay or straw. This is one example how some of the more industrious pioneers helped to make life a little more enjoyable on the rough and undeveloped frontier.

At noon, having concluded my purchases, I retired to the shade of my wagon and dined sumptuously on crackers and cheese and a handful of dried apples washed down with cold clear water drawn from a shallow Fort Dodge well.

Immediately after eating, I undertook to locate the Sergeant. My way led to the frame (wooden) quarters occupied by some of the married soldiers and their families. His wife, a good-humored woman of unmistakable Irish origin, directed me to the Post blacksmith shop, where I found him supervising the

242

shrinking of a wagon tire. He was grateful for the promise of the fresh buffalo meat and we spent the greater part of an hour renewing acquaintances and carrying on small talk. Here I met the blacksmith, a genial and talented fellow, whom we continued to know afterward as "Smitty". He was probably the most accomodating man I have ever known around an Army Post. Smitty expressed a taste for buffalo tongue and liver. Before I left, I found myself promising him those portions of my next buffalo.

When the conversation finally got around to the Indian situation, I found the Sergeant disturbed and pessimistic. "As an army man," he elaborated, "I ain't supposed to talk this way, but being as its Tom Powers and you fellows that may be concerned, I'll say this. Things sure don't look good, we've had incidents, you might say, almost agin the walls of the Post and there's been fellers attacked and killed up and down the trail, off and on all spring, and the same things are occurring above the Smoky on the railroad. No big trouble yet, but believe me, it's a brewin'. If I was Tom, I would bring Mrs. Powers and them kids in here 'til things kinda quiet down. Quarters are crowded here now, but we can put 'em up, one way or another. A man in my position has to be careful how he sticks his neck out, but in this case I'm sure the Major will feel the same way; as a matter of fact, he will likely recommend it."

When I left the Fort, my mind was filled with events of the day and in particular the foreboding words of the Sergeant. I must confess to a certain amount of imagination in my nature, but I have rarely let that influence my logic. The fact remains, however, I was worried, and to make matters worse, I took the main trail along the river. At places, the foot of the limestone dotted buffs came close to the ruts of the Old Trail and I noticed for the first time how easily a cunning enemy could lie in ambush along the eroded slopes. After a coulpe of miles along this route, the mules suddenly perked up their ears for some reason that warned more of caution or alarm than mere curiosity. I stopped and looked intently about me, but nothing unusual could be seen or heard, although the team continued to show an unexplainable nervousness. Along the trail ahead of me there was no heavy cover, but willows near the river, small ravines and gullies, as

243

well as tall clumps of grass, could easily conceal an enemy. Call it fear, caution or some instinct of self-preservation, but all of a sudden that trail along the river had become mighty lonesome. With my foot I nudged the scabbard holding the Henry rifle, along the floor of the wagon bed where it would be in handy reach and at the first easy slope to the north, I guided the team off the trail and gave them the reins; the mules broke into an easy lope and I let them go until we were well up on the slope, then I slowed them down to a walk and looked back. Nothing out of the ordinary was to be seen behind me, but I saw no reason to change my course, so I continued on my way across the flats at a trot until I pulled up at the soddy. I will never know whether my alarm was justified that afternoon, but I will always think it was. That old mule team by some sense greater than mine warned me of a hidden danger.

As soon as the groceries and supplies were unloaded and the team taken care of, I got Tom by himself. I didn't tell him about my little adventure on the way home, but I told him exactly what I had found out at the Fort and the Sergeant's advice in regard to Mamie and the kids. Tom's face paled and I had never seen him so wrought up.

"My God, what have I done abringin' the woman and kids a way out here in Indian country. I wish't I'd never heard of Dodge and western Kansas. If I hadn't been such a blamed hawg we could have found a better place back in the edge of the settlements." He went on then and blamed the Army, the Indian Bureau, and finally wound up criticizing the President, whom he accused of pursuing a shilly-shally Injun lovin' course;" and after all, he warn't much mor'n a Democrat to begin with." His diatribe having gotten on politics, a subject he knew little more about than the average muleskinner, soon exhausted his "repertoire", so he paused and glared broodingly at the perfectly innocent landscape. Sometimes Tom had a knack, providing he talked long enough, of absolving himself of any blame when ventures failed, no matter how headlong he may have blundered into them.

I stood by now, without commenting until he showed signs of returning to his usual reasonable frame of mind. Finally, he asked gruffly, "Well, Jack, what do you think we ought to do?"

"In the first place, it's not gonna do any good to stand around and blame yourself or someone else. It's too late to do anything about that now. For the present at least, I think you should take the Sergeant's advice. He's in a lot better position to know about trouble than we are here. But first, Tom, I think we should go to Mamie without any more beating around the bush, and tell her exactly how matters stand. In my opinion she is entitled to know and needs to know the facts."

Upon consulting Mamie, we found her not unduly alarmed, but concerned enough that she readily agreed to do whatever we thought best. She spoke her mind. "If it t'wasn't for the kids, she would just be switched if she would move a foot off that ranche."

Next morning bright and early we hitched the best team of mules to the light wagon and an hour later we started for the Fort, with Mamie and the kids; Tom, on the driver's seat with his trusty double barrel at his feet and I riding escort on old Blaze. We were armed and prepared as best we could for any emergency. Thus, it was not surprising that our trip was relatively uneventful. We encountered nothing more dangerous than a two foot rattlesnake, which Sid decapitated with a shovel, while his mother screamed orders for him to be careful and to let the menfolks shoot it. "Shucks," gloated Sid. "tain't nothin' to get excited about. I killed two of the varmits t'other day bigger'n this'n and with the same tarnation rock."

At the Fort we found the people sympathetic and generous in their concern for the Powers' family. Though quarters were limited and crowded, a community effort was made to find room for the new arrivals. On the south side near the river bank was a row of unimposing adobe and dugout quarters occupied by married soldiers. Generally the wives of these men served the Post as laundresses, it being considered a privilege to hold such a job as the pay was welcome and entirely adequate for that time and place. Here a pair of accomodating soldiers, who fortunately had enjoyed our hospitality at the soddy, a Private Gleason and Corporal Driscol, came up with a solution of how to house the Powers family. A tent was procured and set up near Driscol's quarters for the troopers use and the two women moved in the Corporal's place, leaving the former Gleason domicile for

Mamie and the kids' use. Of course, Mamie insisted that she and the kids didn't deserve such generosity and they would be mighty happy to stay in the tent. But she was over-ruled by the soldiers who claimed it was no imposition on themselves as they would still be next door to their families. Besides, Mrs. Gleason, a sad-eyed frail young woman, was "expectin'" and in the parlance of Fort Dodge's Soapsuds Row, was "right poorly" and needed the care and attention of another woman. Mamie didn't give up without having her say, declaring she and Mary would take care of Mrs. Gleason's washin' and ironin', and so it was settled.

At noon, having gotten the family settled in their quarters, we were all invited over to the Sergeant's for Sunday dinner, where we dined on buffalo hump roast, brown beans, hot cornbread, and as a special tidbit from Mrs. Powers, some of her delicious blackberry preserves.

The next few days at the ranche were spent to some extent in adjusting ourselves to a life without the services of our cook and housekeeper and tophand. While Bid was with us the daily routine had rarely been a problem, just a matter of time. As the weather became warmer we had once more taken to driving the stock to water each day. With Bid's skill and experience, it was no great chore, merely time consuming, an element we usually had plenty of. But now, with the necessity of keeping someone at the ranche, I had to take over the chore by myself, as Sid was needed to handle the water wagon. We partly solved this problem by using one of the larger wagons, loaded with every container available that would hold water, thereby reducing the necessity for these trips to only every other day. During Bid's stay, handling the loose stock had generally been a lark; through his tutorship and lots of practice, I had become a pretty fair mule wrangler. It was lucky that I had developed some skill along this line because I now found myself plenty busy keeping some of the more skittish animals in a controllable bunch with the others. Tom had a gentle old buckskin mare he called Ruthie. She was not very large, but possessed a lot of grit and determination, so much so in fact that no mule in the herd dared stand up to her, a lesson more than one of them had learned from colt-hood. With these qualifications, old Ruthie made an ideal bellmare; as in the horse and mule society, he (or she) who rules also usually leads. At least we found this true in Ruthie's case. I would start Sid on ahead with the wagon at a fast trot, leading old Ruthie behind, with the bell tied to her neck jingling melodiously and the rest of the stock would follow with the persuasion I could add, bringing up the rear. In this manner we were usually able to control our little "remuda" very well.

In the past, Sid had never been allowed to carry a gun, although he was more than willing and in his own opinion was able to handle one with the best of them. But now, short handed as we were and danger from Indians seeming likely, Tom and I decided we were going to have to make a man of this fourteen year old boy in a hurry. In those days on the frontier, the six-shooter, though occasionally displayed "for show", was not the symbol of romantic glamour it has become in late years. In the old days it was carried primarily for protection because it provided six ready shots. Although its capabilities have been greatly over-rated, it was an impressive looking weapon and when displayed prominently on one's person, it bore a warning somewhat like a coiled rattlesnake that knew no language barriers. At least it was this sort of thinking that prompted Tom and I to dig out the old .44 caliber Starr we had taken at the Indian fight on the Little Arkansas, and teach Sid the use of the cap and ball six-shooter. I carefully cleaned and oiled the big pistol and tested the cylinder, hammer and all moving parts. Everything seemed in good order, so I loaded it from a packet of paper cartridges we had purchased at the Fort, slipped the primer caps on the nipples and handed it to Tom for a trial shot. Sid stood between us, tip-toed and eager, eyes bugging with excitement. Tom was no crackshot with a pistol but he had a steady hand and was familiar with the heft and feel of the longbarreled old handguns. He aimed at a chunk of sod sixty feet away and missed the first shot; but at the next shot, the dirt flew as he grazed the edge of the target. He now handed the gun to his overly eager son and cautioned him in the manner of holding and cocking it. Sid took hold confidently, aimed, shut both eyes and pulled the trigger. The bullet cleared the target by about four feet and kicked up dirt eighty yards away in the cornfield. By the time he had pulled off three more shots, with the muzzle of the old banger jerking a little higher with each successive shot, Sid's ardor had cooled considerably and from then on he had to be coaxed to

247

fire the gun at all. By experimenting with loose powder we found that loading with a slightly smaller charge reduced the recoil without effecting the power of the load a noticeable amount, so this is the way we continued to load the gun for Sid's use. After firing a half dozen more rounds with the reduced charge, Sid's marksmanship had improved to the point, Tom allowed "the cornfield warn't in nigh so much danger from a wild shot"; and we put the gun away for the day. Before we made our next drive to the river, I made a weather-tight holster from some spare canvas and laced around the seamed edge with a thin leather strip. With the pistol belted to his waist and tied securely at the bottom, Sid thought he was a sure-enough Injun fighter, despite his new found knowledge that the Old Starr packed a wallop at each end.

On this particular drive we had our first real brush with Indians. We had watered the stock, filled all the water barrels and containers and started home. Sid was ahead with the wagon, leading old Ruthie and followed in a haphazard manner by the rest of the stock, with me bringing up the rear. As was my habit when leaving the river, I took a quick look around the country side. About a mile away I saw a group of horsemen, followed by what appeared to be a small wagon. At that distance I knew they could be white men; but I had learned some lessons well in my short stay on the frontier, and I figured the safe assumption was that they were Indians. As we had a good start on them I didn't immediately alert Sid, figuring we could reach the soddy well ahead of any danger, but before we were half way home I looked back and saw the strangers, after a brief consultation, had turned and were following in our direction. I yelled at Sid to hurry and he urged the team in a fast trot spilling and splashing water as he went. As we approached the soddy, Tom came running out of the corral where he had been working, knowing at once that something unusual was brewing. We quickly corraled the loose stock and unhitched the team, turning them in with the others without unharnessing, and beat a hasty retreat for the house. Inside Tom and I brought out all our weapons and made sure they were properly loaded, while Sid opened a front window and kept watch. Then with rifle in hand I climbed the lookout ladder through the roof opening and went out on the roof where we had placed a pair of gunny sacks filled with dirt, at both the upper and lower edges for just such an emergency as this appeared to be. I laid down behind the bag of dirt on the top edge facing our callers and took a close look. They definitely were Indians and I counted seven or eight of them on horseback as they shifted back and forth at a fast walk, surrounding a light wagon carrying three more of their brethren. I recalled the Indian with the team and wagon Bid and I had seen the other day and then I remembered also having heard how the Government "on a splurge of generosity" had turned a number of used ambulances over to certain chiefs as a gesture of peace and good will.

Upon nearing the sod house the Indians halted and held a brief pow-wow. Then the wagon, or more accurately a stripped-down ambulance, approached with the occupants each holding a hand high in the sign of peace. One of them, a wrinkled old character sitting next to the driver, wore a battered hat with his gray streaked hair hanging tousled and unbraided under the brim like some slovenly old woman. I could never forget that face and get-up.

"Tom," I called through the opening in the roof, "one of these fellows is old Red Bear that Barney took us to see at Larned. I think we can trust him, so I'll get down and find out what they want."

"Alright, but tell 'em they cain't get no closer. I'll leave the door open and if they try anything, get inside as quick as you kin and we'll give 'em a dose of hot lead."

I dropped easily from the roof on the lower side and hurried around the corner and faced the Indians, motioning with my rifle to stay where they were. The driver, a middle-aged brave with a hard and hungry face, made signs professing friendship as he stepped to the ground. Immediately three or four of the younger and more irresponsible bucks commenced having trouble holding their horses. They pranced around in a frisky manner obviously intended to impress us, although they stayed in the background and were careful to make no threatening moves, for the cold double muzzles of Tom's ten gauge confronted them across one window sill and Andy's big Sharps from the other. With this kind of armament backing me. I addressed Red Bear with confidence. but got nowhere. as the old man pretended he didn't remember me and couldn't understand English. However, the

Indian on the ground was more cooperative and made a great effort to converse with us in the sign language, all of which was mostly Greek to Tom and I. Meanwhile the young bucks continued to have trouble with their mounts and eventually wound up in the edge of the garden where they trampled around for pure cussedness, talking and gesticulating in an arrogant manner. I knew that was getting under Tom's skin as well as my own, although I pretended not to notice their shenanigans and concentrated on Red Bear in an effort to break up his silence, but it was no use; the old reprobate stared straight ahead "no savvy."

In contrast his companion went on earnestly with his hands, attempting with apparent skill to find some medium of communication with his thickheaded white brothers. He laid his hand reverantly on the battered ambulance then pointed to one of our good wagons and grasping a wheel hub dramatically he wound up grinning owlishly, hanging on to both ears. I shook my head emphatically, as it occurred to me that he wanted to "make swap" for Tom's wagon. Not in the least discouraged, he grabbed the wheel hub again, released it suddenly and spit on the palm of one hand and rubbed it against his other, apparently denoting smoothness. I shook my head again, "that's pretty smooth, old boy, but we're not about to swap a good wagon for your battered up old rig."

By now the young Indians were having a great time wheeling their horses and cutting up amongst the vegetables. Tom growled from the window, "tell their chief if they want peace around here to get them varmits out of that garden and damn sudden." I shared his sentiments one hundred per cent and with a few motions with my rifle and some forceful words in the English language, I turned to the sign talking Indian who read me instantly and ordered the show-offs to let up and remove themselves from the garden patch. The manner in which they obeyed indicated he was the man of authority among them. Perhaps because he was the acknowledged leader of this band may have had something to do with Red Bear's unwillingness to unbend. Red Bear, I knew, had his good points or he wouldn't have held the respect of white men like Barney Balaam and Smokey Joe. I was tempted to give him a plain and fancy tongue-lashing, as I had been exposed to the efforts of some artists along that line recently, and certain words came readily to my mind, but I managed to subdue the impulse and tried a shaming approach instead.

"Red Bear," I said, speaking slow and clear, "I was told you were great Chief who kill buffalo and take much Pawnee 'har' when you young buck. But now has Red Bear become old woman and afraid to sit in council with men and talk Whiteman's savvy to his white friends?"

For the first time he unbent a little, looking a bit gotten, he grunted, "Red Bear, she hol tongue—she keep frien'."

"No, Red Bear, hold tongue too long, she lose friend. In this lodge we have plenty fast shooting guns—or we have plenty big hearts for our red brothers." I laid it on thick. "Now, its up to you to tell us which you want. Do you savvy?"

He nodded, "Umm, mebbee savvy now." He dismounted from the seat, some what ludicrous in his Gov'nment overcoat for the sun was shining brightly and the temperature was ninety degrees in the shade. Stamping around gingerly for a while to get the circulation back in his rheumatic joints he finally walked over and laid a hand on a wheel of the ambulance and in understandable English he explained to us what the Chief had been trying to make clear all along.

*"Little goddam she ki yi yi heap lak hell, plenty no grease on wheel."

I set my rifle butt on the ground and choked back a belly-laugh. "Just a minute, Red Bear," I told him as soon as I caught my breath, "and I'll get you plenty of axle grease."

I went to the lean-to and came back with the pail of axle grease and told them to help themselves. Instantly the space around the ambulance became a bee-hive of activity, a pair of husky braves lifted the rear wheels off the ground and they were quickly removed. The chief reached in the pail and got a handful of grease and smeared it liberally on the dry and worn axles and when finished wiped his hands carefully on his pantleg

* According to Red Bear's translation of the English word "wagon"—from listening to many muleskinners and bullwhackers use of the word.

much to the horror of Sid who watched the proceedings wide-eyed through the bedroom window.

While the Indians were occupied with the greasing job, I stepped over and talked to Tom. We agreed a further friendly gesture might be wise so knowing the Indian taste for knick-knacks, we gave them a few pounds of dried fruit and some brown sugar, which they disposed of in short order. Red Bear told us they were on a friendly trading mission with the whites, having with them a pile of odorful, partly tanned robes. We encouraged them all we could as to the many fine opportunities for trade they would have at the Fort and along the Santa Fe road, but warned they should make all haste or other Indians would grab all the bargains. They evidently believed us for they soon departed with gestures of friendship and good will, of course, taking with them the partly emptied pail of axle grease which was all we had and was a necessity sometimes hard to come by on the frontier.

They started back along the trail to the river and we were congratulating ourselves on being rid of them when suddenly four of them, the same four who had caused trouble before, turned their horses and in a dead run make a big circle around the soddy and corral. Twice they circled the premises yelling and displaying fancy horsemanship and for the sake of pure cussedness, managing to trample the corner of the cornfield in their wide circles and scare the daylights out of the hogs who were enjoying a siesta in the shade of the sod wall north of the corral. Bedlam broke loose as the hogs scattered squealing and grunting in every direction, and the chickens flew up, cackling and going on at a great rate. One of the mules cut loose with a desperate bray and the other stock circled the corral in wild abandon. As the savages came around on their second circle, they each gave the lonesome little privy on the slope a loud whack with their ropes. Then Tom came tearing out of the soddy with fire in his eyes and thumbing back both hammers on his ten-guage. On the roof where I had gone immediately, I dropped to my knee ready for any emergency. But the redskins saw their error before it was too late; and they pulled their ponies to the left and with a final yip yip ayay they headed for the river as fast as they could go.

Tom lowered the hammers on his shotgun reluctantly. He

was still mad as a wet hen. As soon as he got his breath, he spoke long and fervently, although it was some time before he became fully coherent. I gathered that from now on, he was on the warpath agin them Indians, in particular, and all others in general.

That was the last Indians we saw for a while, but the next few days we went about our regular chores with some apprehension, because we realized how vulnerable we really were; our place had been exposed to the enemy. I suppose as human nature goes, we had entertained some naive hope the sod ranche would remain unknown to the Indians, situated as it was on this broad expanse of gently broken plains. Perhaps in a land so big and empty and so much the same, such a hope wasn't illogical, but it hadn't worked out that way. Now we would need to be more alert than ever.

CHAPTER VIII
Buffalo Hunting

In the matter of a couple of days having seen no more Indians, things returned to normal. I took Tom aside and voiced a proposition; one by the way, I had been considering some time. Why not go in the meat hunting business? After all, we could usually find buffalo in a few miles of home and there was a market at Fort Dodge within easy driving distance with a team and wagon. As I saw it, there could be but two obstacles to success in such a venture: first, the always possible danger from Indians; second, the certainty of meat spoilage this time of year if we didn't move quickly. But, Tom, sometimes, when he was in the right mood was a sucker for a get-rich-quick scheme and was rarely one to give any such scheme the thought and consideration it deserved. Money was fast becoming a scarce commodity in the Power's household and he was anxious to try anything to turn an honest dollar. Tom had explained to me some time ago he would be unable to pay my wages until the expected money came from his land sale in Missouri. As he explained the deal to me, he had received one half the first of the year, at the time of the sale, on the balance he had taken the buyer's note with the agreement another payment was to be made on April 15th. Here it was now June and his debtor wouldn't even answer his letters. There is no need to delve futher into this business of Tom's only to say he was understandably concerned. As a matter of fact, he saw red every time he thought about it. As this matter affected me it worked no great hardship; my part in this pioneering venture had been the biggest adventure of my life and I had enjoyed almost every minute of it. Besides, as of the present, our life at the soddy had become one of partial leisure, hardly enough actual hard work to warrant wages.

Accordingly, in no time at all, Tom and I worked out an agreement and decided on a plan of action. He would furnish a team and light wagon with Sid as driver while I was to furnish my horse and rifle and do the hunting and butchering with, of course, Sid's help. When available I was to continue my regular

254

ranche chores without wages and we would share even on all profits from the hunt.

When the rains were plentiful and the grass was green, this was possibly the greatest meat-game country on earth. Buffalo and antelope were in abundance; deer and even elk were to be found along the creeks and rougher country. Hunting in such a land required no great skill and offered thrills and excitement aplenty, as well as a reasonable opportunity for profit. The next morning by the time the sun was half an hour high, Sid and I were striking across the flats northwest of the ranche, eagerly scanning the countryside for game. For two hours we saw nothing of importance save a small flock of antelope and they were off on the wings of the winds so far ahead of us that a shot would have been useless. Later, riding well ahead of the wagon I was about to turn more to the east, for we had promised Tom not to get too far from home on account of the danger from Indians. I had topped a small rise and looked down on a wide draw that ran in the direction of Saw Log Creek; a herd of, perhaps, a hundred buffalo grazed in the short grass a long rifle shot away. I slipped off my horse and waved Sid to a halt and then led my horse quietly back to the wagon where I tied the reins and commenced a cautious stalk on foot after warning Sid to stay put and not move a muscle until he heard me shoot. I was lucky the wind was in my favor and I found an old deep grass-grown buffalo trail. I crawled within easy rifle range and dropped a two-year old heifer first shot; but with my next two shots, I only wounded a larger cow and she disappeared in the bunch as the herd rumbled off in a northwesterly direction. Sid drove up in a hurry and we dressed and quartered the heifer. A half mile further we located the wounded cow and dispatched her, as she was a large animal we dressed out only the hind quarters. In that day when buffalo were plentiful, some hunters saved the hind quarters only. These were usually removed at the first rib and were called a saddle by the professional hunter. The balance of the meat was left to spoil or be eaten by the wolves. From the start I preferred to quarter the carcass, as the meat cooled better and was easier to handle. For this purpose I usually carried besides my butcher knife and stone, a small hand axe and in the wagon, Tom's carpenter saw. Whenever there was any possible use for the meat, we always liked to save the front quarters

255

although sometimes they were hard to sell especially when buffalo meat was plentiful and cheap. Buffalo as dressed at the site of the kill, rarely set an example of sanitary meat handling. But Tom and I, possibly because we were amateurs, took more pains than the average hunter, especially in warm weather. We usually carried a large keg of water for cleansing, besides keeping the wagonbed covered with clean coarse hay and covered the meat with cloth canvas.

By the time we finished dressing the buffalo it was still early and I was tempted to stretch our "promise" to not venture far; and follow the buffalo herd. Being interested in what I had heard of the Sawlog area north of the Fort, it seemed a good time to see some of it. Accordingly I struck out scouting some distance ahead of the wagon, blythfully heading across the buffalo grass divide. Eventually I came to the edge of a little valley that dropped away rather suddenly from rocky bluffs. Dismounting I led my horse to where I looked down on a little creek with patches of hackberry and other timber the upper end of which was pretty well cut over judging from the many stumps. Shallow wagon ruts meandered in the valley from the general direction of the Fort. I judged this was one of the many wood trails used by the soldiers to haul firewood and etc. Sid soon came up with the wagon and was duly impressed. "Gollie!—I wish't Paw had found this place and built the ranche here. We could've had a rock house I betcha and plenty wood to burn and all the water we need right down there in that crick."

"Well Sid, I don't imagine the Government would allow any settlers here. As I understand it, this part of the domain north of the Fort for twelve or maybe even fifteen miles was surveyed some time ago for the Military Reserve, partly so the Soldiers could have all the wood and stone and grass."

"Sure don't seem right though."

"Of course its right Sid. Without those things that are a part of this reserve, the Fort couldn't carry on and protect the Santa Fe Trail and the Stage Line as well as you and me."

We turned our attention again to the valley and pretty soon noticed scattered dark forms that were buffalo moving slowly down the creek amid patches of trees and brush. Sid was all for

256

going after them but remembering my promise to Tom and certain forebodings of my own, I commenced to get cautious. The scene below held as much allure for me as it did for Sid, but having had a few good Indian scares lately and knowing it would take several miles and a good deal of time at the least, to handle another buffalo, I suddenly had no desire to venture any further away from civilization, especially in a place with so much cover it could easily hide a small band of Redmen ready willing and able to take a cheap scalp or two. I explained the situation to Sid as I saw it and suggested instead, as it was near noon, that we eat lunch and then proceed to Fort Dodge with our meat. As expected Sid was always ready to eat and so it was later in the afternoon we reached the Fort and quickly disposed of our meat at five dollars for the large saddle and two dollars per quarter for the smaller. We kept one quarter which was divided among our friends and benefactors the Sergeant and Corporal, and Private Gleason. While there of course we visited with Mamie and the kids for a while.

"My land," the good woman said, "it seems like we have been here a month. 'Though the folks are all mighty good to us, it still ain't home. And these here younguns, they nigh wear a body out; if they ain't somewheres out behind a tryin' to get in the river, they're gallivantin' around followin' some of them troopers a listenin; to their swearin' and some of 'em drinkin' and playin' cards too, or I miss my guess—I declare, I've always said town is no place to fetch up younguns."

I joshed her and told her she was just a country gal and it was going to take a bit of gettin' used to, life here in the "city". But the last thing she said as we left was, "now, I want you to tell Tom to come in the first chance he gets. I want to talk to him."

There was no question that Mamie was already a little homesick and she could have talked on steadily for another hour, but I knew Tom would be worried if we didn't show up soon, besides a dark and threatening cloud was fast building up in the west. We bade Mamie goodby and stopped at the store for a few items of groceries and were on our way home.

The cloud moved quickly and when we were within a mile of the ranche, we had the mules in a gallop. Pulling up at the corral

I left Sid to unhitch the team and I mounted Blaze and rode to help Tom bring in the stock. Just as we closed the corral gate behind them the storm struck and the rain came down in torrents. Tom and I were drenched as we dove in the door of the Soddy. But he was jubilant, "jes what we need fer that corn and taters," ——and the rain came down. The thunder boomed, the lightening flashed and the water ran from the sod walls and streaked the windows with muddy lines——"but let 'er rain."

The next day Tom and Sid drove to the Fort and late that afternoon; when they returned, Mamie and the kids were with them. "Never saw nicer people than the soldiers and the woman-folk," Mamie declared, "but I sure am glad to get these younguns away from that town life."

The recent rain, besides its benefit to the crops and range, also filled the waterholes near the soddy and it was no longer necessary to drive the stock to water. Thus relieved of that necessity and encouraged by the ready sale of meat, we entered into the buffalo hunting business with new enthusiasm. The first day things went well, but from then on our problems mounted. As to be expected, our kills occurred a little further from the market place and we were rushed to get rid of the meat before it became tainted. On several occasions I hauled meat to the Fort after dark in order to get it there in saleable condition. Being well aware of the Indian situation, I made these trips with a certain jittery feeling. But I was well armed and had a good husky team of mules on the light wagon and took all possible precautions. This procedure necessitated arrival at the Post after dark where I would help my customers cut up the meat and place it in barrels of brine or at least hang it in some cool place where it would have to be disposed of in a hurry. Of course, all this would have to be done by lantern light or some more crude system of light. Anyway, it was usually near mid-night by the time I parked my wagon behind the Sutler's store and fed the mules a little corn, which cost me at the rate of two dollars a bushel. The mule tender would always give me some fresh hay in return for some buffalo tid-bit. I would give part of the hay to the mules and put the rest in the wagon and crawl in with my blanket and spend the balance of the night under the stars. Just before sunup I would arouse and clean the hay out of my hair and clothes and report to the stage station, where I would be served a breakfast of fried sidemeat, spuds and warmed over coffee, unfailing, for forty cents. But I rather enjoyed the change and made some new acquaintances and met some interesting people. Some of the famous scouts like Apache Bill, California Joe and Wild Bill Hickock were in and out of Dodge that summer, but these illustrious characters were a step above a simple buffalo hunter like me and I never actually knew any of them. However, I did business and became well acquainted with some of the stable members of the community, men who never attained the notoriety or romantic appeal of those I have named, but nevertheless had a much more important role in the true history of the area.

It has been said that all good things must end and my career as a meat hunter ended in about ten days. As has been noted, meat spoilage was the greatest problem of the buffalo hunter in hot weather. But as far as my business was concerned, other hunters in the area soon brought competition to the point where there was little profit for anyone. Although the venture was not as rewarding as we had hoped for, we actually didn't do badly. I made some welcome pocket money and Tom's share netted enough cash that he could buy a little needed grain, as well as staples in the grocery line.

In particular, the grain was needed for the hogs, as the other livestock got what sustenance they needed from the short but nutritious buffalo grass. Although Tom belonged to that school of Missourians who habitually let their hogs run loose, there just wasn't enough of the elements a porker needs in the short grass to make a good growth. And in recent days, Tom and the kids had their hands full just keeping them out of the corn and garden. A few times we brought in buffalo entrails which they cleaned up in short order. Tom even hauled in some of the wasted meat we had left on the prairie. But Mamie soon put a stop to that. She informed us in no uncertain terms, "she would just be switched if she would allow any stinkin' dead animals drug in around ary place of hers for the hawgs to fight over." So that settled that and on Tom's next trip to the Fort, he bargained for some not so cheap corn.

As the spring months lengthened into summer, weather conditions remained good. Rain, the most unpredictable and precious blessing affecting life on the Great Plains, continued to fall when needed, at least in our immediate area, although some of it was of a purely local nature. Tom, as was his way, regained his good spirits and loudly praised the country. The little corn field stood out in the draw, a green oblong of wonder. "Never saw corn look any better'n this in June, not even on them river bottoms back east." The vegetable patch continued well nigh a miracle in this land. On every trip to the Fort, Tom took baskets loaded with onions, lettuce, radishes, peas and beans. For a time this was about the family's only source of income. The vast buffalo range became a sea of grayish green and down on the river bottom the tall meadow grass gave promise of luxuriant hay. The mules and horses, with little to do but graze, became slick and frisky. The same was true of the few head of cattle and the old milk cow was giving better than three gallon a day on grass alone; milk and butter was regular in our diet. The orphaned buffalo calf, Bull Run, was kept in a pen for awhile but we managed to teach him to slurp skim milk from a bucket and he became tame and gentle as a pet. When ever Sid and I would venture in sight with a bucket in our hands, he would come running and the playful nudgings of his short stubby horns earned him many a hearty cuff.

The accumulation of these good things, plus the simple healthful life we led, gave me a satisfaction I had never felt before; only the constant and nagging threat of Indians gave cause for concern.

CHAPTER IX

Bid Buys Himself a Mule

One day late in June I was leaving the river after watering the stock and I heard a sound like a dog barking. On investigation it proved to be a lean, shaggy and very hungry dog. With a little coaxing, he came to me and wagged his tail and whined so friendly I took him home with me. In a few days, after his hunger had been satisfied, I found he was about the luckiest find I had ever made. Someone somewhere had done a very good job teaching him the trick or tricks of stockhandling. After "Shep" as he was immediately christened, became acclimated and learned his place in the way of life around the soddy, the hogs rarely ventured south of the corral fence and even the most contrary mule in the herd walked with one ear cocked warily when Shep was on the job. He liked to take his position in front of the lean-to and stretch out head resting lazily on his front paws, where he could see the draw before him as well as the corners of the sod corral and the house. If anything moved around those corners, one ear would suddenly go up and business was likely to pick up. Tom allowed, he was worth an extra hired man.

The last days of June slipped by uneventfully, three or four times we saw Indians, but we were not bothered. One day a band of a dozen or more passed along the ridge north of the house. I watched them through the field glasses and they were girded and painted for war, but they paid us no heed. This was probably well for them, as we had a little forewarning and were ready. Some of them could very well have bitten the dust. That day we found another virtue of Shep's—he had an instinctive aversion to redskins and it was largely his actions that warned us of their nearness.

At the Fort rumors flew thick and fast of Indian depredations. Early in June a large force of Cheyennes had raided the Kaws near Council Grove in eastern Kansas close to the western edge of established settlements, an area ordinarily considered safe from raids. War and raiding parties ranged openly from the

Solomon and Saline settlements west to Cheyenne Wells, Kit Carson, and Fort Lyon. The severity of their raids were often exaggerated, for an "Indian Scare" never failed to bring with it a certain amount of hysteria. Everyone knew of some blood curdling incident that had taken place in his own area. But on the other hand, a large proportion of these incidents were not without some basis of facts. Individuals and small parties were ambushed and murdered along the Smoky Hill and Santa Fe Trails far too often. Although, no doubt, some of these tragic happenings occurred because the victims failed to arm themselves properly and take wise precautions, the danger was there. Careful freighters and travelers liked to band together for protection; but even then, there was risk of losing livestock and property. Actually, the situation became so bad the Stage Line operating on the Santa Fe Trail by Ft. Dodge shut down because of the constant risks and costs involved in keeping the line running. General Sheridan was in charge of the military in Kansas and there was talk he and General Sully would move a large body of troops to Fort Dodge and proceed against the Indians. As to whether this was likely to happen, we had no way of knowing, but there was a lot of troop activity around the Fort and anyone with a little experience could draw rations and military pay working for the Army.

One morning the first week in July, we looked up and greeted old Barney Balaam on his faithful mule. The old scout was out of a job and having no desire to work for the Army, he reckoned, "he would jest ride out and see how Tom and Miz Powers and the young'ns was amakin' it." Having once tasted Mamie's cooking, we had little trouble persuading him to stay; home for him was apt to be where he hung his hat. Unpretentious in his habits, a bed of hay in a wagon or better yet, a haystack and a square meal or two a day was heaven to him. Like many men of his kind, he was inclined to be lazy as far as routine and regular hard work was concerned. On the other hand, when he wasn't resting or spinning tall tales of his younger days, he was apt to be out prowling around, either hunting or scouting the countryside, in this respect he was in his natural element and had few peers. The old man had some opinions on the local Indian situation. "Right now," he calculated, "thar's more Injuns north of the river than thar is south. Ie doggies, a man mought be safer on the Cimarron now, then up hyar."

Barney had been around for a few days when one morning I saw a horseman approaching from the southwest. I climbed the corral fence and watched him. As he came closer, the easy way he sat in the saddle and the familar stride of his horse brought back not too distant memories. With real pleasure, I dropped to the ground.

"Bid McClaine! You onery old son-of-a-gun!"

"Well sir, Caroliny, he said, as we grasped hands, "I see yo'all taken my advice and hung onto your hair."

I was surprised at seeing him so soon and said so. He gave me a typical half-grin. "I wouldn't a'missed thet visit with my kin folks for nothin', but after a few weeks I commenced to get restless, besides there was too much bossin' and abickerin' to suit me."

Of course, the Powers family urged him to stay for a spell, but he was politely noncommittal, saying he had run acros't Mustang in Dodge and he reckoned they would be together for a spell. Later in the privacy of the corral he told me what he had on his mind.

"You're a'gonna figure I'm a damn fool and I spose in a way I am, but I been hangin' around Dodge for a couple a'days and I got the straight dope on thet black horse and them mustangs from a pair of soldiers who was huntin' strays south the river t'other day. These two waddies was with a squad over there for two days and they run acros't the same bunch—the way they told me, as we chased in them canyons last spring. Then last night a ox train come in from the "Jornado" and they had seen the same hawses on the big flats nigh the haid of Crooked Creek.—I reckon I'm never gonna be satisfied until I get another chance at thet bunch."

As usual I was interested in anything that promised adventure and seeing the country, so we sought out old Barney and asked him about the "Jornado" and the chances of trouble with the Indians south of the river. I made the mistake of mentioning wild horses; on that score, we got a monotonous and highly colored account of his own experiences catching mustangs that contained no information we didn't already know and probably little real truth. But when we finally got him sidetracked back to reality, he gave us an accurate description of the country along the "Dry Route" of the Santa Fe Trail as far as the Lower Spring of the Cimarron. On a piece of paper he drew us a map showing all the streams in an area almost one hundred miles long and over fifty miles wide. Bordered on the north and beginning at the Arkansas River it covered roughly the southwest corner of Kansas, a vast unpopulated domain so wild and remote and "worthless by reputation" that the enterprising politicians at Topeka had not seen fit to map it into counties. Although Barney's map was not without errors, it was remarkable for a man who could neither read or write and that part which had to do with the Santa Fe Trail was well done according to scale, considering the old man was always a little vague when it came to miles or measurements.

When we pressed him about Indians, he was of the same opinion he had been the other day. "A man's har mought be safer on the Cimarron than up hyar." That's what we wanted to hear and I told Bid I was ready to join him, providing Tom had no objections. Tom wasn't exactly enthusiastic, but down deep inside he could appreciate the streak that motivated us; besides with old Barney at the ranche, he felt fairly secure from Indians. "The lazy old cuss was worth a squad of soldiers in that respect."

The balance of the day Bid and I spent watering the stock and putting everything at the ranche in ship-shape order so Tom, Barney and the boys could manage in case of any emergency. Bid insisted on Tom keeping his rifle, the seven-shot Spencer, saying he had along an extra six-shooter and wanted to travel light "nohow". The next morning I packed a light bedroll, extra shirt, socks etc. and coffee pot, frying pan, and a good supply of jerky. Then Bid and I were off for Dodge where we were to join Mustang, and 'outfit' for our coming adventure on the wrong side of the river. Arriving at the Post, Bid reckoned he ought to see a man about a mule; he spoke of a deal "hangin' fire since day before yestiddy and he might just be able to pick up a cheap mule to pack some of our plunder". He led the way beyond the big cavalry corral to a small, temporary pen of poles on three sides and completed on the other by a large wagon and van-like vehicle parked end to end. He turned to me with a grin, "Did'nt you tell me onc't you bought Old Blaze from a man named Glimp?—Well, there's the crafty old devil right now, big as life and twice as uncertain."

The pen contained a couple dozen animals of various sizes, shapes and forms, but mostly mules. The good Colonel, himself, in once immaculate trousers, vest, white shirt and, of all things, a top hat, (albeit somewhat battered by time and climate) stood beside his little black van. In one breast pocket, there were fancy cigars, the other was stuffed with legal looking papers, and in his hand. he held a small jigger of reddish brown fluid which steadily diminished as he surveyed his little domain with evident satisfaction. Yes. it could be no one else but Colonel Glimp.

"Well, Colonel, it's a small world." I said, offering my hand, "I'm Reynolds, the fellow that bought the blaze-faced bay from you in Kansas City last spring."

The old trader took my hand limply, with a blank and unenthusiastic stare. "Ah yes, they come and go, but it seems ah can nevah recall the names."

But in Bid he recognized a customer and he was all attention. "Ah say, my friend, it gives me pleasuh to deal with a gentleman of youah profession. Ah assume yo'all come to bahgain for the little roan trotting mule?"

But Bid could turn a cold shoulder too when he felt like it. He carefully ignored the Colonel's outstretched hand and when he spoke his tone was polite, though deliberate and blunt. "No. Mr. Glimp, I came to offer you, once and for all, ten silver dollars for thet inbred, throw-back-of-nature, with them mean and evil eyes thet don't track; and which also I know for a fact, yo'all redeemed from one Clint McCandles—and at his presuasion."

The conversation was enlightening to me and I looked around, and sure enough there stood the same mean, little cross-eyed mule that everyone with the McCanles train had known so well. The Colonel lost his composure for a minute and a little of his calculated accent too. "Young man," he snapped irritably, "are you trying to tell me my business, trying to tell me about mules? Why, I've dealt in mule stock for thutty years and I simply cain't be fooled. I tell you in all honesty, young man, that mule is a true double purpose work animal, equally familar with harness or pack and only appeahs unruly when 'unduly' disturbed. Ordinarily, he's a pictuah of abject humility."

"Double purpose, Hell," replied Bid emphatically, "thet mule wouldn't work in harness if his life depended on it. I spent one mighty hawd day with the double purposed son-of-a-bitch and I know him well and so does nigh every other teamster from here to Kansas City, and if yo'all don't find a sucker for him directly, Mister Glimp, he'll be on your hands 'til summer freezes over."

Bid, having thus made his offer and spoken his piece, had little more to say. But for a long time we listened to the harangue of the old horse trader as he vehemently denied all of Bid's allegations. True, though he finally admitted, he had redeemed the mule from McCandles "foah full purchase price," but only because he had been threatened with bodily harm and not because the virtues of the animal had in any way been misrepresented. But finally, the Colonel came to realize that his rantings had no effect at all on his customer other than evoke an occasional unsympathetic grin, then he changed his manner and after a further period of futile dickering, he gave in and accepted Bid's offer.

As soon as we were out of the Colonel's hearing, I said to Bid, "you certainly opened my eyes on how to deal with Colonel Glimp; but, on the other hand you didn't get any bargain either. What makes you so sure that damnable mule will work any better under a pack than in harness?"

"Because the tarnation little Devil never was anything but a pack mule to start with and if McCandles would have ever bothered his head to taken a good look at him, he would've knowed so too. My guess is, his pappy was one of them cactus, tough little Mexican jacks and when you cross one of them with a good Missoury mare you got yourself a go-gitter."

Bid glanced at the sun. "Maybe we better go over to the store and lay in a supply of chuck to take with us and sumthin' for dinner. Then we kin go on out to camp: eat, packup, and be on our way."

At the store we purchased a liberal supply of the usual essentials, plus a few tid-bits like dried fruit and a little canned goods. The store was unusually well supplied with a reasonably fresh stock of goods from Hays City on the new railroad, so we laid in a supply of cheese, crackers and bologna, enough for several meals.

With the eatables packed carefully in a pair of canvas bags, we rode back to the Colonel's camp and got the pack mule. Leading him behind Bid's horse we started for the camp located about two miles up the river.

Bid appeared well pleased with his bargain. "See, 'Old Satank'," (as he* had already named the little mule) "leads jist like a damn pony."

"Yeah," I said with deep misgivings, "as near as I recollect, he always led well and kept his place in the remuda, too, like a solider. But just wait 'til you get a pack on his back. "

"Aw hell, Caroliny, you're a regular wet blanket. If I ain't mistaken, he's gonna take to a pack like a duck takes to water."

Bid and Mustang had thrown in with a Mexican ox-train which had come in a few days before from the "Jornado" and was resting up before starting the next jaunt towards Larned. To the west of the wagons was the ashes of a campfire; a small tarp, bedrolls, and camp equipment were piled nearby. On the slope above the wagons, a considerable herd of oxen grazed; hobbled among them were a few mules and horses, evidently the caravans riding stock.

"The rawboned buckskin yonder is my spare hawse." Bid explained, "I picked him up in Colorado. He ain't much to look at and not overly smart either, but man, he's got a 'mile eatin' gait."

"Tell you what," he continued, "as I recollect, you're a right smart cook, so why don't yo'all make a fire and bile some coffee whil'st I see if I can locate thet triflin' Mustang."

---

* Satank was a Kiowa chief, considered by many of the whites who came in contact with him as one of the trickiest and most dangerous Indians on the Plains.

267

Presently he returned with Mustang and the Mexican boss, both in a frivolous state, the former clutching a half-empty bottle of whiskey. I could see Bid wasn't happy about the condition of the two, particularly Mustang; but in the presence of the wagon boss, he made an effort to be cordial. He accepted a drink as a matter of courtesy and Mustang passed the bottle to me. On an impulse to be sociable I took a drag, manfully bracing myself as the fiery liquid drained down my throat.

As a matter of social principle we felt called upon to ask the Mexican to share our dinner and he willingly partook of our bologna, cheese, crackers and coffee. Then he and Mustang continued their conviviality until the bottle was emptied. Bid led up the mule and with my help, he expertly put on the pack. Everything we didn't have a place for elsewhere, Bid put on the mule, topping it off with nearly a bushel of corn equally distributed in two bags. Even then "Old Satank" was not unduly loaded. As our "dinner guests" still hadn't taken the hint, we brought in the horses and saddled them.

"There's a time fer drinkin' and a time fer leavin' it alone," Bid muttered disgustedly over the back of Mustang's pony as he tightened the cinch.

Finally we got Mustang on his horse and amid the wagon-boss's best wishes and hearty "adios" we were on our way up the trail. Bid went ahead leading the pack mule.

"I'll lead him at first," he said assuredly, "whilst you fellers foller along behind until he kindly gets adjusted and then I've gotta hunch the ornery little bastard 'll tag along just like he's s'posed to."

CHAPTER X

The Cimarron Adventure

Mustang, when sober, was inclined to be untalkative unless the proper spirit moved him, but now he was just drunk enough to be a nuisance. For the next hour I listened to tales of all the mean broncos he had ridden and tamed and how once't down on the "boadah" he had whupped a whole roomful of greasers. The tales in themselves wouldn't have been so bad, but they each required a comment from me or otherwise his rough face and whiskey-flavored breath was thrust uncomfortably close to mine, accompanied by a gruff "hunh!" or "ain't that so?". Before long I commenced to get my bellyful and gave him a few sharp answers; then he became sullen and quarrelsome. Bid knew well what was going on, so he soon called a halt and suggested I go ahead with the pack mule; it being well apparent by then "Old Satank" was going to be less trouble, at least this afternoon, than our friend, Mustang. Bid had even less sympathy for a drunk than I and showed no mercy when his companion complained of the heat and the slowness of our progress, and hooted with derision at his loud and profane threats. But once I heard him say clear and to the point, and bluntly so, "Charlie, yo'all ought never to take a drink of whiskey."

"Yo're a great one to talk," muttered Mustang, sullenly; Bid made no answer.

As the afternoon wore on, the effects of the whiskey commenced to wear off and Mustang became drowsy and quieted down. Several times he swayed in the saddle and appeared about to fall off his horse, but always managed to arouse enough to catch himself at the last instant. The first few times this happened it was a little comical. I looked at Bid and he grinned unconcernedly. Finally I suggested "he's liable to fall off one of these times. Don't you suppose one of us ought to ride alongside and hold him on his horse?"

"Hell no, I don't! Might jolt some sense in his haid if he does."

Later in the afternoon the heat abated somewhat and

269

Mustang commenced to feel a little better. As the pack mule continued to hold up, we kept going until sundown when we approached some substantial adobe buildings* situated back a little way from the river. This had been one of the better stations of the stage line; but now deserted, except for two Government wagons with a six soldier escort on their way back from Fort Lyons. We camped with our backs to the river in a stone's throw of the buildings and where the grass was good. The pack mule had done surprisingly well all afternoon and seemed to realize the day's work was over. He dropped tiredly to his knees and started to roll before we had a chance to unpack him. Bid caught him before he had a chance to do any more damage than bending the handle of the frying pan. A hearty kick to his belly applied with the proper appelations brought the wiry little mule to his feet, although the look in his eye was murderous. I gave Bid an "I told you so" look as he cautiously removed the pack.

Near the buildings was a shallow well with clear cold water. I fetched water for camp and stopped to talk with the soldiers. They said they had seen Indians all day long until about five miles of camp and expressed surprise that we had seen none. "Better sleep on your arms tonight," they advised. We took what precautions we could and hit the hay early.

Next morning Bid and I were up; and before the sun rose, the smell of bacon, spuds and coffee filled the air. The horses were led up and fed helpings of corn. Across the way Uncle Sam's boys stirred sluggishly, but Mustang still lay in his blankets soaking up pleasant rest and recuperating from the effects of the day before.

"On your feet, man," yelled Bid unfeelingly, "when you was a'ridin for Clint McCandles he woulda busted your lazy ass fer such as this." Mustang rolled over and reached grumblingly for his boots. An hour later we rode our horses in the river at one

* This was probably the Cimarron Ranche stage station established by the illfated Hartwell brothers in 1866. It was the scene of many severe Indian attacks. One of the brothers and a partner were killed in 1867. It was built of sod and doby somewhat like a fortress with two round lookout towers. It was ordered to be abandoned in the summer of 1868.—References Louise Barry Kansas Historical and R. M. Wright.

of the famous *Cimarron Crossings. For an instant, Old Satank held back when he was in foot deep water. Mustang gave his wrangler's yell and popped him on the butt with his rope. The pack mule took a couple of healthy jumps as Bid quieted him down with vitriolic oath and we crossed the river without difficulty.

"What did I tell yo'all." Bid grinned at me, "now ain't he a 'pictuah' of abject humility?"

We pulled out on the old "Dry Route" following the wheel ruts laid off by wagons forty years earliers. On the sandy rolling countryside, tall uneven bunchgrass grew and frequently, sagebrush dotted the rises and hollows. As we moved briskly along in the cool of the morning, prairie chicken and quail with broods of young birds scattered ahead of us. After a while we gradually worked out of the low sandhills and came out on the buffalo grass flats that stretched on and on in the apparently unlimited distance. Although we had seen no water since leaving the Arkansas, the grass covered land before us was not the desert I had expected on this so-called "journey of death." Buffalo grazed on the fringes of the hills a mile or so away, antelope and coyotes were seen more than once and jackrabbits frequently darted out of the sod-grown ruts ahead of us. Then we passed a large prairie-dog town that must have covered over a hundred acres. The well populated settlement of the gregarious little varmints seemed ugly and desolate with its yellow earth heaped, mounds contrasting with the smooth short grass prairie surrounding it. But everywhere there was animal life of many shapes and sizes. In its way that particular morning the first stretch of the Dry Route seemed a land of abundance.

We stopped for a rest and a discussion of our plans. From old Barney, we had a rough idea of the main geographical features of the area. We knew that once west of Mulberry drainage, no other stream of any consequence drained toward the Arkansas with the exception of Bear Creek far to the west. All other streams flowed to the Cimarron. The soldiers Bid had talked with were sure the wild horse band would be found on the upper draws

* Cimarron Crossings, not to be confused with the Cimarron River. The crossing places on the Arkansas River for the Dry Route which led to the Cimarron.

and breaks of Crooked Creek, which flows some forty miles southeast to the Cimarron. Accordingly, we left the Trail and turned our horses almost due south. Soon the prairie became more rolling and we came to a large draw leading southward. This, we agreed, must lead toward Crooked Creek. Following this we came to a stale water-hole near a scraggly cottonwood tree much rubbed by buffalo. Close by, we found the remains of a campfire and shod hoofprints.

"See, them was made by the soldiers," Bid told us, "let's just mosey on a ways; this is either Crooked Creek's head or a branch and we're bound to find better water soon, and mebbe them mustangs."

The draw became quite a little valley and in another mile or so we came to a better waterhole where we stopped and watered our horses. On the bank were more shod hoofprints, indicating the soldiers had also been there. But no other animals had watered there since, not even buffalo. To my partners this seemed assurance there was plenty of good water below and in all likelihood, the wildhorses too. Half an hour later we came to a fine waterhole that appeared to be spring fed. Nearby was a little bunch of cottonwoods. We filled our half empty canteens and decided to make our noon stop at this pleasant place.

"We-ll," said Bid, after we had eaten, "bein' as I'm the only one with a spare hawse, why don't you fellers stay here and let your'n rest up and graze whil'st I take the Goddam buckskin and smell around fer a spell."

The idea of keeping Mustang company didn't exactly appeal to me but I knew if we succeeded in capturing any wild horses, we were going to have to conserve our mounts as much as possible. From the shade of the trees we watched as horse and rider moved into the distance amid shimmering heat waves. Our attempts at conversation generally failing, Mustang finally got up and went to his saddle where he carried his slicker and came back with a full quart of whiskey. I looked at him in surprise.

"Hev a drink with me, will you, Caroliny?"

"No, not me. This is no place for that."

"Hell, this is some of Tapan's best. None of thet barr'l whiskey fer me when I kin get this kind. A little old jolt of red likker will make us both feel a heap better."

"Nope," I said positively, "I don't want any. Better put it up and save it in case someone gits snakebit."

"All right, by Gawd, if that's the way you feel about it." he growled peevishly, and put the bottle away. "I ain't gonna drink alone, but I won't be askin' you agin."

From then on conversation came to an end between us. I tried to break the ice a time or two, but got only a surly grunt, so I got my field glasses and trudged up the slope to look for Bid. In the shimmering distance, I located him riding our way alternately in and out of sight, as he followed the slight undulations of the creek valley.

He soon rode in with the news "he hadn't turned a bit of hawse sign, and as he knowed them soldiers hadn't lied, we had best scout back along the haid of the creek some more and see if we could locate some tracks."

We watered our horses well and filled our canteens before heading back up the creek. For nearly two hours we followed the far reaches of the watershed until it became little more than a grass covered draw, then we discovered day old horse droppings and the faint tracks of a considerable herd of horses. The tracks led in a southwesterly direction and following them, we soon came again to the Santa Fe Trail, which they joined and followed directly up trail. We concluded we were several miles southwest of where we had left the road that morning.

"I'll be damned," puzzled Bid. "I cain't figger why they would haid up here on the flats unless they know where water is."

Following this assumption, we struck straight up the trail until sundown approached, looking in vain for a camping spot. But not a bulge or a hollow, not even a soapweed or any faint landmark was in sight, save the deep and worn ruts of the old trail. We finally stopped alongside the main set of ruts and made a dry camp. Fortunately, the last hour it had become cooler and the animals were holding up well. For ourselves, we carried a canteen apiece, besides a pair of large ones on the pack mule, which all told, provided us with more than enough water for our evening meal and coffee for breakfast.

We hobbled the horses out, except for Joker and Blaze, who could be depended upon to stay close to camp. The mule was put out to graze on a picket rope, Bid explaining "he had no hankerin' to have his daylights kicked out while fitting a pair of hobbles on the little so-and-so."

"Why, you're an untrusting soul," I jeered, "I figured you would have him eating out of your hand by now."

"Aw, go to Hell, will you Caroliny. I'll tell you one thing though, I ain't never had any illusions about the sunnabitch's downright meaness."

We turned in under a clear and starlit sky, almost a complete silence enveloped us. Not even a cricket chirped or any insect stirred. Except for the slight movements of our stock, you could have heard a pin drop.—Mustang's profane mumblings regarding the hardness of the ground and the flatness of the land and Bid's unsympathetic rejoinder. "Hell, what'ya expaict, a featherbed?" were the last sounds I heard.

Shortly after sun-up, we stamped out our buffalo-chip fire and were once more following the tracks of the mustangs. Bid rode the lanky buckskin with the pack mule's lead rope dalleyed around his saddle horn and dependable old Joker following side by side with the mule, while Mustang and I took turns bringing up the rear. Our plan of action was a simple one based on the assumption we could eventually wear the wild horses down and drive them in a canyon or ravine where hopefully some of them could be roped. For this reason Bid rode the buckskin so that Joker could be saved for the finish, because he was the better rope horse. Mustang, who also could handle a rope, rode a lively and tough little brown mare. I, of course, hadn't mastered the use of the rope yet, so my job was to help bunch and contain the herd. What I lacked in skill and experience, perhaps my horse made up for.

Gradually the cool of the morning turned to the heat of the day. One thing I noticed, Mustang appeared to be in better humor this morning. He hadn't been hitting the bottle, so I assumed the effects of his over-indulgence the day before yesterday was worn off. My first impulse had been to alert Bid in regard to the bottle he kept hidden in his slicker roll, but in the peculiar code of this frontier country, to break a confidence, even though it was but an implied one, was considered an unmanly act, if not downright effeminate. So my friend was going to have to find out in his own way, and I knew he was smart enough, he would find out quickly if any more whiskey trouble occurred.

For miles the trail of the wild horses following plainly in the ruts of the wagon road led gradually southwest. A few times it was plain they had spread out and grazed for awhile before moving on. All morning we moved through a country almost as level and flat as last night's campsite. The low uneven blur of the sandhills to the north had long disappeared and the only perceptible change in the montonous prairie was the occasional shallow buffalo wallow. Some of these showed unmistakable signs they had held water not long ago, from the many hard-baked hoof prints on their surfaces. But so far, all we came to were dry, a condition more usual than not for this was "The Dry Route", and not so called, without reason. As the day grew hotter, the horses became thirsty and we looked anxiously ahead for water. Although we had some left in our canteens, we knew whatever way the mustangs led, it was still a long way to the Cimarron or even Sand Creek.

I rode nearly a mile to the northwest in the hopes I could find some sign of water, but all I saw was the usual mirage and I came on an area of considerable size completely covered with cactus of the low spreading prickly-pear variety. The country definitely appeared more desert like as we moved westward. And I noticed the condition of my horse who had been well toughened by the spring and summer riding. When I dismounted to tighten the girth, his flanks were white with sweat and his head drooped slightly. I felt almost ashamed as I took a healthy drag from my canteen.

Later back on the trail with the others, the slight south breeze, hot and dry, seemed to have a faint scent. Old Blaze pricked up his ears and so did the pack mule. "Whoa, now!" Bid said suddenly, as if to himself, "they went thataway." And he pointed to the ground where the smudge of the mustangs' trail left the road and turned south. A half a mile in that direction we came on a small pond, which was fed by a number of buffalo trails; a small pool of stale water remained in the center. Fresh tracks showed the mustangs had drank here, perhaps as late as last evening. The pool was a little roily and inhabited by tadpoles, but it was the first water our horses had tasted for twenty hours, so we let them drink. Finding this water, poor as it was, raised our spirits and gave us something to feel thankful for, because under the broiling southwest sun, it should have been evaporated long ago.

We stopped here for noon. As our canteens were low and the sun was hot, the thought of bacon, jerky or anything along that line held little appeal so Bid cut the top out of a large can of tomatoes (by the way, a rarity at that time and place), which we ate from our tincups along with some hardtack and dried peaches.

The horses were unsaddled and the pack removed from the mule so the animals could roll and rest. So far, Satank had behaved far beyond expectations; had even exhibited little of his ingrained ill nature. Bid's hopes that he would follow without being led hadn't panned out, but considering the animals reputation, we certainly couldn't complain—so far.

After an hour and a half's rest we were once again on our way. With well practiced eyes, we had little difficulty following the tracks of the mustangs which soon again mingled with the ruts of the Santa Fe Trail. "By Gawd," said Mustang, "this shore don't seem natural to me. Hits almost like they was bein' druv by somebody."

"Seems thet way alright," Bid agreed, "but I don't reckon no one can predict for sure what a wild hawse will do. Take me and Caroliny heah, we trailed this same bunch, I reckon, last spring in them canyons south of Dodge and they taken us purty much where they wanted to."

"Yeah, and as I recollect, they very nearly took us right into an Indian camp."

276

"Injuns, hell," declared Mustang, "I figger they're the least of our worries. No-good-fer-nothin' buck Injun would venture out heah on these Godfersaken flats, as hot as it tis now, jist to chase some hawses when he kin steal them a damn sight easier from some fool citizen."

Gradually as we traveled up the trail, sometimes one of us riding considerable to one side, we commenced to notice a change in the lay of the land, as the nearly level flats became a little more rolling. Scouting some distance to the south, I began noticing in the hazy distance the broken outlines of the opposite side of a large valley. I came to the head of a draw, which led in that direction. With a sudden interest I turned my horse and followed it as it sloped rapidly away from the flats. It soon became a rugged ravine with washed sand and gravel bottom; soapweed, sage and tall bunch grass grew on the pebble and gravel outcropped slopes. The ravine or gulch proper, grew deep enough to hide a man on horseback. Suddenly, a large gray wolf emerged from a sandy cut-bank, where he had been lying in the shade. He gave me a wild and injured look as he glided down the wash with his tongue hanging out. As I reluctantly pulled back on the flats, I had the feeling that in the valley where this draw led, and only a few miles from the old and sometimes well traveled Trail, lay a wild land that as yet had seen little of any White Man.

As I caught up with my comrades, the plain commenced to slope to the south and we looked down on a comparitively broad valley, where the short grass of the flats partly gave way to Bluestem, soapweed and sagebrush. We were approaching what appeared to be a moderately-sized stream, but as we came near the main crossing, we saw only a dry sandy ravine. This was Sand Creek, or at least was known as such on all maps of the time. More properly, it was the North Fork of the Cimarron as it is known today. Apparently, most of the freighters and map-makers of the Old Trail did little exploring and knew little of the extent of Sand Creek for none of the old maps I have seen correctly showed its length or course.

At the crossing the creek was dry, but our hopes got a lift as the horse tracks, clear and distinct, turned directly up the channel. "Keep your shirts on, boys; it ain't fur to water now." Bid surmised.

We followed, strung out in the dry creek bed, alternately deep and then shallow. In time we came to a sizable mudhole, which we detoured by climbing out on the bank. Before us lay quite an expanse of thinly grassed, green meadow, from which came the faint scent of saltgrass. As the flat grasslined channel bent its way across the meadow, we caught the clear sparkle of a long, shallow pond of water. Our horses eagerly headed that way.

On the opposite side stood a few low sandy bluffs that reached perhaps twenty-five feet above the level of the stream. From the highest most vantage point of these, the wild Black Horse watched us like a sentinel, statue still and majestic. His appearance was as if some unseen and mysterious rider held him in check. Then I was brought back to reality as Mustang reached hurriedly for his rifle. "Look yonder! Thar's a gawd-damned Injun."

"Hold on there!" It's thet Black Hawse, sure as shootin'!"

At Bid's words Mustang relaxed his grip on his rifle and we all set there slightly transfixed for a moment. Then the Black Horse lowered his head and trotted disdainfully out of sight. Bid was the first to regain his calm.

"Now, fellers, it t'ain't no use gettin' worked up yet. We knowed we was bound to ketch up with them hawses sooner or later. 'Course, I didn't expect it just this way, the point is they're all just over the bluffs the way the black went and if we was to take off helter-skelter after 'em, they would run the laigs plumb off us. We had best jist mosey over to the crick and take on a little water, then pull in behind and keep out of sight. There'll be many a mile yet atwixt us and hawseflesh."

We drank and filled our canteens from the clear, though lukewarm water and allowed our thirsty horses only part of their fill. Old Satank, the packmule, suddenly took it on himself to lay down and cool off. Fortunately, Bid caught him in time and amid a shower of maledictions, the two Texans jerked and lashed him out of the water.

"Why Bid," I deplored, "what's the matter with you fellows? The poor critter just wanted to cool your blankets. 'Afteh all, he's a pictuah of abject humility'."—There is no need here to degrade the ethics of English literature by repeating Bid's reply; but it wasn't nice.

We scouted from the top of the bluffs until we located the Black and the rest of the herd trotting southwest, heading up on the flats beyond Sand Creek. We followed, barely keeping them in sight for a few miles until they disappeared in a long draw that ran due south towards the Cimarron. From there, they led us two miles until their tracks once more intersected the Santa Fe Trail, where apparently without hesitation they turned up that road again. We worked back up the slope to keep out of sight and not crowd them too much. From pretty well on top, we watched through the field glasses as they left the Trail and moved down near a big bend of the Cimarron which bent in close to steep, rugged bluffs dotted with browse and brush.* Moving on, we rode near the Trail again, which came out on a sort of divide, but where soon it started angling across another large draw. On the draw's slopes was plainly visible three parallel ruts of the old road, as on a comparitively easy grade it crossed this deep canyon-like dip in the prairie and stretched on in the more proper valley of the Cimarron. Below we could see the glisten of a narrow stream of water, looking cool and inviting. I decided to pass up a drag from the tepid water of Sand Creek in my canteen, in favor of the greener pasture below us.

Again, we focused the glasses and located the wild horses where they were grazing, contentedly on a little strip of meadow near the stream. We watched them for twenty minutes, carefully keeping our distance. From all appearances they seemed relaxed and apparently were not aware we were near. We had definitely come to more interesting and exciting country. Still, I wondered at the wisdom of an unlimited chase in this direction, for we were probably over ninety miles from any settlement, in a wild and remote domain whose only pretense at security was the wagon ruts of The Santa Fe Trail, a thoroughfare by the way we had traveled the last two days without seeing another human being. I was the rookie of the expedition, something I probably

* The reader must remember there was no visible timber one-hundred years ago in the general area of Wagonbed Springs and the bluffs approximately a mile east.

realized more than anyone else, so I cleared my throat apologetically.

"As you fellows know, I never saw a mustang or wild horse until a few months ago, but it seems to me this band is more settled and satisfied now than they have been at any time we've been on their trail. Why wouldn't it be wise to move on up the Cimarron a mile or two above them and make camp and try to work 'em down stream tomorrow."

Bid glanced at the sun. "It's the only thing we kin do. It'll be a gettin' dark before long and down there," he pointed southwest, "nigh to the bend of the river must be the Lower Spring*. From what 'Uncle Balaam' told us, they'll be a plenty of grass and water there."

Detouring to the west we came down the slope of the valley through scattering bunch grass and angling across a shallow ravine with a few whitish rocks outcrops, we struck the Cimarron below the Spring. Here in the sandy channel ran a clear stream of water, not over ten feet wide and a foot deep, but clear as glass and tasted cool and satisfying. Crossing the stream, we found good grass and prepared to make camp. Above us near the bend of the river was a considerable marsh or bog, covered with bull-rushes and fringes of willows; this along with the springs was a constant source of water. If ever any timber of consequence existed there, it had long since been utilized one way or another or burned for fuel. But the grass, like the water, came from an unexhaustible source. It might be eaten and trampled to almost nothing, and even more than once burned off; but when given a little rest, it always came back.

Leaving my partners to take care of the stock, I rode downstream in search of fuel where I soon found some driftwood of which I lashed a good supply on my accommodating horse and started to mount when a five-point buck jumped out of the brush and bounded off about sixty yards and stopped broadside to me. He made a beautiful target but I remembered the mustangs only a mile or so downstream who would likely be disturbed by a shot, so I rode back to camp with the wood.

As I rode in, Bid was unlimbering the camp gear and grub

* Better known now as "Wagonbed Springs."

sacks. Mustang had already spread his bedroll in a choice sandy spot next to a clump of sagebrush. He rolled his saddle over carelessly, and the full bottle of red-eye slipped out of his slicker roll. I knew Bid saw it and so did Mustang; although the former never batted an eye as Mustang, looking a little guilty, quickly slipped it under his blankets.

After a hearty supper, we sat around the campfire and discussed the subject most on our minds, "how the Black Horse had looked as he stood on the bluffs at Sand Creek and showed off for us," even Mustang unbent and proved himself a prince of a good fellow. He produced a small mouth organ and entertained us, proving again that in spite of a rough exterior, he was a born musician and I wondered if his actions sometimes didn't expose the temperament to go with it.

Just before bedtime Bid had to answer the call of nature and delicately retired some distance downwind where he squatted only partly concealed in the sage. Mustang and I, being in a frivolous mood, amused ourselves tossing pebbles at his bare bottom and got cursed roundly for our efforts; and warned, "jist wait 'til your time comes". The night was only partly dark and I could see Bid plainly as he groped for a rock to fire back at us. Suddenly he stiffened and his drawl had an edge to it. "Boys, heah's a big, Goddamned rattlesnake." Mustang, suspecting a trick, gave him a profane horse laugh, but I, naive as usual, ran to his assistance carrying a long stick of driftwood and in a way, was a little relieved to see there actually was a big rattler coiled and ready to strike as Bid backed warily away.

"He kinda had you in an uncompromising situation, didn't he, Bid?" I laughed, after dispatching the snake.

"Hell yes, he did, but if I hada been as mean and unprincipled as some fellers I know, I would've tossed him right over there for you hombres to play with."

Needless-to-say, before turning in we searched the camp grounds well because none of us fancied the thought of a rattler for a bed partner. The thought possibly effected Mustang most of all, at least in the sanctity of his own blankets he silently drew forth his bottle and stealthily took a drag of preventative. Bid seated on his bedroll in the act of pulling off a boot, appeared not to notice, but his voice came dry and casual, "Best put thet bottle up, we don't need none of thet heah."

I recalled two or three times when that would have been good advice for Bid himself—but there was a difference.

CHAPTER XI

A Prayer for Bid

We slept soundly that night for when we awoke the next morning our horses had strayed, hobbles and all, some distance from camp. Even the pack mule had pulled the picket pin and joined them. At my whistle Blaze came running and I told Bid to go ahead and take him to bring in the others. With the wood chopped and the fire going, I set the coffee on and sliced the bacon in the frying pan. We had flour, meal, and all the ingredients for flapjacks or bread of a sorts, but again I put that off for a later, more leisurely time as we had supplied ourselves well with plenty of hardtack—it was more convenient.

Mustang aroused, and as was his habit early in the morning, appeared to be in a bad humor. As he pulled on his boots he cut loose with a string of obscenities directed at his little brown mare, "strayed off, did she? Put the whole bunch up to it, so she did. Jes wait 'til I git a saddle on her back and I'll larn her a thing er two."

He started to make up his bedroll and noticed the whiskey. He picked it up and looked at it, then pulled the cork with his teeth and took a drink.

"Starting kinda early, ain't you?" I suggested.

"Hit's none of yo're Goddamn business if I am, Caroliny!"

I shrugged and put the bacon on to fry. Better humor him for the present, besides, it was too nice a morning along the Cimarron to stand around and bicker. As the top rim of the rising sun cleared the rolling flats in the east, Bid came in driving the three horses and mule ahead of him at an easy trot, with hobbles and picket rope in hand. He made a picture of devil-may-care self confidence that I will never forget. Bareheaded and sitting on old Blaze with the ease of a lifetime on horseback, he was in the flesh what a "would-be cowboy" only dreams of.

Well, I may have been in a poetic mood that morning but not so Mustang. He grabbed his little mare by the mane and with many

283

a savage jerk, he bridled her and threw on the saddle. Cinching up tight he drew back and gave her a hearty kick in the belly and brought her quivering back to earth with a heavy hand on the reins and an ugly oath. Then he swung in the saddle and headed south as fast as she could go.

Bid looked on calmly saying nothing until Mustang disappeared in the riverbed and came up on the other side, still lashing his horse with the reins. Then he confided to me, "Now thet's sure as hell a tom-fool way to shape up a hawse for a hard day's ride."

He led up the mule and carefully started packing the tarp and bedrolls for we were anxious to get started while the day was still cool. Pretty soon I handed him a plate of bacon and hardtack, with a cup of coffee. "To the devil with Mustang, he could have his breakfast cold; we had wild horses to catch today."

The Cimarron, a changing stream over the years due to the sandy nature of its course and the violence of its floods, makes an irregular double bend near the Lower Spring, sort of a gigantic and mis-shapen "S". We were camped in the north curve of the "S"; inside the south curve is a narrow belt of high grassland that rises some height above the river banks. To one not familiar with the stream at this point, the narrow peninsula conceals well the channel around the bend. Munching bacon and hardtack we watched Mustang as he disappeared over the little divide and then suddenly reappear heading our way, riding harder than ever.

"Why, the damned fool ain't got a lick of sense this mawnin'" Bid allowed.

But by the time horse and rider crossed the river again, we saw something was wrong. Mustang had lost his hat and was waving excitely. Bid, with his usual presence of mind laid aside his eating utensils and went back to packing the mule. Mustang rode into camp with his curly black hair almost standing on end. He plowed his puffing pony to a stop and slipped out of the saddle like a relay rider. "Git them hawses saddled and let's git to Hell outa hyar! The whole damn bottom's full of Injuns t'other side of that bend!"

284

I hastily dumped the coffee pot on the fire and tossed the bacon on the ground and stamped out the embers. Bid tied the cooking utensils on the pack, expertly tested the hitch and went for his saddle. As he bent to pick it up a big rattlesnake coiled up beside it struck viciously. Instinctively, with the saddle in hand, Bid drew back, then slammed down solidly with the stirrups and as the snake lay partly stunned, he smashed the deadly head with his bootheel. Mustang, with the lead rope of the packmule dalleyed around his saddle-horn, was waiting. In a minute Bid was mounted and we waited while he briefly took in the lay of the land.

"We best get down in the cover of the river bed and haid for them bluffs yonder." He said, pointing east.

We strung out at a canter so as not to raise a dust, skirting the edges of those occasional deep ponds and most of the time staying clear of the narrow stream of running water. "Keep your eyes peeled fer quicksand," Bid warned Mustang, who was in the lead with the pack mule. Some distance downstream we came to a place where the north bank was low. I rode up a way and looked back. Vision was limited, but south of where we had camped, a thin trace of dust was rising, indicating the movement of a body of horsemen. Realistically, the Indians wouldn't be long in locating our campsite and by the same token, as the art of trailing came natural for them, it wasn't likely they would be puzzled any great length of time by our maneuvers in the stream bed.

Ahead, the channel cut in close to the bluffs on the south side and we skirted to the left to avoid a deep pool of water with moss and bulrushes on its edges; then the bluffs rose abruptly, broken here and there by rugged ravines. At one of these, Bid whistled a halt. He pointed above where the mouth of the ravine had in the past disgorged a steep incline of sand and rubble. "Haid up in there." he said to Mustang.

"Powerful steep lookin'." the other objected.

"G'wan. we can make it. Give thet mare the spur and she'll climb a tree."

Mustang took one look, then headed the mare across the

narrow strip of water, straight up the bank, and bogged his spurs. "Ya-a-ah," yelled Bid, popping his rope like a pistol shot over the rump of old Satank, and the two animals exerting every muscle, lurched over the bank, followed obediently as if his life depended on it, by the buckskin. Then old Joker, with a forlorn look dug in. For an instant it looked like he wouldn't make it, then he got a foothold and went up and over. The steep, sandy passage almost impassable from the start wasn't improved any by use, but old Blaze, clawing like cat was almost over when a small section of the bank gave way. I slipped off and rolled over and over to the edge of the water. Unhurt, I looked up as Blaze was just clearing the top. Then, I clawed my way to the top on hands and knees.

We had entered a steep banked little canyon, brush and rock dotted the sides and strangely a couple of scrubby little hackberry trees were in sight. We were in an almost totally different environment, though the main cut wasn't over a few hundred feet long.

Bid was dismounted and leaning heavily against his horse as I came over the top, and I expected to be greeted by the derisive grin he always seemed to reserve for such occasions, but a dead seriousness was in his look and his face had a peculiar color.

"Boys, we better hole up here, I cain't go no futher. Thet rattler done got his fangs in me back there at camp."

We helped him up the ravine to a more comfortable place and sat him with his back to one of the little trees. The thumb of his left hand where he had been bitten was already swollen twice normal size. I cut his shirt sleeve off at the shoulder and fashioned a tourniquet, although the poison had already spread and his arm was puffed and discolored. "Open my knife, will you Caroliny, and I'll slash thet thumb and suck the poison out."

"I'll do it for you. I'm supposed to be the doctor around here, but this ought to've been done a long time ago."

"Didn't have time. Remember, the Injuns was afteh us."

"Bid, you blamed fool," I told him passionately, "if you wasn't so bullheaded and would've told us about this at the start,

286

we could have stopped and treated this thing and still beat the Indians here."

"Goddammit, Caroliny," he said, with a trace of his old grin, "get on with the cuttin', I cain't feel a damn thing in this here thumb nohow."

Mustang was as much surprised and shocked as I to learn the snake had bitten Bid, but at the latter's suggestion, he clambered to the top of the bluffs to look for the Indians. Shortly, he reported back, "nary a hide ner hair of Injuns." He took one look at Bid's face and departed immediately for his bottle. Whiskey has long been a popular prescription for snakebite, actually believed by many to have the power of some miraculous cure. But medical science has proved it has no curative powers, but is beneficial only as a stimulant of temporary duration, while at the same time contending, if taken in substantial amounts, it can be very harmful. However, I well knew the futility of arguing these points with a man like Mustang, although as it turned out, I had little to worry about because Bid was too sick to take little more than a sip. But not so Mustang. He followed Bid with a healthy jolt for himself and meaningly stared at me. Then his eyes shifted to the rugged brushy slopes of our hideaway. "Looks like a damn good place for snakes hyar too," he observed and took another long pull for prevention.

I climbed the slope and with field glasses, studied our back trail, Mustang was right, there were no visible signs of pursuit. Below us well beyond the bluffs in a big flat near the river, I located the wildhorses less than a mile from where we had seen them last night. From the bluff there was a good view of some of our immediate surroundings, perhaps two or three men well-armed as we were could defend the place in daylight. But the prospects didn't look promising for night especially with one of our number completely out of action and likely dangerously ill. In short, we appeared to be in a pretty tight spot.

I cut a bough from one of the trees and laboriously tried to brush out our tracks up the steep incline from the river: for in the main channel just the other side of the narrow stream of water, were numerous tracks the wild horses had made—perhaps as recently as early as this morning. Hopefully, even an Indian would have trouble telling our tracks from theirs. But I wondered too, if even then some redskin wasn't lurking near by, laughing at my efforts.

We put the horses behind Bid where there was a little good grass, and they were pretty well protected. Mustang insisted on picketing the packmule on the opposite end near the mouth of the little canyon to serve as a watchdog!

"I'll jist tie the cock-eyed little bastard down hyar so he kin stand guard fer us. I found out with McCandle's remuda he had a powerful keen nose fer Injins."—That was probably the wisest move he made all day.

Mustang's idea of our best defense was to lay low and keep quiet, but I had little hopes of the Indians not being able to find us, hidden though we were. The possibility of being caught like sitting ducks seemed likely if we didn't take positions up near the ravine's edge where we could detect any enemy trying to slip up on us. But an attempt to reason with him got me nowhere for he had taken another drink and was commencing to get touchy.

"Whata'ya tryin' to do, Caroliny, ramrod this here show? I've fit and trailed Injuns half my life and no fool easterner kin tell me whut to do."

"Alright, do as you damn please then, but me, I'm gonna guard where I can see what's goin' on."

I selected a position where I could look well over the top from behind a clump of stunted soapweed that hung on the edge of the rocky soil. I kicked out a secure foothold and made myself comfortable. For the present there seemed little we could do in the way of defence, but wait and see. It was bad enough, I reflected, to have Bid "hors de combat," but now it was apparent my other partner was about to drink himself into a state of uselessness. One way or another I determined to put a stop to that. Ninety feet away I heard him cough as he again set the bottle down and the line of amber fluid was a little lower. I picked up my rifle and started down.

"Hist!" Mustang's voice came in a hoarse whisper, "look at that damn mule!"

Old Satank's long ears were pointed forward and his nostrils were distended and he backed up slowly to the end of his rope, then he deliberately rared back on his haunches until the picket pin gave way. Mustang made a futile dive for the end of the rope as the mule dashed up the ravine with the iron pin banging and dancing behind him, then for some reason he reversed his course and came running down past us and in spite of all we could do to stop him, he went on by and made a flying leap in the streambed where he landed in the soft sand. But "hard as nails" he dug himself out and went up the other bank and with a few hearty and spectacular bucks he soon divested himself of the remnants of his pack and lit out cross country like a racing animal. Just then a series of bloodcurdling yells came from the river bed and a dozen Indians painted and stripped for action broke over the bank and took after him.

For a minute Mustang and I forgot our feud and looked on, completely speechless. Poor Bid who was so miserable he could hardly set up finally broke the silence.

"There goes anothah ten dollars shot all to hell," he groaned weakly.

I went to him and tried to make him more comfortable, but he would have none of it. "Never mind me, boys, just keep your eyes peeled for redskins. It's up to the good Lord to take care of me now."

Mustang, shookup enough that he used a little common sense for awhile, went up and stood guard and I scouted around on the bluffs and the little ravine just above us, slipping along on my hands and knees and belly until I was sure no Indians were hiding there. From appearances the Indians had all gone in pursuit of the pack mule and with some satisfaction we watched them go over the hill, well behind Old Satank. If they had any real desire to catch him, it was going to take them a long way from us. This unrewarding chase after the pack mule was an example of how unpredictable the Indian nature could be. Perhaps they were in doubt as to our actual strength and took this opportunity to put on a grandstand show rather than risk losing some of their braves in an attack on us. At any rate, we were glad to be rid of them if even for a brief respite.

289

Mustang called me from down in the hideout. "Best come down here right away; Bid 'pears to be wuss." Bid indeed looked bad. The swelling seemed to be effecting his neck and face, the sweat poured off him and a faint slobbering froth came from his mouth. We laid him on his side with his saddle blanket to rest his head and I wiped his face with a wet cloth and fixed another for the back of his neck. I racked my brain for some simple remedy that might be helpful, but I remembered the first rule of snake bite treatment was prompt attention.—I looked helplessly at Mustang.

He had taken another drink and was becoming talkative again. "Knowed a feller down on the Nueces once't that got hisself bit by one o' them big timber rattlers, when he commenced a foamin' at the mouth he didn't last no time a 'tall. But Bid, he's the toughest feller I done ever saw, hit shore ain't like him to get this fur gone no matter what happens to 'im." He shook his head, mystified and serious, and reached in his pocket for a chaw of tobacco.

"Give me a chaw of that too," I demanded suddenly, "now, let's just chew a gob of this up good and then apply it to Bid's thumb."

"By God," he said in sudden disbelief that this simple though miraculous cure had been overlooked by both of us. "Why in tarnation didn't we think of thet sooner?"

"It likely wouldn't have done any good if we had used it from the start; the way the poison has spread now, it's even more unlikely to help."

"Why're yo'all so ready to use it then if yore so damn shore it won't work?" He asked, glaring at me as he laboriously worked his chaw.

"Well—its reached the point where I'm ready to try most any 'old wives' remedy"."

After chewing silently for a minute, I retrieved the shirt sleeve that had been used as a tourniquet and dumping the double chaw in it I applied it poultice-like to Bid's swollen thumb and secured it from slipping with a wrap around the wrist. Mustang watched, belligerant as ever, then he picked up the bottle and measuring its contents with his finger, raised it to his mouth and took another drink.—"Now whut'sa matter with me a drenchin' old Bid with a good jolt of this whiskey?"

"Forget about the whiskey, unless you want to kill him quick."

"Alright, if yore so danged smart what kin we do?"

"If I knew that, I would be a working on it. This is mighty serious, not only for Bid but you and me as well—and it looks like the only thing we can do now is trust in Providence."

"Whuta yo'all mean—Providence?" he ask suspiciously.

"I mean bow our heads and pray sincerely to Almighty God; if that's any clearer."

"Well then, by Gawd! Git to prayin'!"

"That's precisely what I intend to do," I said, bowing my head awkwardly, and self-consciously mouthing a silent prayer.

Mustang's half drunken stare turned suspicious. "Jist whut did yo'all say?" he demanded.

I only partly held my temper. "What d'ya suppose I said?"
"By Gawd, I don't know. But Mister, you pray fer my podner now; and you pray so we kin all hear you." His long barreled pistol came out, aimed carelessly at my stomach, as he gave me my orders.

"This is ridiculous," I told him heatedly, "we've got far bigger problems here than carrying on this kind of foolishness."

"Pray, damn you!"

So I prayed, briefly it is true but to the point. "Lord, help our friend Bid to quickly recover, for underneath it all he is a good man and if he has sinned, forgive him for he has meant no evil or disrespect.—And Lord, also forgive my inebriated friend across the way and help clear the cobwebs of likker from what he has that passes for a 'brain', for he knows not what he does.— Amen."

Mumbling to himself Mustang somewhat reluctantly returned

his revolver to its scabbard. Disregarding his presence, I took Bid's wrist and felt his pulse. It seemed strong and regular. After all I concluded, "here was a man of more than ordinary stamina, he was just too tough to succumb to a simple snake bite even though our feeble attempts at treatment had been delayed until they were of little help."

Mustang, sitting sullen and suspicious across the way, kept my temper "hair trigger"; so I got up and walked away and climbed the slope to simmer down. I, again, scanned the countryside for Indians and again no sign of them but I knew we dare not relax our vigilance for long. By now the sun was bearing down on our hide-away, but I hardly noticed as I came to a couple of conclusions. First, the pistol episode was just a drunken bluff; and second, I was going to get rid of that whiskey before it caused any more trouble. Carrying my rifle loosely in my left hand, I came down unconcernedly and walked over to where Mustang relaxed against his saddle with the bottle in easy reach. He gave me an unfriendly stare, but before he could move I took the bottle by the neck and tossed it neatly over the edge of the bluff. He came to his feet in a rage, as I stepped back and let him rave, disregarding all the references he made of me and my ancestry.

"Alright you've had your say now. Is it more important to you to stand here and bluster or are you interested in hanging on to your scalp a while longer? If you are, how about climbing that slope and helping me watch for Indians for a change."

"By Gawd, I ain't interested in no skelp but yourn right now, and I aim to take it one way or a'tother."

"Do you think you can take it without your gun?" I jeered.

"Hell, yes, I kin take it with one hand tied behind my back."

"Alright, if you won't be satisfied any other way, it'll sure give me pleasure to see you try it."

CHAPTER XII

A Little Rough

Meaningfully, he removed his gun, knife, and spurs and hung them on a limb above Bid, while I stacked my weapons on the ground; then we squared off on a moderately level little spot. I admit to some reservations of judgement in settling our differences in this manner, particularly when we needed to be united against a common enemy, but "my dander was up". Mustang, though short in stature, was powerful built with long arms and bull-like neck. I had a height advantage, but he was considerably heavier and none of that was fat. However, I was in perfect health and due to months of rigorous exercise, I was in better shape than most professional athletes, besides the man I faced could never carry his liquor well and he already had enough to effect his steadiness.

We circled each other warily until he rushed in with a wild haymaker. I ducked and got in a right to his check; as he came in again I swung a solid left to his eye, and he lost his balance, as much from unsteadiness as from the force of the blow and fell down. He got to his feet more embarrassed than hurt and rushed in again. By now I knew my advantage was sure foot-work and quickness and I played it to the limit. We traded solid blows back and forth for some time, I managing to keep him off balance on the uneven ground so that he could never get his full strength in any blow. It was pretty even so far with the edge a little in my favor, but he had learned his lesson and kept his short, powerful legs so well braced I couldn't get him to go down again, although I got in a few telling licks to his face. But, strong and agile though he was, he simply wasn't skilled with his fists, especially in his present state and when he saw he was getting the worst of it, he rushed in and got hold and took me to the ground with sheer strength and fury. For a time I had my hands full keeping him from getting a killing hold on me, as he was like an animal. The glare in his eyes, furious and merciless as a wolf's warned me of his intent better than words, as we rolled and thrashed about over the bottom of the hideout. He tried his best to get his hands on my throat, but I read his purpose and managed to fight him off, although eventually he did get his arms around me in a mighty bear hug and started bearing down. My right arm was free and I felt my fingers touch a bush below us. I grabbed hold and pulled for all I was worth and rolled us over and over downhill. But still the bear hug only loosened enough for me to breathe. Desperate, I knew that hold had to be broken and I got my chance as he threw out a leg to stop our rolling, then I brought my knee up in his crotch. He grunted and slackened his grip enough that I rolled free and on my feet in a little washout. He rolled over and faced me on the other side, although he must have been pretty sick for a little while he stood his ground. "I'll get yu fer that," he promised between breaths. Then he noticed the iron picket pin which had lost from the mule's rope and lay in the grass on the edge of the washout. I dodged his first wild swing, but with a speed and dexterity I didn't expect he swung back-handed and I saw stars as the iron pin cut a gash in my scalp. He rushed to swing again but thoroughly mad now I got my back against the bank and with both feet in his belly, I catapulted him backwards against the opposite side and before he could get set, I vaulted out of the washout. Blood was running down my face from the cut scalp, but with satisfaction I could see the marks of battle on his face, too, including a partly closed eye.

"Come on outa that hole, you polecat, and fight like a man," I invited.

For the first time he showed a little sense of reason and flung the picket pin to the ground, then sprang out of the washout to face me. "Don't git gay with me, Caroliny," he warned, "I aint' half through with you'uns yet."

He talked confidently, but he was breathing heavily and it was easy to see he was tiring. Maybe his whiskey diet was telling on him. Clearly, my wisest course was to wear him down, but I had to take some chances and fight his style, at least part of the time, which included crushing, gouging, choking and dangerous body maiming holds. I had learned well the lessons of rough and tumble wrestling from larger brothers and cousins, but that was a game, albeit a rough one, with certain civilized rules which

294

Mustang completely ignored.—The next time he clinched, I used whatever means necessary to avoid those crushing arms and dangerous holds he was striving for. We went at it like a pair of tomcats, except for the noise which he kept to a minimum. We rolled and tumbled first one on top and then the other. He tore my shirt to shreds and once he got a handful of hair in an iron grip and I would have lost it too, if I hadn't managed to roll him in a bed of cactus. Eventually we wound up at the mouth of the ravine near the edge of the bank. The fast action was telling on him and I was getting the best of it. Then, in a split second of my carelessness, he got a leg and slowly twisted with a vise-like grip. At first I managed to turn with him, but he brought the leg up and I could see his face. It was cruel and taunting, the pain was getting worse as he very deliberately applied the pressure and leered down at me with an ugly grin. Important as it was, this fight wasn't worth losing a leg for and with clinched teeth I said "Uncle". He only laughed and as I felt my knee joint almost ready to give way, I pled with him to loose his hold, but there was no mercy in him as he deliberately bore down on my leg.

In this last round of our rough and tumble action, we had worked to the very edge of the river bank. As a last futile effort, I dug the heel of my free foot in the ground and tried to push us over the edge. That didn't work, but suddenly that portion of the bank did give way and caved off in the deep channel. To me it was a wonderfully welcome deliverance from a painful experience, that would have no doubt left me a cripple, and I rode the chunk of earth and sand to the bottom and landed with no more than a bump. But Mustang tried to fight it and fell with a solid jolt next to the freshly opened bank and before he got to his feet, he was showered by a small avalanche which partly covered him. I got to my feet and tested my twisted leg and found it would bear my weight and could walk quite well on it. Instead of severe pain there was more of numbness, which seemed natural considering the punishment it had taken. I watched Mustang and waited patiently until he dug himself out of the sand and debris and got to his feet, where he stood spraddle-legged and shook himself like a dog. Then I moved and like a ball of fury I hit him with my shoulder and knocked him flat on his back and lit astraddle and pinned him down. The late happenings had apparently taken some of the fight out of him because for the first time he couldn't overpower me and I held him in spite of his efforts. The thrashing about opened the cut on my head and it commenced to bleed in a steady drip. The blood dripped down on Mustang's somewhat humiliated face and he tossed and squirmed to avoid it. I grabbed him by the hair and held his head so he got the benefit of each steady drop. Though ordinarily tough and hardy to the extreme, he was not without weakness, I found now. The constant drip, drip, of my blood on his face was a punishment he couldn't take, surprisingly it seemed to take most of the fight out of him. He turned, twisted, and cursed for all he was worth, but with an iron grip on his hair I would bring him back. "My Gawd, man," he finally implored, "fer Gawd's sake, let me up! I cain't take much more of this."

"You son-of-a-bitch," I told him, "it's a lot of mercy you showed when you were trying to break my leg."

After what I had been through, his 'begging' was music to my ears and I thought while I had the opportunity, I would teach him a good lesson. Then, from almost on top of us came the sudden sharp crack of a rifle. In a matter of seconds we were both on our feet. Above us stood Bid with legs braced and the Henry rifle in his hands, which he had fired in the air. He was deathly sick and keeping his feet with an effort as he stood bareheaded in the broiling sun, with week old beard, sweat and grime streaked, and in his face and eyes the strained and dangerous look of a wild man. He was too weak to call out, but I followed his eyes across the stream and less than a hundred feet away, astride their sweating ponies, were once more our Indian vistors. Halfnaked and motionless, with hard and impassive faces, they watched us like a pack of hungry wolves.

For a full minute I suppose, we stood and stared at them and then for some unexplainable reason known only to themselves they turned their horses and rode single file downstream and out of sight. Why they passed up three comparitively easy scalps, I will never know; but it is probable as we looked then, they figured we were three deranged and completely mad white men and the "wild Injun" was said to have a superstitious fear of the mentally disordered.

Disregarding each other, Mustang and I clambered up in the ravine and helped Bid back to his blankets, where about played out, he half whispered "I tried to warn you two damn fools sooner—'bout them—redskins."

By mutual agreement, without speaking a word or exchanging a glance, the fight was over and we each kept to our side of the ravine and ignored each other as much as possible. I got a blanket and draped it on the sparse limbs of the little hackberry tree above Bid for shade and noticing Mustang hovering near on the other side, I went up on the bluffs with my rifle and field glasses. The wild horses and Indians were both gone. Not a trace of dust was visible to indicate where they had disappeared, but in my mind I put the two together—where one had gone so had the other, and those redskins were in for a long, hot day with their run-down ponies trailing the fresh mustangs. I had the feeling we had seen the last of both.

I got my horse and rode up the ravine to where it was little more than a gully and then across to where another and smaller ravine sloped with an easy grade into the stream bed. From there I crossed and picked up the route of the runaway mule and retrieved the scattered pieces of pack and equipment. Here was a belt of meadow-like flood plain with scattered dry drift and cottonwood poles deposited from high water many years past. I resolved to ride back over here for a load of wood, which I did, hauling in a pair of long, slender poles hooked to old Blaze "travois" fashion. By then, it was noon and I was hungry, but more noticeable was my numerous irritations and battlescars making themselves felt in no uncertain way. Plainly, I felt like and looked like I had wrestled a wildcat. I got my spare shirt and a cake of soap I had luckily brought along, and went down in the creekbed in the clear, shallow water and thoroughly cleansed myself of the grime and blood of battle. I then felt a hundred percent better, even though my knuckles were stiff and sore, one leg was a little lame, and I had a knot and gash on my head, along with numerous unplucked cactus spines and minor lacerations.

Back in the hideout I checked on Bid and found him quiet and apparently resting. Mustang had disappeared, which right

297

then suited me fine; I didn't care if he never came back. It was too hot to think of lighting a fire, so I made a meal of jerky, dried peaches and hardtack.

The day was becoming more hot and sweltering and in the west a dark and threatening cloud commenced building up. I became drowsy sitting beside Bid until the low rumble of distant thunder warned me I should be preparing some kind of a shelter. Fortunately, a year's service following Lee's Army had given me plenty of experience in erecting temporary shelters. I picked a place nearby where the dirt and rocky bank of the hideout dropped straight down about shoulder high. I cut small stakes from brittle cottonwood limbs and pegged one edge of the tarp (off the mulepack) securely to the ground above. The lower end I staked down with rope, tent fashion and drawn over a horizontal pole about two feet off the ground and supported by two short sections of weathered cottonwood poles, chopped to length with the hand axe and set in holes gouged out with my butcher knife. The finished shelter, though not large, was big enough to protect all of our gear as well as ourselves, providing in case of a severe storm too much rain didn't come in around the open sides. But now the cloud was close enough it was evident we were in for a violent thunderstorm. I lugged all our gear, food and bedding under the shelter; that is, all but Mustang's saddle which I didn't touch. He had gone off and left his rifle, a Springfield carbine, along with a box of cartridges lying on his saddle: those we might need, so I put them under the shelter too. Now—the problem was how to move Bid, but he had at last fallen into a troubled sleep and I decided to let him alone for awhile. Lately he had been a little light-headed as a result of the spread of the poison, I suppose, and the heat. Certainly he was now too weak to help himself and he was too heavy for me to move uphill and under the shelter, except by dragging and that would surely do no good.

Now the thunder was booming regularly and the sun was obscured. Worried, I got up and went on top; when viewed from there it looked even more threatening. "Why couldn't that no-account Mustang be around just once when he was needed?—Well, I would wait a little longer." While I was waiting I decided the manner the tarp was pegged down on top could be improved, so I carried rocks and piled on it. As I finished "WHAM" the lightening struck across the river and the whole ground seemed to shake. Then there was sudden calm and a very few scattering raindrops fell. Making a last check to be sure the horses were secure, I hurried down to Bid.

The crash of thunder had aroused him and he stared curiously at me, as I offered him a drink in the tincup. "Bid, its gonna rain here directly, and it looks like a real bad one. I've made a shelter up near the rim and if you can wrap your arms around me and hang on, I'll get you up there."

"Hell, Caroliny, I ain't skeered of a little old rain," he answered. And then he lapsed into broken talk halfway between reality and delirium, "git afteh them steers—yo'all—and bunch 'em in the mesquite yonder, it's gonna rain like hell."

From then on he was only half consicious and I was debating whether to try to manhandle him to the shelter when the storm struck. The rain came down in torrents along with marble-sized hail, the lightening struck all around us and the thunder rolled and crashed. I pulled the blanket from the limbs above us and held it over our heads, but it only provided partial protection from the hail. In minutes we were soaking wet. A figure suddenly emerged from the storm, stumbled over Bid's legs and sank to the ground on the other side; the eyes protruding from a swollen and rain-splashed face were hard to recognize as those of Mustang. He yelled something as he slumped down which I couldn't understand, but I judged he was so disturbed by the violence of the storm that even my companionship was preferable to braving it alone.

When the rain finally let up, water rushed down the ravine beside us and the slopes and hillsides all about were streaked with streams of running water. The flat across from us was a sheet of water mixed with shallow drifts of hail and the river channel itself was already a third full of swiftly billowing, muddy runoff.

The rain and soaking he had received seemed to revive Bid and now he seemed fully rational and even stronger. Mustang and I, self-consciously avoiding normal conversation, got him to his feet and laboriously moved him uphill and under the shelter, where we removed his wet boots and clothes and rolled him in dry blankets. Of course none of us had thought to bring along extra trousers, but Bid like myself, had a spare shirt and socks. We got these on him because the air was becoming quite chilly. Ironically, I thought how a sip or two from that bottle would be a welcome tonic for Bid now,—or even a hot cup of coffee. But wood and buffalo chips were hopelessly soaked; if only I had thought to put some of the wood in the dry. Perhaps somewhere along this range of bluffs was a protected spot where some dry fuel could be found, even though it was but grass and twigs,—at least I could warm up while trying.

It was late afternoon and the main cloud had moved on east, but we were still covered with an overcast and scattered rain-drops fell, accompanied by a cool breeze off the main cloud. I climbed out of the ravine on the east side and started along the top of the bluff and as luck would have it the first thing I saw, lying on its side in a crevice, was the unbroken whiskey bottle, cork and all and nearly a fourth full.—Here lay the root of an awful lot of trouble this day, but perhaps what was left might indeed prove a blessing.

I continued on and explored the next ravine of any size, and found a small cave dug back a few feet in the sandy wall. Near the front, partly covered by sand, was the charred remains of an old campfire, possibly many years old, but inside was an armful of dry wood and nearby a nest of grass and twigs where some wild animal had made his lair more recently. But more interesting yet was a rusty old butcher knife sticking in the sandy wall. On the wooden handle and carved irregularly was the word "SANTOS". I wiped the rusty blade and stuck it in my belt; then I gathered up the dry wood and all the grass and twigs I could carry and headed back.

Half an hour later the frying pan and the coffee pot simmered on a little fire by the canvas shelter, and all the wet wood we could cut and stack beside it was steaming and drying for future use. And I thanked God for SANTOS, whoever he had been.

CHAPTER XIII

A Picture of Abject Humility

Mustang and I managed to put away a full and satisfying meal without the social exchange of a single word of conversation. I knew this situation was foolish, as well perhaps he did too, but I remembered how he had been the cause of all the trouble and more especially, how he had tried to break my leg, and I would "just be damned if I would be the one to say the first word."

About dusk I got up and climbed the bluff east of us and returned with the whiskey bottle and in the way of "offering an olive branch" I silently set it down beside Mustang, who was trying to dry his boots over the coals of the fire. He looked at it in the strangest way and worked his Adam's Apple, "Well, by Gawd," he said, and a little later Bid was enjoying a jolt of medicinal corn spirits; then Mustang carefully put the bottle away until Bid needed another shot and no one else touched its contents. Now I don't want to imply that Mustang and I indulged in any great cordiality that evening, but the ice was broken, and we did share the same shelter, one on each side of Bid. Out of my wet clothes and into a dry, though skimpy blanket, I was about to doze off when I heard Mustang clear his throat. His voice was a little apologetic, but plain and distinct above the roar of the Cimarron and Bid's heavy breathing. "Say, Caroliny, whut in the Hell does 'inebriated' mean?"

The morning broke with clear sunshine and promise of a fine summer day. I rolled from my blanket, stiff and sore as an old man, and pulled on my sodden shirt and pants, but with the luxury of dry socks in my wet boots. The river had fallen during the night to not over a few feet deep, indicating the storm had not been heavy very far west. Bid awoke clear and chipper, but still woefully weak. He insisted on an eyeopener before breakfast, and he downed a couple of swallows manfully and smacked his lips. "My, my," he winked. "they ain't nothin' like a good shot of whiskey to cure the affaicts of snake bite." Thereafter, he took his first nourishment in twenty-four hours, a slice of bacon and some coffee.

After yesterday's setbacks, we all realized that our wild horse chase was one grand failure. Bid's hard luck alone was enough to guarantee that, as it would be many days before he would be in shape to rope and handle mustangs. Therefore, we put our horses out to graze on the blufftops and spent the greater part of the day recuperating. We sat around in the early hours, drying out and mourning our hard luck. although frankly, I felt mighty lucky we had fared so well considering some of the dangers we had escaped. Especially welcome this morning was the warm balmy sunshine. And after Bid's pants and boots had a chance to dry, he insisted on dressing and walking around a bit, although he accomplished the latter in a shaky manner. He was, no doubt, the most disappointed one among us, and because he was unused to weakness and physical frailities, he seemed to feel he was the one who let us down.

"I'm the one who ramrodded this here damn-fool, wild-goose scheme, and talked you fellers who should've had more sense into comin' along," he lamented.

"Yeah, that's so," I grinned, rubbing my stiff knuckles, "but I wouldn't have missed it for anything."

"Well, I reckon we all could've missed yestiddy right easy," he allowed dryly. "But all thet stuff aside,—it just seems like Providence ain't inclined to give us no decent chance't at them mustangs a'tall. Tho', if it wasn't for the Black Hawse, I don't reckon I would give a billy-be-damn."

Bid put away a hearty meal at noon and that afternoon, after the day's heat had hit its high, he announced that by the time we "could saddle and pack he reckoned he would be ready to ride." We brought in the horses and as a substitute for the mule we tied the pack on the buckskin, then helped Bid on old Joker and were on our way. We crossed the river half a mile above the bluffs and headed due north, aiming to strike the Arkansas in a little over thirty miles. This was approximately the route of the age-old Government *Survey known then as Brown's Trace. Our horses stepped right along in the cool of the evening and we made several miles before we stopped for night in a wide shallow draw near a buffalo wallow.

After a leisurely start next morning, we continued on, keeping to the west of the shallow draw and saw numerous buffalo on the slope of the other side. By the middle of the morning we reached Sand Creek (North Fork) and crossed near the zenith of the big bend. Evidently the storm which struck us with so much fury had been much lighter on this watershed, because only a shallow flow of nearly clear water ran between the low grassy banks where we crossed. This seemed a pleasant little creek, coming from the southwest and meandering through green little meadows. It was bordered on the south, though well back from the channel, by a low broken line of hills covered with soapweed and bunch grass.

"Mighty purty cattle country heah, if it just had a mite more cover," Bid commented.

We had just crossed the creek and started up the half-mile long hill on the north when we heard a low and disconsolate bray. Looking back over our shoulders we beheld coming towards us like a long lost friend. none other than old Satank, the pack mule. A little thin and haggard looking, to be sure but for once in his wicked life, glad to be among friends. As he snuggled up against Old Joker like a colt, even Mustang had to laugh. I had never seen the occasion before when Bid couldn't come up with a proper and fitting oath, but this time he could only pull up and and stare. Here was a mule he had called every name in the book and given many a hearty and deserving whack, a mean and untrustworthy critter he had never suspected of having one decent animal instinct. But his loss of words was only momentary, for Bid was a born mimic, and the classic words of the shady old horse trader again seemed most appropriate—"Satank, if you ain't a pictuah of abject humility."

Several miles further on we stopped for our noon break in

* In 1825 the U.S. Government commissioned an engineer Joseph Brown to survey the then new Santa Fe Trail. He surveyed a route almost due south from the Arkansas through the Sandhills, following Bear Creek for a short distance and then across the flat prairie crossing the North Fork and thence on to the Lower Spring.

303

sight of a scattered herd of buffalo on one side and on the other a smaller band of antelope. Neither paid us much attention, particularly the antelope who lay scattered about on the hot flats, apparently mostly concerned with their midday siesta. Ordinarily we would have eagerly unlimbered our rifles, but we had plenty of grub to get us back to civilization and in the heat of the July sun, in this God-forsaken land, the thought of fresh meat held little appeal to any of us. We were more concerned with the fruitless thoughts of cool water and the many hot and weary miles separating us from the Arkansas. The last in particular because we commenced to make out through a dancing haze and mirage the low outlines of the desert Sandhills.

Soon we struck the ruts of the old Brown Trace and followed them to the big basin of Bear Creek, where we found a wide area covered with fine grass and stale waterholes. The animals took advantage of the welcome water and drank their fill, but we finicky humans drank the now warm water of Sand Creek from our canteens. Mustang called attention to the dainty manner Satank waded out in the water and sipped like a gentleman. "Look at thet contrary li'l son-uv-a-bitch, if he had a pack on him, fust thing he would do is lay down in thet mud hole and roll."

Bid grinned reproachfully. "Aw now, what do yo'all expect from a pore begotten jackass, afteh all he done outrun the best the Kiowa Nation could throw at him, and whilst he was at it, maybe savin' our unbeholden scalps."

We moved on and soon rode in the dry channel of Bear Creek. A chapter could be devoted to the vagaries of Bear Creek and still not tell it all. One might tell how it starts on the high flats of Eastern Colorado, in sight of lonesome Two Buttes and flows northeast nearly one hundred miles towards its original outlet, the Arkansas River. And how somewhere in the unknown past it has all but lost its way in the jumble of shifting sandhills, we were about to enter, and how in historical times it is apt to divert its rare but massive floodwaters over a vast flatland to eventually flow in the big north draw* that leads to Sand Creek.

As we rode along a shallow section of the channel where our heads were well above the banks, our attention was drawn a

* Lakin Draw and into the North Fork of the Cimarron.

mile or so west where numerous buffalo could be seen grazing along the flats. A horseman appeared riding rapidly in our direction being pursued by a half dozen others. The leading rider suddenly turned north where the valley floor appears to rise rather abruptly towards the Sandhills. With the field glasses we could see puffs of smoke as he fired at his pursurers and made out the distinct color of his white horse before he rode out of sight over the ridge. We saw enough to know that a lone white man was in a heap of trouble. but other than sympathize. he was too far away for us to help. I remembered then. he was the first of our own kind we had seen in five days.

With our eyes peeled and guns ready, we continued through the Sandhills, following the indefinite channel of Bear Creek. A cloud built up in the west and soon came between us and the sun, and our ride became more pleasant. We finally came out of the sandhills into a large flat and soon came to the river which we stayed near until we saw a large island with cottonwood and willows for cover. This seemed a pleasant haven so we forded the shallow waters and camped there for the night.

Two days later we rode into Fort Dodge, as bewhiskered and disreputable looking trio as was ever seen. We made the near eighty miles without incident, yet times, we had our doubts. The first few miles after leaving the island we congratulated ourselves that at last we were nearing civilization and old Barney's prophecy had already been repeated in a caustic imitation by Bid, "Yas Sir, ay-ee doggies. a man's har mought be safer on the Cimarron than up hyar." But then, we commenced to notice that no one else was on the road and we made ten miles before we saw another soul. A single horseman approached us from the east. As he came closer he watched us very carefully until he was sure we were white. He proved to be a civilian dispatch rider going to Ft. Lyons. He told us the Indians were killing and pillaging all over the country and intimated that only a few brave men like himself dared venture out without an escort. It was apparent that his courage was bolstered somewhat by the liquid variety, but he was confident his fortitude would hold up for the entire trip because the two canteens he carried on his saddle were not filled with water. According to him a small caravan had been ambushed near the Cimarron Crossings a few days ago, and the wrecked and partly burned wagons could still be seen from the trail. After this tragic incident, traffic had almost come to a halt along the Santa Fe Trail. His words gave us food for thought, but we concluded to take them with a grain of salt until we found out better. But by late afternoon, having met no further travelers, we were not so sure. That night we picked a campsite with our backs to the river and a large and clear open space in front. The next morning when we approached the vicinity of the Crossings, sure enough in the distance were the scattered wrecks of three or four wagons. Later we came near the line of low bluffs which border the river bottoms on the north. Realizing these were ideal cover for an ambush, we pulled to the right nearer the river. When nearing the Point of Rocks*, three Indians on horseback appeared along the crest and were in sight at intervals for a mile or more. No doubt they were aware we were well armed and ready because we were not molested.

Old Fort Dodge was used to the presence of rough lookng citizens, but in the summer of '68, a lot of new troops were in and out of there and some of these were fresh from the states, or at least a more settled area. Some of these lounged near the Sutler's store and they stared at us curiously. We ran across a few fellows we knew and they plied us with questions about the Indians south of river and we in turn asked about the happenings around the fort the past week.

A traveling photographer was at the post and we posed for pictures with weapons in our hands. The photographer's helper, a bright-eyed young man with goggle-eyed glasses, and an unsatiable curiosity, noticed Bid's somewhat wan appearance and questioned him directly about it. Now Bid was the type of fellow who sometimes resents a direct query, but only a gleam came in his eye as he admitted with apparent reluctance he had "taken an arrer on Sand Creek". Then the young man wanted to see the wound, but Bid politely, though firmly, refused. "No sir, I'd ruther not talk about it nuther," he said sadly. "Two times them Kioways forced us in the kiver of the bluffs and two times we repelled them with turrible losses—and I kain't bear to think of

* Not to be confused with Point of Rocks on the Cimarron.

306

them poor comrades we planted in the shifting sands of the Cimarron." He shook his head dolefully and Mustang and I silently followed suit.

We reported to the proper authorities, the lone horseman we had seen pursued by Indians near Bear Creek on the south edge of the Sandhills. No one knew of a man or horse fitting that description. Later we tried again to get information regarding the same incident and met with the same result. His fate has always remained a mystery to me, as well as did his identity. In those days records were kept that supposedly covered all citizens killed by the Indians each year. These records have been quoted as official and correct. Official they no doubt were, but they can hardly be considered correct (or should we say complete) because on the frontier, communications were poor: much of the area was too remote and human nature too capricious to know with any certainty of all the isolated killings.

The worsening Indian situation created a demand for experienced men to serve as scouts, carry dispatches and similar chores for the Army. Our old aquaintance, the Sergeant, looked us up and made us an offer, explaining he could issue us arms and ammunition and five days rations if we would remain on call at or near the Post. After some discussion, Mustang accepted and Bid and I rode on out to the ranche. Before we left, Mustang called me to one side. I guessed what was coming, as some time earlier I had seen him in earnest conversation with Bid, and from the stern set expression on the latter's face, I judged they weren't discussing the sunrise.

"Say, Caroliny," he said gruffly, "I want to say I don't hold nothin' agin you fer what happened down there on the Cimarron. Hit musta been the whiskey thet made me mean like I wuz. And I wanta say right here I wouldn't fight yo'all agin fer a hundred dollar hawse with saddle and bridle throwed in."

"And I wanta say," I agreed as we shook hands, "I wouldn't fight you again for a hundred dollar buggy mare with a mule colt by her side."

CHAPTER XIV

The Hay Meadows of the Arkansaw

At the ranche we were greeted warmly by the Power's family as they had almost given us up for lost. Old Barney was still at the ranche and they had been left to themselves by the Indians. We gave them, at first, a somewhat deleted version of our adventures which we gradually elaborated to Tom and Barney. We found the family living well, off the bounty of the land: fresh antelope every few days and Tom and Sid had caught a big mess of catfish down at the river. Everything in fact was well, except the cantankerous nature of Western Kansas had finally asserted herself and hot winds and lack of rainfall was fast drying up the cornfield, with the exception of a couple of acres that lay well on the bottom and caught the runoff from the spring rains. This small patch was still flourishing and now in tassel, giving promise of roasting ears soon to come. But Tom, a pure farmer at heart, took the loss of the main patch more seriously than its size warranted.

"Dunno what happened," he mourned, "never saw corn fire so fast in all my born days."

"Shecks," old Barney informed us privately, "I knowed all along he couldn't raise no corn in this hyar place."

But if the corn prospects were doomed, the land offered still other opportunities. For example, the broad meadows of the Arkansas were covered with thousands of acres of heavy and luxuriant grasses. In the sixties, portions of this had begun to be utilized as hay, particularly in areas near the military posts, and for that matter at any time and place along the Santa Fe Trail there was always a demand for hay and it usually sold for a premium price. For many years the reaper and the mowing machine had been used and out here the mowing machine had truly found its place. Man had not yet successfully grown culti-vated crops west of Larned, but with the help of new and improved machines, he could readily profit from those crops nature grew so bountifully. Therefore it wasn't surprising that Tom hadn't finished mourning his corn crop until he became "all hepped up" over prospects for making some easy money in the hay meadows. "And I reckon," he wound up, "if a man had a machine and crew together, he could start in a couple of weeks or less."

I have no right to criticize Tom for as a matter of fact, I was as enthused as he, possibly because I had envisioned the possibilities since early spring. Accordingly, the very next day Tom and Barney drove to the Fort to talk business. In a remote settlement such as Dodge, the Sutler and his associates were usually some of the most important and influential men in the area, not only as far as the military was concerned, but also to the civilians. Such officials sometimes serving as advisor, confidant, and perhaps even banker. If he was a man of integrity, he soon held the trust and confidence of the community. If he was unable or unwilling to help a man business-wise, he could perhaps direct him to someone who could, if he deemed the proposition feasible. Tom's activities this summer had earned him a reputation for courage and hard work. And when he came home that evening he was elated because he had just negotiated a handshake agreement to fill a sub-contract for Government hay, wherein he would be advanced the money to buy a new mowing machine and lumber necessary for hayracks and etc. at 5% interest and all he and I needed was to sign a note. The Indian situation at the time appeared so threatening to the successful filling of hay contracts that the contractors were as eager to sub-let as we were to accept Two days later Bid and I. with three empty wagons and ten head of mules, were on our way to Hays City in company with a small wagon train and a *six man trooper escort. At Hays we were to pick up freight for Dodge, purchase a little lumber and supplies for our haying venture and incidently bring back a brand new McCormick mowing machine that was supposed to be waiting on the dock at the Union Pacific E.D. (Kansas Pacific) depot. Near the crossing of the Pawnee we had the opportunity to take on a couple wagon loads of wood for Hays City delivery. The delay only cost us half a day and the hauling charge made a little money for Tom. A little over a day and a half later we drove into Hays despite all the Indian talk, without having seen a single redskin.

* Probably a detachment from the "soon to be famous" Seventh Cavalry.

309

That night we had just seated ourselves at a table of the new town's best restaurant in anticipation of steaks, ham and beans, lightbread and berry pie, when who should appear but our former wagon-boss, Clint McCanles. The rough and rugged wagon-boss was in good humor and if he held any hard feelings from our last meeting, he didn't show them as he clomped over to our table and greeted us.

"Well, By God, if it ain't old deacon Power's two right-hand men. You fellers still a'gaddin' mules fer a livin', I reckon?"

We agreed that was our present occupation.

"Occupation maybe," he scoffed, "but at a Goddamn niggers pay, I'll betcha. Why fellers, I'm a freightin' out of Sheridan, the new town at the end of the line, to Denver; and I kin give you an "occupation" a'workin' fer me at wages you never heard of— two dollars and a half a day and board. Now, what in the hell do you think of that?"

We agreed that was mighty good wages, but we liked our present jobs and couldn't leave Tom in the lurch, nohow.

"Aw, you sanctimonious bastards," he grinned sourly, "I knowed you'd say that, but jist keep my offer in mind, it'll be good 'til the railroad opens up again next spring and then old Clint will get him another gradin' contract and'll still be apayin' top money fer men and mules".

"Think it over," he advised, "and if you change yore minds, you kin wire me collect at Sheridan." Then he elbowed his way roughly out of the room.

Bid grinned reflectively, "Well now, if he wasn't in good humor. The last time I saw Mr. McCanles he wasn't nigh thet sociable."

The next day we loaded our two big wagons with freight; and the other, which was just the bare running gears, we pulled over to the lumber yard and loaded with enough rough lumber to build two eighteen foot hayracks. Early the next morning we were out on the road again, headed for Fort Dodge, with the spanking new mowing machine oiled up slick as a ribbon and

310

trailing behind my wagon and behind that a riding hayrake of the latest design.

A week later we pulled over on the Arkansas bottoms about three or four miles from the ranche and set up our hay camp. We had a crew of seven, not counting Tom and Sid who spent their time between the ranche and haycamp. The regular crew consisted of Mustang, a pair of Mexicans, Jose* and one Ramon, an Irishman and ex-freighter Pat Gillespie, who had fallen out with his boss at the Fort and a big, hard-working Missourian by the name of Luke, who was the stacker. besides Bid and myself. Bid and I didn't trust anyone on that mowing machine but ourselves and we kept it and the rake going, switching back and forth like a pair of kids with a new toy. Old Barney, like Tom and Sid, plied his time between the ranche and haycamp, the policy being never to leave the ranche without at least one man and a rifle, at any time. As has been mentioned before, Barney knew Indians and their ways and in some situations his services were invaluable. Although we hadn't been bothered lately, there was a lot of Indian movement and unrest in the country. Almost any still day we could see what we took to be signal smokes and Barney usually came up with a pretty shrewd assessment of what they meant.

Bid and I aimed to keep the mowing machine going from sunup until sundown. This necessitated constant vigilance and good care, but we got a few spare parts with the machine and two extra sickles. Tom usually came over long enough each day to sharpen a sickle on the grindstone, as it was usually necessary to change for a sharp one every half day.

We were fortunate in getting a good crew and we set them a good example. Of course, this was in the days before the modern buckrake and mechanical stacker and all the hay had to be pitched out of the windrow into wagons and hauled to the stack. This was hard work, but the crew was up to it and luckily the first few days during the breaking in period, were moderately cool and pleasant.

Everything went so well the first five days, we estimated

* The same Jose who had been cook and roustabout with the McCandles train.

311

our contract was over half filled. But that only spurred us to more effort because hay was selling from thirty to sixty dollars a ton and hard to get at that. There was no lack of a market, whether it be Uncle Sam, the stage company, or some private freighter.

On the sixth day we moved camp and started cutting on a new section of meadow. Tom thought the hay would be a little better if we would wait a couple more weeks for it to mature, but no one, least of all him, suggested we wait. After all, we had a crew now, the weather was fine and there certainly wasn't very much wrong with the hay. At our new camp we set up the tent and wagon with the river protecting the rear, as was our custom. Over a quarter of a mile to the north we posted a lookout on the bluff whenever anyone was available to fill that position. And the new stackyard was started on a slightly elevated piece of bottom land between camp and the bluff. It was a rather pretty piece of bottom land as viewed from the bluff if one had the time to sit and enjoy it. Bid started mowing on the new land about the middle of the afternoon and there was little for me to do as the rest of the crew was finishing stacking at the first camp, so I mounted my horse and rode north a few miles and shot a big fat buffalo calf and brought the saddle back for camp meat.

The next day Tom had to go to the Fort for grub and supplies. We figured it was unsafe for one man to go alone so we pulled Pat off the hay wagon to go with Tom and sent Mustang over to the ranche until they returned from the Fort. I guess Tom gave the commandant a big song and dance about all the danger we were in, "while procuring hay for the benefit of the army", and suggested they should send at least two or three troopers to protect our hay camp. He was promptly informed that if everyone in danger was furnished a guard there wouldn't be any soldiers left at the Fort. But in the end he was issued two long range Springfield rifles and fifty rounds of ammunition with the admonition to keep his "damned mouth shut, as this was strictly off the record and the less heard about it the better for everyone concerned". The two rifles were a welcome addition to our armament, but they were of the type recently modified to breech-loaders using metallic cartridges and the trapdoor mech-

312

anism didn't provide reliable ejection of the empty cartridge which reduced their firepower accordingly.

Tom and Pat brought back disquieting news from other hay-camps that lay above us. According to the stories, 'at least', the Indians had raided some of them repeatedly, wounding a number of haymakers, killing oxen and mules and stealing stock, as well as burning hay. Tom warned us that so far we had just been lucky and advised us to keep our arms by our sides at all times. This was advice which none of us belittled, but just try pitching hay all day in the heat of summer time with a three or four pound pistol strapped to your side. So the men usually took their six-shooters off and hung them in their scabbards on the wagon standards or left them at the stack. Bid and I wore ours on the mowing machine and rake, but in order to keep them in a working condition, it was necessary to wrap them with rags to protect them from the dust and our rifles were left in camp from necessity. Of course, at no time were we over a half mile from camp and we were constantly vigilant in all directions. We figured in case of a surprise attack the odds were still greatly in our favor of beating the enemy to the camp.

The first few days went well at the camp, although the hay was very heavy and the mowing was necessarily slow, the tonnage per day was even better than it had been. Tom was forced to drop his daily visits to camp because of the danger in leaving the family at the ranche unguarded. But Barney continued his trips back and forth, though we never knew when to expect him. Sometimes he appeared suddenly on top the lookout bluff, with all the stealth of an Indian and giving us a momentary chill. I think the old man got an inward chuckle out of his tricks, but it wasn't funny to the rest of us, particularly Luke, the stacker. Luke was a big husky fellow and an outstanding worker, but he wasn't overly blessed with raw courage and being fresh from Missouri his knowledge of wild Indians was based entirely on the tall stories he had heard. After two or three of Barney's sudden and sometimes dramatic appearances he became so agitated that he neglected his work and spent most of his time peering in the distance for "Injuns". He even talked seriously of quitting, but I assured him if he did, he would have to walk back to the Fort on his own, as we couldn't possibly afford him an escort. The prospect of this scared him even more than staying. The success of the whole haying venture depended on our help and possibly more so on the stacker than anyone, so we had to keep him one way or another. In the interests of this, the pleasurable pastime of telling hair raising Injun stories to an easterner was strictly forbidden. Bid and I went out of our way to convince him the stories of Indian atrocities were nearly all exaggerated and that as well armed as we were, about the worst we could expect was to have our mules run off, the hay burned and a lot of yelling and showing off. All of our talking didn't completely placate him but he did stay on the job, probably because he couldn't get away.

One evening about an hour before sundown, after Barney had left the lookout and returned to the ranche, twenty-five or thirty Indians appeared on the high ground to the north and made a mad dash towards camp, screaming their war cries. I probably saw them first, but as luck would have it I was taking my turn at the mower and was at the far end. I knew that racing the Indians to camp with the mowing machine would neither do that contrivance any good nor improve my chances of getting there alive. So I took a few precious seconds to unhook the traces and fasten them over the mules backs. Then I vaulted on the big red and let the neck yoke ring slip off the end of the tongue, and headed for camp at a dead run. Bid was on the rake nearby and Mustang and Jose were loading hay in one of the wagons. They all made it easily where Bid directed the others to take care of the mules while he went for his Spencer. Although my two big mules were stretched out and running like a chariot team, three young bucks attempted to cut me off and they almost made it. Bending low over the red mule I dug my pistol out of the scabbard, hastily wiped the rags off the mechanism and cut down on the lead Indian at about thirty paces. Twice I fired as fast as I could thumb the hammer, but he paid no more attention than if I were throwing rocks; however, a lucky third shot stumbled his pony and spilled him on the ground. As he tried to scramble out of the way I deliberately ran him down and as the big mules passed over him I took a snap shot at his twisting, squirming body at a range of only a few feet. I must have missed him completely, for upon glancing back I saw him limping and lurching to his feet, undoubtedly scared and a little dazed, but still plenty active. Disgusted, I felt like throwing the pistol away. In the meantime Bid ran out from camp a hundred yards, shooting at the other two Indians with his Spencer. On his fourth shot he dropped one of the ponies, which discouraged their attempt to cut me off and I rode in and plowed the team to a halt behind the shelter of the hay wagon.

Over at the haystacks, things weren't going too well either. With their wagon half unloaded, the men first decided to stay in the shelter of the stacks, but the main force of Indians riding on the sides of their ponies circled the stacks shooting arrows wildly at them. Bid and I opened up with our repeaters at long range and soon put a stop to their activities between us and the stackyard. Pat slapped the mules on the backs and headed toward us at a run, followed by about twenty of the savages. Ramon, kneeling in the hay at the back of the wagon, kept them at a distance with his six-shooter, but unaided by big Luke who was so excited he had jumped in the wagon and left his gun lying on the ground by the water jug. As Pat wheeled the half-loaded hayrack into camp, I saw the shaft of an arrow sticking in the off mule's side and the red froth from his mouth told me he was hard hit. For a few minutes it took three men to handle the stock and keep them behind cover which reduced our firepower for the time being. But the Indians, wise in the ways of their kind, soon discovered we were well armed and stayed out of effective rifle range, where they rode back and forth, yelling and shooting just enough to keep us on edge. Every so often one better armed than his brethren would drop off his horse and carefully lob a rifle ball towards our hay wagon shelter. The distance was too great for accuracy and the bullets were pretty well spent, but they still had enough force to cause a nasty wound in man or beast. We retaliated with the Springfields and while we didn't score any direct hits, they moved back.

I turned to see Pat and Jose helping Ramon to the ground. The young Mexican's face was a sickly color and a bloody splotch spread over his shirt front, shoulder high. He had caught a bullet on the way from the stacks. Upon examination we found the bullet had gone clean through, apparently causing only a bad flesh wound, but serious enough to put him out of action for a couple of weeks at best. The little black bag came out and I bandaged and treated him as best as I could and gave him a shot of whiskey to top it off. Ramon, a little shy among the "Anglo" had been well liked by the crew because of his willingness to work and his easy grin. In the short dash from the haystacks to camp he had wielded his six shooter with enough authority that no one suspected he had been shot until it was discovered he was unable to get up. From then on every man in camp went out of his way to show him some little act of kindness.

The Indians were by no means through with their deviltry. Some of them quickly located the mowing machine and hitched their lassoes to it and dragged it over the meadow as close as they dared come to tantalize us, jerking it first one way, then the other, and even up-side-down until they played their ponies out. Their tactics hit Bid and I where it hurt because that machine was our special pride and joy, but we knew it would be suicide to retaliate, so we contented ourselves with name calling. To complete the day they set fire to the hay stacks, but fortunately a light rain had been falling and they got only the finished stack to burn, and this in spite of the shower of bullets we poured over there at long range. Luckily, the green stubble, damp from the shower wouldn't burn and we were spared that fearsome menace. But as darkness descended, the fire in the big stack lit up that end of the meadow in a spectacular show. Someone yelled, the Indians were creeping up on us along the riverbank. Bid and I slipped behind the tent and found a place where back to back we could command as far as we could see in the semi-darkness in either direction along the river. After an hour or more there, we decided that warning of danger was a false alarm, but the riverbank provided the only cover for an Indian to get in close and we rested none to easy. Alert, until hours after dark and all signs and sounds of the Indians had vanished, every man kept his place on guard, one man at a time slipping back to the tent to grab a bite to eat and check on the wounded man. Fortunately, the rain let up at sundown and it wasn't an unpleasant evening and after the big haystack finished burning, we had reason to hope the party was over, at least for the night.

It seemed probable that we had made it hot enough for our visitors that they would be content with the mischief they had done and leave us, but to relax our guard on that assumption would be foolish. Although we had forced the attackers to retire, Bid and I were disappointed with ourselves, for despite our repeating rifles and Springfield breechloaders, the Indians had been able to inflict some serious damage. One of our men was wounded and out of action, one mule about to die, a couple hundred dollars worth of hay burned and our mowing machine likely wrecked beyond repair. And perhaps what rankled worst, the other side had escaped with nothing worse than two or three crippled ponies. Grimly we tried to console ourselves with how much carnage we would have made "IF. them so-and-so's would have just had the guts to come in decent rifle range."—But, regardless of how we disliked his tactics, his propensity for showing off, and worse, his all compellng urge for blood and gore, the wild Injun was sometimes a mighty cagy fighter, rather than a fool or a coward. And that was a bitter pill we had to swallow whether we liked it or not.

Late in the evening we divided our force into watches of three men each, one group guarding while the other caught a little sleep. We posted one man in the hay wagon to scan the starlit meadow and the other two covered the more dangerous river bank. But the night passed calm and clear, and morning broke with no signs of Indians.

All night long I was worried about the folks at the ranche. Had they been attacked? If so, we best give up the haycamp completely and go to their assistance. We had been unable to hear any sounds of firing from that direction, which gave us some reason for cheer; still, the distance was several miles and you could never tell. At daybreak, Pat and I left on horseback for the ranche. We were less than a mile from camp when we saw old Barney coming our way. Everything was fine at the ranche, although the folks were greatly worried as they had seen the glow of the burning haystack and heard the guns firing. I told Barney to return at once and by all means, to stay alert and on guard and that we would report later and bring the wounded man over to the ranche if he was able to travel.

Ramon was loaded in one of the partly filled haywagons, pulled by our best team, and he with Pat and Jose left for the ranch. The rest of us stayed at the hay meadow, determined to try to pick up the pieces and continue haying as best we could. Under modern circumstances the extent of our damages might not seem severe, but here we were faced with the dilemma of a broken down machine for which there were no repairs closer than Hays City, perhaps even Kansas City, or the outside chance we could put it in running condition again. We hauled it into camp and looked with despair at the bent and twisted sicklebar, the broken tongue, dislocated seat and other miscellaneous minor battle scars. I was about to throw up my hands as Bid shook his head and walked away, but presently he returned carrying the sledge hammer in one hand and helping Mustang with the five foot section of railroad iron we had picked up at Hays (our only substitute for an anvil).*

"Fellars," he said, "there's just no two ways about it, we're gonna have to fix this battered up chunk of iron"—And we went to work.

Later, Pat and Jose returned from the ranch with the the empty haywagon and we put them to work hauling hay out of the windrow to the partly finished stack the Indians had been unable to burn, and stationed Mustang on the bluff as guard and lookout. One note of encouragement today was the attitude of Luke, the stacker, who having survived yesterday's fracas without a scratch, had learned a moral lesson he wasn't likely to forget. The quiet gritty manner the Mexican boy had taken his wound without fuss or bother, had a chastening effect on the big Missourian who talked no more of quitting and made a determined effort to keep his fears to himself.—And by the way we picked up his six-shooter, covered with a little hay where he had so ingloriously left it when the shooting began.

Bid and I with our crude and limited assortment of tools spent a sweaty and knuckle skinning day, putting the battle scarred mowing machine back into working order. But by late

* A 'moonlight' donation from Union Pacific E.D. via the ingenuity of Bid. The railroads were considered big and unscrupulous and any small item the common citizen could lift off them was held to be strictly legitimate, providing he didn't get caught.

318

afternoon we blocked her up and turned the drive wheel and the sickle worked slick as a ribbon. We looked at each other in silent approval, but voiced a few choice appellations toward Indians in general and those in particular who took a special delight in molesting men, beasts and mowing machines. The slick running mower had been the pride of our hay crew and the special joy of Bid and I, neither of us having had any previous experience with anything more efficient than the old reapers.

The next morning we took to the meadow with our patched and battered mower purring like a sewing machine, but due to our reduced crew we had to drop one haywagon. However, by mid-afternoon, we once again had both wagons going with a spare man besides. This stroke of luck came about in this manner; the so-called Wet Route of the Santa Fe Trail passed near the Arkansas bottoms where we were haying, although travel on it had been reduced to almost nothing due to the Indian menace. We looked up this morning and beheld about a dozen large ox-drawn wagons approaching from the east, with two mounted men riding well in advance. The train turned out to be a well-heeled outfit bound for New Mexico. The wagon boss politely enquired if it would be alright to pull off the trail and camp near us along the river. After our recent experiences, any white man looked good and I bade him welcome as long as they didn't graze or trample the uncut hay. He told me they only wanted to stay and rest up until the next morning before pulling on to Dodge, as they had been worried and harassed by Indians off and on since leaving Larned. A pair of young men from the states were traveling with them for protection and doing odd jobs for their board. As soon as I learned this I sought them out and offered them jobs. They were country boys so it turned out, but tender-feet, pure and simple. They said a paying job sounded good, but insisted they were headed for "The Wild West". As soon as I caught my breath I informed them "this was it!" and as they had seen enough Indians since leaving Larned, they were not too hard to convince and I hired them at a dollar and a half a day. We were paying our present help two and a half, but they were, for the most part, experienced men and furnished their own weapons. These tenderfeet were an ill-assorted pair, Dave rather short and solidly built with a ruddy complexion and a gift of gab while his partner was a big stolid fellow named Gotlieb, with a bashful grin and little to say. Their only armament was an old English made Adams revolver which Dave called "Ida May" and said his pappy had carried her at Mine Creek. He brought Ida May forth from his bedroll and explained her salient features and modestly admitted if properly held, she could hit a cat in the eye at half a quarter and while he was at it, he volunteered that he wasn't adverse to trying Ida May out on a real live "Injun". I wasn't impressed and advised him that we had men to take care of the shooting in case of an attack and that all we expected of him was to follow orders and keep out of the way. I had sized him up to be a knowing lad and I figured we just as well straighten out once and for all who was in charge here. Our haying crew were pretty well armed to handle any ordinary attack, but we could always use a couple of non-combatants to help take care of the stock. Undaunted however, Dave was waiting when Bid pulled into camp with the mowing machine for the noon stop. By the time the team was unhooked and fed, Bid had undergone a thorough interview from Dave and the pair of tenderfeet unconsciously earned themselves, nicknames, "David and Goliath"; Bid named them, and David and Goliath they were as long as they were in our brief employ.

The pair of new men, despite David's brashness turned out to be willing and able workers. For the next two days we made good progress at the haycamp, as with a full crew we were able to work out a more orderly schedule than we had in the past. Old Balaam was dependable as lookout and scout, so we put our extra man in a wagon and pressed Jose into service as cook, a job he had filled very well with the McCanles wagon train. This relieved Bid and I from this monotonous and demanding chore and provided us with a man in camp for those unexpected jobs that continually arise in such a venture. Jose, despite a rough exterior and an uncertain past, was as dependable a fellow as could be found.

We kept on the alert for Indians and knowing their preference for a dawn attack, we made it a practice to be up and preparing for the day's work well over an hour before sun-up. To make up for this early arising, we took off a full two hours at noon, which incidently, benefitted us with more of the cooler hours of the day for work.

Although the work was hard and the days long and hot, life at the haycamp was not without its rewards. We had plenty to eat with as much variety as possible under the circumstances. The nights were cool and sleep came easy and pleasant under the stars. But perhaps the event most looked forward to at the end of a long, hot day's work was the dip in the river just a few yards behind the tent. This time of year the river was low, but luckily here we had a hole about waist deep with a clear sandy bottom; no Roman Bath, mind you, but for our purpose we wouldn't have traded that water hole for a half interest in Niagara Falls.

No doubt we were scouted by the Indians and our habits were probably well known by them, because at breakfast time on our last day at this camp, a half dozen of the raiders managed to slip in close along the riverbank. At the same time a larger band appeared across the meadow, a pair of them dragging a flaming gunnysack and riding towards the stackyard. Luckily we had the foresight to bring the stock in of a night, because we had nearly all of Tom's Stock at the meadow on account of the availability of good grazing and water. The mules we were actually working were haltered to the hayracks and the other animals were in a small rope corral next to the haywagons. With one exception and that was "old Satank". The pack mule (on account of his disposition and his known ability to take care of himself) enjoyed unlimited freedom and had the run of the meadow. He toiled not and neither did he spin, but he had the confidence of the two Texans who firmly believed he could smell "Injuns half a mile down wind." Satank took full advantage of the situation and could usually be found where the meadow grass was sweetest and most nutritious, or else with his nose stuck in the haystack following the shade around on a hot day. He waxed fat and lazy and lived the life of the proverbial Riley. His only claim to his salt being his alleged prowess as a watchdog. This morning he had taken his usual stance at the small haystack near where we were finishing breakfast. Suddenly his long ears went up and he sniffed the cool morning air toward the riverbank, then he snorted like a locomotive letting off steam, wheeling in his tracks he sped past our breakfasting crew, scattering bits of hay in his wake and headed for the wide open spaces. within Satank the instinct of self-preservation was strong and he had a lot of faith in the ability of his legs to get him out of trouble. But to his credit his noisy antics and sudden departure gave us enough warning to grab our guns and be ready for the redskins along the river and a few quick shots soon sent them high-tailing. The big danger now appeared to be to the haystacks across the way. Pat and I quickly took positions in one of the hayracks and cut down on the bigger band at long range. Bid. joining in with his Spencer and despite the distance we must have made a few hits, judging from the way they scattered; but not before they touched off one of the haystacks which commenced smoking lazily.

These Indians were evidently expecting a surprise raid and our fire power quickly discouraged them; most of them abruptly withdrew to the top of the bluff. Some of the more adventurous ones on perceiving the flight of the pack mule, had taken after him with wild whoops, in a probable fruitless but face saving chase. Soon they disappeared from sight over the slope of the valley. "Thar goes the last of your damn mule," yelled Luke. But the rest of us were more concerned with the smoldering fire at the haystacks.

"Hitch the big team to thet empty wagon, you men, as damn quick as you can make your fingers fly!" Bid ordered Luke and the two new hands. "Me and Mustang'll load thet barrel of water and we're gonna put thet stack fire out."

In a matter of minutes they were on their way, pounding the mules into a gallop. Pat and I stayed in camp, perched on top the other hay rack with our rifles and kept them covered. At the stacks the men went to work with their pitchforks and wet gunnysacks and soon had the fire under control, aided by the light morning dew, which had made the hay and stubble slightly damp. Pat and I kept the Indians on the bluff at bay by elevating our Springfields and lobbing a few bullets in their midst and soon they retired from sight. By eight-thirty old Barney appeared on the bluff and gave us a wide sweeping wave and we knew the Indians were gone and everything was all right at the ranche. "Well, if there ain't Balaam on his ass," drawled Bid with porker-faced good humor.

In a very short time the mower was clacking busily and our crew was forking hay in the windrow. We had got off lucky this time.

At noon there was speculation among the crew as to the fate of Satank but we who knew him best were unworried. Bid even offered to bet he would show up in camp before morning. "Why," he assured us confidently, "the ornery devil knows a good thing when he sees it and the fear of Injuns ain't gonna keep him from this grubstake long."

That afternoon we moved camp to another meadow about a mile and a half away. We profited from our experiences and arranged things a little differently. As usual we setup with the river to our back but here, the near bank was very low and provided no cover or hiding places. The channel was over four hundred feet wide and the opposite (south) bank was high and steep with no easy means of descent, thus making it difficult for any enemy to make a surprise attack. The stackyard was placed next to camp, so close in fact, some of us slept on top of the stack with our rifles by our side when the weather permitted.

I calculated already we had considerably more hay than we needed to fill our contract, but hay in the stack was a valuable commodity and we decided to cut at least this last meadow while we had a good crew.

The next morning, on hand to greet us before the rising of the sun, was our erstwhile pack mule "Old Satank". He appeared somewhat used up and stiff and sore from over-exertion on his softened constitution, but otherwise without a mark on him. From then on, there was never any doubts as to the crosseyed little mule's knack to anticipate and outrun trouble.

By mid-morning I temporarily caught up with the raking. I saddled my horse and rode across the river, bent on scouting and exploring the south side hoping to bring in some buffalo or antelope meat. I located a narrow break in a steep bank and Old Blaze climbed out on the other side. Not far away in a sandy hollow I discovered a considerable thicket of sand plums that for size and profusion were the best I have ever seen. They hung on the branches almost like some overgrown species of grapes.

323

Although they were not dead ripe, they were delicious and sweet to the taste (providing one didn't dwell on the rind). After months of mostly a meat and potato diet, these were far more welcome than a saddle of fat antelope. I carried a burlap bag tied behind my saddle and in a short time I picked nearly enough to fill it. I was so pleased with my find I helped Jose prepare a mess of them for dinner, although it took nearly half of our total sugar supply to season them. I knew Mamie and the folks at the ranche would be delighted to have the balance of the plums so with this for an excuse I delegated the cook to take my place on the rake and left for the soddy. Upon coming near home, I found Tom and Sid had been busy with corn knives cutting the drought stricken corn for fodder. but for the time being they were enjoying a long dinner rest with Barney and Ramon on the shady side of the soddy. They had no idea I was near until old Shep announced my presence.

"It's a good thing I wasn't a war party on the prowl," I reproached them, half seriously, "or there would likely be some short haircuts among you fellows."

"I-ee doggies, Jack," rejoined Barney, "don't you know Injuns is like coyotes when it comes to hot weather, they ain't likely to prowl around any more than they jes have to."

"Maybe that's what makes me so mad. Here we whites strain and sweat all day in the sun trying to make a few honest dollars and then they move in on us in the cool of the evening or early morning and try to steal our stock and burn our hay. In this way I can agree whole heartedly with Clint McCandles in his distaste for their thieving habits."

I got a good look at Tom and he seemed soberly worried so I changed the subject and explained what I had in the bag behind by saddle. Quickly, thoughts turned from the nagging dread of Indians to the tasty tidbit at hand. Soon Mamie took a hand and shooed away young and old alike, explaining "she would just put the rest of the plums up in butter and preserves afore the bunch of you get a bellyache from gorging yourselves with them raw." I told them where the plum thicket was located and it was agreed when the haying was over, we would go "plumming."

Although he had little to say on the subject, I could see Tom was badly discouraged over the continually worsening Indian situation. To be faced with a problem over which he had no control, left Tom with a desire to be shut of it, to not think or talk of it any more than possible, in the vain hope somebody or something would come along and clear the whole thing up. Plainly, he had believed all spring and summer long the Government could and would control the Indians. And now it was clear they either could not or were not really trying. Word had spread to Fort Dodge that settlements west of Salina on the Saline, Solomon, Republican and Smokey Hill had been raided. And all of this just a few days after being supplied arms and ammunition from Larned. No doubt these first reports were exaggerated and the number of women and children murdered and the other atrocities were out of proportion to the facts. Still, it was bad enough, in fact, very bad indeed.

Without doubt the reaction from these events had much to do with the eventual punishment of the "wild tribes", and unfortunately the innocent among them as well as the guilty suffered. Because these raids were for the most part, on innocent and unarmed people. Settlers and their families who had a legal and just right to be where they were, and that was largely in a land that had never been claimed, at least with any validity by the members of the tribes who carried out the raids. Furthermore, they were carried out with a barbarious cruelty and vindictiveness typical of the worst element of the Redmen. The public was aroused, from Topeka to Denver they cried out for protection and "revenge". Travelers and settlers alike near the frontier were scared and they were "mad".

But to get back to Tom. I could see his worrying had reached the point where I feared the next little event of a discouraging nature might cause him to toss away everything he had worked for all spring and summer, and pack up the family and go back to civilization. For, though he was a hardy soul and a good industrious worker (when the spirit moved him), occasionally he needed a little encouragement and perhaps someone to lean on. And this was one of those times. From then on I avoided all talk of Indians and dwelt instead on the good progress we were making with the hay and of the prospects for some extra money we had. All of this cheered him up a little, but not much for he was down in the doldrums so deep, I think he feared the hay would all go up in smoke before the red-tape of Government approval and acceptance was completed.

About an hour later I started back to camp with a sack full of the last of the late corn and a small pail of fresh butter. As I turned to wave back at the family I realized "in the rush of haying" it had been over two weeks since I had last set foot on the sod ranche.

That evening, near sundown, two riders leading a pair of mules, came in sight from the east. At camp, we had no reason to suspect them of being other than ordinary citizens, but Old Satank, below camp and near the river where he had found a choice grazing spot, suddenly came dashing into camp, a little stiff from his last run, but with his eyes flashing fire. For once I was sure his instinct had failed him, but when the two men rode up they were none other than my old acquaintance, Smokey Joe Smith and a pure-blood Kaw Indian, with the unlikely name of "Deer John". They were hunting strays for the stage company and spent the night with us. Satank was suspicious and unsettled until the two rode out of sight the next morning. In the later discussion of this little event, some of the crew remembered the evening the Indians raided our first camp. They had noticed the little mule acting "powerful funny", but at that time they knew nothing of his peculiar powers of perception and thought no more of it. From then on Satank became the chief topic of conversation among the hay crew and "Satank watching" became a kind of a game. If he had been of a different disposition he could have had affection but he wasn't that kind of a mule. Satank was mean and orney and there was no getting around that. The only language he understood was a hearty kick in the belly and a blistering curse; these applied with the proper emphasis would result in a certain amount of reluctant obedience, and respect. Any attempt to caress or pet him was down right foolhardy and no one ever tried it twice. Furthermore, it was never safe to venture in his immediate rear unless you knew that he knew, you were prepared to commit mayhem upon him. For these reasons Old Satank never became the camp pet.

The next few days things went well at the hay meadow and on the sixth of August we stacked the last of the hay. By then, Tom contracted with a civilian dealer at the Fort to deliver twenty-five tons of hay at top prices. We paid off Luke and David and Goliath and started delivering on this contract. Indians in substantial numbers were known to be moving up and down the Arkansas, especially in the more broken land on each side of the river. We took no unnecessary chances and always moved two wagons at a time; Bid and I riding horseback with our repeating rifles, and the men on the wagons armed with revolver and rifles. We put four mules strung out, on each wagon so we could move in a hurry if necessary. Late the second day we met ten Indians just as we were leaving the stackyard with our last loads. It turned out their leader was the same chief who had visited the Soddy in June with Old Red Bear. He recognized me and we said "How" and heap "hook-ah-hay" (which I had picked up from Barney) then we shook hands. We had with us a few pounds of coffee and some sugar; as a goodwill gesture we shared this with them and parted friends. I felt pretty good after this piece of diplomacy and told the boys we wouldn't have any trouble with that band of Indians.

"Maybe." Bid said sarcastically. "especially if y'all sweeten em with sugar and coffee once or twice' a week."

"Well, it's cheaper than powder and lead at that."

"That's so," he agreed, matter-of-factly, "but it's a damn sight less permanent."

CHAPTER XV

A Plumming We Did Go

By the following day we finished hauling to the Fort and hauled and built a sizeable stack at the ranche. This finished the hay work, so we paid off the crew, having collected from our civilian contract, more than enough to pay all hands, plus other operating expenses. Bid and Mustang agreed to stay for awhile longer, although for the first time in weeks the former mentioned his obligation to report to work for Mr. McCoy in Abilene. I knew this was a commitment which he had delayed several times for our benefit, but one, despite his careless manner, which he fully intended to honor. Early the next morning he, with Mustang, Pat and Jose, left for the Fort with one of the heavy wagons which required some blacksmith work. Our friendship with the Smithy and the Sargeant usually led them to wink at Army regulations when Tom's equipment needed emergency repairs.

Ordinarily, Ramon the Mexican boy would have left along with Pat and Jose, having recovered enough from his wound to be on his way, but he had made a good impression on the Power's family and by mutual agreement he stayed on. Probably in all his life the young man had never been treated so well; certainly never by "Anglos" and he insisted on working out his board and care. He observed the need to herd and drive the stock to water and as much of his life had been spent among the "sheeps and caballada" of his native New Mexico, and as that was where his talents lay, he could be of useful service to "Senor Tom".

With these circumstances suggesting a near idle day at the ranche, the family remembered the wild plum patch I had discovered while haying, and insisted this would be an ideal time to go there. Tom took to the idea with more enthusiasm than he had shown for a long time. It was against my better judgement, but I didn't advise against it. Besides, Mamie and the younger children hadn't been off the ranche for over a month and the prospect of a jaunt just a few miles down to the river seemed like an exciting outing to them. Sid considered himself about grown up and insisted on staying at the ranche to help Ramon with the stock, the pair had driven the animals to water and back so many times it was routine with them. Both boys knew enough to keep their eyes peeled for trouble and what to do in that event.

Mamie packed a picnic lunch of two young fried chickens and other home goodies and we were off with Barney and I on mule and horseback respectively, providing an armed guard. Well, before noon we crossed the river below our last hay camp and were soon among the plum bushes. With all hands busy it didn't take long to fill all the containers. As the day was pleasant and cooler than we had been accustomed to, we relaxed and enjoyed ourselves. The kids chased each other, yelling and screaming, up and down the ravines and through the bushes with Mamie advising them loudly to look out for snakes. We found a shady bank and Tom drove the wagon over and we unhitched the team and fed them some hay. Mamie got out the lunch basket and I skinned down the steep river bank and got a pail of clear cool water. Then Tom admonished his kids to settle down and fixed a stern eye upon them until they did, whereupon he bowed his head and said grace. He dwelt for some time expressing his appreciation to the "Almighty" for his graciousness, in particular the bounteous harvest he had bestowed upon us, alluding in part to the baskets and pails filled with the red sand-hill plums. Which brings a point to mind regarding human nature; here we were on the Redman's side of the river, but outside of being a little concerned for our own personal safety, I don't recall that any of us had the slightest twinge of conscience or shame or any feeling whatsoever that we might be trespassing on the Indians.

We were just finishing lunch when young Tommy emerged excitedly from the bushes carrying a brightly colored feather. "Oh looky, maw, I found me an Injun feather."

As soon as Barney and I got a good look we exchanged glances and withdrew to the other side of the wagon.

"That feather," said the old man ominously, "'pears to be Kioway and its been drapped right recent, since that little shower last night fer shore."

"We know Indians are going up and down this river whenever they feel like it. Just what do you mean?"

"I mean I'm afeared Injuns is clos't, mebbe in hearin' distance right now."

"That's great and we've been making enough noise around here to rouse the dead for a mile."

Barney saddled his mule. "I'm gonna scout around over yonder." And he waved his hand downstream and towards the hills. "You and Tom best get that team hitched an' Miz Powers and them kids started home pronto."

Tom, already a little curious, tossed away a last drumstick and came around the wagon just as Barney was leaving. I explained the situation as the old scout viewed it and saw the sickly look on Tom's face that always came when he feared for his family.

"Maybe we best keep still about Indians, but we better pull out of here at once." I glanced at some thunderheads building up in the west. "We can tell them we don't want to get caught in a rain."

In a few minutes we were hitched to the wagon and on our way, despite the disappointed wailings of the youngsters. Tom and I would feel a little less uneasy when we had put the river behind us. For the first time we felt like interlopers in a forbidden land.

When we reached where we had crossed in the morning, Tom crowded the team down the bank a little too fast and then had to hold back and caused a weakened hame strap to break. He managed to get the wagon level in the stream before we had to stop and fix it. Standing in about a foot of water, we managed a makeshift repair with whang leather, and then proceeded on across the river. A quarter of a mile on the other side I glanced back and saw old Barney start across with his mule splashing sheets of water in her haste. I told Tom he had better hurry and turned my horse to help the old man. Before I reached the river I saw Indians riding along the south bank looking for an easy descent into the river. Pulling up in a little ravine, I dismounted, rifle in hand as the old scout cleared the bank. He spat out a liberal chaw, "Like to rid square into a hornet's nest," he observed, glancing back at the Indians.

It seemed like a poor time to catch up on our visiting, especially as his doughty old mule could never win any horse races. "Go on and catch up with the wagon," I advised him, "I'll stay here a little while and see if I can't slow 'em down."

The river was well over four hundred feet wide at this spot, a little out of easy range for my Henry. But I held it a little high and as the lead Indian started down the opposite bank I fired and must have nicked his horse because he quickly pulled back and held a brief consultation with his brethren. Then they tried it again in two groups a few hundred feet apart, apparently trying to keep more out of range while attempting a circling maneuver. Contenting myself with a couple of quick shots, I mounted old Blaze and left them amid a scattered volley of shots. I waved my rifle mockingly and gave them the Rebel yell. In just a little while they were left far behind.

It took me some time to catch up with the wagon and then Barney and I stayed about fifty yards back, one on each side. Tom was crowding the mules for about all they had and it was plain to see unless some accident befell them, the Indians couldn't possibly catch up. A more likely danger was the chance of hitting a chuckhole or washout and wrecking the wagon. I pulled along side. "Take it easy, Tom," I yelled, "you're gonna make it alright without ruining your team." Mamie was begging him to slow down and between us he finally got the message and slowed down to a trot. Mamie declared afterwards she was more frightened of the ride than the Indians.

The Indians followed us to the top of the low ridge southeast of the soddy and they watched from there as the wagon drove into the shelter of the sod walls. Evidently they had scouted the ranche pretty well and knew its connection with the haycamps and feared a large force of defenders, because they never came close and soon retired in the direction of the river. We watched them with the field glasses from the watch tower until they were out of sight. Not long afterward a big smoke appeared down river several miles and we didn't have to be told they were burning the haystacks at our last haycamp.

At dusk, Bid along with Pat, came in with the wagon, but minus Mustang. Bid was tight-lipped and said little and I knew him well enough to not question him. I got Pat off to one side and he supplied the answer. "Old Musty was a hangin' on a big one an' him and Bid had words. Bid said to Hell with him and called him a drunken bastard and said he wasn't bringin' him home among'st decent folks."

But Tom had somehow taken a liking to Mustang, who had been on his good behavior during the haying. He accosted Bid a little gruffly, "why'nt you bring him home? I've seen drunks before."

"Not like him, you ain't." Bid answered, "besides, I was thinking of Mis Powers and the kids."

"Well." Tom allowed, somewhat mollified, "we kin get him tomorrow."

"Forgit him, Tom," Bid advised, "he ain't worth it. I quit him once't before for similar reasons, not thet I ain't gone a bit fur myself a few times. But Mustang, when he gets too much whiskey is sloppy and mean as a fightin' hawg. I warned him afore noon when he taken his first drink, but there was no stoppin' him, once't he got started."

CHAPTER XVI

Scared Out

That evening at the supper table Bid casually mentioned. "Oh yes, Tom I nigh forgot, but we run across Andy Cooper. He had just got in from Hays City with a load of freight. He aims to rest up his teams a bit before heading back—said he would likely be a droppin' in on us tomorry."

Tom perked up at this news, "good old Andy," he said, "I sure will be glad to see him." Then he relapsed into unaccustomed silence, taking little interest in the conversation around him. Tom was worried and was never very good at disguising his feelings. I suspected he was in the painful process of making a hard decision. He knew as well as I did that Bid and Pat were deliberately sparing him and the family unpleasant news of Indian activity. For at that time no man could spend a day at any army post west of Abilene and not hear of some new outrage, whether true or not. The Indians were active and they were hostile. And the news media of the Plains, no matter how sparse and undeveloped, someway always managed to quickly spread any word that might create fear and horror. Tom with a family to think of, had enough of that. The situation was becoming intolerable to him and as the head of our little group, he was going to have to make a decision that would effect the lives of all of us. The next morning before breakfast as we were tidying up at the outside wash basin, he "sprung" it on us.

"Boys," he said bluntly, "I've done made up my mind, we're gonna have to get the woman and kids outa this here country. I'll move 'em up on the railroad some'res maybe Saliny, or Abilene, for the winter and until things quiet down. I kin maybe freight back and forth to Dodge here, and make a livin'. Besides, these here young uns need to be someplace where they can get a little schoolin'.

For a while no one said anything. Tom's announcement was sudden, but no one was surprised or could disagree with him. Our isolated position, miles from Fort Dodge, and with no instant means of communication with that outpost, was certainly no place for women and children; perhaps not even for well armed men.

Immediately after breakfast, the womenfolks went to work with pots and pans, sugar and water, putting up the plums gathered prior to yesterday's little adventure. While we of the crew were soon busy greasing and repairing wagons, fixing single-trees, neckyokes, harness and etc. preparing for our move to the railroad. Just before dinner a familiar one-mule shay hove into sight and soon Andy Cooper was with us again. Andy in new hat, brand new jeans and black cowhide boots was his usual calm and cheerful self and appeared to have enjoyed a prosperous summer. He tactfully touched but little on the Indian scares, but reported the freighting business was booming between Hays and Dodge. He said the talk was; General Sheridan, who was spending a lot of time in Fort Dodge, was preparing for a fall campaign against the Indians south of us in their own territory, with General Sully in field command and some thought a new post would likely be established a hundred miles or so south on the Canadian. But more important to Tom, Andy offered a proposition that was a possible solution to our present problem.

"Why Tom, I've got just the place for you there in Hays. Bought it cheap last spring when the boom was still on at *Coyote. It's a two room frame house with finished attic and cellar attached and there's a pretty fair rough stock shed on the property too."

Andy went on to say he would be glad to sell or rent the property if he could reserve enough room in the loft for a bunk and to store a little gear as he was getting tired of batching. His final clincher, delivered with the assurance of a true "town booster" was, "I'll tell you fellars, Hays City is a gettin' to be right civilized, we're even aimin' to start a school this fall."

That afternoon we started preparing for our move to Hays. By evening two days later the wagons were all lined up and loaded, with wagonsheets in place and ready to go. The few articles of furniture, including the kitchen range, were placed in the wagons. The corn was husked; the potatoes, onions, and turnips were

* Coyote) No, not a ficticious place but a boom town (tho short-lived) on the new railroad many miles west of Hays.

dug; the beans, peas, tomatoes, watermelons and pumpkins picked. The best hayrack was kept intact and loaded to the limit with hay. In fact, everything was ship-shape for the road early tomorrow morning. Old Barney and Jose had agreed to hold down the soddy until Tom and I located the family in Hays City and returned to Ft. Dodge with freight. From then our plans were to use the soddy as sort of a base camp for our fall and winter freighting business.

Shortly after sun-up the next morning, August 24th, (I find on checking my old notes) our little train was strung out on the short cut across the slope towards Ft. Dodge. Tom, ahead in the big wagon lightly loaded with a crate containing the old sow and two young gilts, (his future brood stock) about twenty bushels of ear corn and some corn fodder. Then came Mamie with the covered "kitchen wagon", and then came Sid and Ramon with covered wagon carrying food supplies, mostly the home grown products from the garden, also extra bedding and etc. Next in line was myself with four good mules strung out on the hayrack, and then Pat, with odds and ends we knew would be needed at our new home and establishment on the railroad. At our rear came Bid, lounging lazily in his saddle, guiding the little "cavvy" which consisted of four head of spare mules, the milkcow and her progeny, plus Bull Run, the young buffalo, tame and gentle as a domestic but possessed of the usual obstinacy of his kind, he was almost impossible to herd or drive, although he followed the cow family perfectly "when he felt like it", which fortunately was most of the time. And of course Old Satank the pack mule. independent as usual, but keeping his place with little guidance, as Bid said, "he knowed a good thing when he saw it."

From my seat high on the load of hay, I couldn't help grinning at the sight of our little outfit strung out in all its glory and headed for a new home, with high hopes. At the top of the ridge I looked back for a last glimpse of the Sod Ranche, my grin faded and I felt almost a touch of sadness as I wondered if this was the end of the most satisfying period of my life.

We swung a little to the north and missed Ft. Dodge and soon came on to the Hays City Trail. A mile ahead, lumbering slowly along, was a train of a dozen ox-drawn wagons, accompanied by a couple of six-mule teams, one of which was Andy Cooper's. By noon we caught up with them in the Sawlog bottoms. The Sawlog was a scenic little stream with its patches of timber, including hackberry, elm and cottonwood, scattered over the bottoms at the foot of rugged brakes. But at the crossing was already evidence of the price paid for the advancement of civilization. This place had, not too long ago, been heavily timbered, judging from the many large stumps scattered about. No doubt some of this timber had been utilized in the construction of Ft. Dodge and in the even earlier posts in the vicinity, but it is likely that much of it had been used as firewood. As coal was not available without hundreds of miles of freighting, wood crews were regularly at work, not only at Dodge, but all other military posts on the plains, cutting the timber along the creeks for fuel. It is little wonder many of these timbered little streams were pretty bare by the time of the country's settlement.

At the noon camp on the Sawlog, we met our old "compadre" Mustang in charge of an ox-team. He greeted me with an embarrassed grin but to Bid he gave only a sullen and disgruntled look. The latter returned this lack of sociability with a studied unconcern, perhaps suggesting in his careless glance what they both knew well, namely that it was no promotion to step from the muleskinner's profession to that of an "ox-gadder". Later in the day Bid mentioned the occasion to me and I knew he was more concerned about his former friend than he let on.

"He thinks it bothers me to get his cold shoulder," he said referring to Mustang, "but he's just sore at what happened the other day. He thinks I ought to've stuck around and kept them soldiers from throwin' him in the guardhouse." And then he added, as if to clear his conscience, "if he thinks I'm gonna come a'runnin' to kiss his ass every time he gets in trouble, then he's a bigger damn fool than I think he is."

And that was the last Bid had to say on the subject until we reached Hays. In the meantime he and Mustang continued to ignore each other as much as possible.

That afternoon we moved on ahead of the ox-train and camped early, on Buckner Creek, above the crossing where the grass hadn't been grazed and trampled by the Ft. Dodge freighters. The Buckner, like Sawlog is a branch of the Pawnee and was another interesting break in the monotony of our journey. Some timber as well as wild plums and grapes, grew along its banks. The grapes were large and sweet so we picked a water pail full, and cut Mamie a couple weeks supply of firewood before dark.

After an early start the next morning, we moved on at a lively pace as with the exception of my hay-wagon the loads were light, and the teams were in good shape. Before noon we came to the *Pawnee Crossing. Here the deep natural channel had been made into a fairly tolerable crossing but with heavy use it required regular repair, especially as the stream was liable to flood frequently during the summer. However all our wagons crossed without problems until it came my turn with the long load of hay. Aware of a deep chuckhole half way across, but having supreme confidence in the big four-mule team, I held them back to reduce strain on the wagon, with the result one of the rear wheels settled solidly in the chuckhole. Unfazed, I gave them the reins with a loud Yaa-ah! The big mules dug in with a mighty heave, when suddenly one of the leaders slipped and the wagon rolled back and settled again in the hole, more solidly than before. Before that, any of us who worked for Tom Powers, firmly believed those four mules could pull anything that was movable. But not so; in spite of all my efforts of encouragement they only budged the load enough to make matters worse. Finally Tom had to hook his team on ahead and with four men standing in nearly knee-deep water, heaving on the wheels, the load came out of the creek and up the bank where we had to stop and re-rope our hay.

Later, that afternoon we approached the main Walnut Creek crossing with some apprehension, but luck was with us and nothing worse happened than the creaking and groaning of the overloaded hayrack. Stopping near a sod-shanty about sundown, we made camp hoping the worst obstacles of the trip were over.

It was a clear star-lit night, just a tiny tinge of coolness,

* This was before the well known, O'Loughlin log bridge was built there.

337

perhaps a hint of coming fall, stirred the air and reminded us it would be a fine night for sleep. Bid and I got our blankets and with rifles by our side, we made our bed on top the load of hay. Working myself into a comfortable hollow in the hay, I pulled up my blanket and drowsily reflected on the happenings of the summer. One thing was certain, the old days on the Arkansas were gone forever and we were about to open a new chapter in our lives.

End of Part II

MAP OF THE AREA
1868

NEBRASKA

Republican River

Beechey Island Battle Field

Arickaree Fork

S. Fork

Beaver Cr.

Sappa Cr.

Prairie Dog Cr.

N. Solomon

S. Solomon

N. Smoky Hill

Saline River

Sheridan

K.P. Railroad

Coyote

Big Cr.

Hays City

Ft. Wallace

Smoky Hill River

Ft. Hays

Twin Butte Cr.

Punished Woman Fork

White Woman

Walnut Cr.

COLORADO TERRITORY

KANSAS

Pawnee Cr.

Buckner Cr.

Trail to Hays

Sawlog Cr.

Ft. Larned

To Ft. Lyon

Granada

SANTA FE TRAIL

Sand Hills

ARKANSAS RIVER

Ft. Dodge

The Rattleshake

Butte Cr.

Bear Creek

Sand

DRY ROUTE S.FT.

Mulberry Cr.

Sand Arroya

Sand Cr.

Lower Spr.

CIMARRON RIVER

Crooked Cr.

Bluff Cr.

Medicine Lodge

Pt. of Rocks

Middle Spr.

INDIAN TERRITORY
NO MANS LAND

Cimarron River

Beaver or N. Canadian River

Scale: 5½ in. = 200 miles

340

PART III

The Arickaree Campaign

CHAPTER I

"Fort Hays and Hays City"

Moving on again early the next morning, we clunked steadily along over many rather uneventful prairie miles and pulled into Hays City late in the afternoon of the 26th of August. The wagon-load of hay was the source of about our only problems of the three-day drive. And I wouldn't again recommend freighting hay in an ordinary light hayrack over nearly a hundred miles of unimproved trail, especially where it is necessary to cross a half dozen streams. On the flats it was fine and the four mules handled the load in good shape but at every creek we had problems. It was usually necessary to lock the rear wheels with a pole when going down the steeper grades and once we had to hook on an extra team to complete the crossing. Two or three times the wide unwieldy load threatened to tip over on its side, and I remember distinctly of breathing a sigh of relief on finding a bridge of sorts at Big Creek on the outskirts of Hays. And, thankfully, we made the entire drive without seeing an Indian.

After crossing the creek we rested our teams and waited for Andy; but as he was observed well over a mile behind, we pulled the whole caravan on down main street, where opposite one of the main trading stores Tom and Mamie went inside and attended to some much needed shopping. The rest of us sat a little conspicuously on our wagons, as the passers-by stared at us. Hays City was used to wagons and freighters, but apparently a family-type caravan such as our wasn't seen every day. Of course, the "cavvy" with the buffalo calf was the biggest attraction as it soon drew several spectators. Buffalo were old stuff to Hays residents, as common as wagons and mules, but a live and tame one on main street was something else.

"Where did you get him, stranger?" asked someone. Bid,

341

with one leg wrapped over his saddle horn, was in his element.

"Why," he answered with a straight face, "me and my podner there took him off'n a daid Indian."

About then, Andy grinning from ear to ear, pulled past with his six-mule team and we fell in behind and followed him past the edge of town to our new home.

The next morning we were occupied until nearly noon unloading the wagons and moving into the new premises. Mrs. Powers was having some problems with her youngters, besides getting everything situated to her liking. To spare her further trouble, Bid, Pat, and I borrowed a team and the light wagon and drove downtown for our dinner. Entering the same restaurant we had found to serve good food on our earlier trip to Hays City, we seated ourselves at the only empty table. The place was crowded and the table behind us was occupied by three men in uniform and one in civilian buckskins. In contrast to most of the other patrons, these mens' conversation was reserved and quiet, yet we couldn't help but overhear all that was said. Their topic was of the organization of a company of civilian scouts to be under regular army command, especially equipped and outfitted to fight Indians and hunt them down, in their own territory, if necessary. I detected a note of envy in the officer's voice behind me. "Some of my men might be induced to show more enthusiasm for their jobs at the thought of fifty dollars per month compensation."

The man in buckskins across the table chuckled. "Well, you can see it works that way with me too. Twenty-five a month, per head, makes me right enthusiastic about parting with the company of my horses."

"Yes, I noticed," gibed one of the military men, "but I hear you have competition now."

"Oh, you mean Glimp—that rascally old cypher. But power to him, I ain't got a pony left that I would have the gall to lease to the Govn'ment for twenty-five a month."

"It's a strange thing," chimed in another, "during the past two years I've been in and out of a number of these frontier outposts and it never fails, when word gets out of some Government money to be had, but Glimp or someone of his stripe is sure to show up."

At the mention of Glimp, Bid and I exchanged grins. After the men had finished eating and left, we discussed what we had just overheard and without attaching any significance to our remarks we were in agreement 'that maybe the Government was on the right track for a change.'

"Well," said Bid, as we stepped out on the street, "thet crick water they served in there sorta left a bad taste in my mouth. Yo'all reckon we ought to test the whiskey they have hereabouts." He grinned at Pat. "We got old Caroliny heah to lay the hand of moderation on us."

I knew there was no use trying to deter a Texas drover and an Irish muleskinner from taking an occasional drink of whiskey when it was so freely advertised as it was in Hays, but I had my say. "Well, I know a blame sight better than trying to reform a pair of heathen like you two. You're too far gone for that, but I'll trail along anyway to keep you out of mischief."

We picked the most respectable looking place on the street and entered. The place was clean and business was slack this time of day. Bid selected a table near the bar and ordered the best whiskey in the house. My friends drank moderately and we were about to leave when a tousled lad in his teens came in distributing handbills. He dropped one on our table. In bold print it read something like this: ENLIST WITH COLONEL FORSYTH'S SCOUTS. $50 A MONTH PER MAN, MAN AND HORSE $75.— ACT NOW!

Bid and I glanced at each other without comment, but Pat's liquor had touched a chord.

"B' Jasus! Boys! If I hadn't promised me blessed mother in Salina that I niver again would serve in the 'military' I'd be tempted to jine."

We joshed the Irishman good naturedly. Bid nodded to the bartender and paid for the drinks, then we left for our team. I don't recall that any more was said on the subject as we drove back to Andy's place and helped Tom and Andy rebuild and enlarge the corral. But gathered around the supper table where Mamie served some of the niceties of semi-civilization, the conversation got around to talk of the civilian scout troop being organized. Tom, who had cheered up now that the family was safe at Hays, spoke up with some of his usual candor. "By golly, I think it's the smartest thing the Govn'ment's done lately and if I was a young feller and foot loose, danged if I wouldn't be right in the thick of it."

I made a half-joking rejoinder of agreement. Pat stirred his feet and stared at his plate while Bid went on calmly eating. But Mamie, ladling the fried apple pies out of the pan raised her voice.

"Tom Powers, you wouldn't do no such thing; go out there in the wilderness somewhere and maybe get yourself scalped and it ain't right for you to set here and encourage these younger men to put themselves in no such danger."

"Doggone it, Mamie," Tom said, a little exasperated with his good wife, "you know I didn't mean it that a-way. But someone is gonna have to give Roman Nose, Old Satanta, and Injuns of their like, a blame good lacin'. And the dad-blamed Army don't appear to have the guts and determination to do it."

The talk resolved into a reserved but brief agreement with Tom. That is all agreed but Mamie, who "woman-like" could see none of the thrills and adventure of Indian fighting.

"I couldn't sleep of a night knowing a boy of mine or even kinfolk was out there bein' stalked by them bloodthirsty heathens," she told us forcefully.

The night was clear and pleasant. We of the Powers crew got our blankets and retired to the haystack. "You know," I finally said, stirred by an afternoon's thoughts and the discussion at the supper table, "I may sound like a fool, but having always had a hankerin' for adventure, maybe sometimes more than is good for me, still I feel an urging to find out more about that scout troop."

"No, you don't sound like a fool, at least no more'n usual," Bid answered. "I've had them same kinda urgins ever since I been

344

big enough to chew tobaccy and take a drink of whiskey. And right now it ain't all because we're itchin' to give the Indians a damn good lacin', 'though God knows they need it."

"Alright," I answered a little too eagerly, "let's go down in the morning and find out about joining up, or at least, learn a little more about the thing."

"Whoa, now Caroliny, I said I have had them urgings, but I hope by now I've learned a little sense. Afore long I'll be thirty years old and I gotta be thinkin' one of these days of kinda settlin' down. And, if I was yo'all, I'd take me a good night's sleep on this afore you jump into somethin' you may be sorry about later. As for me I aim to forget the whole blame thing and make plans to catch the cars for Abilene the next day or two."

I took a good night's sleep on it, but the next morning the "hankerin' and the urging" was still with me. For the first time since coming to Kansas I felt free to leave Tom and the family, now that Pat a good reliable hand, was available to take my place. After breakfast Bid and I strolled out towards the barn. I think he knew I hadn't changed my mind, but he waited for me to speak.

"Bid." I said, trying to keep my voice calm, "I've slept on it and I've made up my mind. I'm going down and locate the recruiter and find out some more about "Forsyth's Scouts" and if I like what I hear, I think I'll join."

Bid leaned back against the fence and with his pocket knife carefully dug the mud out of his bootheel before he answered. When he did speak it was forcibly and to the point. "Alright—you damn jackass, then I'm goin' with you."

An hour later we were in the presence of the recruiting officer at Ft. Hays. The purpose of the formation of scouts was explained to us and we were told our service would be in the nature of employment through the Quartermaster Department, and our mission was to seek out and destroy marauding bands of Indians.

We signed our names and were receiving final details on when and where we were to report for duty. When the Scout who was serving as clerk called the officer's attention to an apparent oversight, namely the addition of our names to the roll call, exceeded the authorized compliment of the troop. This called for considerable discussion between the two which was carried on in an earnest undertone.

Presently the officer turned and spoke for the benefit of us, "Men, I'm sorry for this apparent mix-up, but disregard all you may have overheard. The names of Scouts McClaine and Reynolds will be temporarily stricken from the register until this matter can be resolved. But in the meantime you two gentlemen consider yourselves officially sworn in as members of Forsyth's Scouts. Your names and the date of your enrollment will be made a matter of record—I personally will assume full responsibility for your employment."

Bid signed on with his horse for $75 per month and was allowed to use his own saddle. But I, having left my horse at the soddy, would be paid $50 and would have to procure a mount for which $25 would be allowed the owner. The clerk suggested I see "one Anthony J. Glimp" whom he assured me would be happy to furnish a mount for the monthly Government compensation.

We rode back across Big Creek to Hays City where we parted, Bid to send a telegram to Mr. McCoy at Abilene explaining his position and I to see the redoubtable Colonel Glimp about a horse.

For a change the old horse trader was not "in his cups" and I considered myself fortunate in being spared some of his usual blarney. His riding stock had been pretty well picked over, but I finally selected a sturdy bay. I wasn't elated at the look in the animal's eye but he seemed well broken and had a bearable gait. The Colonel signed the official papers, then we shook hands on the deal and I mounted the bay and rode him home, leading Bid's buckskin. I rode up to the little barn at Tom's new head-quarters, feeling pretty good about my horse deal, when suddenly the younger Powers boys dashed out the open door, yelling like a pair of demons. My horse jumped sideways, then shied the other way and suddenly reared upon his hind legs, whereupon I kicked free of the stirrups and hit terra firma on my hindquarters, still hanging on the lead rope of the buckskin. Andy ran up and

346

grabbed the reins of the bay and held him as the disturbed animal trembled in every limb and cast wild-eyed glances in every direction.

After things had settled down a bit and the horses had been turned loose in the corral, Bid rode in and we explained we had joined Forsyth's Scouts. The eyes of Sid and the younger boys bugged. "You mean," one of them blurted, "you and Bid are sure enough sojers?"

"That's about it," I assured them, "we're sure enough in the Army now."

Bid unsaddled and turned his horse in with the others. I followed, curious to learn his opinion of my new mount. He hadn't been told of my being "unloaded" and I bided my time about mentioning it. The bay had settled down, but stood in a far corner by himself. The Texan looked him over and shook his head.

"I wish't now I hadn't told Tom to use the buckskin. You would've been more'n welcome to him."

Knowing Bid's prejudices about certain types of horses I was a little put out. "Thanks a lot, pardner, but what in particular is wrong with this horse?"

"Well, in the first place, the son-of-a-bitch looks to me like he had been nippin' on the loco weed."

I made a clean breast of things then and told him what had happened when I rode in. He swore softly at Colonel Glimp. "Why thet crooked, connivin' old bastard, I'm afeered he's done worked you this time, Caroliny. I should have rid over there with yo'all."

"Well, maybe he'll work 'out' alright." I said, studying the appearance of the bay hopefully. "Besides, as far as Glimp is concerned he never had any other horse I would have accepted as a gift."

"Thet's just it. The onery old Devil worked this critter off on you and the Govn'ment, with never a thought but linin' his own pockets. When, if he had owned a speck of honesty, he would've sent you somewheres else."

347

We were all given the day off except Sid and Ramon, who were sent to graze the work stock on Big Creek a mile away. I got paper and pencil and wrote a short letter to the homefolks. When about finished I observed Bid with rope in hand walk out in the corral and catch old Satank. Then I saw him and Pat in earnest conversation. More than a little curious I laid aside my writing and walked over to see what was up.

"I aimed to leave this damn mule with Tom over the winter," Bid explained, "but he nigh kicked Pat here into the next township this mawnin'. Which convinced me that maybe he ain't safe where kids is bound to be underfoot, so I reckon I'll just see if Mister Glimp might be persuaded to deal for him once again. I would certainly admire to give that connivin' old scalawag a taste of his own medicine."

I looked at Bid. "Are you cold sober this morning—or have you been out in the sun a little too much lately?"

"Go ahaid and belittle my efforts to make an honest dollar," he grinned, "but this is gonna call for some right sharp and indirect bargainin' and thet is where Pat comes in. And it's likely gonna take a right smart of trickery besides, which I aim to handle myself."

He went to his saddle and brought forth a full quart of whiskey, which he held up to the sun and studied the contents. "I've observed that Mr. Glimp has a powerful weakness for the best bourbon. This cost me two and a half bucks this mawnin' and I ain't one to take them kind of costs lightly."

I soon returned to my letter writing, where with my back to the haystack and a book over my knees for a writing pad, I settled down where I could watch the proceedings. Tom and Andy were liesurely setting posts at the far end of the corral for an extension of that structure. They were so busy discussing old times in Missouri they never noticed what was going on, but I could just see enough to arouse my interest. I saw Bid go to the house and come back with a small pan of stove or chimney soot. Soon I could see him applying the black substance to Old Satank's hide while Pat held a firm grip on the halter rope. To my amazement they appeared to be doing an artistic job in transforming

348

the commonplace appearance of the mule. Finally I could stand it no longer and again laid aside my pencil and walked around the corner of the barn where the two were admiring Bid's handiwork and laughing to themselves. The pack mule had suddenly been changed from a dirty grayish roan to one of black and roan; and ridiculous as it seems, he still retained a certain natural and realistic appearance.

"Why, you son-of-a-gun," I gasped, "he's the first pinto mule I ever saw."

Bid modestly stifled a last chuckle. "Well, they ain't common," he agreed.

I could only guess as to the details of his upcoming deal, but knowing Bid I figured they would be good and 'might even work'. He wasted little time in putting them in effect. As soon as dinner was finished he saddled his horse and left for Colonel Glimp's camp. About an hour and a half later Pat left on Bid's buckskin, leading old Satank, he also headed in the direction of the old horse trader's camp. And I noticed he kept to the back way avoiding people as much as possible.

Well before dark, the two conspirators rode in completely satisfied with themselves. Pat pulled forty dollars from his pocket and they split it then and there. When Pat finally quit laughing so I could get a word in, I got the gist of the story.

"Mister Glimp," Bid explained with a relish, "besides having a weakness for good bourbon; he don't fancy drinkin' out of the bottle like the common man. He sips his'n from a fancy little jigger. Now, at his rate of intake it takes considerable time to get him good and drunk, but with the proper encouragement it can be done. It so happened the old gentleman was right dry today and whilst I was a holding my jigger in my fist a pretending to fill it every time I did his'n, he was actually a downin' three or four to my one. Why, thet old man liked to of killed that full bottle of whiskey by hisself, but by that time he couldn't tell a mule from a Tennessee Walkin' Hawse and his tongue was agoin' like a tame magpie's."

Bid, true to his Scotch ancestry, appreciated the value of a dollar and could hang onto one too, but when the notion struck him he was generous to a fault. This was such an occasion; he was happy to split even with Pat for his part in their illicit deal—forty dollars for a ten dollar mule. BUT then, on the other hand, as pack mules go, Old Satank was worth forty dollars or more, providing one could cope with his cantankerous disposition and no one knew that better than Bid.

old "Satank"

CHAPTER II

First Days with the Scouts

We had our orders to report early the next morning to Col. Forsyth for active duty. Before supper Bid and I went over our belongings and crated all except the few articles we would take with us, and stored them in the loft of (Andy's) Tom's house. Every dollar we possessed we had with us, so that was counted and most of it left with Tom and Andy to deposit in the safe at the general store managed by a friend of Andy's, with instructions if anything happened to us to see that our next of kin got it. This was all duly receipted and accounted for in a business like way. My spring and summer take was just over $250, which of course didn't include my share of the Government hay, hopefully which would be accepted and fully compensated for by Uncle Samuel's bureaucrats before the Indians got around to sending it all up in smoke. I finished the letter to my folks and explained briefly that it might be some time before they would hear from me again, as I had joined a troop of Indian fighters and would leave in the morning on a long scout, with the expectation of some excitement, but of course "little likelihood of encountering anything really dangerous."

We hit the hay early for a good night's sleep and the last I remember was Bid saying, "I cain't help but wonder what Mister Glimp is gonna think when he sobers up in the mawning and finds his paint mule has begun to fade."

We were up and had our horses saddled and ready before daybreak. After breakfast we led our horses up and the folks all gathered to see us off. Tom, Andy, Pat, and even Ramon shook hands cheerfully and wished us well. I noticed Mary in the background sniffling and Mamie, good woman that she was, attempting to smile through her tears. And Sid and his younger brothers, big-eyed, sober, and shuffling from one foot to another. I experienced a sudden lump in my throat similar to what I had felt when I left my home early that spring and I realized how attached I had become to this family.

Over at the Fort the newly recruited scouts had already begun to gather, most of whom had been in camp for a few days. Some of the men experienced in this type of organization got us together and lined up; where the first sergeant called us to attention and introduced Lieutenant Beecher, who spoke a few words explaining our mission. The roll was called, then Colonel Forsyth, our commanding officer, stepped up with proper military precision and gave us a short talk reminding us though we were civilian scouts, we were under Government employment and a certain amount of discipline would be expected. As we were enlisted primarily to fight Indians, parade ground manners would be kept to a minimum. But we would function as a troop of cavalry, under accepted military rules, and orders must be obeyed without question. We were then marched over to the supply depot and outfitted.

As outfitted, we were a walking arsenal, each man being issued a seven-shot Spencer carbine, with 140 rounds of ammunition, a 44 caliber Colt's revolver with 30 rounds, all of this to be carried on the person. Besides equipment consisting of a blanket, saddle, bridle, halter, rope and picket pin, haversack, tin plate and cup, butcher knife and etc. In addition, a small pack-mule train was assigned the troop which carried camp kettles, picks and shovels, medical supplies, extra ammunition, salt, coffee, and dry beans and army hardtack and other small supplies.

We lugged our "artillery" and equipment over near the stables and spent the next hour fitting and arranging all the paraphernalia to our saddles, and getting acquainted with our fellow troopers. Naturally, there were interesting characters in the group, most of them having served in one Army or the other during the late war or had experience with some of the State Indian fighting regiments in recent years. Above all, they were frontiersmen, tough, rugged, and independent. Probably one of the least experienced, as I remember, was a young man of Jewish origin from the city and way back East. He had little to fit him for the tough job ahead save a year or so spent knocking around from Kansas City to Hays, plus the fact he was very broke. He explained to us, in his peculiar accent and comical manner, how he owed his job solely to the Post Scout at Hays, who had pulled wires getting him enrolled so the latter could draw Government pay on his horse. I don't remember his name, only that it was too much for Bid who promptly dubbed him "Ikey". Unfamiliar aboard his horse, especially one burdened with cavalry equipment, Ikey had a mighty hard day or two before he finally commenced to get the hang of it all. A little help from some of us but mostly determination and perserverence on his part pulled him through and in time he made a first-rate trooper. Another character Bid sort of took under his wing was of a different type, from a newly settled lower Solomon and Saline area, he was a big, green, country-type boy, good-natured, likeable and brash. To Bid, this young man became "Paradise" and before long we lost track of his real name. And then there was "Irish", a devil-may-care sort of fellow as you ever saw. He was no tenderfoot—he knew his way around. In him, Bid about met his match when it came to pranks and horseplay, there was a rivalry between them from the start and a sort of a grudging respect. By his real name, "Irish" made the history books and with Forsyth's Scouts was where he done it. Probably the most qualified man in the group was A. J. Pliley. Not given to blowing his own horn and enrolled as a common scout at $50 a month, his fame was nevertheless well known among his comrades and we weren't long hearing of some of his exploits. Our surgeon was Dr. Moers, a Hays City physician, and as has been mentioned, our second in command was Lieutenant Beecher.

Forsyth's Scouts as a group probably had as little pre-field training as any military aggregation ever sent forth to do battle. They called us together and mustered us in, outfitted us, then again called us to attention and we stood inspection and were pronounced fit for duty. Shortly after we were mounted and on our way. Colonel Forsyth had received the following terse message.

"Fort Hays, Kansas   August 29, 1868

Brevet Col. George A. Forsyth, Commanding Detachment of Scouts:

I would suggest that you move across the headwaters of the Solomon to Beaver Creek and thence down that creek to Fort Wallace. Upon arrival at Wallace, report to me by telegraph.

Yours truly,

P. H. SHERIDAN, Major-General"

"No bands played", no flags waved and no crowds cheered as we rode in an irregular line out of Ft. Hays. Only some of the citizenry and itinerant freighters stared as we clattered by in the general direction of the Saline River. In a matter of hours we were beyond the bounds of civilization.

Bid and I had seen service in the Confederate Army, mostly in the supply and transportation arm. Bid had seen considerable horse and mule herd duty, as well as that of a teamster. But still neither of our war records were those of distinction; besides years as independent civilians had left us a bit rusty as to military methods and procedures. Hence, on being suddenly transformed from muleskinners to mounted troopers, it behooved each of us to keep a wary eye on our leaders and fellow scouts as a sly and covert indoctrination in the ways of a Cavalry Troop. However, many of our comrades were in the same boat, which, though not

354

conducive to our training, was a source of solace to us—for whatever that was worth.

Our Colonel led the troop with an erect and proper military bearing, and was copied a bit rustily by the First Sergeant. But the Lieutenant,* who was a seasoned Indian campaigner, sat on his horse comfortably and relaxed like a true frontiersman. However, I will say this much for our leadership, no matter how important the proper "soldierly bearing", they refrained from insisting on strict military procedure from the hastily organized and somewhat green troop. Forsyth, although himself a long time professional soldier with a remarkable record, nevertheless had little experience with Indians and at first relied heavily on Lieutenant Beecher and some of the more experienced men in the company for advice and everyday campaign tactics. At the same time, he managed to plainly convey to all of us as to who was in command of the expedition.

Knowing now the unbalanced nature of my horse, I kept a wary eye on him, fearing I might be the victim of one of his sudden fits before the eyes of the Colonel and the whole troop. Bid gave me some useful pointers on what to do in case he did throw one of his conniptions. But outside of prancing needlessly and tossing his head, "Loco" seemed to be on his best behavior around other horses and I had no real difficulty with him that first day. After several steady hours in the saddle, we noticed the Colonel had lost some of his erect cavalry bearing and the first sergeant even more so. About that time, a short halt was called. Bid and I being used to hard work and the saddle had hardly felt the ride, but the afternoon was humid and my horse, being soft, worked up quite a sweat. I dismounted, cut some bunch grass, and gave him a light rub-down. Bid led his horse over near the end of the line and helped "Ikey" untangle some of his gear. Pretty soon he motioned to me. There was a look of disbelief on his face as he pointed toward the little group of pack mules.

"Do yo'all notice anything familiar about them mules?"

* Lt. Fred Beecher had spent much of the last 18 months in the vicinity of Ft. Wallace and had been in charge of scouts. He was lame as a result of a wound he received at Gettysburg' but he managed well astride a horse.

We led our horses over for a closer look and there stood "Old Satank"!—big as life and decked out in a new government pack.

"My God," Bid groaned in my ear, "my chickens have done come home to roost."

Tell-tale streaks of soot still remained on the old mule's hardy hide as he turned and gazed at us as if he was in no way at all surprised at once again being in our presence. A trooper spoke up, "By God, boys, that's soot on that mule sure as sartin'."

"Yeah," I volunteered for Bid's benefit, "it looks like some blame prankster must've tried to color him."

At the next halt, Bid out of the goodness of his heart, approached the scout who had charge of the mules with a word of warning. He cleared his throat. "Mister, yo'all want to watch out for thet roan mule, he'd as soon kick you as look at you."

But the scout who had aspired for a more pleasant assignment than his present one cut the Texan off grouchily with the comment, "that he reckoned he knowed enough about mules in general and packmules in particular that he didn't need to be advised by every Tom, Dick, and Harry in the detachment."

Bid shrugged and walked away and when he rejoined me on the march he had little to say. It took him fully two days to get the mule off his mind, but by that time, by subtle questions and crafty sleuthing, he had come up with some answers. As we lay in our blankets the second night, he confided in me. Information straight from the horse's mouth, so he said, was "that Col. Glimp had agreed the day before he bought Satank, to furnish two well-broke pack mules to the Army Quartermaster Department at a set price of $60 per head."

"And there I was, a pourin' drink after drink down him and me a hurtin' inside 'cause I realized that old man has a sickness for bourbon whiskey and cain't always control his cravin' for it. If he hadn't been such a schemin' and conniving old crook, I coulda never gone through with it," Bid sighed, "and him all the time a knowin' he stood to clear twenty bucks on the deal. It's a good thing I didn't let my conscience be my guide or he would've took me, shirt, and all."

He felt so badly about the deal, I felt compelled to remind him of some of Satank's good qualities. Half seriously, I suggested, "Maybe we should enlighten the Colonel that he has in his possession the best Indian alarm in the country."

"No," Bid advised seriously, "the best thing fer you and me is to keep our blamed yaps shut about thet mule. For if this here Army is anything like the one I served in for "Uncle Jeff Davis", you and me are likely to find ourselves in the Goddamned mule detail."

To keep the events in their proper order, I will return briefly to the first day's march. After a short rest with time to eat, we continued on after dark and didn't make camp until late at night. We had encountered a light drizzling rain, the bane of cavalrymen, cattle drovers, and outdoorsmen in general, who are subject to the vagaries of the weather with little protection except hunker down and bear it. We finally camped in the dark near a stream where we had a little shelter from bushes and cut banks. After satisfying our appetites with cold rations, we fell asleep in the most comfortable positions we could find. A small guard was ordered, but I think every man of them promptly fell asleep, which was probably just as well. As one of the scouts grumblingly expressed it, "no Goddamn Indian would be dumb enough to be prowling around on a night like this."

After a short night we awoke the next morning, our enthusiasm for our adventure slightly dampened. Lieutenant Beecher accosted Irish as the latter huddled in his blanket against a steep bank. "You look disconsolate as a wet hen this morning, Jack. What happened?"

"Lieutenant," said the other, as he arose grimacing and shook the water from his hat, "some damned idiot must have left the window open last night."

But after breakfast, topped off by hot coffee, we felt a lot better and by eight o'clock were once again on the march—and once again in a drizzle.

In time the sun came out and we soon dried off, every man in the outfit rejoiced and soon became appreciative of the vast, slightly rolling grasslands surrounding us from every direction. At the next halt our dampened blankets were spread atop the grass to dry in the warm sun and that night we would not have exchanged places for all of the comforts of home.

After the first few days of adjustment we settled down as seasoned campaigners. For some of us used to riding and hard work, our duties took on something the nature of a lark. To one who has endured the searing heat of summer, early fall on the high plains sometimes comes as a welcome break. The days are shorter and the nights cooler; and the vegetation seems to respond in its own special way to the relenting will of the weather. For the area stretching north and west of the Smokey in the fall of '68, this seemed especially noticeable, not all outright scenic to be sure, and certainly not all drab and monotonous, but possessing an attraction and excitement of its own. The flat, nearly level, reaches covered with buffalo and gramma grasses stretched on and on, finally blending with rolling hills dotted with tall bunch grass and yucca, which eventually terminated into rugged brakes and dropped suddenly into the gray-green valley of a stream. It is the streams that made the high plains interesting and liveable. They not only provided a weclome break in the monotony of the flats, but there the thirsty traveler could replenish his water supply and rest his weary limbs, while his horse grazed knee deep in the meadow grass. Sometimes colorful rocks outcropped from the bluffs, and wild grapes and plums dangled appetizingly from the vines and bushes. Usually a few scattered trees grew in the valleys and now and then a small but unexpected belt of virgin timber flourished where it was not "yet" accessible to the axeman. This was the greatest game country on the North American Continent. Here the antelope abounded and buffalo was king; and deer and even elk were not uncommon. The gray wolf and coyote always lurked near the great buffalo herds. Bobcat and an occasional black bear or even puma hid out in the rougher areas of the bluffs and streambeds. Prairie chicken and quail were plentiful where herbs, grasses, and cover were to their liking, and wild turkey frequented the areas where a little timber grew. And, of course, the jack rabbit was everywhere.

There were few among us who were not hunters at heart and

358

while our pace and formation as a fighting detachment was at best a far cry from a stalk, we frequently saw wild game that was rarely observed in miles of the most advance outposts of civilization.

We crossed the Saline, the South Fork and the main fork of the Solomon, the Prairie Dog, 'so called' Short Nose Creek, the Sappa Fork and on to the Beaver.* Each one a little different than the others and we approached each with an inner excitement and caution for we never knew when to expect Indians, or wild game, or some unexplored or unexpected feature of this "beyond the frontier", where settlement didn't exist and even a wagon track on the prairie was a rare sight. The days were long and at times the sun was hot, but always the nights were cool. At first we had our share of drizzle and rain, which was miserably disagreeable but when the sun came out, our spirits and our bodies quickly revived. And in time we hardened to anything we encountered.

At the noon and evening camps, we nearly always had some free time and with fellows like Bid, Irish, and Paradise in our little clique, there was usually "something a doing". Paradise had seen little of the outside world, even the ride on the train from Fort Harker to Hays was a memorable occasion for him. Once, a few years back he had seen a steamboat on the Kaw River stuck on a sandbar. He had never forgotten the excitement of that day and he was always eager to tell the story to anyone who would listen. When things became a bit dull in camp, Bid or maybe Irish was apt to speak up as if it was a matter of greatest importance. "Say, Paradise, why don't you tell us about the time you saw the Steamboat stuck on the Kaw River?"

Paradise was always willing to oblige and he would go into detail, waving his arms, illustrating the gyrations of the paddle-wheel, and puff and blow through his teeth, imitating the steam engines. Both Bid and Irish possessed the control of their emotions and facial expressions generally attributed to good poker players, but rarely either of them could hold out through one of Paradise's recitals without breaking down like the rest of us. Paradise, good

---

* Many other lesser known streams were along the way of the long scout, some of them fully as interesting as those named.

natured and unashamed of his own greenness would join in the laughter. Whereupon the High Command would rise up and look our way obviously wondering what all the merriment was about.

One evening we pulled into camp near a stream of clear water. As usual we were dry and thirsty. I noticed Bid filled his canteen before drinking then he stretched on the ground and drank his fill. When he arose he grimaced and remarked loudly that the water was alkali. I had thought it was good and I knew something was up. We gathered wood and soon had a fire going— Paradise, Ikey, Bid and I, and tonight joined by Irish and a fellow named John. The day before, Irish had gotten the laugh on Bid; and I knew the Texan had'nt forgotten. The coffee pot was set on the fire and was soon steaming away when Bid suddenly remembered. "My God, boys—thet alkali water, we'll sure have to settle the coffee tonight." Grabbing a handful of dried rabbit pellets of which there was a quantity near some scraggly plum bushes, he threw them in the coffee pot and stirred them up well with his butcher knife. I could gladly have kicked the whole mess in the fire, but I had been forewarned and I knew my duty, so I matter-of-factly filled my tincup. At first both Paradise and Ikey rebelled at the idea of drinking such a concoction; but seeing Bid and I sipping unconcernedly, brought them around. Irish drained his cup with a visible effort and accepted another cup as if he liked it, knowing full well his whole meal was ruined. He, as well as myself and Bid, too, for that matter, were particular about the water we drank. BUT Irish had made the mistake more than once of making an issue of his "finicalness". The next morning Irish and his partner were conspicuously absent from our fire. They had deserted our mess for one more compatible with their tastes. But Paradise learned quickly. Before anyone could stop him he threw a generous handful of none too clean pellets in the coffee, with a big guffaw. Bid was shocked, but kept his composure.

"Paradise," he drawled reproachfully, "yo'all wouldn't needed to done thet this mawnin. The alkali done settled to the bottom over night." Never-the-less, we drank the coffee as we had the night before. As a matter of fact army coffee brought to a boil over a campfire was usually so strong it took more than a little rabbit dung to noticeably effect the taste; some veterans of many

360

a campaign liked to cut it with a little water rather than drink the stuff straight. But from then on, no matter what condition we found the water, it was never again necessary to settle the coffee.

On the third day out some buffalo were killed, but as we were on rear guard the shooting was all over by the time we got there. When we came near the butchered beasts the smell of blood set my horse off on one of his loco-ed fits. Fortunately, Bid was near and grabbed him by the bit and held on until he calmed down. I led him up on a little knoll away from the slaughtered animals and kept watch until the meat was taken care of. Most of the carcasses were wasted as there was no way to prevent spoilage for very long. Lew Farley, who was a crack shot and the oldest member of the Saline Valley contingent, brought us a tender portion which we cooked over a slow fire that night and enjoyed our best meal of the scout.

We had been issued what was supposed to be seven days rations, but it is hard to understand what the Army expected of healthy outdoorsmen in the saddle from ten to twelve hours a day. By the sixth day we were almost out of grub despite the buffalo meat, and welcome addition of wild plums and grapes we found along many of the creeks. On the seventh day, the 4th of September, we had little breakfast or dinner. We followed tributaries and camped on Beaver Creek* after night, with only a kettle of soup and a little hardtack for supper. After covering over forty miles on such short rations we, as well as our horses, were tuckered. Some of the country the last day or two had been **very broken and some** of the rest almost a barren desert, **which** only added to our hunger and fatigue. Needless to say after partaking of our soup, none of us were much concerned about Indians and immediately sought our blankets.

As our purpose was to fight redskins, it is not surprising that at least once every day someone came up with an Indian alarm. Although this type of enthusiasm seldom extended into the night when it was common practice for most of the guards to go to sleep at their posts. On this scout, I began to suspect

* Most of the scouts called it Beaver Creek and tributaries, but it may have been Sappa Creek.

I had developed an unusual talent for discerning danger. One similar to that of "Old Satank"—a sort of inner feeling or warning of the presence of Indians. After a few of those false alarms when some of the more experienced men were fooled, I found myself calm and skeptical. I can only explain this by the fact that for the last five months nearly every one of my waking hours had been spent with an alertness for Indians; a tenderfoot habit that stayed with me and apparently not shared by many of those who had spent years exposed to the same danger and had grown used to it.

When we broke camp the next morning, we moved in a southerly direction. Late in the afternoon we started down a valley* with a grassy meadow in which a number of haymakers were at work. A halt was called and we observed from a distance, that they clearly took us to be Indians as they all rushed into camp and commenced corralling their stock. The Colonel took in the situation and ordered Irish and Scout Pliley on ahead to identify our force. Shortly afterward we followed them into the haymakers' camp. Some of the hay crew were known to members of our troop and we were made welcome and invited to light and share their hospitality. Which, the Command gratefully accepted as we had ridden all day with nothing to eat save a few remaining scraps we had managed to find in the packs. The boss apologized for their lack of variety; but he insisted they had plenty of fresh meat, spuds, and coffee—and we were more than welcome to it. Fifty "some" hungry men took him at his word and wished him well.

After eating and giving our horses a short rest, we bade our hosts "so long" and moved from the haycamp toward a line of bluffs. Suddenly there was the cry of Indians and the troop charged in a run towards a few skulking figures partly concealed in the brakes. For me, there was none of the creepy sensation one usually feels when encountering hostile Indians, but nevertheless I kicked my tired pony into a run and yelled as hard as anyone. It was all over soon after it started as the hostiles turned out to be members of the Hay crew returning from Pond City

---

* No reference seems to identify the valley, but it would appear to have been the North Fork of the Smokey Hill, or some of its tributaries.

362

with grub and supplies. Unfortunately, in the false charge, a horse fell and one of our men was injured. He was attended to as humanely as possible by Dr. Moers and placed on his horse with the doctor and another scout riding escort. We, then, continued on our way, determined to reach at least the vicinity of Ft. Wallace that night. Nearly midnight we were hailed by the guard and rode in among the wagons and buildings of the Post. For most of us, as soon as our horses were taken care of, our saddles and blankets next to the corrals made a welcome bed for the rest of the night.

Erected by
L. Troop 2 US Cav.
and
E. Co. 2. U.S. Inf.
In memory of
the Soldiers
killed in action

ERECTED 1867

Fort   Wallace
Cemetery

Monument in Fort Wallace Cemetery for soldiers killed by
Indians in 1867.

CHAPTER III

At Fort Wallace

We were awakened the next morning by the blare of a trumpet from the parade ground. Rubbing the sleep from our eyes we rolled our blankets and reported for breakfast. Then, as we had rest duty for the morning, we took our first look at Ft. Wallace. This comparatively new Army Post had been laid off rather ambitiously with a couple of large barracks, the hospital and other buildings constructed of a distinctive pinkish stone peculiar to this section of the South Fork of the Smoky Hill. It was said to be easily worked with carpenter tools, but hardened on exposure to a very durable material. Some of the construction was only partly completed but work was still going on when men could be spared from more soldierly chores. Mess-halls and other barracks were of wood frame construction, as were some of the officers quarters, stables, and etc. Just south of the fort was the river, the source of water supply. To the north a quarter of a mile was the cemetery already well-dotted with graves, victims of the violence of the frontier.

Wallace County, a vast unsurveyed area, ninety-nine per cent uninhabited, had a "sworn-to" population of over 600, including military and had already been accorded the status of a legal county. Bordered on the west by the boundless plains of Colorado Territory and all other sides by the like plains of Kansas soil, its legal designation seemed a travesty in the name of state and local government. Pond City, located a couple of miles or so west of Ft. Wallace, (originally a stage station) was a cluster of frame, sod, and adobe buildings, dugouts and tents, including a fairly substantial stone store. It had the honor of being the temporary county seat with officers already commissioned by the Governor. One, John Whitford, was Justice of the peace and upheld the dignity of his office with an Enfield rifle. Roving bands of Indians created a constant danger to the town and when the citizens were not engaged in protecting themselves, they were not adverse to committing acts of violence against one another. More than one grave in the cemetery was proof of that.

365

Ft. Wallace was the most westerly of all Kansas Army posts, located only about twenty miles east of the Colorado line. It served as a base for supplies and operations for a territory stretching nearly to Denver. Despite its remoteness and, to some, desolate location, it was not an unpleasant spot. In fact, for Forsyth's men, it promised an enjoyable change from the week we had just spent in the saddle. The Sutler's store, well stocked from the railroad only a few hours away by wagon, Pond City with its saloon and other diversions, and just a stone's throw away, a swimming hole on the Smokey, all suggested pleasant ways to spend our time while resting up for our next assignment.

In the afternoon of our first day, a group of us filed down to the Smokey and took advantage of the swimming hole. After getting our fill of the water we sat on the grassy bank and talked. Paradise, young Farley, and some of the older men from the Saline Valley area spoke of their claims and their hopes for the future. I, in turn, told of some of our experiences the past summer on the Arkansas. One word led to another and we soon had quite a discussion on the merits of different locations. One of the older fellows pretty well summed it up. "Well sir, I come from the east. A place where you could go out in the woods and pick fruit, berries, and nuts to your heart's content. And any kind of wood you wanted to build a house or a barn was there, all you needed was an axe, saw, and hammer, and plenty of help from your neighbors. But, you know—I wouldn't trade my claim on the Saline fer the best damn farm in that country."

Bid, who rarely took much part in such bull sessions, expressed his opinions. "Now me," he said, "I was born and raised in Texas and my folks came there from Virginny; generally I got nothin' agin Texas, but since seein this nawthen country, I'll never be satisfied there again. Take this country right heah, it's the comin' cow country. Find yourself a crick with runnin' water, some bluffs for protection from storms, a patch of hay meadow and a hundred head of cows, and you've done got yourself a start. And the best part of it, fellers, is it's all fer free, soon as we get the tarnation redskins cleared out."

From the swimming hole, Bid and I stopped at the corrals. Nearly all of the Government stock was being herded on grass a

366

mile or two away. A bunch of our horses and mules were in one of the big corrals feeding on prairie hay. Among them was our one-time pack mule, "Old Satank". We climbed the fence and Bid directed a few choice words of abuse towards him, delivered in his usual conversational drawl. The little mule cocked one ear and looked our way. "Look!" I said, "he knows us."

"No better'n we do him I hope," Bid grinned.

A pair of young cavalrymen, on fatigue duty, who were liesurely policing the corral, wandered over. "That roan mule belong with your outfit?" one of them enquired. Bid nodded guardedly. "He's the meanest damn animal I ever saw," continued the calvaryman, "already he's the boss of everything in the corral."

We stayed and visited with the young fellows awhile and learned the daily routine in handling the stock. Before reporting back to our temporary quarters we volunteered for herder duty for the morrow.

The next morning we reported, as ordered, and drew Government mounts, and rations for our lunch. Then, in company with the other herders detailed from regular troops, we moved the herd a mile and a half from the post, well up on the flats. A small guard of colored cavalrymen accompanied us and posted lookouts on the higher ground, as raiding parties of redskins were known daily to be in the general area. Bid was dissatisfied with the horse he had drawn and besides he possessed some of the prejudices generally attributed to the Solid South.

"First time I ever had to play second fiddle to a Goddamn nigger," he said resentfully, referring to our black escort.

"Well, maybe you'd like to send 'em back to the Fort," I countered argumentatively, "and leave us out here to look out for trouble by ourselves. Personally, I have nothing against a black man guarding me, if he does his job."

"Maybe you ain't been around 'em and seen how they live and act and all thet," he grumbled.

"I'm from the South too, remember. I recall playing with

367

the darkey boys when I was a kid and I remember very few I wouldn't trust."

"Trust! What's thet got to do with it? Goddamnit, Caroliny, ain't you got no pride?"

"Pride? So that's it," I laughed, "you and your Texas pride."
Bid had no answer as he spurred his horse to bring a pair of strays back in the herd. I began to feel a little sorry for what I had said and began to think of something I could say to take the edge off my last remarks without committing myself to a real apology, but the Texan beat me to it.

"Caroliny," he said, "yo'all probably got a right to jeer at my pride, but I come by it honest; it runs in my family. Just what we got to be so damned high-headed about, I don't rightly know. Likely some of our forebears weren't much mor'n hawse-thieves or whore-chasers, and more likely both."

It took a little while for the herd to settle down to steady grazing and then all we had to do was keep an eye on them to see they didn't scatter. Again we saw the remarkable grazing qualities of the short dried-up buffalo grass.

"Man, I never saw the like," marveled Bid, lighting up one of the cigars he had purchased at the Sutler's. "Down home a hawse would starve to death on grazin' twice't thet tall."

"Barney Balaam, who as you know is a colorful man with the truth, told me a tale of a little rocky canyon on Bear Creek. The old man claims he spent three weeks there one winter resting up their teams and repairing wagons, and the oxen actually got hog-fat on grass alone."

"That," said Bid, lazily removing his cigar, "sounds like a crackin' good place for a ranche. Or take thet yonder," and he pointed toward the brakes of Pond Creek and the hazy outline of the Smokey.

"I'll go along with you on that proposition, but how do you plan to take care of the buffalo herds and the Indians?"

"I reckon we're a fixin' to take care of that last problem directly, but neither of them headaches is gonna be cured overnight. If a man aims to make it in this country, he's gonna have to do like old Tom Powers, grab the bull by the horns and take a chance."

As always Bid's talk of ranching in this big grass country touched a responsive chord in me and we spent the rest of the morning building an imaginary herd on one hand and living "The Life of Riley" on the other. Before we realized it was time for lunch; and a little later our replacements rode up.

Herd duty had been a snap, but soon after returning to the Post, time began resting heavily on our hands and when the opportunity came for a ride on a freight wagon to Pond City, we took what was known among the Scouts as "border leave" and went along, bent on "seeing the elephant". Paradise showed up about that time and climbed in beside us for the ride. We helped the freighter unload at the stone store and then wandered down the street of the little hamlet taking in the sights. In a matter of minutes we had seen the town and wound up where the action was—the saloon. The place was well patronized by a rough and ready crowd. On my suggestion, we decided to keep our noses clean and ordered only a beer apiece. Bid and I, interested in our own idle talk, paid no attention to Paradise for an interval. When we looked for him he was in the far corner occupied with a pair of the local bullies. Now, to look at Paradise you had only to see "here was a big, green, goodnatured, country boy". Obviously, the two bullies, though half drunk, had read him well; they were engaged in teasing him with insults. Guessing from his clothing and equipment that Paradise was connected with the army, a little, whiskered tough was berating him. "Now, lookee hyar, boy, don't try to make out you'ns is an Injun fighter. Them red bastards'll sick thar squaws onto the likes of you'ns."

Then the big man beside him laughed high-pitched and cackling. "Whoa, naow," he said, deliberately nudging Paradise's elbow, causing him to spill beer on his clothes, "be keerful thar, sojer boy, yo're done spillin' yore beer. Thar's no call to be nervous." And he clamped a hand roughly on the boy's shoulder.

I felt my temper flare in a minute, but I looked at Bid and took my cue from him. He sat his glass on the bar and walked easily over to the big man and tapped him calmly on the shoulder and spoke gently as if apologizing.

"I certainly would appreciate it if yo'all wouldn't jostle my friend heah."

The big man turned and looked at Bid and what he saw in the Texan's eyes belied the gentle voice.

"Naow Mister, I wuz jist a funnin' the boy."

"Funnin', Hell," said Bid, calm as ever, but with a little edge to his voice, "yo'all was afixin' to buffalo him."

The big fellow was undecided as he watched Bid warily and mumbled a few words to himself. But the little, whiskered one whom it was plain to see was the real trouble maker, urged him on. "Git in there, Newt, you'ns don't have to take that sass offen no dam waddy. He's jest atryin' to run a blazer on you'ns."

Thus encouraged, Newt spoke up threateningly. "Don't push me, feller, or I'm liable to haul off and lam you one direct'ly."

So Bid pushed him—just a gentle push over a chair and up against the wall, which shook from the impact. Newt lunged back from the wall and the ball was opened. The big man was no match for Bid, who punched and pushed him at will with no intention of really hurting the fellow. But then, one of the by-standers, displeased with the turn of events, took up the fight and things got a little rough in the barroom as Bid began to punch in earnest and would put first one of his opponents down and then the other. "Little Whiskers" darted around the sidelines with a bottle in his hand, yelling encouragement to his friends. My dander was still up; besides, I hated to see Bid doing all the battling for our side, so I started for Whiskers who retreated behind some spectators. As I went after him, someone grabbed me from behind, twisting around. I broke loose and confronted a medium built redhead with buck teeth. He was partly drunk and not in as good a shape as myself, and I felt pretty confident as I forced him back against the crowd, landing a solid right and then a left, when wham! from behind, Little Whiskers had slammed me over the head with his bottle. I sat down on the floor, conscious and faculties clear, but unable to make my legs

370

work. I saw Paradise, who had been standing back goggle-eyed with a shocked expression, suddenly bound into the middle of the ring with Little Whiskers in his grasp and forced him to the floor; a look of blind rage was on the farm boy's good humored countenance.

The crowd wasn't overly friendly, and it looked like we might have more on our hands than we could handle. But three negro soldiers of the 10th Cavalry had been sitting in a corner minding their own business. They jumped up and with one of them wielding a chair menacingly, they moved over to our side. But then, through the open door burst a tousled-headed citizen, waving an Enfield rifle and proclaiming he was the law and demanding an immediate end to the rucus. Anyway, the fight was about over. I was temporarily out of action, Bid's two adversaries had about enough and Little Whiskers was effectually under the control of Paradise. The troublemaker had a knife in his belt, but one of the cavalrymen took it away from him and he was now yelling at the top of his lungs for someone to "pull him off!".

From the tenor of the voice and the look in his eye, the "law" didn't appear slanted exactly in our favor, as I pulled myself dizzily to my feet and confronted the Enfield rifle which swung from Bid to me. My eyes weren't tracking too well, but the bore in the end of the barrel appeared large as a half-dollar. I tried to speak, when I realized the bartender was telling his side of the story. Through a haze of faces I made out a pair of our comrades standing near the door, Irish and John. The Irishman was grinning with delight, for he dearly loved a good fight. Studying the situation for an instant, he put his pleasant personality to the fore and stepped over to the lawman and explained (exaggerating easily) that he had seen the whole fracas from start to finish and that we were only defending ourselves from a dastardly attack. And diplomatically he told how we were all members of Lieutenant Beecher's Civilian Scouts* how our only duty was to protect Pond City from bloodthirsty Cheyennes, Dog-Soldiers, and any other redskins who might molest them.

---

* Lieutenant Beecher was well known and liked in this vicinity and this was why he was referred to the scouts as Beecher's rather than Forsyth's command.

The muzzle of the Enfield was elevated and the butt struck the floor with a thump.

"Well now, that's different," opined the voice of the law, "that bein' the case, you are within your rights and there'll be no charges pressed agin' you fellars. But as for you other men, git out of this here barroom and stay out of trouble, or I'll place the whole kit and kaboodle of ye in the hoosegow—now move!"

When the law and most of the crowd had left, we shook hands with Irish and John and the black soldiers. "Sure do appreciate your efforts," Bid grinned at Irish, "but you're a damned liar."

They, then got some water and soap and washed my head and applied some liniment. "One thing about it, Caroliny," Bid consoled me, "when you get in a fight, you certainly use your head."

We all lined up at the bar and I noticed our black friends hanging back. "Here," I said, nudging Bid at the same time, "you fellows step right on up here, if you don't drink nobody's gonna drink cause we're all tarred with the same stick around here "The U. S. Government."

Bid took my cue and done the honors. "Here's to you Mighty obliging fellars from the 10th Cavalry, and to 'Beecher's' Scouts and the Pond City law."

Frontier whiskey, shipped in fresh from the nearest distillery, had a bite to it that induced even the confirmed drinker to proceed with caution. That served at Pond City was no exception, pretending to savor the stuff like some of my fellow celebrants, I got a few swallows down before the full fiery force of the concoction hit, from then on it took a manful effort to finish my glass. But I no longer felt the knot on my head and my mind cleared immediately; so clear in fact, I had the good judgement to politely pass on the next round. Fearing this might turn into a debauch, I managed to get my partner's attention and he responded with the good sense he could use when he wanted to. "Fellers," he said setting down his empty glass, "me and Caroliny and Paradise are over heah without passes, so I reckon we're a gonna have to leave yo'all and report back to the Fort."

It was nearly sundown when we left, and as no wagons were available, we struck out afoot, the three of us discussing the incidents of the afternoon, laughing and carrying on all the way back. Paradise was in an especially jovial mood and we had a little difficulty keeping him on the trail. When we got him back to the fort and he had his supper, we put him to bed and we weren't long in following.

When we arrived back at our quarters that evening we were pleasantly surprised to find in our short absence, four-men tents had been erected for us on a clean stretch of buffalo grass outside the Post's main defense perimeter* and near the corral holding our horses. Besides the luxury of tents we snuggled up in fresh extra blankets. And further we owed our suppers to the thoughtfullness of A. J. Pliley and the old scout, Lew Farley; these two accommodating comrades knowing we were absent and guessing about where, used their influence to draw our rations, for which we were extremely grateful.

Despite a tolerable knot on my head and a long day behind me, I was just dropping off into restful shut-eye when I was interrupted by the drowsy voice of Bid, "I'm sure glad yo'all suggested leavin that saloon when we did or some of us would wound up considerable drunk an' I reckon them niggers woulda been about the first to go—not that I ain't right obliged to them, but I never saw a black fellar yet thet could carry his whiskey like a whiteman."

"I don't know about that Bid, but your wrong on one thing, me and Paradise would have been the first to go."

Bid chuckled to himself and rolled over and went to sleep.

* Although there are records of a number of engagements with Indians in the vicinity of Ft. Wallace, especially in 1867, there was little danger they would attack the Fort itself with its strong buildings and corrals.

CHAPTER IV

Detail to Sheridan

To the east of Wallace, some 12 or 14 miles on the North Fork of the Smokey Hill, was the end of the rails in "68". This was "the" to-be "infamous" freighting town of Sheridan, recently risen from nothing to a settlement of considerable size and already doing a tremendous volume of business. Sheridan was unique among frontier towns of Kansas, as its happenings were recorded by no local newspaper and its citizens protected by no law. The fact that it was the temporary (nearly two years) end* of the line for the Union Pacific Eastern Division was the main reason for its importance. The town became the starting place for freight and human transportation bound for hundreds of miles beyonds the rails. With all this booming business came the exchange of much money, so came the population drawn like flies to a molasses barrel. It is likely no man came to Sheridan because he savored the climate or enjoyed the view. The working man and the industrious and the greedy came because the pay was high and money was to be made; the crooked, the illicit, and the sharpers came to fleece the former category. Add to that the adventurous and the rowdy, then throw in an unlimited supply of whiskey and plenty of firearms and you have the makings of the town. For the next two years it did a mighty business as a

---

* Afterwards renamed the Kansas Pacific.

legitimate supply point and from the beginning earned the reputation as a tough, very wild and wicked community. No records were kept of those who came to violent ends there; but gun play was ordinary and ammunition was plentiful to say nothing of the knife, or even the spade and the shovel and finally, the railroad trestle on the outskirts of town, which according to one former resident, bore monthly and sometimes daily fruit.*

Early in September of its first year, Sheridan consisted mostly of tents, sodhouses and dugouts, with perhaps a dozen or so frame buildings of recent construction. Nearby was the cutbank channel of the nearly dry North Fork, spanned by the newly built railroad trestle. Toward the west, a pair of low buttes broke the monotony of the plain. Like lonely sentinels they overlooked the town and still serve as ageless landmarks to the site of Old Sheridan.

On September 8th, having risen with reveille, we reported for formation, had breakfast and stable call, and were idly putting some of our equipment in order when in walked Bid with a broad grin on his face. "On your feet, men," he said importantly, "I've been authorized to select three of you no account waddies to accompany me from here to Sheridan with orders to repair and inspect the wires of the Western Union Telegraph system."

"How in the world did you wangle an assignment like that?" I asked him suspiciously.

"Nevah mind how I did it, them's my orders. I've observed though, for the enlightenment of some of you other fellers, if a man keeps his eyes and ears open and displays the proper attitude, he'll stand a better chance of makin' it in this heah army."

"Well, I can see by the gleam in your eye that I'm already in. I just hope it doesn't include any more barroom forays. I sure don't need another busted head."

"Twasn't nothin' said about barrooms and such in the orders," Bid grinned, "but, of course, a fellow never knows when a slight diversion might be adviseable."

In a short time Bid had the detail mounted and we were on

* W. F. Webb—Kansas Historical Quarterly, Vol. XXXIV, 1968.

our way. We drew Government horses and rations for one meal and were furnished with the necessary equipment for the job, a lineman's belt and harness, a pair of wirecutters, a small roll of wire, some insulators and a short handled spade. Besides Bid and myself the detail included Paradise and John, possibly as inexperienced a crew as ever repaired a line. Our orders, however, included the advice that we also keep our eyes peeled and scout for roving bands of Indians. We rode easterly along the line of poles that stretched across the prairie. Bid and John ahead scanning the line for defects, with Paradise and I bringing up the rear. All the while me trying hopelessly to explain the mysteries of telegraphy to my companion.

We rode for miles without finding a single imperfection; finally we stopped at a pole where the wire sagged loosely, unattached to the insulator and intermittently swayed back and forth. Bid and John had been briefed slightly by the telegrapher at Wallace on where to look for trouble spots and the latter took his job seriously.

"That," said John, appraising the swaying line, "had ort to be fixed. A dangling like that from belly to gut is bound to cause a break in the circuit and interrupt transmission, sure as shootin'."

"Well, I dunno about thet," Bid allowed, "but we best tie it back onto the insulator anyhow." He dismounted and awkwardly donned the lineman's belt and started up the pole, his booted feet gripping the wood ineffectually, but through main strength and agility he reached the top where he swayed back on the belt and grinned down on us. "Don't tell me headquarters didn't use good judgment when they picked this here detail to improve transmission on the Western Union Lines."

A few miles further on, a pole had been pushed over by buffalo and the next one leaned at a sharp angle. For a stretch the wire touched the ground. We dug a hole and reset the first pole and straightened the other. We proceeded on, me explaining as well as I could how Samuel Morse developed the telegraph and all about Ben Franklin's experiments with electricity. But Paradise continued completely mystified. He still "couldn't figure how one feller could talk to another over a danged little ole wire."

Bid reined up and studied Paradise thoughtfully. "Why, there's nothin' to it if yo'all know Morse Code and I reckon I could show you right easy if I ain't forgot the blame code."

He rode on to the next pole which was tall, willowy and full of splinters. That would have discouraged some men, but not Bid when he scented a victim. He dismounted and donned the belt, eyeing the pole with misgivings, then gritting his teeth he pulled himself to the top, where, before adjusting himself to a more comfortable position, he first addressed a few unkind words to the splinters his skin had just absorbed. Feeling better then, he leaned back on the belt, testing it. When he was sure the top of the pole would support his weight, he placed his right ear against the line, cupping one hand tightly against the wire and ear as one practiced in the art of eavesdropping. Then he became perfectly motionless for so long our horses became restless and stamped impatiently, but still, he never moved a muscle. Knowing Bid, I made up my mind to not be the first to break the silence if he stayed there until he petrified. But Paradise and even John were visibly impressed by his performance. "Ary a thing a doin'?" queried the former in a hoarse whisper.

"Hist!" came the answer dramatically from the pole, "theah's a message a comin' over the wire—'going west, mixed train pulled by Engine 109, left Hays City at 8:40, arrives in Coyote 10:50—Stop'."

Poor Paradise's eyes glowed as one witnessing a miracle and John shook his head in disbelief. When Paradise got his breath, words of wonder gushed from his mouth all at once. But Bid raised a hand. "Quiet boys! Theah's more a comin', he said awesomely. Then his voice came in a lifeless, coldly official tone, pronouncing each word separate, "Alert all personnel—alert all personnel—Indians sighted east of Monument—believed to be Roman Nose and the Dog Soldiers—I repeat, alert all personnel'—." And then, after so long a time, "Thet's all boys! The line's done gone daid."

"By God, boys!" said John, dismounting hurriedly and pulling his cinch up tight, "if that's so, we best git the Hell out of here."

"No hurry," advised Bid, sliding stiffly to the ground,

"Monument is a right smart piece from here. Besides our orders were to ride this here line to Sheridan and as long as I'm in charge, thet's exactly what we're gonna do."

But to Paradise the wonder and the mystery of telegraph banished all fears of Indians. "I sure would like to listen jist once't to that wire."

Bid, not about to be caught off guard, assured him, "twouldn't do yo'all no good if you can't understand Morse Code."

"I know, Bid," persisted the other, "but I'd jist like to hear that little ole wire go tick-tack even if it 'tis just Morris Code."

"The trouble is," Bid told him, expanding easily to fit the occasion, "you couldn't even hear the clatter of the wire. They tell me only about one man in fifty kin pick it up. It ain't thet I'm any smarter than you or John or Caroliny here, it's not thet a'tall. It just so happens that I'm one of them damn freaks in fifty with 'negative polarity', where a perfect normal feller has a hearin' of positive polarity."

I had to get off now and tighten my cinch.

Paradise still completely perplexed, shook his head. "It sure beats thunder out of me."

Bid allowed himself a condescending chuckle. "Paradise, you sure ain't like 'Wes Cantwell' who rid with the Trail Outfit last summer. Well sir, when we hit the railroad west of Abilene, there was the damn telegraph wires a runnin' right aside of it, so I clumb a pole and listened just like I done here, AND—do yo'all know to this day 'old Wes' thinks I was jist a spoofin' them."

To Paradise, such a thought was incredulous and he laughed aloud at the idea. "Why, the damned fool," he chortled, "that feller thought you was jist a spoofin'!"

After that, Bid and I both got off and checked our cinches.

Before us the buttes above Sheridan showed up. We rode on at a fast canter and after a few more miles we entered the town. First, we reported to the boxcar that housed the telegraph office. There we left our tools and carbines. Before dismounting,

378

Bid winked at me "Best not mention what I heard on the wire about them Injuns or the whole pack of us may be in trouble for listenin' in on official Government messages."

After leaving the telegraph station we tethered our horses on main street, leaving Paradise in charge of them (the populace was such we feared they might be stolen). The rest of us made a tour of town taking in the sights. About half of the establishments in town sold whiskey in one way or another. One big tent held a saloon and gaming tables, with every conceivable gambling device plus the added attraction of painted women. Business was conducted with a carnival-like air. Glib tongued hawkers presided over the tables and roulette wheels. Whiskey was drawn from spigots in large wooden barrels and a number of full ones were held in reserve. A shelf of fancy bottled goods were on display, but the big business came from the barrel at two-bits a drink. Everything was wide open and business was flourishing.

We came to Sheridan already aware of its unsavory reputation and the appearance of some of its citizens bore this out. As a group, their movements were strange and suspicious and in their eyes was a restless, uncertain look. Although we heard no promiscuous shooting and witnessed no mayhem, there was no doubt about it the place was tough. I reminded Bid of my sore head, he rubbed his swollen knuckles and John looked wise—we did not imbibe.

Although there was a difference, it was roughly true, "if you saw one whiskey joint in Sheridan, you had seen them all". So, soon tiring of this pastime, we got on our horses and rode over toward the railroad works where we found a shady spot and got out our haversacks and ate our noon meal. While at it, we entertained Paradise with exaggerated tales of what we had seen on our tour of the saloons.

The terminus of the railroad was in a partial state of construction. Flatcars loaded with ties, lumber, and equipment stood on the siding and other material and equipment was piled along the right-of-way. A handcar with section hands aboard came smoothly down the track, four men working the handles with easy rhythm. They rolled past without deigning to give us a glance, thence on up the tracks. In a little while they were back, a worker along the line threw a switch and they glided down the siding near us. They left their car with one of their number to watch it and under the guidance of a burly foreman, they swaggered up the street in search of liquid refreshments. We discussed the handcar with interest, as it was of the latest type none of us had ever viewed at close range; a far cry from the common light push car. We walked over and examined the vehicle. Noting the well-greased gears and smooth mechanism, John voiced a thought, "I don't know about you fellers, but I sure would admire to ride on one them things."

Bid looked thoughtful. "You know," he drawled carefully, it's just possible thet could be arranged."

"Yeah," I started out, "if you keep your eyes and ears open and display the propah attitude."

Bid ignored my remarks, "you fellers really like to give thet little car a fling?"

"No," I said promptly, scenting mischief, "I remember the last fling I had with you." But our comrades were impressed with Bid's leadership to day and gave me no heed.

"Looks like you're outvoted, Caroliny. 'Course, if you think the ride won't agree with yo'all, you kin stay heah and look after the hawses." Bid winked at the other boys. "I figure we kin stretch our orders a mite and utilize this here contrivance for our own convenience." So saying, he assumed a proper military bearing and walked over and accosted the little old Irishman in charge of the handcar. Bid cleared his throat, the old man sitting on a pile of ties smoking a corncob pipe looked at him calmly and continued to puff away. "I say, my good man, you in charge of this handcar?"

The watchman nodded without speaking.

"I'm Sergeant Reynolds of Forsyth's Scouts from Fort Wallace," Bid asserted in an authoritative manner. "I'm in charge of this detail with orders to inspect and repair the telegraph line, and on authority of the U. S. Government, I'm forced to requisition this here hand car for official use."

The Irishman's pipe came out of his mouth and he came to

380

his feet. "B'Jasus, man, and Mike O'Rourke's will not be a thinkin' kindly O' that."

"I'm sorry, Sir, but Mister O'Rourke's feelings are of little concern to me. I have certain duties I'm bound to perform and then Mr. O'Rourke can have his little old car back safe and sound and with apologies from Uncle Samuwell."

We checked our horses and made sure they were properly tied and admonished the watchman they were Government property and we expected him to be responsible for them. Then, despite the old man's protests we mounted the handcar and with all four pulling on the handlebars, we glided down the siding and out on the main track and soon were gradually climbing the slope towards the high flats. After a time we stopped for a rest. The other fellows thought the whole thing was a lark, but I had misgivings from the start and continued to gripe and prophecy a bleak end to this thoughtless and unnecessary adventure.

"Aw now, Caroliny, you're a helluva hard feller to please. I figured a little ride in the fresh air would clear your head so yo'all could think again for a change."

"My head is clear enough to realize how big and mean that section boss and his crew are and how many friends they're liable to have around the yards and how kind the Colonel over at Wallace will be when they Court Martial you."

But the others laughed at my doleful predictions and we soon continued on eastward, for as John said, "we won't get busted any harder for playin' with the blame thing two hours than we will an hour and a half." Having commenced to get the hang of it, we pumped the handles liesurely until miles ahead we observed the heavy smoke of an oncoming train. We reversed directions and pumped along at an easy pace, I having decided to be just as calm as my partner. Suddenly I noticed the eyes of John and Paradise were absorbed with the panorama behind us. "Fellers," Paradise finally blurted, "that old engine is a gettin' powerful close." We turned and looked and sure enough, it was in sight about half a mile away.

"We better ditch this thing and let the train go by," I suggested, noting the town with its sidings was still nearly two miles distant. But Bid, taking another quick look around scented a challenge. "And have them Gandy dancers laugh their heads off at us. No sir, not for me, its mostly downhill and if we pour on the wood, we kin beat 'em easy."

He was probably right if everything had been predictable, but unfortunately the engineer and fireman were a pair of reckless spirits, too. Observing us pulling for all we were worth, they opened the throttle and commenced closing the gap. We approached a stretch of higher grade, and the shrill whistle of the old woodburner sounded almost on top of us. It was too late to jump now, we had already committed ourselves. Bid bore down on the handles like a superman. "Pump, you sons-a-bitches!" he yelled, one of the few times I ever knew him to be excited. And pump we did, as the little handcar seemed to slowly pull away from the puffing monster behind us. (We realized afterward the engineer had to start slowing for the station ahead.) As we raced the handcar up the tracks that marked the main thorofare of Sheridan, we noticed about a fourth of the sporting population was out watching the race and they gave us a cheer as we went by. But at the other end of town near our horses, a half dozen grim-looking railroad men, headed by the redoubtable Mike O'Rourke were waiting for us. I saw the short length of pick handle in the latter's hand as we came near; and the little old Irish watchman, pipe still between his teeth as he crouched expectantly on the pile of ties. But Bid never lost his head in an emergency and now it was working clear and sharp. "Indians!" he yelled at the top of his voice, as the little car ground to a halt, and he hit the ground running. I followed his example precisely, as well as did John and Paradise.

"Whar, whar?" roared Big Mike, rushing up a little skeptical, and fondling the pick handle in his hand.

"A couple of miles east of town" yelled John, who was nearest and was nervously trying to untie his horse, "git your guns and put the women and kids inside, there's a passle of them a comin'."

Somehow we got our horses untethered. Mounting, we left in a dead run for we knew it wouldn't take long for the train crew to squelch our hastily improvised Indian scare. We dashed around a warehouse and then cut back to the boxcar and picked up our rifles and repair equipment and left Sheridan at a gallop and didn't slow down until we were a good two miles from town. Paradise who kept an anxious eye on the back trail, announced all was clear behind and we reined down to a walk and let our horses blow.

"Dumb engineer," John said, out of a blue sky, "he could've got us all killed. I could see him stickin' his head out of the cab and grinnin' like a monkey eatin' paste."

Bid looked at me without speaking, a sort of a sickly grin on his face, and I suspected remorse was chewing at his soul.— Ironically, we heard the next day, Indians did raid two miles east of Sheridan and two hay teamsters were supposedly killed.*

The following day we were glad to take it easy at the Fort. We were sore and stiff and our hands were blistered from the adventure on the handcar. After mess, word got around we would be moving out on a new assignment the next day. "That suits me fine," I told Bid, "a few more days resting up like the last two and I'll be glad to get out on the trail to recuperate."

We went over and checked our mounts and while I engaged the trooper in charge of the stable in conversation, Bid slipped our horses a liberal portion of grain. We knew the horses of the Scout troop were being slighted in favor of the regular Cavalry and the Scouts resorted to all sorts of trickery to get a little grain for their mounts. As we were leaving, a soldier stopped us with orders to report to Colonel Forsyth at headquarters. I looked at my partner.

"What do you suppose he wants us for?"

He shrugged, but refuse to speculate. Still, it made a fellow wonder. Word of our escapades the day before had pretty well gotten around and we had already taken a good deal of joshing.—I certainly hoped we weren't about to be charged with stealing a handcar and falsely reporting an Indian attack.

We were ushered into the presence of the commander along

* During the first two weeks of September, "68", Indian activity was so common around Forts Wallace and Dodge that an accurate date for each occurance may vary as much as a day or two on official reports.

with seven or eight other scouts, among them, Irish. With the Colonel was Lieutenant Beecher and the new guide and chief scout, "Sharp Grover".

The Colonel cleared his throat. "Men, I asked you to come here partly because I believe you are fairly representative of the troop. I also want to commend some of you in the manner you have conducted yourselves during this rest period. Some of you have cheerfully volunteered for extra details, which under the circumstances of our stay here, were beyond the normal call of duty. Gentlemen, on behalf of myself and Colonel Bankhead*—I thank you. Tomorrow we will once more be on the march in quest of an elusive and dangerous enemy, and I know I can depend on you fellows for your usual unselfish devotion to duty. HOWEVER, it has come to my attention (I rammed my elbow into Bid) there has been some indulgence in mischief and horseplay, while here in Wallace, that may not have always been in the best interest of the command. But understand, I am not condemning any of you because I believe no malice was intended, little damage was done and it was mostly in the spirit of fun. NOW, I know you men are as well aware of the dangers of campaigning against the Redman as I, and I mention this as an admonishment. You are well aware that the odds 'are' all who leave here tomorrow will not be returning. For that reason, if for no other. I would suggest that there be a little less levity in the ranks, hereafter—. That is all, men."

* Colonel Bankhead was the commander at Fort Wallace.

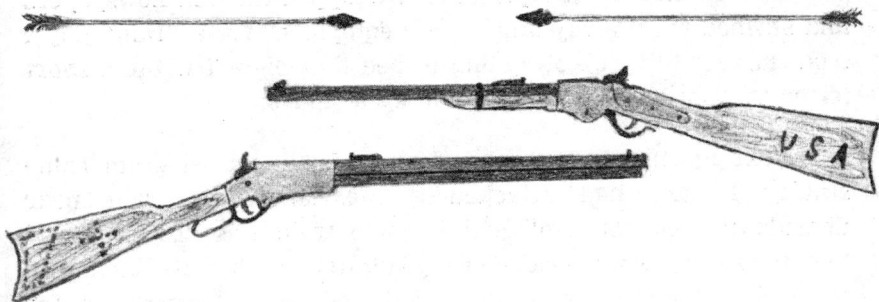

CHAPTER V

With the Colonel in Charge

We returned to our quarters and a little later some of us got permission to try out our Spencers down near the river on the rifle range. Unlike Bid who owned one, I had never learned to completely like the Spencer Rifle. The carbine model we were armed with was a short ruggedly built repeater; designed strictly for rough service with none of the niceties of balance and appearance I admired in my Henry. But despite my likes and dislikes, the Spencer had its good points. The seven shot carbine handled the potent .56 caliber Government cartridge through a proven fairly dependable mechanism actuated by an awkward ring lever, and considering its short barrel and plain sights, it was extremely accurate. With all its lack of refinements. it was the best Indian fighting arm of the "60's" and the early "70's".

We fired about twenty rounds apiece and also unlimbered our .44 caliber Colt side-arms and burned several rounds of Uncle Sam's ammunition in them. Returning to our quarters we cleaned and oiled our guns, taking special care with the revolvers before we placed them in the Government holsters and carefully closed the flaps. I had learned from Bid the prudence of keeping one's six-gun well oiled and dust-free.

After evening mess, we strolled over to the Sutler's store and purchased a few goodies such as candy and etc.; remembering the shortage of food on our previous march, I purchased a side of bacon for emergency rations, feeling confident we would find a use for it before we hit civilization again. We cut the salty, strong, cured bacon into smaller pieces and wrapped them in newspapers and stashed them away among our equipment for a "rainy day". And the last thing before going to bed that night I wrote a short letter to Tom and the Powers family at Hays.

Next morning as we prepared to march, a telegram came stating Indians had attacked a Mexican wagon-train near Sheridan; stock was stolen, the whole train was disrupted and two teamsters were dead. On consultation with Col. Bankhead, our original orders were discarded and we left posthaste for Sheridan. When we arrived at the scene of the attack we found two very dead Mexicans, turned over-wagons, scattered freight, and dead oxen—some still in their yokes were lying on the slopes and bottom. Arrows protruded from the sides of the needlessly slaughtered animals and stuck in the wagons sides and covers. The human victims were laid out much as they had died, but someone had taste-fully covered their bodies with a soiled wagonsheet. On our arrival, the canvas was pulled back and as the troop crowded forward amid the dust from our horses hooves, we viewed the pale and gruesome faces of the scalped teamsters. As I recall, no word was spoken, only a grim silence prevailed. Most of our men had seen similar scenes; "sometimes even when innocent women and children were the victims."—Then the wagonsheet was laid back in place and the Sergeant's voice boomed, "Attention!"

The Colonel turned his horse, facing us. "Men," he said, "this will require some investigation. Why don't you dismount and let your horses rest until you are called upon."

He led the way and held a consultation with the first Sergeant, Lieutenant Beecher, and Sharp Grover. The latter two were well-qualified to judge "Injun sign", particularly Grover who was probably part Indian himself and, anyhow, had spent a lifetime in contact with them.*

When we arrived at the scene, a pair of wagons and mule teams were there with a handful of men gathering up scattered

* Grover was said to have a Cheyenne wife. He had just recovered from a wound received from the Indians while returning from a scouting mission on which Bill Comstock, former chief of scouts under Beecher, had been killed.

freight and equipment. In charge of this detail was none other than our ex-wagon boss, Clint McCandles; with him was our one-time companion "Mustang". The former greeted us with his usual salty gusto. "Well now, by God, if you fellers ain't hard up fer a job." Then he laughed, "but I shore never figgered you'd jine up with no damned yallarstriped Colonel."

Bid looked calmly across his saddle. "Aw, I don't know, Clint. Sometimes I bin mighty careless "WHO" I jined up with."

As I shook hands with Mustang, for once, I felt genuinely sorry for him. He wore a dejected look, his jeans were tattered and worn and his boots sloppy and streaked with manure. Whatever else he had been previously, he had always shown some pride and neatness in his appearance. Bid must have had similar feelings, for he unbent a little and shook hands and passed the time of day with his former friend. Someone gave the signal to mount and as we swung into the saddle we bid farewell to our old companions.

"Now you fellers hang onto yore hair. I'll be needin' a pair of good mulewhackers come spring." McCanles called after us.

A careful study of the ground indicated there were not over twenty-five Indians in the raiding party. With Beecher and Grover at the head of the column we rode off; the men in front easily following the trail at a trot. On and on we followed, the trail gradually becoming less distinct. At almost dusk we made camp in a ravine.

On going into camp, as a rule each man took care of his horse by seeing to it he was properly watered (if water was available); then the animal was unsaddled and allowed to roll, if such was his inclination. Then, if the rider was particular and had time, he would grab a bunch of long grass or a gunny sack and rub the horse down. Next, the picket rope was uncoiled and a good piece of nearby grass was selected and the tired and hungry animal was picketed out to graze. Experience and necessity demanded the use of the unwritten rule, that no man picket his horse in an area where he could overgraze in another's path. This was to prevent the animals becoming entangled in their picket ropes—close together, yes, but not too close. Horses, the same as people, like company. Besides, it was well to keep them in as compact a group as possible and as close to the campfires as practical from a security standpoint, in case of an attack or some unexpected fright from wild animals. This night, horse procedure was little different from our former march. By the time the chore was taken care of and we had gathered a little wood and chips for a fire, darkness was gathering in the little valley. After supper Bid and I, with the attitude of "get-it-over-with so we can have a few nights", volunteered for the first hitch of guard duty. Our outfit called this "running guard", from supper to midnight and from then until morning. We took our positions at the top of a little knoll by two large soapweeds about 400 feet from the Colonel's bunk, with the picketed horse herd between us and camp. Near the edge of the horse herd, the little band of pack mules were staked out by themselves. As we walked by, we made out Satank and he followed us to the end of his rope. I stopped, amazed!

"Well, what do you know about that?"

Bid stopped too, probably as surprised as I, but his fertile mind was working. "Wait a minnit," he said feeling his way along the mule's rope to the picket pin. "I got an idee how we kin save ourselves a few hours sleep." He pulled the pin and we guardedly coaxed the pack mule up on the knoll next to the soapweeds and picketed him out. "This contrary devil is a sight better sentry than ary one of us," Bid said. We allowed ourselves a hearty chuckle apiece, then crawled in our blankets and went to sleep. On the other side of the draw the other two sentries likely went to sleep too, but not as peacefully and secure.

At midnight we were relieved by Irish and John who brought us up with a few sarcastic words of criticism. We made no apology for our apparent dereliction of duty; but at early dawn, Irish was accosted by the irate muletender. "How the Hell did that mean little mule get staked out way up here on the hill?"

"Ask me no questions, my friend, and I'll tell you no lies," returned the puzzled, but wary Irishman, "but according to my recollection, I haven't the damnedest idea."

After a hasty breakfast we were once more on the move with

Beecher and Grover scanning the trail about fifty yards in advance. The trail became dimmer due to the Indian's trick of gradually dropping out of the main band whenever they passed a piece of difficult to trail terrain. Our progress became slower and in a few hours the guides came to a standstill. Beecher turned his horse facing the command. "Disappeared," he explained, without embellishment. We were halted and dismounted with orders to let the horses rest and graze while the Colonel and his staff held a long consultation. Everyone agreed the Indians knew we were on their trail, yet no one in our outfit had seen the slightest sign of them save the faint pony tracks which had now disappeared. The Colonel, realizing his own inexperience in trailing, listened carefully as Grover and McCall somewhat monotonously aired their separate conclusions. Lieutenant Beecher, unwilling to guess wildly, said little and refused to express an opinion. But not so the other two, who after much talking and gesturing, finally came around to similar viewpoints. As nearly as we could determine from the snatches of conversation we overheard, they were sure our Indians were in the process of joining a large war party and that it would seem best to exercise great caution in advancing too far to the north lest we risk overmatching ourselves. Colonel Forsyth listened politely until his impatience began to show.

"Gentlemen," he interrupted, "it has been my opinion that a push to the north towards the Republican River will be necessary to find the main portions of the Cheyenne and Sioux who have generally been the perpetrators of trouble in the settlements. And I want it clearly understood that I am determined to track them down and punish them no matter what the odds are against us. We are fifty some strong, the best equipped and capable force in the west. If we can't whip them, at least they can't annilihate us. Futhermore, this command was intended to fight Indians and that is precisely what I intend for it to do."

With that speech the discussion came to an abrupt end. Our own little clique, of course, had no part in the discussion, but we were close enough that we heard much of what was said, particularly the Colonel's last remarks. As we moved out, I asked Bid his opinion of the pow-wow, knowing he wasn't greatly impressed by the Colonel whom he considered too much of a brass-bound Yankee blueblood.

"Well, in the first place I like the way Lieutenant Beecher said it—he didn't know the answer and kept his yap shet instead of givin' out with a lot of bullshit like them other two. But," he grinned, "I sure admired the way the Colonel brought the discussion 'precisely' to an aind."

Pushing northward, generally without trace or trail and beyond all signs of civilization, we camped that night on what our guide proclaimed to be Beaver Creek. We had completely lost all signs of our original Indians, but the prevailing opinion was we sooner or later would cut fresh sign. Good grass and water was available here, so we staked our mounts out early and got ourselves a welcome meal topped off by plenty of hot coffee.

CHAPTER VI

A Little Lesson in Manners

For two more days we moved here and there in a general direction of north. The command sometimes spread out searching for sign and even hunting game. It was long days and sometimes great distances between water. The element of a pleasure outing was more subued this march and horseplay was not so frequent, but still all that happened was not "dead serious". Among the scouts was one who made himself obnoxious from time to time by a monotonous habit he had of moaning about the state of his physical well-being, and his inability to look at any situtation from any but the darkest side. It was no wonder this fellow went by the name of "Gloomy". He first came to the attention of some of us for remarks he made on our march from Hays when he noticed among the camp equipment carried by the packmules was a pick and some shovels and spades. As was his nature he could conceive of but one use for these tools and he never failed, at least once daily, to speak forebodingly of the sinister implications these simple tools aroused in his imagination. "Fellers," he would say, "I sure wish't they'd a left them blame shovels at the Fort. They wasn't hung on there just to dig fer water."

Irish, after becoming acquainted with Gloomy's peculiarities, usually made it a point early each day to enquire of the other's health, as—"I say there, comrade, how are you this fine morning?"

"We-ll, I ain't right well this morning," Gloomy would respond, "my rheumatism is a pullin' at me somethin' awful and I got a naggin' pain in the pit of my stumick, but I reckon I always feel a mite porely of a morning."

"Well now," persisted Irish, "don't you feel just a 'mite porely' all day long too?"

"As a matter of fact, I do," agreed Gloomy, "take my family now, none of 'em ever reached a ripe old age. Even us young uns, too, had our troubles. My pore step-brother was laid in his grave afore he was twelve. The Almighty has seen fit to let me reach the prime of manhood, 'though much of it has been amid woe and sorrow. If by some lucky chance't I pull through this here campaign, I suppose it'll be back to the old grind fer me—a plowin' and a plantin' and a diggin' and a storin'—too hot in the summer and too cold in the winter and—."

By this time "even" Irish had his fill and walked off, leaving Gloomy reciting his unhappy past and doleful predictions for his future.

One night around our campfire, Gloomy came to a minor downfall. Among our comrades was a grizzled ex-trapper of probable French ancestry who was known as Old Pete. Pete was not especially gifted with the social niceties, but he had a simple good humor that made him well-liked. Gloomy got along fine with Pete, likely because the ex-trapper put up with his constant moaning better than any one else. Gloomy wasn't long in showing his friendship by detecting symptoms of dread physical ailments in the hardy frontiersman who in all probability had never been ill in his life. This night, however, Pete did show up after supper a little indisposed and complained of a "bellyache"; caused most likely by too many wild plums and tanking up too heavily on water. But Gloomy never considered such a trivial ailment. "Mighty peculiar," he allowed to the group of us, "I never knowned them symptons to p'int to but one thing, and THAT, fellers, I hate to mention here 'cause you all know what an epidemic like this kin do to the troop, especially in our position. But, boys, it cain't do no good to try to hide things like this, so's I'm gonna bring it right out in the open—I'm afeard Old Pete has done been teched with the 'cholera'."*

His diagnosis was so ridiculous that some of the boys laughed outright. But not Irish and Bid. They agreed solemnly there was a possibility Gloomy could be right; anyway, the first thing to do was get him over to Dr. Moer's right away. Irish volunteered to take Pete to the Doctor. The ex-trapper being convinced by now that he really was sick, and the two departed at once. Bid by some trumped up excuse, coaxed Gloomy to go with him and look after the horses, where they succeeded in stumbling around in the

* A terrible epidemic of cholera occurred in the frontier Plains country the previous summer (1867). A large percent of the cases were fatal and for many years it was remembered as the most dreaded of diseases.

392

dark for some time and eventually being challenged by the sentry. Then Bid took advantage of this diversion and had a prolonged visit with the latter. In the meantime, Doc got out his medicine bag and fixed Pete up with a proper dose for the bellyache and topped it off with a small slug of brandy—and, of course, in the interests of best social behavior, Doc and Irish took one too. The Doctor then advised Pete to go on back and sleep it off; and as luck would have it, in fifteen minutes the old trapper was flat on his back, snoring away. I got a blanket and laid it reverently over his sleeping form covering him from head to foot. Irish studied the situation seriously and shook his head. "Set over there beside him," he told Paradise, "and nudge him easy-like in the ass with your toe and see if he won't stop that damned honking."

It worked and Pete's breathing smoothed out into a quiet sleep. Irish grinned confidently, "stay right there beside him" he advised Paradise, "and whenever he breaks his easy gait, give him a little of your toe."

A little later Bid and Gloomy came in. The latter cheerily discussing horses with Bid and in such good humor for once in his life that he paid no attention to the still, stretched out, and blanket-draped form of Old Pete. Someone silently offered him a chaw of tobacco which he accepted with a "thank thee kindly", for as an habitual "bummer" of the fragrant weed, he was not used to such generous offers. All was silent around the still form of our comrade—you could have heard a pin drop. Paradise sat tense as if in mourning, while he kept his toe against "Old Pete's" behind to quiet any sudden outburst of snoring. Bid stepped over in plain view, staring solemnly at the ground and had a few whispered words with Irish. Gloomy busily masticating his chaw, commenced to notice the gravity of the situation. "What's goin' on around here, boys—what'd the Doc say about Old Pete?"

No one answered. but Bid leaned over and raised a corner of the blanket and gazed briefly at Pete's quiet face. then gently laid the blanket back and stepped away. hat in hand. Irish stood up. cleared his throat. and spoke in the grave and studied tones of the clergy. "Men," he asked, "is there any amongst you who can say the Lord's Prayer?"

Gloomy nearly swallowed his chaw as he came to his feet. "My Gawd, fellers, not Old Pete!" he said incredulously, and badly shaken he roughly jerked back the blanket. Pete, who had spent much of his life in the wilds, was touchy about such rude awakenings, and raised up in alarm pulling his six-shooter.

Poor Gloomy sat down amid roars of laughter. Finally he got hold of himself and walked away dejectedly. "Fellers, I didn't think you would do this to me," he moaned.

After Gloomy had gone, one of the boys spoke up that he "sorta felt sorry for the pore devil".

"Not me," said Irish, "did'ye notice how downright disappointed he appeared when 'Old Pete' raised up out of the dead?"

Returning to the serious part of our mission, we continued on, sometimes perhaps half the troop spread out and searching for Indian sign. Probably a third of the force was qualified to track and trail and a third more of us were ready, willing, and learning fast. Our eyes grew sharper and our senses more alert, no mark on the ground or unnatural object escaped someone's observation; every hoof mark or even disturbance in the grass came to have a meaning. The very nature of our methodical advance hardened us to the knowledge that we were embarked on a systematic and deadly manhunt, one in which the enemy was almost certain to outnumber us. We moved so far off the beaten path that we found ourselves in an almost unknown country. Even Sharp Grover, our guide, exhibited a doubtful familiarity with the terrain. At places, the draws and brakes became deep and precipitious as we approached the Republican—but what stream was the Republican?* Actually, no man among us could identify it for sure; a determination by size and amount of water flow seemed our best bet. Finally, we struck a sizeable stream with cottonwood trees and other species along its banks and willows and bushes crowding the edge of the water. Under other and more favorable circumstances it would have been an interesting stream to explore. For the last day or two, our extensive scouting

---

* The maps of the Republican were not completely accurate and Grover's knowledge of that area aroused the skepticism of some of the other scouts.

had flushed no game, an almost sure sign, the old timers said, that "Injuns" were in the area. Scouting along the river banks, we ran across a few false leads and then someone discovered an Indian wickie-up among the thick willows. Examination indicated it had been occupied by two Indians, possibly the night before. Soon a small but fresh trail was located. That night as always, a guard was posted, but this time no one slept on duty; this was Indian country.

Although the new trail had developed fast and was by all signs the most promising since the first day out, more than one man wondered before we hit our blankets, if it wouldn't peter out before we had a chance to burn powder. But the trail became better next morning as it converged with other trails and for the first time it was clear we were following a sizeable body of Indians. A quiet feeling of excitement was felt among the troop. At last perhaps, we were nearing the climax of our campaign and "maybe after all, we'll get to square a few accounts with them red devils".

The Colonel silently studied his men.

"He cared not whether the odds be five or the odds be ten."

"It mattered not the numbers for he feared no vagabond band."

For his was the ridingest, shootingest, fightingest force within the entire land.

Forsyth's fighting fifty.

CHAPTER VII

"Trailing"

At the first rest break as we led our horses through scattering willows to water, Bid and I found ourselves side by side with Old Pete, the ex-trapper. The latter was known to have had a world of experience with Indians and with the trail getting hotter mile by mile, I yearned for a more educated opinion than my own.

"Well, Pete," I asked, "when do you think we'll catch up with the Indians and will they fight or scatter?"

He looked at me, his face working half serious and half humorous before he found an answer. "I think," he finally said, "we will catch up with heem only whan he isa ready to fight."

I thought of his answer later in the day as the trail continued to broaden and it was clear the Indians were not concerned with the sign they left behind them. Their course of travel became a trampled path wider than a wagon road, scored with the marks of lodgepoles and travois, indicating squaws, children, and whole villages had recently passed ahead of us. Some of our older and wiser heads watched the trail unfold with misgivings. Only a day or two before the Colonel had enjoyed the complete support of the troop in his determination to push doggedly on. But now more than one man questioned the wisdom of following too closely a band that could easily number more than ten times the size of our force. Eventually, things reached a head and at the next stop a group of the more concerned approached the Colonel and openly questioned the wisdom of the present tactics. Forsyth, a little surprised at their presumption, nevertheless listened to what they had to say before he made another of his little speeches that brought the matter to a close.

"Men," he said, "I sympathize with your concern, but you are assuming no risks that I, Lieutenant Beecher, Dr. Moers, Sergeant McCall, and others are not willing to take. Further, in my opinion, it is better to advance and do them battle rather than attempt to return. And I ask you all in clear conscience, did you not each and all hire out specifically to fight Indians?"

The dissenting group, of course, had no answer to the Colonel's final remarks. Although they disagreed with the policy of pressing too closely on the heels of a potentially powerful enemy, it would have looked little short of ridiculous if not downright cowardly for our mobile and well-armed force to turn tail just when it appeared we had tracked the Redman to his "lair". No one felt this any more than Colonel Forsyth, although I think it was shared to a lesser degree by the whole force. Anyway, the protest had no apparent effect on the Colonel's studied determination to attack the Indians, regardless of costs, but it probably did influence him to exercise extreme caution in our continued advance. On the afternoon of September 15th, with every man quietly alert, we entered the silent valley of the Arickaree.

By this time, of course, the South Fork and the main Fork of the Republican had been recognized for what they were. On pursuing the Indian trail up the latter and thence up the south-westerly course of the Arickaree Fork, we traveled in three states*, a fact most of us never knew until later, as their lines were imaginary nothings in a boundless wilderness and were really unimportant insofar as our mission was concerned. When we went into camp along the banks of the stream that evening, we were near the last of our rations except coffee, some beans, a little hardtack, salt, and etc. Our horses were in a worse way, some of them being so jaded they would hardly graze. The hunter's thrill of an expected bout with the Indians was somewhat dampened by the realization of our horses' condition, our shortage of food, and the probable odds against us. But there could be no turning back now; we had passed the point of no return. And we had to accept the fact, whatever happened to us lay with our commander and how well we really measured up as a fighting force.

But all was not gloom in camp as we sat mostly silent by our little fires, munching hardtack, crackers, and sipping a last cup of coffee. The irrepressible Irish walked by a neighboring campfire which illuminated the faces of "Gloomy" and Old Pete

* The three-corner area of Colorado, Kansas, and Nebraska.

Trudeau with the youthful Jack Stilwell, reclining easy and unworried beside them. The slightly bald pate of the ex-trapper shone like a new dollar. "How, how, cola,"* laughed the Irishman, "you'd better keep your top side undercover, Pete, or some Cheyenne squaw is liable to take a hankerin' for it as a fly swatter."

"Listen to thet damned Irish," growled Bid, "he'll find something to laugh about when they open the gates of Hell for him."

Early next morning we were up with a scanty breakfast in prospect. Bid and I with guilty glances around, brought forth one of our little parcels of bacon and soon it was sizzling on the coals of our little coffee fire. I don't know how many of our comrades noticed the scent of bacon in the air. Perhaps, and I hope, more serious thoughts occupied their minds.

Shortly after daylight our mobile and self-sufficient little force was once more following the well-traveled trail of the Indians—like a small dog sniffing on the heels of a grizzly bear. Every effort was made to avoid an ambush. Without extending our advance scouts too far from the main body, we proceeded carefully at a moderate gait, the trail becoming fresher as we advanced. Soon we commenced to notice fresh horse droppings and other signs which told of the proximity of the Indians; yet searching the hills and valley with practiced eyes, no man could detect "hide nor hair" of them. "A bad omen" said the old scouts. Forsyth rode near the head of the column with a thinlipped silence, as we wound our way in and out of the willows, plum thickets, and desert brush that flourished along the stream and foot of the hills. About noon he called a short halt but the site was neither suitable for good grazing or observation. There was, however, a small stream of good water and we refilled our canteens and watered our horses after a brief rest and scanty lunch.

For a week now, we had been on the march with little more than the night times for our horses to rest and graze and for many of them it was beginning to tell. To the man with the responsibility of command, the best strategy for the present was to find a place with good grazing and water where horses, mules,

* Injun lingo.

and men could fill up, rest up, and generally fit themselves for the sterner measures ahead. About four o'clock we came to a pleasant grassy stretch near a narrow island in the sandy, nearly dry riverbed. We were ordered to fall out and graze our horses and make preparations for an early camp. The Colonel was a competent military man and no doubt he would have preferred a more defenseable position, but grass and rest were pressing needs for our mounts. The risks we must take, and there were grounds to believe those risks were about as minimal here as anywhere in the immediate area. The field of view extended on all sides for a reasonable distance without enough cover to hide a sizable enemy force, closer than the foot of the rocky hills. A day spent soul-searching and mulling over a situation for which there was no easy choice, doubtless convinced Forsyth that an early camp here was our most sensible course for the present. Certainly in the next day or two something would have to be done about our food supply. In the meantime rest up, continue to study the situation, stay ever on the alert and, perhaps, await the enemy to make the next move.

Bid and I unsaddled and led our horses down the shallow bank of the stream where a clear trickle of water flowed along the sandy bed, a few inches to a foot deep and perhaps a rod wide. My partner had been unusually silent the last two days. Although he had taken no part in the protest group nor expressed any opinion, I could only guess he realized the seriousness of our position more fully than some of rest of us—Although this feeling was contrary to his sometimes reckless attitude toward ordinary danger. Studying my horse, he broke the silence.

"Thet blame locoed bronc of yourn is sure a holdin' up better than some of them other hawses that's got a sight more sense."

"Well yes, but for one thing you and I have both taken better care of our horses than some of the other fellows. Besides, remember how you stole grain for them at Wallace?"

Ordinarily a remark like my last would bring a grin out of the Texan, but he remained grim and sober. "A campaign like this'n kin be mighty hard on hawses, more so even than men. A lot of us," he forecast glumly, "is apt to be walkin' out of heah—afoot."

He relented a little then and like a couple of kids we took off our boots and waded the shallow water over to the island where we found a grassy spot near a small cottonwood tree and staked our animals out to graze while we stretched out in the shade and wriggled our bare feet in the warm sand. Both of us sensed something impending, from which our outfit would never be the same, and some of us wouldn't be "walkin' out of here"— perhaps, even he or I. Probably we both had the feeling we should be entrusting our last will and testament to the other, but a mutual shyness of appearing sentimental kept us silent. I finally brought myself to say, "We've been pretty close since we've been together, Bid, and there's one thing I'd like to be sure of, no matter what happens here—we stick together."

He took out his pipe and tapped it upside down against a dead branch, and never looked at me, but I knew his word was strong as his bond and a dozen handshakes. "Yeah, Caroliny, thet's the way it'll be."

Later, I noticed some of the boys in camp pointing curiously in our direction and I realized we might be a little out of bounds, so I roused Bid and we pulled on our boots and mounting our horses bareback, we trotted back to camp and staked them out in the big grassy area.

That night a number of guards were posted at strategic spots around the camp with Colonel Forsyth personally overseeing their locations. Careful precautions were advised that every man be particular how his picket pin was driven and that his tether rope be secure. A stampede of our horses was a calamity that couldn't be risked. Orders were to hobble any animal who had persistent habits of bolting or rearing back against the tether rope. This precaution should have been taken with my horse, but we were unable to procure hobbles as they were all in use that night.

We volunteered for first hitch of guard duty and took our post near the riverbank. For rations we drew a cup and a half of dry beans and gathered driftwood for a small fire which we started well before dark. Placing the beans on to cook with a tinplate for a lid and held down with a rock, we kept them simmering until nearly midnight. Under cover of darkness, some

400

of our spare bacon was cut up and added to the beans for seasoning. At guard change we shared our repast with our replacements, John and Gloomy, and enjoyed a satisfying meal; and the last that can be described as such for a long time.

As we were finishing the beans, a dim figure approached slowly, picking his way in the darkness. Bid stood up. "Is that your post, McClaine and Reynolds?" came the Colonel's voice.

"Yes Sir," answered Bid, "we're just now changing guard."

"Fine," returned the other as he stepped closer, "I'm checking all posts and I want to caution each of you to continue ever on the alert. You men are familiar with the Indians habit of an early dawn attack. Keep your arms by your side and your lariats within easy reach. We can't afford to risk the loss of a single horse."

The September nights turn cool in the high plains country, even following a hot day. We went to sleep fully clothed with only our boots removed and the saddle blankets thrown over our feet for extra warmth. My partner reminded me the last thing, "Look out for your hawse if trouble starts, he's just liable to throw one of his damn conniptions."

Gloomy's voice came in a querulous undertone to John, complaining of the quietness of the night. "Tain't healthy; still as this is, it sure don't abode no good."

Sleep came quickly and I knew no more until nearly morning, when I felt Bid's hand on my shoulder. His arm was tense as spring steel. "Hist!" he whispered, "there's somethin' a stirrin' yonder."

I sat up and reached for my picket rope and felt it tighten in my grasp. Sure enough, my horse must have heard it too for the rope was drawn tight. Straining our ears the sound came again; this time clear; a loud snort, then a shuffle of hooves, followed by a strained and muffled bray and next the sound of a horse or mule running wildly in the dark.

"By God! It's Satank and gone again, sure as hell," exclaimed Bid, coming to his feet and staring after the running mule.

I located my picket pin and commenced to reel in my horse

when the sharp crack of rifles came from the other side of camp and the cry of INDIANS went up.

Following the rifle shots my horse reacted as Bid had feared. Straining backwards he pulled me along with my feet braced while I hung on to the rope gripping it desperately for all I was worth. Bid quickly hitched his own rope around his waist and came to my assistance. The two of us dragged the distraught animal to a halt, but he reared back straining and jerking until the taut rope suddenly parted and he fell back on his haunches. While we watched helplessly, he regained his feet and dashed off in the semi-darkness. Then we heard the unmistakeable Yip Yip of Indians and about a dozen of them clattered by the outskirts of camp, jangling bells and rattling hides in an attempt to stampede our stock. A number of shots were fired by our men, but it was still too dark for accuracy, although it caused the raiders to veer away without much to show for their efforts.

"Saddle up, men! And stand by your horses," yelled the Colonel and echoed by Sergeant McCall.

I rolled my saddle, bridle and blankets in as small a bundle as possible and stood by, feeling mighty helpless without a horse. As it commenced to get light, a few of the men were granted permission to ride a little way to the top of a small rise and reconnoiter. I jumped on behind Bid with the faint hope I might locate my horse. We only took a quick look and hastily returned; the country was literally alive with Indians. Sharp Grover mounted on his horse peered upstream as the morning light brightened the valley. "My God! Colonel, I've never seen anything like it in all my life."

A group of mounted warriors all decked out in their "war-getup" charged down on us as if they intended to overrun the whole troop. We held our fire, each man with his carbine in a handy position awaiting the command. "Fire" was the word when they came in long rifle range and the Indians ducked low on their horses and pulled sharply to one side with a few crippled ponies and a little more respect for the range of our Spencers. The effect of this little preliminary engagement gave our troop a temporary lift of confidence. But the awesome advantage the Indians had in numbers left the danger of the situation no less hair-raising. No one realized this more fully than Colonel Forsyth, now faced with the necessity to make a quick decision, which could determine the life or death of his whole *command. He turned at once to Lieutenant Beecher, Sharp Grover and some of the others and a brief consultation was held. Then, almost immediately, came the order. "Men, we'll move over there to the island at once. Then each of you tie your horse securely and take cover.

* Eight years later, on the Little Big Horn, Custer apparently failed to made the proper decision and lost his entire command in a similar situation.

CHAPTER VIII

"The Battle Ground"

In the short time it took to move to our new positions, a few of the scouts under the direction of Beecher and Grover kept up a steady fire, momentarily keeping the Indians at a distance. The narrow little island rising only a few feet above the sandy river bed didn't appear to be any bulwark for defense, but it was the only reasonable choice and we had to make the most of it. As soon as the horses were tethered to the few little trees and bushes where hopefully that scant cover would give them some protection, orders were given to faced outward and "dig in". Much of the area was covered by tall bunch-grass and nearly all the ground was extremely sandy. For most of us the only tools to dig with were our butcher knives and tin plates. Lugging my saddle, blankets, and equipment, I yelled at Bid to follow as soon as he had his horse secured, and I would pick us out a vantage point to fight from. Plunking down my saddle and plunder on top a half buried log of driftwood which protruded possibly six inches above the level, I laid my carbine nearby with the end of the barrel resting on the log and covered the breach with my jacket. Then I got out my culinary tools and went to digging in and throwing up a breast work of sod and sand. In a matter of minutes the island was completely surrounded by a large force of Indians who commenced pouring in a heavy fire of bullets and arrows. By any battle standard "all Hell broke loose". They knew accurately the size of our force and pressed that advantage recklessly for a time. At first about our only protection was the slight cover afforded by the bunch-grass and thin brush. Very soon some of our horses went down. immediately a few of our more experienced scouts crawled in behind the downed animals and commenced to methodically and accurately return the Redmens fire. But still bullets whistled by and thudded into our positions with regularity. Soon several of our men were hit and nearly half of the horses were dead or dying and the effect on the remainder of wounded and terrified animals, with their screaming and groaning and plunging created a horrible and undescribable bedlam. Old man Farley and a few of the other Saline Valley boys held a position on the riverbank where their steady and accurate fire had a very intimidating effect on the Indians. The old man*, personally accounted for several Indians in the early part of the battle and they soon learned to give him a wide berth. But unfortunately he had to operate from poor cover and suffered a severe leg wound himself. He and his comrades bound it up, however, and continued to fight.

It is surprising how quickly a man can entrench himself even with makeshift tools when his life depends upon it. I felt myself making some headway when Gloomy plunked down at the other end of the log and commenced clawing at the grassroots with his butcher knife and predicting in a low and toneless voice that we would all be killed. I was too busy and scared to pay much attention to him, but I did commence to worry about Bid. It couldn't have been more than 40 or 50 paces from where I had left him. So far I hadn't fired over one or two shots, as the opposing fire was so intense, if a man exposed himself by necessity or carelessness for more than an instant, he was asking for a slug or an arrow. My better judgement told me Bid wasn't coming now even if he were alive and well, because it would be sure death to attempt to crawl to my position pinned down as we were. But still I couldn't help feeling a growing fear for his safety.

One of the scouts nearby called out desperately. "Men, if we don't raise up and shoot in earnest, we'll be over-run!"

That did seem reasonable, so some of us threw caution to the winds and rose and took a few quick shots. I took a hurried shot at a young Indian riding recklessly close to our lines, but I missed as he shot at me with a revolver from under his horse's neck. I didn't miss the next time, though, and down went the pony with the young Indian landing on his feet and running like a rabbit for the cover of the bushes at the end of the island; but he never made it. One of the scouts, crouched behind a dead horse, nailed him as he dived for cover. A bullet went splat into my saddle and another kicked up sand where my arm had been, as I ducked down behind the log.

* Lewis Farley may not have been over 45 or 50 years old, but to a young man under thirty, he seemed old. He had a son, Hudson Farley, in the fight.

To my right a pair of scouts lay back to back and alternately dug and took quick shots at the enemy. In my present state of mind I couldn't think of their names, but they worked together as a team and gave me a sense of security from that direction. Occasionally the voice of the Colonel could be heard mingled with the sounds of battle, exhorting us to not waste our ammunition and shoot only at sure targets. I didn't realize then he was exposing himself without regard for his own safety in order to observe and command our defense. By now, I had dug out and erected a sand breastwork large enough for two. My pessimistic neighbor rolled unexpectedly in the depression beside me, explaining that two big Indians with bows and arrows had a bead on him not a hundred feet away. I had worked a peephole in the mound in front of me and took a good long look and couldn't see a thing. "They're out there anyway," he warned, "jist a waitin' to rush our positions and kill every mother's son of us." I looked at him with distaste, for an instant relishing the thought of how well he would look with an arrow in him. He must have noticed my lack of sympathy for he started out again, this time his mental block taking complete possession of his wits. "You don't believe me, do you? You think it's jist old Gloomy a goin' on again as usual, but I know we've already lost half our men, Culver, Gantt, both the Farleys and McCall fer a few, and you know as well as me you'll never see McClaine alive agin."

It was not the time when one whispers "sweet nothings" to remonstrate with an obstinate and blockheaded comrade and I reacted accordingly. "My God man!" I roared in his face, "I'm sick and tired of your predictions of doom and your eternal bellyaching. If you're so sure we're all gonna die, then aim that rifle and die like a man."

Following my own advice I laid my rifle over my peekhole and took a couple of quick shots at a figure behind an isolated sagebrush 120 yards away and I think I made it pretty warm for him. As I pulled my Spencer back, I heard the splatter of retalitory bullets and sand sprayed over the top of the embankment. I looked around for Gloomy and he was gone. Wherever he was, he must have gone in a hurry. I remembered some of the recent things I had thought and said to him and I sure hoped he had made it.

Firing became more frequent from our side and less from the Indians, as most of our men were dug in behind cover now and were systematically picking off any redskin who dared show himself. Some of them had gotten too close to our lines for their own comfort and were now forced to extricate themselves. This is an area where the Indian warrior excelled, being able to take advantage of every little bit of cover, and some of the scouts were still so well pinned down by the superior numbers of the Indian sharpshooters that a quick bead and a snap shot was all that was prudent and possible. As the human targets became pretty well concealed, the Indians turned their attention to the remaining horses and mules and soon made short work of them. Their methods evoked no love from those of us who had to lay more or less helplessly by and see the slaughter done. One wounded horse, straining desperately, pulled loose from where he was tied and plunged directly towards me, where he was hit again and fell in twenty feet, mortally hurt and unable to raise. Some Indian boys, out of sight behind a sage—covered bank, amused themselves by lobbing arrows into the unfortunate animal. When the first arrow struck his belly, he twisted his head and looked straight at me, silently and imploringly. It was Bid's horse, Old Joker. Another arrow struck with a thud and the poor animal flinched and stared as if he realized I was the only one who could help him. But that power wasn't in me; I could only draw my revolver and put him out of his misery. Then, venting a little emotion, I sent a couple of probably useless shots towards his tormentors.

When the last horse was down, someone from the Indians' ranks yelled out in clear English, "There goes the last of their *damned horses." Another sound not commonly heard from an Indian attack force was the blare of a bugle which was heard several times that day on the Arickaree.

Finally the firing abated some on our side of the island and I got a chance to visit with my neighbors in the next pit. They told me that from the talk being passed down the line, Colonel Forsyth was wounded twice and several of our scouts were dead, but they weren't sure of the names.

"Could one of them have been McClaine? I asked anxiously.

* It was speculated that one of William Bents "half-breed" sons was with the Indians. Though educated and with many reasons for a decent life he was a known renegade.

"No, sure don't recollect that name. He's the tall, blackheaded feller with the Texas saddle, ain't he?"

"That's the one. Have either of you fellows seen him or got any ideas what has happened to him? He's my partner and we agreed to stay together."

I could hear them talking between themselves and pretty soon the nearest one called back. "We're sure sorry Reynolds, but neither of us can recall seein' your partner since we moved across the river, but likely he's on the other side and ain't been able to get in touch with you either."

A bullet thudded into the saddle just above my head and the conversation was terminated. I was pretty depressed about Bid, but the sound of the bullet reminded me that self-preservation was the first order of the day. It appeared that my position was "zeroed in" by a sharpshooter armed with something the power of a big Springfield or Remington for the last bullet tore clean through the heaviest part of the saddle and sprinkled me with sand. Very carefully I moved to the other side of the shallow pit and worked out another peephole. I soon found that my neighbors, too, were under siege, and apparently from the same Indian. We conversed back and forth in an effort to locate his position. By one man shooting and drawing fire, while the other two watched, we were able to determine his approximate location; a comparatively open spot over a hundred yards away. He apparently lay in a shallow depression, situated in such a way that he had a view advantage over us. He certainly was an expert at utilizing what cover he had and he was a remarkably good shot. My eyesight was good as any man's and after a careful study I detected a slight mound which must hide his position. I described the spot to the boys in the next pit and asked them to watch while I tried a little ruse. With my butcher knife, I pushed the top of my army cap over the sand bank. Nothing happened, so I wriggled the cap back and forth and finally in desperation I pushed the brim and all above the sand. But our opponent was too smart for an old trick like that. I, then, told the boys I would "smoke him out" and stuck the barrel of my Spencer over the peep hole and was raising up to take aim when "spang!" the barrel bounced up minus a thumbsized chunk from the forearm and I got a mouthful of sand and wood splinters.

"By golly, you're right!" one of the boys called back, "that's the place, sure as shootin' "

I didn't laugh at his little pun, if it was so intended, but pulled my carbine back to safety and spat the sand out of my teeth before answering.

"You all right over there?" evidently fearing I had become a casualty.

"Yes, I'm alright, but I got a little careless. Why don't one of you fellows stick your gun over the parapet just like you intended to shoot, but stay low, and don't expose your head for that redskin has a deadly eye. While you keep him occupied, maybe I can see what's going on out there."

Our ruse worked again, but with less danger, although the Indian's bullet hit accurately in a few inches of the gun barrel. Observing closely, I saw what was happening. Immediately upon firing, he would roll over quick as a flash to another position a few feet away. During the brief lull in the shooting, we discussed the power this one Indian had over our little sector of the battle. Something had to be done; he was immobilizing at least three men and judging from the uncanny accuracy of his shots, it would only be a matter of time until some of us became casualties. We decided for each of us to alternate in firing a quick shot to get his attention while the other two would try to pick him off when he made his quick flop. It would be difficult shooting with some risk, we knew, because we were dealing with a smart and tricky customer who might be too cagy to follow his regular pattern. During the past summer, I had became pretty confident of my markmanship and I felt now that I could nail the "savage" if I could just get in position for a quick and steady shot. In that respect he literally had the Injun sign on us, for he and his brethren out there weren't apt to give us that kind of a break without considerable risks to ourselves. In my previous encounters with Indians, I realized I had held an advantage in gun, position and markmanship. Here, that was all pretty well reversed. An untutored savage was demonstrating that he was a better shot and a smarter one.

Before we could try our plans, our positions commenced to draw more fire with the result we had to content ourselves with a few hurried and inaccurate shots and hope for the flurry to soon die down. Awaiting a lull in the shooting, I tried something different, pushing my carbine ahead of me and hugging the ground like I was part of it, I crawled out of the rifle pit and through the grass just behind Bid's horse. From here the ground was slightly higher and a better view of "Deadeye's" position was possible. I carefully eased a little sand out from behind Old Joker and slipped into the shallow depression. So far, so good. Apparently I had made the move without being seen. I was afraid to risk giving myself away by rising up to take a look, but finally I screwed up courage enough to very carefully raise my eyes above the level of the dead horse. The next move was to get my rifle in position which I accomplished by forcing the barrel slowly along the still warm body of Old Joker. Just then, one of my neighbors fired another shot. Quick as a flash came "Deadeye's" answer; and as he made his quick flip, a shot came from the Saline Valley contingent on the river bank. The Indian raised halfway, his heavy rifle slipped from his grasp and he spread-eagled on the sand beside it. That was the best shot I have ever seen and for minutes, not another one was fired in our area. And then we heard the wailing of the squaws from the hillsides.*

My mission accomplished, I crawled thankfully back into my rifle pit. One of my neighbors told me calmly. "Tom's been hit."

"Bad?" I enquired.

"Can't tell, it's in the arm and bleedin' right bad."

"Hold on a minute. I've got some bandages in my haversack, and I'll be right over."

We dressed the wounded man's arm as best we could. He was painfully hurt, but not seriously—the heavy bullet going clean through and luckily missing the bone.

As I crawled back to my hole, a familiar figure wriggled

* Survivors of the Beecher Island fight told how the Indians squaws and noncombatants assembled on the hillside where they had a grandstand view of the battle. They came to cheer and stayed to mourn.

along pushing his saddle ahead. In place of his hat, he wore a bloodstained bandage. "You fellers certainly are raising considerable Hell over in this neck of the woods," he drawled.

To hear Bid's voice again was sweeter than music and I felt like jumping up and hugging him. But as soon as I got the lump out of my throat so that I could speak properly, I said, "it's about time you was showing up. Now that I got all the heavy digging and housekeeping done."

"It appears to me," he commented, as he crawled over the edge, "thet it could stand a right smart more diggin' if it's to accommodate two fellers with all of the comforts of home."

He explained his tardiness by describing how he had tethered his horse so he might have a better chance for survival. Then he and a couple of other fellows walked right into a hot party the redskins were giving and "I got this little souvenir up the side of my haid and the next thing I knew, me and them other fellers were down on our hands and knees a diggin' to beat hell." He wound up, "Then Gloomy came a slippin' in there about an hour ago sayin' you was asking about me."

"How is old Gloomy?" I asked, "when he left here he was sorta dejected."

"Never saw him so willing to put his shoulder to the wheel. He was doin' his share of diggin' and shootin' when I left. I reckon he was like the rest of us, too damn scared to do otherwise."

Although the whole band on the island were entrenched in an area within yelling distance of each other, the fight was so hot and heavy, those on one side were seldom sure of the situation on the other. Bid was a little better informed than I in regard to casualties because he had been nearer the center of the fight. Colonel Forsyth, he knew was wounded, although as we both knew, he was still actively in command. "He's a gritty cuss alright—the way he stood up on his hind legs and gave orders whilst the rest of us was diggin' like badgers to get under cover," my partner acknowledged.

"How about Ikey, John, and Irish and Paradise? Have you seen or heard anything of them?"

411

"Ikey and John, no; but Irish has done took Paradise under his wing and put the boy to work a diggin' while he does the shooting. Thet lucky Irishman'll make it if any of us do and'll likely come out of this a smellin' like a rose."

The battle continued never letting up completely and never giving a man a chance to relax or even fully appraise himself of the situation on the other side of the island. We took turns with our Spencers when fighting would permit and the other partner would busy himself enlarging and deepening the rifle pit. The Indian casualties by now had been heavy and as their reckless tactics at the beginning had not succeeded in demoralizing us, they became more cautious and were eventually forced to find better cover a little further from our lines. Their arrows were no longer effective, although every once in a while one would drop in our vicinity to remind us of their danger. Most of the men dreaded the arrows more than the bullets; they made a very nasty wound and could kill you just as dead.

The sun beat down on us and with the strain and exertion of carrying on the fight since early dawn, our thirst became almost unbearable. Gloomy and I had long since emptied my canteen and Bid had left his with the boys on the other side of the island. In the next lull in the shooting, we discussed how the water in the stream divided at the head of the island and we both agreed that it must flow in at least a few feet of the bushes and tall grass on one side or the other. At the beginning some Indians occupied that area, but we knew none were there now, except possibly "Good Indians" as some of our scouts were posted in 50 or 60 feet and we were little over double that distance ourselves.

"I'll just collect a few canteens and crawl over yonder and see if I cain't reach the water," Bid volunteered through parched lips.

"You will like the dickens," I said, "since when did you get any better at crawling than I am. Besides I don't make as long a target as you."

He looked at me for an instant, but the strain was too much for his usual grin. "I sure as hell don't aim to toss no coin with yo'all."

We settled the matter by drawing a marked cartridge out of my cap and I won. So gathering up my canteen and those of our neighbors, and slinging them on as best we could, I crawled out of our pit. My way was dotted with scattered bunches of bluestem, stunted brush, four or five dead horses and a few sandpiled rifle pits which provided significant, but spotted cover. But by carefully choosing my route I expected to avoid detection, at least until the very edge of the water was reached. As I figured I needed both hands for locomotion I left my rifle in the pit, taking only a revolver and butcher knife. We had worked out observation and rifle slits in our entrenchments and now Bid and our unwounded neighbor were standing by with a pair of fully loaded Spencers apiece to provide instant fire cover if and when I needed it. Taking advantage of every bit of cover, I crawled in close to each rifle pit and talked to the other occupants, most of them I knew by their first names as Will, George, Slim, and so on. They all wished me well and I picked up more canteens, but had to turn some of them down as I was offered more than I could handle. Slim and his partner, dug in behind a dead horse, were near the end of the line for me. Slim told me he had made his way through the bushes shortly after the Indians had been driven out, but was unable to reach the water, though it was little more than an arm's length from the edge of a thick stand of young willows.

"If a man had a short pole, he could tie a canteen on the end and maybe reach through the willows to water," he suggested.

"Any of those willow sprouts long enough and stout enough?"

Slim and his partner were as dry as the rest of us and said they would try about anything to get some water, so Slim insisted on going with me and the two of us slithered the rest of the way to the willows. Here we were pretty well concealed from the Indians, except possibly a few isolated ones at long range on our flanks and back from the riverbanks. I was really more concerned that the Saline Valley boys concealed along the river bank knew our identity. Having already seen enough of Lewis Farley's shooting, I had no desire to be mistaken for an Indian by him. On the other hand, their position pretty well assured us there would be no Indian fire coming from that angle.

413

As we maneuvered around the last obstacle, the body of a brown horse still tethered to a bush. There lay the nearly naked remains of the young Indian killed earlier. He was hardly more than a boy, smooth of face and in his way handsome. One hand grasped at his belly where he had been gut-shot from a rearward angle and his insides spilled out where the heavy bullet had gone through. It was a part of war that is never a pretty sight, but neither of us felt any remorse. I only remember feeling grateful he hadn't fallen in the water and polluted it. Moving on by, I carefully parted the willows and peeked through to the crystal clear stream of water, perhaps eight inches deep, disturbed only by the slight flicker of the current and the occasional flash of a minnow.

One glance was enough to deter anyone from pushing past the cover of the willows to attempt to fill the canteens. With luck, one canteen might be filled before a barrage of bullets came our way. But Slim's idea of a pole seemed workable. We conversed in whispers, although an ordinary tone couldn't possibly give us away; this was sort of a no-man's-land, only a hop, skip, and jump from the last rifle pit, but one infinitely less hospitable. Selecting a willow six or seven feet tall and nearly an inch at the base, we chopped it off, using our sand-dulled butcher knives axe-like. Slim happened to be one of those fellows who are particularly dexterous with twine and knots and in no time at all he secured a canteen to the pole with simple slip knots that we could undo in seconds and tie another one on. I carefully parted the willows and shoved the canteen on the end of the pole along the sand, so as to avoid detection and into the water. It took a bit of doing, but Slim had done such an expert job of fastening the canteen to the pole that I soon got the knack of filling them in the shallow water and in a short time we had several regulation canteens, nearly full of water. We stopped and drank our fill and emptied nearly two of them which I immediately refilled. As I pushed the last in the water, I noticed what appeared as a roilly cast upstream, but I was so elated at our success that I gave it little though at first, and then it dawned on me that something was wrong. Glancing upstream I saw the reason, two Indians stripped of all but the bare necessities crawled, half-submerged down the shallow stream of water not over forty yards away. Apparently they were so engrossed in their own progress they hadn't noticed the canteen and pole in the water. I pulled the pole and canteen back through the willows where Slim had the canteens arranged together for us to drag back to the rifle pits.

"We better get out of here," I advised him tersely, as I hastily untied the last canteen. "You take all the canteens but this one to your place and I'll cover the rear and meet you there in just a little while."

Slim took one look at me and didn't argue. Then gathering up the canteen straps he took off like a badger. I turned and took another peek through the willows. The Indians, moving very slowly, had probably advanced less than twenty feet since I had seen them last, evidently relying on their unmatched ability for a quiet, patient stalk to get them past our field of observance. I wondered what they hoped to gain; they couldn't possibly be armed with more than knives, and bow and arrows. Remembering the Redman's dread of his comrades falling into the hands of the enemy, I concluded they hoped to retrieve some of their dead—the young warrior at the edge of the bushes, for example. I knew if I had my rifle I could have got them both, but with the hand gun, I had little confidence of accuracy; however I could certainly spook them out of the water, though, where some of the boys in the rifle pits could give them a hot time. Again I parted the willows and took one careful shot, followed by two more quick ones. Not waiting to see the results, I flattened myself on the sand and wriggled my way out of there as bullets sung by and splattered in the sand. Then the boom of the Spencers joined in and the battle was on again. I could only guess that some of my fellow Scouts had a pair of lively targets.

Back in our own pit, Bid and I were just settling down again when word was passed down the line that Dr. Moers had been hit and was dying. This was especially disheartening news, with all our wounded, to learn now that our doctor was gone. The scout who passed the word to us was noticably upset.

"I wonder, boys, has God deserted us?" he asked, "the Colonel says if any amongst us can pray, we'd best do it, but I'm powerful afraid the Lord ain't on our side today."

"Funny attitude some fellers take just because we've lost a few our our best men," Bid commented soberly to me, "but this is a mean fight and I've felt mightly obliged to the Almighty more'n once this mawning for sparing my hide and—." His comments were cut short by a burst of rapid fire from the opposite side of the Island and almost immediately two young daredevil Cheyennes dashed by on fast ponies between us and the riverbank, giving their piercing yells and shooting their six-shooters. Catching us by surprise they were almost through before we got our guns unlimbered and to our shame we apparently didn't score a hit. It was a dangerous and reckless stunt, either designed to demoralize us or more likely to show off the bravery of the two Indians who took part in it. But they got away with it— although it was noticable they weren't foolish enough to try the same stunt again. The incident did focus some attention on the little group of Saline Valley men on the riverbank as not a single shot was observed coming from their position. We knew they had some wounded, but so far their fire power had been the most effective of the command. Now they must either be in bad shape or running low on ammunition, or both.

After almost every conceiveable trick and type of attack known to the Indians failed to dislodge us, they changed their tactics somewhat, and it soon became clear they were about to put forth their strongest effort, as mounted warrriors in large numbers began gathering at a safe distance beyond the range of our rifles. Their chiefs in fancy feathers and headdresses rode among them with much gesturing, arranging them in formation for a grand charge. As this went on, the firing around us gradually ceased, either by pre-arrangement or because the beseiging Indians were fascinated by the preparations for the impending event. For the first time we found it safe to gingerly poke our heads above the fortifications without drawing fire. For many of us it was our best view of the battlefield, for the day. Some of the Scouts claimed they could identify the different tribes in the gathering formation by their battle apparel; Cheyenne, Sioux, Arapahoe, and Kiowa were all said to be represented. Watching them, no one in our lines doubted that we were in for our sternest test. Colonel Forsyth, despite his wounds, was propped up in his pit where he gave the situation his careful study. And orders were soon forthcoming to make preparations for a heavy frontal assault on our positions. Every man was to make sure his revolver was properly loaded and ready to fire, also his carbine magazine was to be fully loaded and a cartridge in the chamber. All of the disabled men's Spencers were to be made ready, likewise, and held in reserve by some of the able bodied and eight or ten of the lesser wounded who could still handle a carbine in a pinch. Some of these "fighting wounded" were our most determined defenders. And morale was generally at its highest among the Scouts. We were entrenched now and had our "second wind"—"let the sonsabitches come, we're ready for them."

The Indians started slowly in a well-organized body while those on the ground surrounding us cut loose again with a heavy fire, aiming to keep us pinned down (but was otherwise ineffective). As the clear peal of a bugle was heard, the mounted warriors gradually increased their speed until they were in a dead run, then they bore down toward us with the wildest of war-whoops. The rifle fire around us died down and we got ready. Soon the Colonel's voice came loud and clear—"NOW!" The crash of the Spencers came almost at once and gaps opened in the ranks of the onrushing Indians. Prominent among the Indians was their leader*, a tall powerfully-built warrior, mounted on an outstanding horse, whirling his rifle above his head and yelling a savage defiance, he completely ignored our rifle fire.

Our defenses 'though' covering the greater part of the island, faced outward in roughly the shape of an elongated circle. For this reason, only about half the men comprised the approximate front line of defenders. On this group fell the burden of the initial assault and they did a tremendous job. They worked the levers of their carbines and aimed with remarkable accuracy, considering the circumstances and never budged from their positions. While those of us on the far side of the circle were at a greater range and were forced to shoot between them and over their heads. Consequently, when their magazines were nearly emptied, we still had several rounds left. When our time

---

* Roman Nose at this time was one of the most famous Indians on the plains. He was said to be the leader of the Dog Soldier band of Cheyennes.

417

came, not to be out done, many of us advanced from our pits and kneeling in the sand, poured our fire into the yelling, maniacal horde as accurately as we could aim. When the Indians reached almost to the end of the Island, the firepower was just too much for man or horse to face and they involuntarily broke and split, some going on each side of us. Among the many who never reached the island was their leader; he had made his last charge.

Some of our carbines were empty, as the Indians dashed desperately by, but we drew our six-shooters and with yells wilder than their own, we blasted at them with our forty-fours. Then the Indians on the ground commenced firing at us again and we remembered the battle wasn't over and dropped down and reloaded our weapons. The mounted warriors crowded their ponies around the river bend and counted their losses. It wasn't long until we heard the anguished cries of the squaws and non-combatants.

When the firing died down again, we got an idea of the Indian losses, although most of the wounded had already crawled away and concealed themselves. For some distance back, the sandy river bed was scattered with dead horses and Indians who hadn't made it. On the other hand, our side apparently hadn't lost a man. Then word was passed along that Lientenant Beecher had been hit and was dying.

Later the Indians re-grouped and charged again and again, but the terrible losses they had taken the first charge apparently had drained them of their leadership and confidence and we forced them back every time. Sharp Grover insisted from the start that the prominent leader killed in the main charge was the famous Cheyenne warrior, Roman Nose, but this wasn't known positively until later.

When the sun finally went down and darkness came, we had our first respite of the long day. But the mourning cries and shrieks of the Indians and the low moans of our wounded continued on into the night. First, we took stock of our losses. Lieutenant Beecher and two of the scouts were dead. Dr. Moers was not dead as reported; but was seriously wounded in the head, and there was no hope for him. About ten men were severely wounded besides Colonel Forsyth, and eight or nine others injured, but not disabled. Our first order was to bring in all the wounded and make them comfortable as possible. A group of us sneaked across the river and brought in Lewis Farley and his companions. The old scout had a severely wounded and broken leg and he had to be carried back. The pain of being carried without a stretcher must have been an ordeal for him, but he hardly uttered a moan. With our Doctor dying and nearly all his equipment and supplies lost in the confusion of the morning stampede of some of our pack mules, it was impossible to dress and treat the wounds of the disabled men. But every effort was now made under the protection of darkness, to improve the liveability of our positions and especially that of the wounded. Water was brought in from the river and more importantly, a well had been dug inside the entrenchments. Some way, two of the shovels (that had been such a worry to our friend, Gloomy) were still in our possession and with willing hands, they were put to good use. We dug a large pit near the center for a "hospital" and placed the wounded there on their blankets. The saddles, blankets, and all equipment was brought in from the dead horses and every bit utilized in one way or another or laid aside where it could be used later if needed. In a collective sort of way we prepared for a "Robinson Crusoe" type of a future. A light rain commenced shortly after dark and as the day had been hot and dusty behind our sand barricades, we rather welcomed it at first. We became used to the darkness and were able to see (and feel) our way around rather well. In this manner we connected all the rifle pits with shallow trenches, piling the sand on the outside. The saddles were placed on the breastworks where they would do the most good. When all this was completed, we felt pretty secure for anything the Indians could throw at us.

By this time, having been over twenty-four hours without food, we were nearly famished. Of course, the only food available was the meat from our dead horses and mules. No matter how distasteful that might seem under normal conditions, here we had no choice and we made the best of it. Wood was available for campfires, but the rain had made most of it too wet to light and some of the fellows ate the horseflesh raw. But our bunch was still a little finicky and fortunately for our tastes, we found dry wood in the log that formed part of my original breastwork. We found one of the picks and split off chunks for ourselves and some for the other boys. I thought of the portion of bacon I still had in my haversack and couldn't help mentioning it to Bid as we sharpened our butcher knives on a borrowed stone. Of course, neither of us had the courage to seriously think of eating such a civilized morsel, under the present conditions and surrounded by half famished companions.

Bid said half humorously, "sometimes, Caroliny, I almost wish you didn't have such a pore opinion of the Quartermaster Department's idees of a proper ration for a Government Scout. Bacon—it's a wonder you didn't think of a dozen aigs, too."

Not a word had Bid uttered about the loss of his horse, although no man in the troop valued his mount more highly or had a greater sentimental attachment. To his practical mind, it was second nature to accept the dangers and the heartaches of frontier life and recognize the futility of "crying over spilt milk." But it would be only as a last resort to save us from starvation that he could bring himself to use a knife on what was left of Old Joker.

Accordingly, as a true horseman, he now led to where he remembered one of the mules had fallen, a particularly lazy and stupid animal, but in better shape than any of the others. We found Irish, John and Paradise there before us.

"Might a knowed you finicky fellers had your eyes on these steaks," Bid grumbled.

"Hell, McClaine, help yourself," invited Irish, "it's first come, first served around here as long as it lasts."

So we helped ourselves and the five of us cut off a good portion of mule meat, which was cut in thin strips and spread on the bushes for future consumption. And back in our pit, we lit our fire and cooked supper. We probably made out better than many of our comrades, as I remembered a little salt I had drawn the night before with our beans. We shared this with the fellows around us and a filling meal was had by all. Most of us would have given half our worldly possessions for a cup of coffee, but that, along with the company supply of salt and medical supplies had been lost in the early morning attack.

After our appetites had been satisfied, some of the boys felt like talking and the discussion soon turned to the loss of the supplies. It seemed strange this loss had occurred when supposedly we had been prepared and trained for just such an emergency. Still no one expressed any blame on anyone else; it was just one of those things that shouldn't have happened—plain bad luck. John was positive he knew exactly where the supplies were, and he described the position. "Why, I could walk there and back in the dark in ten minutes," he declared.

"If you're so sure, I'll go with you," Irish volunteered, "and let's go get 'em."

John began to hedge. "Too many blamed Indians a layin' out there awaitin'. Besides, a man would have to crawl on his belly through the grass and would get wetter'n a drowned rat and would nigh chill to death before the sun comes out."

But danger held a certain appeal to Irish. "There's not many Injuns out there now," he argued with some logic, "they know they've got us holed up and most of them's pulled backed around their campfires, where they can carry on their damnable, heathenish rituals until daybreak."

John avowed Irish might be right, but he sure wouldn't risk his hair on the chance of it. I was inclined to agree with John. Irish's reasoning sounded plausible, but he could be wrong and the idea of playing hide and seek with the Indians in the dark sent the cold chills up and down my spine. Besides, I remembered taking a look at our last night's campground just before dark, and there wasn't a thing to be seen such as John described; a dead Indian pony or two the only objects in the area. Evidently the Indians had already made off with the packs. We were still discussing the subject when A. J. Pliley approached. "Boys," he said quietly, "I need a couple of volunteers for burial detail, the graves are already being dug."

It was a sad chore that probably every man of us dreaded, but we all volunteered at once. Pliley smiled grimly. "Fellows, I wish we could all honor these comrades that gave their all that we might survive, but some of you are needed to guard our lines. Jack, I'll take you and John here, as you fellows knew both Wilson and Culver*. Now, as for you other men, the Colonel thinks where possible, two of you should occupy a pit, one watching while the other tries to get a little rest as we know we can expect another hard day tomorrow."

We stayed in our rifle pit with Paradise stationed next to us until Irish returned. John's partner had been wounded and either he or Irish would team up with the younger man. We felt a sort of paternal duty toward him this first night which I am sure was appreciated, but was probably unneeded, as Paradise had proved himself under fire as well as many an older head. In spite of Pliley's advice, we found the demands upon our minds and physical beings still too great to rest or sleep. The light rain, although of small consequence on the warm, sandy ground, warned us to makeshift some sort of cover for our precious extra ammunition. This and other small chores aimed at making our outdoor quarters liveable, occupied our time.

* G. W. Culver and William Wilson, as well as Lientenant Beecher were killed the first day of the battle.

CHAPTER IX

"Company for Breakfast"

Earlier in the night, while we had been busy working on the entrenchments, the Colonel had called some of the men to his side and asked for volunteers to slip through the Indian lines and try to make their way to Ft. Wallace. The latter place was judged to be a hundred miles or more distant, as no one knew our exact location. Sharp Grover, the head scout who no doubt knew Indians as well as anyone present, advised against it, saying it would be impossible to get through. But Jack Stillwell disregarded the older man's advice and offered to risk it if someone would go with him. Several volunteered, but the Injun-wise trapper, "Old Pete",* was selected. Silent as shadows they slipped out in the night with much of the hopes of our salvation riding on their shoulders. They knew, and every mother's son of us knew, that while Grover's advice may have been overstated, his was the voice of experience; and if they made a single mistake, they were "goners". After their departure, not a sound nor a signal from them was heard and their fate was a mystery for many days. But on the notion that "no news is good news", hope and many a silent and unsaid prayer for them prevailed in the sanctuary of the island.

Lying in our rifle pits thinking of the two men who had gone out into the night, we listened for each isolated sound from the darkness. Once in a while, the clear, sharp yelp of a coyote would be heard, followed shortly by a distant answer or maybe the cry of some bird. To us it was the Indian vedettes talking to one another, but to our relief we heard nothing that would indicate our men had been intercepted. Pretty soon, John and Irish came back from the burial detail. The former, as was his nature, mourning aloud the necessity of burial at such an ungodly hour and place without benefit of clergy. But Irish, for once, was sober and meditative and had nothing to say.

Soon the cloudy overcast lessened and the night became

---

* Pierre Trudeau (Pete Trudeau). Stillwell was still in his teens but well experienced in his chosen profession as an Indian scout.

lighter for a time. Gloomy and another scout came by and said some of the wounded were becoming pretty restless, so Irish, Bid, and I procured some water in a kettle and reported to the hospital pit where we soon got a small fire going and set the kettle to boil. Here, with the help of two more of our able-bodied comrades we were able to dress the wounds of some of our most seriously injured. Some of our walking wounded were willing and able to be of help to the disabled and did all in their power to lighten the long and painful hours of those less fortunate. But in reality there was little that could be done and the wounded appeared to realize this and seemed thankful for the meager care they did receive.

At sunrise, the Indians, true to their habits, renewed the battle and it continued all day long, at times hot and heavy to die down to sporadic firing. We played it cool and suffered no serious casualties. The Indians were still determined and still surrounded us on all sides by vastly superior numbers, their desire for blood and gore and our scalps had not in the least diminished. But apparently they were guided by a leadership that was too shrewd and wise to again attempt to storm our positions in an all-out charge as they had the day before. They tried many small charges which were as colorful and spectacular as only the Plains Indian on horseback could make them. This was the type of warfare which had earned them the title as the "finest light cavalry in the world". But as we held our fire until they were in the deadly short range of our carbines, they always broke when they reached that point and usually circled us just out of effective range and lobbed wild bullets into our positions more for effect than accuracy.

We had, of course, missed our breakfast and by noon were hungry. Some of the boys slipped out and got some of the partly dried horse and mule meat; but Bid and I couldn't forget the little package of bacon I still had in my haversack. We talked it over and decided the cravings of the inner man could no longer be denied. So the package was brought out and the newspaper wrappings removed and there lay the little slab of sow-belly in all its glory, exuding a delicious aroma of smoked hardwood and fat pork. Deliberately steeling myself of all foolish thought of generosity, I drew my butcher knife. Bid already had his out. "Get thee behind me, Satan," I breathed, and Bid said, "Amen." We cut it into slices, rind and all. Paradise and John peered curiously and hungrily from their pit. We tossed them a few slices. "Take them, but there ain't no more," I said.

"I always thought there was some good in you two fellers," John acknowledged by way of thanks.

We ate the bacon raw and never has meat of any kind tasted better. I looked at Bid finishing his and still chewing industriously on a rind. He wiped the grease off his chin with the back of his hand, his face covered with a ten day old black beard; as rugged looking a citizen as you ever saw.

"Now," I questioned, "what was you saying last night about a dozen aigs?"

As the afternoon wore on, it became quite hot again; and after a lull in the shooting, I commenced to feel drowsy in spite of all I could do to prevent it, for it had been well over thirty hours since we had slept. Glancing across at the next pit, Paradise was stretched out in the hot sun sleeping like a baby and John, with rifle barrel poked over the sand parapet, nodded with half closed eyes—about to let go. Bid's voice came sharply, "Keep 'em open there, John, you cain't sleep now." John straightened up like he had been caught with a hand in the cookie jar. I straightened up too, and looked at Bid. "Go ahead, Caroliny,—and catch a few winks. Just so one of us stays awake and I can hold out til' after dark." With the miserable feeling of drowsiness that possessed me, I didn't need to be urged any further and immediately laid down on my side and went to sleep. That delicious siesta must have lasted better than an hour, when I was awakened by the full-throated boom of Bid's Spencer.

"Ha, ha, ha!" he chuckled, "I wish't you could have seen thet, 'cause yo'all will never believe me. But I creased him right square across the topnot and he jumped higher than a blind dog in a stubble-field. Then Irish or Al Pliley over yonder let him have it right in the middle—there'll be an awful wailin' around his campfire tonight."

When darkness came, we again cut and spread strips of

425

horse and mule meat on the bushes to dry and had our usual "steak" supper. We boiled some of the partly dried meat for the wounded and sacrificed the last of my salt. I took over guard duty about ten and Bid relieved me at two. The night was drizzling and chilly, but we had improved our quarters and our blankets had dried out during the day. Experience had prompted us to bring small piece of canvas for bed covers and this we staked above us for some shelter. Thankfully, the sandy ground still retained its summer warmth and I went promptly to sleep and dreamed I was in the warm, comfortable, hay-filled bunk at the Sod Ranche. I never awakened until daylight, when Bid shook me. My right arm and one foot was wet from the night rain, rifles were cracking and bullets plunked into the sand bank.

"Wake up, Caroliny," he said, "we got company for breakfast again."

The shooting gradually subsided, when the enemy determined they weren't accomplishing anything. From then on most of the shooting was from some of their best and more patient shots who lay in some advantageous position, hoping to catch someone careless enough to expose himself. But by now, the scouts were too battle-smart to get careless; patience was a way of life forced upon us by the circumstances. As someone said, "we realized we weren't going anywhere and were in no hurry to get there." The Indians tried innumerable tricks and ruses to draw us out. More than once they shouted insults in English. One time a voice yelled derisively, "You white sons-a-bitches fight in holes with your tails between your legs." Someone from our side yelled back, equally insulting in a mixture of vulgar English and what passed for the Indian dialect. But these tactics drew little fire from either side, as it was too dangerous to get "carried away" and take offense at a little name-calling. At least three dead warriors lay so near our lines the Indians night parties had been unable to drag them away. Knowing the Redman's beliefs in regard to his own dead, we watched these corpses carefully in case they ever became reckless enough to try to recover them. One of the scouts yelled across to the Indians.

"How—brother dog-eater, we've got three of your best braves

426

over here, we're through with 'em now and they're gittin' purty rank."

"Yeah," someone else yelled, "we don't need 'em any more, as we've done took their hair and their moccasins."

The last sally must have been understood, for it brought cries of rage and a flurry of gunfire. The scouts safe in their pits, laughed with savage derision. The Arickaree fight, like many engagements with the Plains Indians, was fought by both sides with the utmost bitterness, without the least compassion being shown by either side. If a wounded Indian would have fallen into our hands, he would have instantly been shot and we knew if they ever succeeded in over-running our island defenses, every man of us would die as unpleasantly as they could manage it. Even now, for all we knew, our two couriers who last night undertook to slip through their lines, may have met a cruel and hideous death.

Later in the day the Indians attempted a flag of truce maneuver which was probably no more than a ruse to get in close to our positions. A. J. Pliley, who was usually anything but foreward in voicing his opinions, spoke up at once and advised against honoring the truce, saying it was an old Indian trick, and he described a similar situation that occurred the year before when he was a scout* with the 18th Kansas Volunteers. The Colonel instantly ordered Grover to address the flagbearers in their own dialect, directing them to halt at once. But the Indians pretended not to understand and continued to advance, whereupon a few of us were ordered to carefully fire a few shots very close to them as a warning. This had the desired effect and they broke for cover and in a little while our chivalry was rewarded by a shower of bullets. Actually, they were lucky; if our commander hadn't insisted on a certain amount of respect for a flag of truce, we would have in all probability picked them all off before they could reach cover. As I remember it, that was the only time any of the nicer rules of "civilized warfare" was observed in the whole battle.

* The battle of Beaver Creek (or Prairie Dog). A. J. Pliley was credited with saving a group of the 18th Kansas Volunteers from a vastly superior force of Indians. Later, because of his part in the battle, he was made a captain. (Reference—Kansas Historical Collections, vol. IX, 1905-1906).

Altogether this day may have been the easiest one of the entire siege. The sky was partly cloudly and the weather moderate. This, coupled with the Indians' reluctance to try a really determined charge, gave us a chance to relax somewhat from the tension of the last two days and nights. Further, we suffered no casualties and our food supply was still edible. However, from then on our difficulties increased day by day until they were almost unbearable.

One of the biggest questions confronting us now was whether Stillwell and Trudeau had made it through the Indian lines the first night. We, of course, had no way of knowing and speculation only added to the anxiety of the entire beleagured force. There was no doubt that the Indians intended to keep us pinned down until they starved us out. And that would only be a matter of time because already our food supply was beginning to spoil. Accordingly, at midnight two more men stole out with another message for help. This time it was Irish and Pliley, two of our most able and resourceful men. We supplied them with enough dried horsemeat for two days; and on their feet, they wore moccasins taken off dead Indians. They slipped quietly away in the blackness with all the stealth of the redman whose footwear they had borrowed. Their orders were to return before morning if they couldn't make it through the enemy lines. By daylight they did not return and no commotion was heard indicating they had run into trouble, it was a pretty fair assumption they had made it through.

It had been a cold, damp night with a light drizzle turning to snow. None of us had got much sleep. But what was miserable for us was likewise for the Indians, and they let us off with only minor activity. As we shivered in our positions, sprinkled with a half inch or so of the season's first snowfall, some of us remembered it was Sunday. I thought of "Pete Purdy", our amateur parson with the wagon train last spring. "Yeah, Prayin' Pete, if he was here, he would be right at home," Bid allowed, "a leafin' through his Bible and aquotin' scripture. But I reckon a little spiritual guidance would be a heap welcome around this layout this mawnin'."

"But a nice, warm campfire with a pot of coffee would do a lot to put me in the proper mood for such guidance."

428

"Caroliny, I'm plumb surprised at yo'all, a havin' such worldly cravings whilst a baskin' in these here sublime surroundings and enjoyin' the first touch of winter's wonder."

"Bid, if this wasn't the Sabbath and we weren't in such a terrible fix and you weren't such a dear friend, I would be inclined to tell you to go to Hell."

Hard as it was for us, the able-bodied, to keep up our spirits, it must have been even more so for the wounded. Although we had rigged up partial shelters for them, from canvas, blankets, and anything available, they were still mostly exposed to the elements. What wood we possessed was damp and fires were for the present impossible. But the wounded men showed admirable fortitude and there was little complaining. Dr. Moers mercifully died before daybreak. His death left us with no one in critical condition, although many were seriously and painfully wounded. Among these, the Colonel was the most voluble, as well he should be; besides being severely wounded, he still retained the responsibility of command. He had been hit in both legs, the bone being broken below the knee on his left leg and besides, he had received a minor head wound which caused severe headaches and dizziness. But he complained especially of the bullet in his right thigh. In time, the pain became so intense that he decided the ball must be removed, but no one would touch it because it lay so close to the artery. Later in the morning, the clouds lifted and the temperature rose slowly. Bid, Paradise, and myself were interrupted in our effort to rustle wood which we hoped to dry out and stockpile for future use. The scout, who had been waiting on Forsyth as orderly, nurse, and what-have-you, approached. "Say, Reynolds," he said, "the Colonel wants to see you right away."

Arriving at the officer's side, I found him in an unpleasant mood. Although suffering considerable pain, his voice was still strong and forceful. He spoke to me quite civilly, however. "Scout Reynolds, I understand you served as surgical orderly during the late war and have had formal medical training?"

"During the war for a time, yes, but I gave the whole thing up before the war was over and have studied no further nor attempted to practice since."

"Well, at any rate," he said a little impatiently, "you are surely better qualified than some of these 'muleskinners' I've had waiting on me. And don't think I'm ungrateful," he hastened to add, "they've served me no doubt as best they can."

Before I could think up an answer, he continued. "My broken leg and aching head I can live with, but this damnable ball has simply got to come out of my thigh. The others are afraid to tackle it on account of the artery. But I've had some experience with bullet wounds and if I am willing to run the risks, why should any of you object?" He laid aside his blanket then and exposed his wounded thigh.

I bent and examined the injury and could make out the outline of the rifle ball imbedded in the flesh. The thing that impressed me most was the correctness of the "muleskinner's" diagnosis. I had seen enough bullet wounds in my time to agree with them. But how to tell the Colonel, I didn't look forward to with pleasure.

"Well—?" he asked.

I braced myself. "Colonel, whoever told you it was dangerous to tamper with that bullet was absolutely right in my opinion."

For an instant Forsyth's pain-filled eyes blazed, before he got hold of himself. "Then you refuse to attempt to extract the ball?"

"I think it would be very dangerous for anyone except a highly skilled surgeon to touch it," I hedged, "especially in a position like this without equipment and surgical necessities."

"Very well, then, there appears to be nothing further to be said. And thank you, Reynolds, for your trouble."

An hour and a half later we learned Forsyth had induced two of the men to help him and using his razor he had cut the rifle ball out himself. Just another example of his courage and determination.

The battle this day consisted mostly of a few scattered flurries of gunfire, with as usual a few of their best shots patiently waiting at long range to pick anyone off who dared expose himself. Occasionally, some of us felt sure enough to show ourselves for a short time. This never failed to bring rifle fire and wasn't the type of relaxation to pursue "safely" for long at a time. The last day or two we had seen and heard little of the squaws and families and had observed some sure signs they were withdrawing. There seemed little doubt some of the braves were leaving too. Although we were still well surrounded and only had to expose ourselves a short time to prove that.

By the fifth day we were almost out of dried meat and the flesh left on the horses' carcasses had become unpalatable, due to spoilage and the unspeakable stench. During the cover of the night, we managed with several men pulling on the hooves, to move some of the worst offenders back a short ways from some of our immediate positions. But this was hard work in our weakened condition, as the combination of battle strain and poor diet was taking its toll on all of us. Some of the men developed bowel trouble from our unsavory rations. For days the only way we could eat the undried meat was by sprinkling it with gunpowder, as we had no salt or other seasoning. Hunger and the fear of starvation became our most immediate problem, because by noon it appeared the Indians were gradually pulling some of their men back from their advance outposts. By mid-afternoon few Indians were seen and those only at a distance. It seemed probable they were withdrawing to more comfortable positions up and down stream, with lookouts posted in the hills above us. They had the upper hand in this respect, being confident we couldn't get away. We hoped they knew we had sent out men to bring us relief, knowing that prospect would keep them edgy. But then, too, there was still that nagging fear among us that our men hadn't made it through and the Indians were only waiting patiently to starve us out.

Long before sundown we commenced stirring outside the entrenchments and sitting on the embankments without drawing fire. Some of us, including Paradise, John, and Gloomy, were sitting around trying to find some cheer in our dismal prospects for survival. Gloomy had lapsed into his old ways and while he said little, all of it was pessimistic. John wasn't in a happy frame of mind (his innards were acting up) because of the ungodly diet he had subsisted on the last day or two. All of us expressed

431

emphatically that we had eaten our last rotten horse meat, no matter what the alternative. In this frame of mind we decided to take our chances and forage a little ways from camp in hopes of finding something fit to eat—anything almost would be better than what we had. Some of the boys started off down stream and three of us tried the upstream side. We progressed slowly, studying the banks carefully and ready to drop to a prone position at the first sign of trouble. By the time we had moved a hundred yards, we commenced to gain confidence in our advance, but there was little cheering in what we observed. In the area of the island, there was almost complete desolation. In addition to the remains of our own horses, many dead animals of the Indians lay where they had fallen along the dry riverbed and upon the grassland. Faded splotches of dried blood marked the spots where Indian casualties had occurred. Even the bushes and saplings on the island were shredded and torn by the action of the battle. The sand was trampled and cut up by hundreds of desperate hooves, leaving a record that appeared without rhyme or reason. What a few days ago had been a pretty valley now appeared to have been blasted by some powerful force of nature. The game animals had long been driven from the spot, not even a sandrat or a mouse was to be seen. Song birds, there were none, and no lowly hawk or skulking buzzard dared come in range of our guns. A horned toad or even a rattlesnake would be a welcome sight now and would soon be a tasty morsel roasted over someone's little fire. Only the wolves and coyotes remained and they were near by the hundreds, drawn by the carcasses of our horses. They were too shrewd to show themselves in range of our rifles by daylight, but haunted the riverbanks and hillsides after dark and tortured our senses with their hideous howls. All these factors, but mostly the stench from the dead animals must have been too much for our besiegers, for we progressed up the riverbed for over a quarter of a mile without incident. Just before turning back, we came to a thicket of plum bushes, the last of the summer crop. We picked and ate plums until common sense bade us stop. But boy-like, Paradise continued to eat until Bid spoke up and demanded sternly that he stop "before he busted his blasted gut." I can still see the hurt look on Paradise's face at the unexpected rebuke, but Bid appeared not to notice. We picked the remaining plums and located a larger thicket back

432

aways from the river. We cleaned that thicket of its scanty crop and headed back to the island with nearly three hatsful of fruit. On the way back we dragged all the dry branches and driftwood we could handle. The boys downstream brought in some plums, too, and that evening we supped on plums, boiled without sugar or seasoning; but they were delicious as far as they went with "forty-some" hungry men.

On the sixth day, I believe it was, a careless coyote came within rifle range and one of the boys got him. Like the plums he was shared by all and his bones boiled for soup. After that the wolves were far too wary to come near in the day, but howled close to our works of a night; sometimes we shot at them by sound, but were rewarded only by a slight break in their infernal noise.

Every day as our hunger increased, our strength lessened, but some of us spent much of the daylight foraging as far from the island as we figured our strength would stand. Once in awhile, we saw Indians but usually at a distance. It seemed probable now that only a small force kept us under surveilance, not daring to charge us, but to make sure we didn't escape. And "escape" did occupy the thoughts of a few of the men, among them misguided and pessimistic Gloomy. Their reasoning was "the able-bodied were entitled to survival and nothing was to be gained by sticking around this stinking hole and starving to death." Most of us refused to listen to them and dismissed the whole thing as idle talk. But some way, word did reach Colonel Forsyth and he immediately called a conference. Bid and I were on guard duty and did not attend and I quote only as reported. The Colonel spoke briefly and to the point. "Men, you know the situation as well as I. It is possible our couriers haven't gotten through and help may not come. The Indian wolves are still out there waiting for us, but it may be possible for you able-bodied men to leave in a group and get through—while we wounded will have to take our chances. If help comes, well and good if not, we are soldiers and know how to die, if it comes to that."*

Most of the group agreed emphatically. "We'll never leave you, Sir, we would never desert you."

* Two or three versions of this affair have been told. Essentially, this is Colonel Forsyth's version.

Sergeant McCall looked hard at the would-be deserters. "No Sir, Colonel," he spoke for the majority, "we've fought together and by God, if need be we'll die together!"

And that settled all talk of deserting the wounded, and some of those few who had at first supported the idea were almost ashamed to hold their heads up the next day.

Foraging for food was never very successful. We soon exhausted the few plums that were in our range, for even if our strength permitted, we never moved out of sight of our earthworks, not only because we considered it unsafe for ourselves, but at the same time it left the wounded in camp largely without protection. Prickly pear cactus dotted much of the landscape away from the river and we plucked and ate this spiny fruit, but it was a sorry way to satisfy a gnawing hunger. At one place along the river we found a water plant belonging to the lily family. We used the roots to brew a tea that might have been tasty with a little sugar. It may have had some medicinal value, but otherwise provided no sustenance. Our best chance for food appeared to be a nearby prairie dog town, but these usually curious little creatures, like all the other animals in the vicinity, seemed to have lost their trust in man and scurried to their holes as soon as one of us came in sight. Whereas their ordinary tactics were to squat on the brink of their dens and chirp curiously at any intruder. As usual, we had no luck when we tried it first on this day. The dogs simply failed to show themselves. Around noon we gave it up and retired to the riverbank where we ate a few prickly pear and drank from our canteens; at least we had plenty of good water. There was still a little dried horsemeat in camp, perhaps enough for another short meal for the wounded and we had agreed they should have it. Talking the situation over, we decided to retrace our steps to the dogtown and try again. This time the four of us, Paradise, Slim, Bid, and I, paired off and allocated certain areas and dens for each one's territory. For nearly an hour, Bid and I lay in the grass, gluing our eyes on the prairie dog mounds, he to take shots straight ahead and I those on the right. Suddenly Bid observed one of the little fellows barely sticking his head above the mound and working his jaws industriously. My mouth watered as I imagined the plump little

434

body attached to the head. At better than 60 yards, the head made a small target, but Bid made a near perfect shot. The bullet barely grazed the top of the mound in a perfect line and I was unable to understand how it had missed.

"The tricky little varmint ducked just as I pulled the trigger," growled Bid disgustedly.

"Maybe you got him and he fell back in his burrow?"

"He-ll no, thet heavy Spencer bullet would've blowed him clean out of the hole. They're just too smart for us, I reckon," he argued discouragingly.

About that time Paradise's Spencer boomed and the Saline Valley boy got to his feet and raced over to a burrow and then trudged empty-handed back to his place.

"Might as well lay here and nap for an hour," I allowed, "by now, they probably think the second battle of the Arickaree has started."

Following my own advice I did halfway doze for a time. Then I was aroused by Bid's whisper. "Yonder, over there on your side, there's one of 'em a stirrin'."

Sure enough, one of the little fellows was exposing brief glimpses of a bobbing head and an upright tail. Pretty soon he sat upright in the typical prairie dog manner and uttered his cocky and defiant little bark. Over the way, a stone's-throw to the left, Paradise answered him back in a perfect imitation. Curiously the dog stayed set and gave me time for a good aim I was closer than Bid had been and the target was good. At the sound of the shot the little animal was blown clear of the mound. "Ye-ow!" yelled Paradise, running back, panting excitedly and holding up the battered trophy of the hunt. Probably it was the first time in days that grins had spread over our faces. It was Bid who brought us back to reality. "Well boys, we cain't stop on one, we best get back on the job and see if we kin get us enough for a meal."

Our confidence restored, we settled down patiently for a full hour and never got another shot. Then suddenly a dog stuck his head above a mound for a quick look and then unexpectedly left his den and darted across to a neighboring burrow fifty feet away. It all happened so quickly we were caught napping, and by the time our guns were ready the dog was safe where we could see the tip of his tail wriggling above the mound. But evidently this hole wasn't to his liking, or else he found he wasn't welcome, for just as suddenly as he had before, he emerged from the mound and started back to his former den. That's where he made his mistake. We were ready and the two Spencers boomed almost at once. He was caught at full speed and rolled end over appetite. Whose bullet had hit him we never knew, nor cared. We were interested solely in the meat. Logically we should have settled down and patiently waited; perhaps we would have got another one or two before nightfall. But hunger and logic doesn't always go together and after fifteen or twenty minutes without any further luck, we gave it up. No doubt each of us thought of the wounded at camp and what a fine kettle of soup the two little dogs would make, but hunger-wise we were in worse shape than the wounded and regretably, no mention was made of that charitable cause.—To divide a pound and a half meal among the whole force was simply out of the question. We retired to the riverbank where a small clump of willows and a slight bend cut us off from direct view of the island. While the other two gathered wood and started a fire, Bid and I prepared the meat for the table. Then we cut a long willow shoot for a skewer and running it lengthwise through the roasts, we waited patiently for the fire to die down to a proper bed of coals. Then we took turns, one on each end slowly turning the meat until we deemed it done, each man drooling in his own fashion while anticipating the coming meal. No one wasted energy with useless words until the last bone was picked. But the little tidbit merely stimulated our appetites and brought visions of platters filled with roasts and bountiful meals of the past. Paradise expressed our feelings.

"Mighty good as fur as it went; sure beats mule meat."

"Yeah,—or even coyote." Agreed Bid dryly.

"Wonder what the boys over at camp think after hearin' all the shootin' and seeing the smoke from our fire?" Paradise mused, "Bet old Gloomy, for one, figgers we've done held out on 'em."

We were all busy with our thoughts and no one commented.

After a while, Bid arose. "Well, boys, we're awastin' time heah, we best get back to the dog town and see if we cain't rustle our suppers."

But the afternoon sun sank low and not another prairie dog showed himself, so reluctantly we gathered up our guns and moved away. We hacked off a few dozen prickly pear and dragged in a little firewood on our way into camp.

I had just settled wearily down in our rifle pit when along came Gloomy.

"Was that you fellers over by the river bank and was you cookin' some meat?" he enquired grumpily.

A mean streak tempted me and I was about to spin a big tale of how we had killed an antelope fawn and cooked and eaten it all at one setting. But I noticed in his face and sunken eyes the look of exhaustion and approaching starvation. When I answered, it was one of the few times in my life I have deliberately lied. "I wish we had of been Gloomy, but we were just burning the spines of some prickly pear before we ate them."

Bid sank down beside me without speaking, pulled out his pipe and little bag of tobacco. He poured the last of the mixture in his pipe, plucked a twig from the fire and lit up. He hadn't smoked for days and I knew he had been saving this last pipeful. He puffed away, silently gazing into the darkness. Finally he removed his pipe.

"This sure won't do. We cain't help ourselves and the others either, the way we've been goin' about it—. Some of us that are strong enough are just naturally gonna have to move out fur enough from this hell-hole to find sumpthin' to eat—Indians or not—otherwise the whole kit and kaboodle of us is gonna wind up flat on our backs if help don't come soon—and thet," he mused, "don't appear likely now."

Certainly his declaration had some risks. In the **first place** no man in the outfit was at near full physical strength. Second, any man who moved very far from our stronghold was almost certain to encounter Indians. But considering the desperate need for food, it seemed worth the risks to move as far out as our strength would permit. Accordingly, we made plans to contact two or three of the other fellows early in the morning and make a determined effort to locate some kind of a meat animal. We both felt we had strength enough to take us at least two or three miles from the island, surely in that distance we would find some game even if it was no more than rabbits or a coyote. Desperate for food we had no worries about our markmanship. Anything the size of a rabbit on up was a dead duck as far as we were concerned "sitting or running."

CHAPTER X

"The Last Day"

We went to sleep with the best of intentions for an early rising, but it turned out we were later than usual. We contacted John who was still fairly strong and he agreed to go with us. We wanted Paradise, too, as he was strong and agreeable to anything we were liable to suggest; but he had already taken off with a companion, apparently for another try at the dog town. John insisted on breakfast before he left. He and another scout had early the day before put out strips of spoiled horseflesh to dry in the sun in the hopes that they would be made edible. Nothing would do but we must all try them for breakfast. Bid and I had little faith in the experiment, but we were hungry enough to try. The stench from our surroundings was strong enough that we survived the cooking and with powder from our pistol cartridges, we seasoned them. One small slice was more than I could handle and Bid would take no more. But John insisted the meat wasn't so bad and finished one slice and started on another before he suddenly discovered that he, too, had enough. Moving out, we decided to try north of the river through the hills, mostly because there seemed less likelihood of Indians in that direction. We proceeded slowly, conserving our strength, but soon passed over the first hills when John became sick. He heaved up his breakfast and then continued to retch and gag until we became concerned and helped him back to a shady spot near some large soap weed. We stayed with him for half an hour when he appeared to be feeling better, but was still deathly white.

"John," I finally asked him, "if we help you back to where you can look down on camp, do you think you can make your way back?"

"Yeah, sure I can," he said, embarrassed by his weakness, "you fellers go on and never mind me. It musta been that damned spiled hoss meat. Never had no trouble like that before."

With one on each side, we helped him back nearly half a

mile to the brow of the main hill that looked down on the Island. But we had to stop frequently to let him rest. We found a shaded place in sort of a rocky crevice and helped him to a comfortable position. I had just straightened up when something caught my eye coming down the hills on the other side of the valley. We soon made out a lone horseman, then soon we saw others behind him. Either relief was coming—or Indians. More likely the latter. At any rate, we better head for camp as fast as our feet and our ill companion could make it. But John, with the new excitement, perked up and followed on our heels. Everything to our worried minds, indicated the advancing horsemen were Indians. They were coming in a hurry and in an irregular formation, as the Indians sometimes did when bent on attack. We realized at the speed they were approaching that we probably could never make the Island, but if we hurried, we could at least reach the cover of some bushes near the riverbank.

"God Almighty, boys" exclaimed Bid, stopping suddenly, "them's soldiers!"

Then we could see the men on the Island jumping up and waving and hear them shouting and cheering for pure joy. Bid, John, and I dropped our guns and wrapped our arms around each other. When we next looked up, we made out an Army ambulance making its way through the brakes. It was accompanied by a small guard which made up the balance of the advance contingent of troops that first reached us. These troops turned out to be Colonel Carpenter's Tenth Cavalry of black troops with a small detachment of scouts. The main force would arrive later with wagons and supplies. As we hurried on to the Island, we found the troops were opening their haversacks and distributing bacon and hardtack to our hungry comrades. We rushed in eagerly for our share. One of the first men to greet us was our old buddy, the indomitable "Irish".

"Bejabbers, man, 'tis about time you was showin' up," Bid wrung his hand, "I swear, I never thought I would be so glad to see thet shady countenance of yourn again."

"Sure must be something wrong with a man who would willingly return to the like of 'yo'all' to be the butt of your coarse jokes and perhaps even drink your abominable coffee," Irish countered piously.

Other men rushed up to shake Irish's hand and express their gratitude and we turned to see a pair of colored troopers approaching and grinning broadly.

"You fellahs remembah us ovah at Pond City?"

"Hell yes," Bid grinned, "Rube and George (remembering their names perfectly). I'd never forget you fellers and Pond City," and we grabbed their hands and we pounded each other on the backs. There were no color lines drawn on the Arickaree that day.

As soon as his wagons arrived, Colonel Carpenter moved camp about a quarter of a mile to a clean smooth stretch of grass and tents were erected for the wounded. Dr. Fitzgerald, the surgeon, gave them his immediate attention. Forsyth's and Lewis Farley's wounds had become very serious. Particularly Farley's, whose shattered leg had to be amputated and the able old fighter survived only a short time after the operation. He died that night to the regret of all who knew him. Otherwise, we went to sleep in peaceful contentment for the first time in many nights.

Colonel Bankhead's men came in about noon the next day.*

After Bankhead's arrival, plans were made to start the return to Ft. Wallace the following day. Preparations were started early for the departure but as many details had to be worked out, it was nearly ten o'clock before we were on our way. Scouts were sent ahead as a precaution against Indians and to find a more suitable trail for the wagons as it was very rough until we got well out of the brakes of the Arickaree. But even then, we reached the South Fork of the Republican for our night camp. Some of our boys, (Forsyth's Scouts) were lucky enough to draw mounts and were with the advance. In the canyons near the river, they surprised a small party of Cheyennes who all got away

* Two different Army commands came to the relief of Forsyth's Scouts. Lt. Colonel Carpenter's from the Denver Road near Cheyenne Wells and Colonel Bankhead's from Fort Wallace about 26 hours later.

as their horses were faster than the mostly tired-out mules of the whites. One of the Indians, however, was afoot and was pursued and wounded. He stood his ground with fortitude until his revolver was empty. He must have realized, then, there was no escape and made no attempt to get away. When the boys moved in on him, he was chanting his death song. According to the story we were told, this Indian was caught redhanded with a woman's calico dress in his possession which in the eyes of the Scouts convicted him of a crime worse than murder.

Not far from our camp was a fresh burial ground. Laid away there were some of the casualties of our fight on Beecher's Island. Our men, battlehardened and bitter toward all Redmen, rolled the corpses out on the ground and helped themselves to any item that appealed to them as a relic worth taking. In this day and age, such behavior seems callous and unexcusable—but that was war. And the engagements with the Plains Indians, though usually small in number of battle casualties, were fought with a ferocity and lack of charity toward none (on the other side). That is hard to imagine now.

The country of the South Republican was an intriguing, wild, and interesting place, but we had no time to linger there. Besides our scouts reported Indians in the canyons, probably in numbers larger than our own. In fact, Colonel Bankhead, on his way to our relief, had been harrassed by them not far from this locality. But he had been able to disperse them with a well-placed shot from a small cannon or mountain howitzer.

The next day we made a long "go" of it and camped at night at a waterhole near the head of Beaver Creek. And the same as the first day, Bid and I found ourselves with the wagons as there wasn't enough serviceable mounts to go around, and we simply had to wait our turn for a horse or even a well-used mule. But I like to think our talents with mules and wagons weren't all wasted in the course of our ride as passengers over this sometimes difficult trip. When the going was rough, crossing some of the brakes and rugged terrain, we often got out and legged it,—more than once, even putting a shoulder to a wheel.

During the course of these two days we got a clear picture

of some of the obstacles the soldiers had to overcome in order to bring wagons loaded with supplies over some of this broken and roadless country. The separate commands and particularly the wagon drivers deserved a lot of credit and praise for their efforts.

On the third day, the wagons and ambulances must have covered nearly thirty-five miles before a night halt was called at some waterholes on a branch of the Smoky Hill. Had the country been level, we were near enough to see the buildings of Ft. Wallace. But the day's ride had been very trying for many of the wounded and the halt was called for their benefit. Bid and I had drawn mounts that day and rode on into the fort after dark with part of Colonel Carpenter's command.

The next day the wounded were brought in to Ft. Wallace's modern, but only partially completed stone hospital where they were put under the best care available. The rest of us were quartered in sturdy tents with clean, new blankets. As our clothing was in terrible shape, we were issued durable fatigue trousers, flannel army shirts, two pair of long-handled underwear, socks, etc. plus a campaign hat and forage cap apiece and cavalry jacket with brass buttons. Thus, we settled down in civilized luxury to rest up, recuperate and await Uncle Sam's and more specifically General Sheridan's decision in regard to our future assignment. From the top brass on down to the lowest private, the military as a whole showed their respect and gratitude for "Forsyth's Fighting Fifty's" services on the Arickaree. Every survivor of that eight day battle and siege on the Island was henceforth considered a full-fledged Veteran Indian Fighter, even though he may have started the campaign as a few month's greenhorn from the east.

CHAPTER XI

"After the Battle Was Over"

Stories of the battle* quickly spread by telegraph, newspapers, and word-of-mouth from Denver to Kansas City and points east. In some cases it was built up out of proportion to its importance. Writers proclaimed the warmaking powers of the Indians were forever broken, although it is almost certain the Military Department never held such views. As a matter of fact, even as we rested at Ft. Wallace, bands of Indians were creating trouble and alarm on the Denver Road and on Beaver Creek and Prairie Dog branches. All in the area of Ft. Wallace's jurisdiction.

My first concern on reaching civilization was to write letters to Tom in Hays City and later to my folks in North Carolina. Then, upon learning we would immediately be issued clean, new wearing apparel, some of us decided we simply had to scrub ourselves of the filth of twenty days hard campaign even if it was necessary to use the now cold waters of the Smokey Hill. But fortunately that wasn't necessary. Some of the barracks had small washrooms fitted with large washtubs which were made available to us on a first come and wait-your-turn basis. Of course, the water had to be hauled from the river, carried inside and heated on wood stoves which consumed much time and firewood; the former of which we had plenty, and the the latter which had to be gathered along the brakes of the Smokey and hauled many miles. But when the rush once started, I know of no one in our outfit who wasn't glad to take advantage of these somewhat primitive bathing facilities. And for that matter, wasn't appreciative of this accommodation by the Command at Ft. Wallace which was somewhat in contrast to the situation on our first stay. Colonel Bankhead and his men went out of their way to see that we had our fair share of comforts the frontier outpost had to offer.

As Bid nor I had received no injuries of consequence in the

---

* Although the endurance and fighting ability of Forsyth's Scouts was probably never surpassed, the battle itself was too small in scope to make much of a dent in the overall fighting strength of the Plains Indians as a whole.

battle, after a couple of days rest and plenty to eat, we were well on our way to recovery from our grueling experiences. Lest life at the Fort become too easy, we commenced looking around for ways to spend our time and make ourselves useful. We spent much time in the vicinity of the corrals and stables. Bid was on the lookout for a good horse to replace "Old Joker," and otherwise, that was generally where our mutual interests lay. There were a number of regularly contracted army scouts around Wallace, then, as well as civilian horse traders. When not on duty this class of citizens were usually to be found loafing around the corrals, bargaining and swapping anything from a chaw of tobacco to a team of horses. Bid had an interest and certain skill in this type of barter and with nothing else to do, I soon got the bug, too. Sometimes hours would be spent in chewing the fat over the barter of a pocketknife or a pair of silver-plated spur rowells. And then, sometimes a good rifle or horse would be at stake. Strangely, the dyed-in-the wool, bottled-in-bond trader was apt to take no more time in making a deal for the valuable consideration than he would for the lesser. One of the Army Scouts had one of the late model Winchester "66" carbines which was similar to and an improved version of the Henry. I immediately took a fancy to the gun and the bargaining began. He was a sharper trader than I, but I refused to be hurried; and unfortunately for him he was a gambler and a poor one and needed the money to pay a gambling debt to one who had a reputation with the six-shooter. After a couple of days I finally bought the rifle for twenty dollars. Of course, I didn't have that kind of money, but I dug up five dollars and as a member of Forsyth's Scouts, the seller knew I was good for the balance on pay day; and he accepted my promise for the same. Cash money was a rather scarce commodity around Wallace between pay-days. Usually, outside of the Post Sutler, some of the well-paid Government Scouts and freighters controlled the most of it among the working class, which, of course, excepted those of the gambling fraternity in nearby Sheridan and Pond City. Consequently, it wasn't unusual around the corrals of Ft. Wallace when a deal was negotiated that required money. The seller would accept an IOU or as in my case, a handshake and a promise. Bid found what he wanted in a horse—a fine three, going on four year old gelding of the tough buckskin coloring that the Texan approved. But the owner, a civilian freighter of doubtful honesty himself, refused to trust anyone without cash on the barrel-head. This, despite Bid's producing Government Service papers which, of course, covered his horse lost in the battle on the Island. The best Bid could get from the freighter was a promise to hold the horse for awhile, "if someone else didn't come along with a better offer." Bid had his heart set on the horse and had made a reasonable and otherwise acceptable offer. To his way of thinking, regardless of the dubious assurances by the owner, the deal was practically closed and we made twice daily treks to the wagon yard where the freighter kept his stock to see that the gelding was properly fed and cared for. And it may have been well for the owner that we did, for much of his time was spent on the road between Wallace and Sheridan. While he was away more than one pair of covetous eyes were cast in the direction of the well-built young buckskin.

Aside from the swapping and horse trading element we mixed a good deal with Irish, John, Slim, Paradise, and others among the original scouts with whom we had become well-acquainted. Any detail we were in was sure to have some of our comrades. Military life within the bounds of the Fort tended to dampen Bid's and Irish's flair for practical jokes, but still they had to be watched, and with fellows like Paradise around we were assured life would never become dull. Someone rummaging around in the Post's very limited recreational facilities came up with a ball, some bats, and a catcher's mitt. Then, Irish, Slim, and I taught the boys baseball. Slim had a good, fast ball and would have made a first rate pitcher. But the busy schedule of the regular garrison, plus the necessity for frequent Indian patrols prevented us from getting anything going along that line. One day, under the pretext of scouting, we procured horses and mules and went hunting on the Eagle Tail Branch southwesterly from Wallace. We were unable to find any buffalo, but by dint of hard stalking we brought in three antelope and a number of prairie chicken which we shot with our rifles. I tried my new Winchester and found it accurate enough to shoot the head off a sitting prairie chicken. In contrast to our first stay at Ft. Wallace, pleasure jaunts to Sheridan and Pond City were not available to many of us because for one thing, we hadn't been paid; for another the Command held a dim view of those two settlements and permission or passes were hard to come by.

Shortly after our arrival at the Post, orders came, said to be directly from General Sheridan, to give first preference to any position "they could fill" to members of Forsyth's force. Gradually a few of our comrades took advantage of this opportunity and we parted with some of them for the last time. Gloomy, our pessimistic comrade from scouting days, left us for one of these jobs and the last we heard he was freighting with a Government train to Fort Lyon. One day we were assembled at the Command Post, where official gratitude was expressed for our services and we were told we had the choice of continuing service under a new detachment of scouts being formed under Lieutenant Silas Pepoon or we could resign and return to civilian life. Military service had already lost most of its allure for Bid and I and recently we had been giving serious thoughts to acquiring some more horses and a herd of cows and starting a ranche. That would require money and the freedom to make our own moves; unrestricted civilian life seemed the only way to go.

In a few days we received pay for our services in the Scout Troop and were officially separated from the military. Knowing we would be leaving soon, Bid, Paradise, and I got permission to visit our former commander in the hospital. Having seen the Colonel but once since our arrival at Wallace, I wasn't quite prepared for the wan, thin face that greeted us from the hospital bed. But his voice was firm and he said he felt well and assured us he was now on his way to recovery. After a short visit, we said goodbye and hats in hand, were about to leave, when the Colonel called us back. There was a slight twinkle in his eye.

"You know," he said, "I seem to recall a somewhat remarkable mule that was in our packtrain when we left Fort Hays in September. I never knew the mysterious connection you fellows had with that mule, but it must have been interesting."

Bid flushed like a small boy before he got hold of himself and grinned a little bashfully as the Colonel continued to give us a good-humored, expectant look. Bid looked at me a little helplessly, but I looked right back.

447

"He was your mule," I said.

Bid straightened up. "Well, Sir, that is, I mean, Colonel Sir, being as it's you, I've a mind to tell you the whole damn sordid story." And he did, even the part where he painted Old Satank with stove-black and got the old horse trader drunk enough to buy him back as a pinto mule. The Colonel appeared weak and in a delicate condition, but he laughed heartily, especially when Bid admitted his humiliation at finding the mule in the packtrain and realizing the old horse trader had made a sucker out of him.

We spent some time, then, discussing the merits of Old Satank and sociably told the Colonel of some of our other experiences with the cantankerous mule. But one thing we didn't mention was the time in camp when we borrowed the little mule and led him up the hill to our sentry post and promptly went to sleep, leaving the sentry duty to the mule. Neither of us were naive enough to think a professional Army officer of Forsyth's type could ever see anything humorous in such a gross dereliction of duty as that.

Leaving the hospital, we went out to the wagon yards where Bid contacted the freighter and completed his deal for the buckskin and received a bill of sale for the same. My partner was disgruntled with the Government for the settlement he received in compensation for the loss of his horse, claiming "Old Joker" as a top cow-horse was worth twice that amount. He had accepted payment with the philosophy that "he about had to, but he sure didn't have to like it."

The next evening after being paid, some of the boys got together and staged a big celebration over at Pond City. All of them getting pretty "full" and winding up by taking over the place. To Bid's everlasting regret we missed the party, as we were busy making preparations for our departure the next morning. I had been in touch with Tom by telegraph and found he was ready to start for Ft. Dodge with four wagons of freight and planned to be there at the Sod Ranche for a week. Quickly, we made our plans. I was furnished a Government horse and in turn we were to deliver dispatches to Ft. Dodge, where we were to be paid the sum of twenty-five dollars for our services. We were allowed to retain our military arms, blankets, mess kit, and equipment until we reached the sister fort.

CHAPTER XII

"Two Men on a Mule"

The celebrants to Pond City must have overstayed their leave that night for our tent-mates, Paradise and John, didn't make it back to their regular residence. But we were unworried, for we suspected from the sounds of hilarity in the early hours of the morning, they had likely wound up in the wrong tent. We were up at five when reveille was sounded. At breakfast, only Irish and John, of our old buddies, made their appearance. They were a woe-begone pair and partook of no nourishment other than coffee. After a few cups of that potent Army brew, Irish perked up considerable and volunteered to round up Paradise and Slim and a few of the other boys to see us off over at the wagon yard.

Half an hour later, packed and saddled, we bade farewell to our friends. Irish did the final honors by presenting us with a bottle of whiskey.

"A little souvenir of Pond City, from your old pals who celebrated well last night, but not wisely. And I trust you boys will dispose of it only in the interests of sobriety. And in that direction," he continued giving Bid a sober half-grin, while addressing me. "I charge you, 'Doc' Reynolds, with the responsibility of prescribing it for medicinal purposes only."

"That I will do," I assured him, and stuffed the bottle in my bedroll. Mounting then, we said our last "so-longs" and turned our horses toward the southeast. We crossed the South Smokey Hill in shallow water below the Post waterhole. At the top of the rise we stopped and looked back at the distinctively tinted stone buildings. Then we cut across the trackless buffalo grass prairie and in less than an hour, were in a completely virgin land so far as our own personal experience was concerned. Before noon the conical buttes* and breaks of Twin Butte Creek appeared. The October sun was shining warm and we stopped

* Not to be confused with the better-known and more impressive Two Buttes in Colorado a hundred miles to the southwest.

449

to water our horses at a clear, rocky pool. The rather picturesque little stream seemed to bear to the southeast, so we followed it until noon. Large numbers of buffalo had grazed recently along the little meadow and flats of the partially dry channel. We discussed the merits of the place for a ranche.

"Here we would be in a day or two's drive of the railroad," I observed, "and there appears to be good water and you can see the grass was first rate before the buffalo reached it. And over there," I stretched my arm (dreaming wildly now) "against those rocks would be an ideal spot to build our shanty or maybe even lay one up with rocks. Why, there's even wood along here."

"Whoa there, pardner," cautioned Bid, "you'all wouldn't want to build no house facin' the north. Always pick the foot of a bluff and build facin' the south for protection agin' the cold."

"How about protection from the heat?" I said, for the sake of argument. "There's two sides to it, you know, as Gloomy always said, 'too hot in the summer and too cold in the winter'."

Bid laughed as we guided our horses next to a shady bank for our noon halt. After hardtack and the "usual", we finished the meal with a can of tomatoes for dessert. Resting our mounts awhile longer, we then rode up the slope to the south and took our bearings. Below us the creek seemed to veer to the north, so setting a course to the south and east, we continued on and were soon up on the flats. In a few more miles we approached the brakes of Chalk Creek*. From a high bluff, we looked down on what appeared to be peculiar geological formations. Most of the water holes were about dry, so we crossed the channel and were about to ride on when I noticed an animal standing near a chalky formation a quarter of a mile away.

"Do you see what I see? Don't look quite right for a horse."

"No, it ain't no damn hawse, but whatever it is, it's a watchin' us too."

"Whatever" it was started our way and soon broke into a faster gait. Bid caught on before we heard that familiar half-

_____
* On some maps called Hackberry. One of the "to many" Hackberry Creeks in Western Kansas.

bray. He slid his Spencer back and commenced to cuss. In a short time Old Satank stood panting before us. True, a much battered and broken-down version of his former self, but unmistakeably the same "damn mule." One ear perforated with a large hole flopped awkwardly to one side, and his hide was splotched with patches of missing hair. His whole appearance was thin and bony like we had never seen before.

Bid's buckskin, "goin' on four old", with ears pointing, watched the approaching specter with genuine fright. But Bid, with a horseman's knack, quieted him down as Old Satank came closer with neck stretched the limit. The young buckskin backed away and clear back on his haunches, as for an instant the two touched noses. Then, as the old mule had strongly suspected, he realized he wasn't greeting "Joker". For an instant I almost felt a twinge of pity, but his mean eye glared and pivoting like a flash, he set his heels dangerously. But the buckskin proved how fast he could move, as horse and rider dodged out of the way. And Bid's "hyar, you son-of-a-bitch!", was strangely without malice.

Our past experience with the packmule had taught us to never be surprised at where he might show up. Therefore, with little more ado we turned our horses heads and started up a ravine with the packmule, like a dog follows his master, trailing at our heels. Following the draw for perhaps half a mile, we abruptly came out on the level. Looking back, we saw a small band of antelope, their lookout alert and watching us curiously. We had apparently passed in less than a hundred and fifty yards of them as we rode up the draw. Bid slid out of the saddle Spencer in hand. He tested the breeze.

"Ride on like yo'all wasn't interested and then fetch a big circle and come onto them on yonder side and I'll slip back down the draw and two-bits says they'll come over the ridge right at me."

"Yeah," I said, very skeptical, "I haven't had any of your money lately so I'll just take that bet." But as luck would have it, Bid's scheme worked just like he had predicted. I rode on, leading his horse with the mule following. On out of sight of the flock, I made my big circle and came up on them from the down wind side and they bounded over the edge toward Bid. Then I heard the boom—boom of his gun and he was busily gutting a two-year-old buck when I rode up.

"You know," he grinned, "I had a feeling they'd do just this. But it sure wouldn't happen every time."

"That's for danged sure," I agreed, as I tossed him my two-bits.

Taking only as much of the choicest meat we could carry handily, we rode up on the prairie and on across a high divide for several miles until we approached the edge of the Canyon of Punished Women's Fork.* We traveled along the rim until finding a buffalo trail that led down a narrow ravine where bushes and brush almost raked our horses' sides and so steep in places we came down with braced feet. Below us we could see the grass-covered bottoms surrounded by the rugged canyon walls, with a clear little springfed creek completing the picture. By accident we had stumbled on one of those rare, delightful breaks in the seemingly limitless monotony of the high plains country. We pulled up on a broad ledge near the bottom and looked about us, pleased with our pleasant surroundings, but instinctively with practiced eyes, studying the area for signs of danger. This place seemed almost too good to be true. Still suspicious, but curious of what lay ahead, we decended to the comparative level and followed the creek bed for a quarter of a mile. But there was no evidence humans had been in the place for years. A few trees grew along the creek and plenty of dead wood was available, but we found no signs of campfires, even years old.

We stopped and talked it over, agreeing that by all signs to experienced plainsmen, the place was safe. It was still early, but not knowing how far to the next water, we decided to camp here. Besides, we thought we might as well enjoy ourselves while we could. We unsaddled, unrolled our blankets and unpacked the camp gear, then picketed the horses out to graze, leaving Old Satank the run of the place. "Sure won't need to stand guard tonight with him around," I allowed, as we gathered enough wood for both night and morning. The October day had been

* Now called Ladder Creek.

warm, but the nights had been increasingly cooler, with the probability now of dropping close to the freezing mark. We chose a camping spot near a sheer, rocky bank and as we had plenty of time, we cut tall grass and placed it under our blankets to insulate them from the ground. Experience trailing Indians had taught us on going into camp to place saddles and every piece of equipment where they could be gathered up and thrown on the horses at a moment's notice. But having so recently gone through the hell of Beecher's Island, we had in a way become used to danger from Indians and took no more than our ordinary precautions. Two or three hackberry trees grew nearby and we hung the antelope there in the shade in the hopes that what was left would be good for the morrow.

While I busied myself preparing a fire, anticipating a juicy antelope roast, I noticed Bid carefully examining our erstwhile packmule.

"You know," he finally confided, "them damn lazy soldiers sure done a helluva sorry job a markin' this mule for the Government. Why, it ain't no more'n a hair brand; I could scratch it off with my knife blade."

"Well," I asked, a little suspicious, "what's that supposed to mean?"

"It means I ain't stole anything from Uncle Sam for some time and I reckon I'll just repossess this animal. He'll make up partly for the short changin' I got on what was supposed to be fair and reasonable compensation for a damn good ropin' hawse."

Over a slow fire and finally a bed of coals, we roasted a cut of antelope meat to a well-browned consistency, and then sprinkling it with salt, (a commodity we had sworn after Beecher's Island to never be without) we enjoyed a fine meal along with dried peaches, hardtack, and coffee.

Relaxed, contented with prospects of a pleasant night in warm blankets, under the stars, I laid a few more sticks in the fire and leaned back luxuriously. "My, ain't a peaceful, civilized life in the wilds wonderful?"

"Too peaceful maybe," Bid drawled lazily, "Surely, as the

poet feller says, somethin'll happen before mawnin' to shatter the tranquility of this here blissful occasion."

The sun was down and dusk was commencing to darken the canyon. I looked about us, realizing something was missing. I straightened up. "Wonder what's happened to your mule?"

We both came to our feet and walked over where we could look up the canyon. Old Satank, tense and alert, stood on a little knoll about a couple hundred feet away.

"Thet," said Bid, "don't look good!"

I thought my fear of Indians was gone, but the same old creepy sensation tickled my spine—-. "Better get the horses," I suggested.

"Yeah, might be a damn good idee—and saddle 'em up."

We got the horses, rolled our picket ropes, bridled and quickly threw on the saddles. My horse, an old cavalry mount, seemed to sense something was wrong. Then Satank came off his perch and headed towards camp. Halfway in, he wheeled and halted, sniffing up canyon. His snort came loud and clear—and we knew the symptons.

"Roll them Goddamn blankets," Bid advised, "and let's light outa here."

We mounted and headed down canyon at a fast trot, leaving our fire burning and meat hanging in a tree, as the packmule bounded up and by us at a run. "Foller close behind-him," Bid hollered, "He ain't ever been caught yet."

We followed, barely keeping the mule in sight in the gathering darkness. After what must have been two or three miles, he suddenly turned to the right and headed up a ravine with a moderate slope and soon we came out on the level. Directly the old mule slowed to a trot and we followed on his tail, figuring for the present we could trust him to break trail same as we had in the canyon. After perhaps a half mile, he halted, puffing and blowing. We pulled up and tried to take our bearings; darkness was less here and we could see some distance on all sides at what appeared to be a flat empty land, perfectly normal for the plains.

"As long as he leads in this direction, we best foller," Bid allowed, "I figger all the time he's been headed back to Dodge and as fur as I'm concerned I got enough faith in him I don't mind putting a right smart piece between us and thet canyon back there."

"Me too. He's never made a mistake yet as far as Indians were concerned. And I agree the more space we can put between us and that pretty little camp, the better I like it. On the other hand, It's possible we could have been safe back there for tonight. I've never heard of Indians attacking after dark."

"Well, for that matter, I ain't either, but the treacherous devils, you cain't trust 'em. Besides, I don't think ary one of us would've enjoyed the night waitin' for them to tie into us in the mawnin'."

The night blackened country was new to us, but we judged the area hereabouts drained to the Smokey Hill and we had a pretty good idea, broadly speaking, where we were and in what general direction our destination lay. So far, our progress was satisfactory and we would have been content to follow the pack-mule further, as his instincts seemed to lead perfectly on the right course, but in another mile his scare had plainly wore off and his worn-down condition began to tell. Pretty soon he dropped behind and after a few more miles across open country, he paused frequently to grab a mouthful of grass. My partner and I exchanged glances; we knew now we were out of danger. During our hasty flight from the canyon, it never occurred to either of us to doubt Satank's judgment. We had never known him to fail to recognize the approach of Indians. His type of warning, coming from anything else, our first thought would have been a bear, panther, or some other wild beast was prowling around camp. But not Satank. He was too hardy and mean himself to get much alarmed over any other four-legged creature; only Indians filled him with fear and distrust.

The night was not very dark, and sure of our directions, we continued over a land that was nearly level until midnight. Then

455

we commenced to notice the chill October air and our rear guard escort began lagging further behind, indicating weariness on his part. On coming to a wide ravine or dry creek that meandered across the flats, we rode down in the shelter of its ten feet high banks, picketed our horses and bedded down for the balance of the night.

Awaking with the sun, we climbed the bank and surveyed our surroundings. To the southeast as far as we could see, the land lay nearly level. But to the north from whence we came, a mirage distorted the landscape. In the distance abrupt, blue-reddish cliffs rose against the horizon, exaggerating spectacularly the region of the Smokey Hill. For a while it was a marvelous picture, but as the sun rose it gradually faded back into reality, a drab distance of buffalo grass and nothing.

Rustling some dry debris and buffalo chips, we soon had a cheery little fire going and prepared our sow-belly and coffee. Then we rolled the blankets and saddled the horses. While I put out the fire, Bid walked over and examined Old Satank, who had just risen stiffly to his feet.

"First time I ever knowed you to lay down of a night when there was anything around to eat," he said unsympathetically, "Kinda tired and stiff, too, ain't you?"

Once more on the move we rode leisurely at a walk, setting our course to the southeast. Instead of speculating profitlessly on the dangers we had escaped the night before, our thoughts turned to that of our greatest interest, namely "ranching". Months before when we first originated this fascinating venture, it was to be somewhere in the cloudy future. But talk had progressed to a point where now we set a date—next spring. Bid was saying, "I've got a cut in the business 'out home', a thing so fur I've never touched. The rest of them's all had their shares so I reckon I'm entitled to mine. If it don't cause no hard feelings, I think I'll just take mine in she-stuff, maybe some in heifer calves. Ought to be somewhere around fifty or sixty haid of pretty good stuff for breedin' stock. And then—as I've told yo'all more'n once, for a thousand dollars a man kin damn near buy a herd of longhorns in Texas."

"That's fine for you, Bid, but I'm afraid I won't be able to match that. When we get paid at Ft. Dodge, I should have about three hundred dollars I've saved this summer and one good horse. And if the Indians didn't burn any more of my hay and if the Government accepts what's left as specified in the contract, I'll get maybe five hundred more. At that rate I'll be lucky to go partnership on a quarter interest."

"You will like hell," Bid exploded, "when we first started talkin' about this enterprise, it was agreed it would be on a strictly fifty-fifty basis and By God, thet's the way it's gonna be. What difference does a few hundred dollars or even a thousand make—one feller can pay the other back first drive we make to the railroad."

I grinned appreciatively. "But in all seriousness, Bid, unless we start out mighty small, this thing is gonna require a lot more capital than both of us have. We'll need a wagon or two, a couple of good mule teams, material for a corral, and some kind of a winter abode for ourselves, supplies, grub, and we'll sure need a string of good horses and enough credit to pay an extra man or two. It could take more than we've got to finance that, let alone buying the cows."

"That's right, and I've done been thinkin' about it, too. As for the hawses, they're a runnin' wild, all we gotta do is ketch 'em and break 'em. And the cows, I venture to say I know fellers in Texas that'll deliver up to three hundred head for a hundred dollars to bind the deal and the balance at the end of the trail at Abilene, Hays, or wherever I want them. And now as to that capital, Mr. McCoy* treated me mighty white last fall in Chicago and I met some of his backers. Them bankers figger the cattle business out here is the biggest thing as ever happened to Chicago. This one banker assured me they would stake qualified and experienced cowmen for no more'n a simple Promissory Note." Then he grinned, "and a mortgage on the damned cows."

"Yes, but that was nearly a year ago. I understand the cattle market has had some setbacks since then."

* Joseph McCoy, the famous cattle buyer, who is credited with establishing the cattle trade in Abilene.

457

"Nothing serious, it ain't. Texas is full of cheap cows and a summer up here on this nawthen grass'll even put beef on a longhorn. And Mr. McCoy and his bankers know this and they know the east is clamoring for cheap beef; out here we can raise it. Them bankers figger what's good for the cowman is even better for them.—It's just thet damn simple."

"Bid, you know I wanta believe in this. All I need is a little reassurance once in a while and believe me, I'll trust your judgment on these matters. You make it sound like the Life of Riley."

He laughed, "better call it 'the Life of Reynolds' with McClaine throwed in for good measure."

As I look back on our enthusiasm that eventually led to the establishment of the Old Frying Pan Ranche, two of our least concerns in the beginning turned out to be our biggest problems— Indians and buffalo. Of course, from the start we recognized these matters, but with the customary optimism of the frontier, we took them for granted and thereby hangs another tale.

Returning to the business at hand, we moved on and soon observed the rolling brakes and tributaries of the Pawnee. We dropped down in a deep draw that led to a spring. As we had made a dry camp our canteens were empty and the animals were thirsty. We paused here for a short break before moving on down to the Pawnee proper. Numerous water holes dotted the crooked channel and good grass covered the valley and meadows. A little scattering of timber grew along the rougher, more protected areas. No prominent landmarks lay along our immediate path to distinguish the stream such as the buttes for Twin Butte Creek and the Canyon of Punished Woman. But we judged from its size it must be Pawnee Creek. We followed its course until noon when we pulled up on a grassy bank and prepared our dinner. Several flocks of antelope had been seen on the high prairie and a few deer after coming into the valley, but none gave us a chance for a shot and we weren't interested enough to try stalking them. A small bunch of buffalo grazed contentedly on the rough slope half a mile from where we ate. But it seemed a waste to shoot one for what little meat we could consume before the balance was almost certain to become tainted. Besides, our "sometimes" faithful packmule was a little too used up to carry a load into Dodge from here. We were uncertain how far we should follow the Pawnee without going out of our way and after a few more miles, we moved on across country in a more direct southerly course. Like most of the plains, it was an almost trackless land. Once we crossed wheel ruts ages old, indicating some white man in the past had used this route for heavy transportation. Perhaps freighters or more likely the Army.

From a high rise we took stock of our surroundings. Mostly the country was rolling and broken as far as we could see in the slightly hazy distance. Then I remembered we still had two pretty substantial creeks to cross before we came near the valley of the Arkansas. There was no way of telling our exact position or whether we were near our right course. But Bid insisted we were "haided right", but couldn't explain why he was so sure. The Old Santa Fe Trail on an east-west line along the north side of the Arkansas, converging with the new Fort Hays road at Fort Dodge and running northeast, as well as numerous wood and stone quarry trails from the Fort, were plain landmarks we couldn't miss. But we made sort of a game of how nearly we could come to a perfect hit. Because we knew Tom and his wagons had a good two days start on us, and knowing him, "if his teams were in good shape and with good luck, he would make the trip from Hays in three days." We wanted to be close behind.

We spent the night on Buckner Creek*, near the foot of some high bluffs cut with little ravines that were grown up with brush and a few small trees. In the creek bed was a clear, fairly deep stretch of water, apparently fed by springs. Along the camp side of the stream were the plain months-old tracks of wagons. As we speculated on the makers of this rare sign of civilization, I stumbled across an object in the grass and stooped to pick up what had once been a fine fishing rod with line and hook intact. "Only some blamed dude, Army officer from back east would pack a fancy fishpole like that around these parts," observed Bid, very confident of his appraisal of the situation.

* Buckner Creek, a branch of the Pawnee.

459

"But why in the world would anyone carelessly go off and leave such an expensive piece of equipment?"

"Most likely for this reason," said Bid, who had continued to kick around in the grass until he picked up an object lying near a rock on the creekbank. He held up a fancy liquor bottle. "I know this here brand and it packs a right smart wallop. With this kind of bankbait and thet kind of a fishin' hole, my guess is he soon lost interest in the latter." He grinned, knowingly.

After a summer on the Plains, I had begun to accept Bid's (and the popular) somewhat prejudiced view of the Army. "It's no wonder they can't control the Indians with the qualities displayed by some of the men sent out as leaders," I opined zealously, and thereby "indicting" an unknown, of a purely imaginary misdemeanor, based on months old circumstantial evidence.

Bid grinned again following my remarks. "Course, we could be jumpin' at conclusions and my 'diagnosis' of the situation could be some slanted. But I will stake my saddle on one thing and that is; nary a one of them common hawseback waddies got to wet his whistle on what was in that there fancy bottle."

Fascinated by the elegant, though somewhat weathered fishing tackle, and the clear stretch of deep water, I announced abruptly I was going fishing. Bid was skeptical. "Ain't apt to have much luck hereabouts. This crick ain't exactly the Colorado of Texas."

"It's not the Kaw of Kansas either, but there's fish in it, I betcha. See those ripples, that's caused by fish hitting the surface."

"Shucks, Caroliny, them's just crawdads a comin' up for air."

But not to be deterred, I grabbed my hat and swatted a pair of late fall grasshoppers and baited my hook with one and cast it in the water. In the meantime Bid walked off to take care of the horses and gather wood for a fire. For the first few minutes, all I got was a few bites and was about to pull out the line when suddenly the bobber went out of sight. I reacted instantly and pulled out a nice hand-sized perch of that species known as sunfish. Nearly as fast as I could catch bait and cast the hook

I would get another one. Enjoying every minute I continued to quietly fish, relishing how I had the laugh on Bid. After I had caught about a half dozen, I could contain myself no longer and held up the string of fish and hollered at my surprised partner. Instantly he dropped what he was doing and came running, grinning without remorse. "Hell, I figgered all the time there was fish in that waterhole."

"Yeah, I noticed how positive you was about that a little while ago."

Bid immediately started hunting for more grasshoppers and was reluctant to stop fishing after we had a string of over a dozen fish—many more than we could possibly eat. We selected several of the nicer ones and scaled and cleaned them on the spot. In a little while a fry pan full of them was sizzling on the fire with plenty of bacon fat and salt. By dark we were still meticulously picking at the bones.

We were putting away our few utensils when a bear came sniffing along from out of the bluffs, frightening our horses, and causing them to pull back on their picket ropes. We grabbed our rifles, but something held us back, maybe a sense of the unknown that might lurk around the next bend of the creek and the knowledge rifle shots would echo off the bluffs like a cannonade. At any rate the bear paused near the creekbank, apparently surprised at seeing humans. He raised up on his hind legs, facing us for an instant (making an ideal target), then he dropped down on all fours and bounded awkwardly off into the darkness. We held our fire, staring at one another in mutual apology.

"Hell-fire," Bid said sheepishly, "I sure ain't lost no bear lately."

"Me neither," I alibied, "if we'ud cut loose with both of our rifles that colt of yours would have probably spooked for good, besides I would rather have the peace and quiet than a few hundred pounds of shaggy bear meat."

"You betcha."

Although our horses came close to being spooked by the

bear, Old Satank merely laid back his ears and rolled his mean eyes. Observing his behavior, we felt safe for the night. After calming down the horses and resetting the picket pins, we rolled up in our blankets with our rifles beside us and went to sleep.

After a leisurely start the next morning, we soon reached the brakes of the Sawlog, or as some military maps still listed it, "Shaff's Branch of the Pawnee". I had never been at this particular locality, but it was near enough home that I felt a certain familiarity. After studying the area from high ground, we both agreed we were well above the Crossing of the Ft. Hays road. We found a good place to cross the narrow channel and decided to follow along the south side for a while. After a mile or two we discovered a small herd of buffalo on the rough hillside ahead of us. "Caroliny," Bid suggested, "I know you been jist itchin' to try that purty Winchester on a he-sized animal. Why don't yo'all slip on afoot and see if you can't injun up on them."

Delighted at the opportunity, but knowing well if I failed it would take a long time to live it down, I dismounted and handed him my reins. "What'll you have, cow or bull meat?" I asked flippantly.

"Jist make it buffalo and I'll be satisfied."

The terrain offered good cover and the wind was in my favor and after a careful twenty minute stalk I came within slingshot range. Selecting a short yearling, my Winchester barked and down went the young buffalo. You can never predict exactly how a buffalo herd will react. This one began to look mean. They gathered around the downed one, grunting and rattling in a great way. One enormous black bull faced me, tail in the air, pawing great gobs of dirt and emitting deep, croaking bellows. I stood up, waving the Winchester and hollering, all to no avail. If anything, the bull appeared more fierce and I commenced to wish for a steep bluff or a tree to climb. Bid, observing my predicament came riding up the hillside at a run leading my horse with the mule following. The big bull took one look and with a last guttural bellow took off humping his back and running as though his life depended on it, with the rest of the herd trying to keep up. Bid rolled in his saddle with laughter.

We skinned and butchered the young buffalo and packed the saddle and hump on the packmule, then rode down to the Sawlog where we found clear running water, there we washed up and ate our lunch. We agreed on our approximate location and decided to head just a little east of where Bid determined to be straight south. Leaving the Sawlog, we were soon up on the slightly rolling prairie where after a few miles we struck the familiar Hays City road. Turning down that well traveled trail we covered a few more miles to a point where the Arkansas River was in view, luck was with us, the first wagons we saw, well back from the outskirts of the Fort, we recognized as Tom's. Tom, Andy and Pat stepped out to greet us and we were genuinely made welcome. Our friends had a cartload of firewood they had picked up on a point near the crossing of the Pawnee and we spent the evening at the wagoncamp, feasting on buffalo hump and reminiscing around a wood fire until late at night. Tom and Andy had made a few freighting trips from Hays in the nearly two months Bid and I had been on Scout Duty and thus had kept pretty well in touch. We learned the Indians had burned our hay at the last cutting but even so, Tom had settled our contracts and paid our note with a profit of three hundred dollars a piece. Besides this we still had hay left which was worth a high price.

We found the Military Post teeming with Soldiers and freighters, the grass on all immediate surroundings was grazed off short by their horses and work animals, tents and temporary quarters were established within a mile or so of headquarters. Everybody and everything pointing to a big push into Indian Territory against the Redmen. Eight or ten troops of the Seventh Cavalry were operating out of Dodge, much of the time from a camp on Bluff Creek and covering the country to the Medicine Lodge. The Third Infantry was gathered at or near the Fort. General Sully, continued as the overall commander but it was no secret the flamboyant Custer held the hopes of Sheridan and the Military. *Sully had already had his chance. The preparations being made brought about the establishment of a new post and

* In September of "68" Gen. Sully left Dodge with roughly the same troops and campaigned briefly on the Beaver where he was continually harassed by the Indians. Apparently fearing for his supply train, he returned to Ft. Dodge with little to show for their efforts.

base of supplies on the Beaver (North Canadian) over a hundred miles to the south of Fort Dodge. This was the beginning of Camp Supply. From there the latter part of November, Custer marched the Seventh through deep snow to the Washita River where he surprised the Indians winter camp and won the Battle of Washita. "But that is another story."

The next morning while Tom and Andy's wagons were being unloaded, Bid and I reported to the proper authorities where we received our twenty-five dollars pay and surrendered my Government horse and our Gov't. guns and equipment, then back to camp we went and strapped on our own 'artillery' which Tom had brought from Hays. We all got together at the Trader's Store and bought cheese, crackers, bologna and etc. and enjoyed a real civilized lunch topped off by red apples from a Missouri orchard. After lunch we concluded Fort Dodge was too crowded for us, besides we all hankered for the wide open spaces at the Sod Ranche. We became concerned about Barney and Jose, who had been left in charge of the ranche following our move to Hays; on enquiry no one remembered seeing them for over two weeks when Barney last appeared at the Sutler's store and purchased flour, sugar and chewing tobacco.

As we somewhat anxiously approached our former homely abode, straining our eyes for some sign of our old friends, we noticed a bay horse grazing by himself below the corral, as we came closer I knew it was Blaze. I could contain myself no longer and jumped from the wagon like a schoolboy and let out a loud whistle, Old Blaze raised his head, ears pointing forward, I whistled again, then he whinnied and came running. I grabbed his mane and swung on top, and away we went making a big circle around the whole layout; Yelling like a Cheyenne as we dashed by the lonesome privy I unlimbered my six-shooter and sent a .36 caliber ball through the open door. Not to be outdone, Bid dropped the mule's leadrope and splintered the roof at eighty yards with his Spencer while his pony pranced and danced. And 'Old Satank', not in the least perturbed by all the commotion, trotted up to the familiar premises and calmly stuck his nose in the haystack. In the meantime two heads accompanied by a long rifle barrel, peeped furtively over the sod wall of the corral and we greeted our old compadres, Barney and Jose.

On the long-legged Colorado hawse

Winding up the "homecoming celebration" almost as abruptly as it started, we settled down for a few days of easy living, being occupied mainly in making plans for the future.—Too soon though it was time for farewells. Bid was the first to go, he was to leave with an outfit for Larned and thence back to Texas, where he planned to contract for a small herd of longhorn cows to be trailed to Kansas in the spring. While my job was to make arrangements at this end and raise what money I could.

The morning came when we gathered to say goodbye. Bid's little string stood saddled and ready, the two buckskins side by side and Old Satank with a small pack containing bedroll and personal belongings, standing obediently behind. Bid swung in the saddle on the long-legged "Colorado hawse". "See yo'all comin' spring." He acknowledged, then he chirped to the young buckskin and tugged on Satank's rope. "Tail Up! you flop-eared jackass, we're a goin' back to Texas where I aim to domesticate you cross-eyed "Indian alarm".

THE END